Country Boy, City Girl

Trials & Triumphs

During the Great Depression

TERESA HOLMGREN

Cover design by Van Holmgren

ISBN: 1530011434
ISBN-13: 9781530011438

DEDICATION

This fictionalized account of my amazing parents, Harley Van Seibert and Mable Bertha Woodrow Hall, as they grew up during The Great Depression, is dedicated to them. My father lived on the farm and my mother lived in town. The tragedies and triumphs they experienced were an enormous influence in molding the character of the tremendous parents they became for me and my two sisters.

It is inspired by actual events.

I had to keep their stories together, so…

Their stories are presented in alternating chapters.

Chapters in regular type are the story of Harley.

Chapters in italics are the story of Mable.

*Dialogue that is in German is translated
on p.416-417*

Table of Contents

ACKNOWLEDGEMENTS

Thanks to my sisters Marilyn Parizek and Sharon Vaipae for their editing help and tolerance, as I fictionalized the story of our parents. "Sister love" is truly a gift from God.

Thanks to my husband, Ronald, for his remarkable patience, German translation, and gentle persistent reminders to get this book finished

Thanks to my daughter, Jenipher Sutherland,
for her meticulous final editing.

Thanks to my teachers, Marilyn Smith and Joan Roberts,
for their inspirational instruction, life-long friendship,
and loving encouragement.

Thanks to NaNoWriMo and Central Iowa Authors for the opportunities provided that allowed me to write this book.

Dawning on the Farm

Pre-dawn silence filled the farmhouse. The dark walnut chest of drawers rested heavily in the dim corner. It deserved a rest, a retirement of sorts. The wizened piece of furniture was just over one hundred years old and had traveled many rough miles to its present location. Lena's ancestors built it by hand in Pennsylvania in the1830's. The dresser was a plain and practical place of storage. Being utilitarian, it was handed down to each next generation, who took it with them wherever they went. They went to Iowa, then South Dakota, then Missouri, and finally back to Iowa. In a covered wagon pulled by oxen, on a flat boat, and by rail, the bulky and burdensome family treasure had crossed the Missouri River four times. It was a bit too large for the little room, but it felt at home in the corner, right next to an east-facing window with heavy ivory lace curtains. That quiet spot in the master bedroom of a small two-bedroom farm home was the proper place for it, for now.

Quietly, a sliver of sunbreak shone down the center of the dresser. On top of it rested a properly wound alarm clock, but it was never set. Real farmers don't need alarm clocks; they know their day starts at the crack of dawn and the good ones usually awaken themselves before that.

Charley and Lena were both awake. They rested easily in each other's arms, eyes closed and ears waiting for the rooster to wake the rest of the farm. There were pigs and cattle, a goat and two horses. The hens kept the rooster company and the dog left the cats alone, as long as they didn't try to get his scraps. The cats could have all the mice they could eat in the barn, but Snowball was a selfish young German Shepherd, and the cats were properly chased and scattered if they came near his treats brought out from the dining room table.

Lena knew her son Harley was up already. She smelled the coffee he had started for her. He would be heading out to start the chores and she would have breakfast ready when he returned. Seventeen years old and still growing, he always wolfed down every morsel of what his mother prepared. Harley was a good son, a serious student, and a hard-worker. As soon as breakfast was over, his Uncle Lynn would come by to pick him up and head back to the dairy farm in West Des Moines. The milk route Harley worked with Lena's brother helped bring in enough to keep the bankers happy for now, but just barely.

Charley kept talking about heading out to Kansas and other places to the west to work on a wheat crew, but Lena dreaded that. She was pleased that Harley was so helpful to his uncle. Lynn's dairy farm made him good money, and he also drove the rural mail delivery route in his area. Lynn helped Lena when he could, but most of the time Charley was too proud to allow her to take any money from her brother. So, Harley worked to earn the extra money, and Charley's pride was preserved.

Lena heard the screen door slam and knew Harley must be back, but it seemed too early for him to be finished. Perhaps she had fallen back asleep; yes, she had, because Charley's side of the bed was now empty. Lena told him many times not to get up and leave her like that, but he said she looked tired lately, and he didn't want to be a widower. He and Harley would both be wanting their breakfast sooner than later, so Lena sat up. Looking out the south bedroom window, she could see Jim and Betty's roof.

Betty, who lived down the road a half mile and was married to Charley's cousin Jim, told her last week that she thought Lena had some sadness and was acting differently. Acting too melancholy and moving slower than normal, she said. Lena had told her to mind her own business and to quit listening in on the party line phone they shared. She had nothing to be unhappy about and that was that. The money they owed the bank for the cattle and for the windmill they had to replace was cutting deep into their small savings, but they could hopefully live off of it until Charley got some of the cattle sold. Hopefully. Worry was what Betty saw on Lena's face. It was the Great Depression and it showed up on the faces of most people, and especially farmers.

Ready to start her day, Lena made her way to the kitchen. Harley had the fresh eggs already washed and on the kitchen table. The stove was warming up, so she got the biscuits mixed and put them in the cast iron skillet right away. There was one last bit of sausage left in the icebox, so that would mean today's breakfast menu was fried eggs with biscuits and gravy. Charley looked up at her over his favorite bright blue tin mug of coffee and smiled.

"How's my little blonde sweetheart this morning?" he said as he grinned broadly and winked at her. She loved his two-eyed winks and a little laugh escaped her mouth.

"I'm just fine, except some big lug of a farmer got up out of bed without his wife again! And please don't embarrass me in front of the boy, Charles."

"I gotta teach him how to talk proper to his girl someday, Lena," the tall and prematurely gray farmer argued. "He's a startin' to get pretty handsome and the gals will be takin' bigger notice of him this fall when school starts again."

"They already do, what with that chirpy little Findley girl popping over here about once a week to 'borrow' something for her mother. Really, she expects me to believe that her mother runs out of kitchen necessities EVERY week? Maxine Findley is not that scatter-brained! That daughter of hers is just trying to grow up too fast!" Lena was visibly flustered and protective of her well-built young son, and her face flushed as she fried the eggs.

"Now just calm down, Lena. She ain't gonna hurt him. He's too busy to bother about women now, anyway." Charley turned to Harley, who was now also flushed. "Ain't you, son? Too busy to mess with no women, that's you, right? Tell your ma."

"I'm too busy, just like he says, Mother. You know I am. Marian just likes to talk and to get out of her chores. That's why she comes clear over here all the time. Her ma always hollers at her and she doesn't like it, so she comes all the way over here." Harley shook his head, "Walking over three miles, just to get far away from her ma. I tell her to go home and do her chores, then her ma won't have nothing to holler about."

"Harley! Use your grammar! Her ma won't have *anything* to holler about!" Lena sputtered. She had her degree from a business school in Huron, South Dakota, and was not going to raise a child who sounded uneducated. Never. Rare were the farm wives with even a high school education, so Lena was an oddity, and very proud of it. It was really coincidental the way she came to marry this Iowa farmer, as she was the only one of her three sisters who did not marry a professional man.

However, she never corrected Charley's grammar. He was perfect for her, she said.

Lena's family had moved back to Iowa from Missouri, walnut dresser and all, and they were all living in Valley Junction, just west of Des Moines. Charley had gone down to the Des Moines rail station, from his farm in rural Grimes, to pick up a new car he had ordered from St. Louis. Lena was there meeting her Aunt Polly, who was arriving for a visit from California.

Trains coming from two opposite directions had brought this pair together. Aunt Polly had needed help moving her bulky travel trunk, and suddenly, Charley loomed over them both, offering to help. He gave Lena her first two-eyed wink, and she actually laughed out loud. Polly frowned at her, but it was too late; Lena and Charley had exchanged glances, as well as their hearts…right there on the rail platform, in front of everyone.

They married six weeks later. Polly encouraged them to not delay because she wanted to be at the wedding; she claimed she was responsible for the meeting. Charley said it was his love of Carlington cars that led them to each other. He would always wink at Lena when he said that, and she would always laugh. It was a wonderful love.

While Lena cleaned up the breakfast dishes and prepared the scraps for Snowball and the chickens, Charley and Harley headed out to the feed lot. The son had already fed the goat, and the pigs, but Charley wanted to help Harley with the cattle. He had to be sure not one of them was off their feed, and that they all appeared to be gaining weight. He surely did not want to leave his family and head west to harvest wheat, but he'd do what he had to do to provide for them and to protect the family farm. His grandfather had bought these eighty acres in 1866, and it was where his family belonged. He would do anything necessary.

"Hey, Dad, I think I saw a rat down in the feed room. Nearly as big as one of the cats!"

"What? We don't need none of them around here. Probably came in with that load of smelly sheep old man Monahan bought for himself the other day. Even rats wouldn't want to hang around those stinkin' critters. Them cats better get rid those vermin if they want to keep their happy home. That's the only reason I put up with them; to keep the rats and mice outta the barn and other buildings! I got no time for cats…or rats." Charley was not kidding, Harley could tell he was mad about having rats. He shrank back a little; not that his dad was ever mean to him, but his dad was a big man and was powerful strong. He threw their bales of hay around for the cattle like they were shoeboxes. Empty shoeboxes. Not like they were hundred-pound blocks of grain.

Harley completely respected his father, and he knew his dad felt the same toward him. He had heard Charley bragging about his "strong-as-a-bull, hard-workin' kid" to his friends at the pig auction in Perry just a month ago. He was proud that his dad was similarly respected by all the other farmers they knew. His father might not be as literate as his mother, but he had finished fifth grade, and was a straight-talking, honest, hard-working man. Charley's tall muscular figure, wearing striped overalls, with a farmer's tan, and that flat-top, nearly silver haircut… it was a striking image standing there in the bright mid-morning sun.

"We'd better get goin' on cleanin' the big water tank, son; don't need no livestock gettin' sick on us. Then we'll need to check that fence up against Jim's pasture. His skinny cows keep a leanin' on it tryin' to git to our corn. Remind me to tell him to feed those animals more!" Charley strode off toward the giant water tank at the base of the barnyard windmill. An early summer heatwave had filled it with green and yellow pond scum or something worse, and his father decided to empty it all out and give the livestock clean water. It would take a couple of hours. By the time they checked out the fence, it would be time for lunch.

At lunch, Harley would have time to see if the new Reader's Digest had come in the mail. At lunch and after dark were the only two times he had to read. His mother insisted he read. Harley was fairly sure his father at least approved of his love of reading, but Charley adamantly frowned on it "during the daylight hours God gave us to farm." So, he read at lunch and after sundown. He loved that what he read gave him a connection with his mother. He would be working with his father all day, and really put his heart and hard work into it, but his mother had always encouraged him to higher aspirations, if that's what Harley wanted. It was what Harley saw on that milk route of Uncle Lynn's that made the young man realize that he did want more.

A Girl with Ambition

"Dad, you know the Yankees are Burnie's favorite team, right? That's just so dumb. I don't understand why he thinks they are so wonderful. Whenever he talks about them, his eyes get kind of glassy, and he starts talking faster. I told him he could go with us to see the Cardinals or the Cubs sometime, but he pretends he is throwing up. If he wasn't my best friend, I think I would kick him when he does that!"

My dad did not look up from our beloved Des Moines Tribune sports section. "Well, darling daughter, who should never kick anyone, it says right here that sports columnist Ted Ashby thinks the Cards and the Athletics will be battling each other in the World Series again this year...so you should be thinking of a better way to settle things with Burnie. You know he will be cheering for the Athletics. He's an American League fan. One of you is going to be crowing, and the other one will be eating crow. Taking off his eyeglasses, he put down the newspaper. "Maybe Mr. Orwig or I would like our cars washed. Or it could involve some fall window washing at the other one's house? By that time, in

October, there will be all sorts of fall chores you two could wager over; raking leaves or putting up the storm windows. The grownups would have to help you with the upstairs windows, but you kids could do the ones on the ground level. What do you think about that?"

"Gee whiz, Dad, I think I am going to be very, very busy with school in October. Senior year is hectic. I'll be swimming on the girls' team and maybe on the boys' team, too."

"What!" Dad pretty much yelled.

Mom stuck her head in from the parlor. "What are you talking about?"

"She's talking crazy, that's what she's talking about"

I guess I had sprung that idea on him before I really took time to prepare him. "Listen, Dad....and Mom, I can outswim all the girls on the girls' team, and I can outswim all the boys on the boys' team. Really, there might be one, or maybe two of the boys who can backstroke faster than I can. That's all. Swimming against the girls is really not that much fun anymore. Most of them don't even want to try to beat me. In fact, Dorothy is the only one who has even come close to my times in the 40 meters and the 100 meters. Coach said I need to get into more meets so I can be challenged. Then I can do even better. If I am on both teams, I will have twice as many meets!" I thought I had laid out a great argument. I was beaming.

Dad, however, was ready to disagree. Mom always let him do the talking when it came to me and my sports. "Mable, I thought you just said you were going to be 'very, very busy' this school year. With girl's swimming season starting in August and the boys' season starting in November, how are you going to have time to do school work and be on the newspaper staff? Or are you going to quit the newspaper?"

I stopped for a minute. That was something else Burnie and I had talked about. Burnie was doubtful at first, but I convinced him I could do it. He just didn't want me to get razzed by everyone at school for even thinking about it.

"Actually, I was thinking of asking Miss Hawn if I could be the editor of the Oracle's sports section." I thought it might help, so I added, "Burnie thinks it's a nifty idea!" I tried to look really calm.

There was dead silence. It was so quiet, I heard my mother sigh one of those "oh, boy" sighs. She would do that whenever she was feeling like supporting me, but still wanted Dad to handle it.

Dad looked at me with an expression that shouted, "Are you goofy?" Then he very carefully went on to explain to me the many reasons why I should not be disappointed when Robert Dodd got the job. Robert was a very good writer. He knew everything about football, baseball, and basketball. He had been on the newspaper staff all four years and this was only my third year. He was also in line to be the editor of the yearbook. He was really smart. On top of all that, his dad worked for the sports department of the Des Moines Tribune. The thoughts flying through my brain while Dad listed all these quasi-facts were more like "Robert is a complete doofus, he walks like a duck, and he likes to think he knows everything about sports because he certainly can't actually play any of them."

Of course, I couldn't let any of those comments out of my mouth or my mother would be shocked and disappointed that I could be so unkind and un-lady-like. However, even she had once said, after meeting Robert in the bleachers at one of my swim meets, that she thought he smelled like boiled cabbage, but I knew this would not be a good time to remind her of that. My mind was racing a mile a minute. It was not the right time to discuss this, but I had let the cat out of the bag. I quickly decided that the best tactic, for now, would be to just let Dad think he had talked me out of it.

I wanted to spend the last few weeks of summer vacation enjoying going to baseball games with Dad, finishing up the swimming lessons I was giving little pool rats at Birdland Pool, and shooting hoops right before dark every night with Burnie in his driveway. There would be time enough for school details when school started.

I managed to wriggle out of the downward spiraling discussion with Dad and Mother when I remembered about promising Burnie to meet him for a quick free-throw contest before dinner. I always thought it was hilarious to watch him trying to make the underhanded baskets that I was so good at. I politely excused myself and left my parents staring at each other across the parlor. Mother had a few splashes of tomato across her apron, from the canning project she had going in the kitchen. She must have been nearly done for the afternoon because, as I let the screen door slowly close, I heard her tell Dad that she would be bringing him some lemonade in a few minutes and then they could relax on the front porch for a little bit. Not exactly my idea of whoopee, but they enjoyed their "porch sits."

As I hurried down the wooden steps and across the browning grass, I knew where I would find Burnie, who had become my best friend immediately after we moved in next door to his family. Back then, I had just finished sixth grade. That meant starting junior high in a much larger school than I had ever attended. The schoolhouse in Steamboat Rock was out by my Uncle Albert's house. It was pretty small and had two grades in each classroom. I had a complete education up to this point. I loved reading and I especially loved to write. Math was not my favorite, but my parents and teachers were intent that I accomplish all the needed lessons correctly, so I did. That's just what was expected.

As the only child, making my parents proud was required. My mother and father meant everything to me. I adored them. My mother taught me how to be a young woman, and my father was my real-life hero. He encouraged me to be an athlete in any sport I chose, and he was as proud of me as if I had been a son.

Anyway, as we drove up to our new house in Des Moines on that late May day six years ago, Burnie was in his front yard trying to get a rope over a high branch in their big elm. His younger sister, who was quite an active little pip of a girl, wanted a tire swing. Her name was Rosie. She was only six, and she thought her 6th grade brother could do anything. Well, he was having a heck of a time with that rope, and as we pulled up, he had just begun to tie a rock to the end of it, so he could toss it up into that elm; hopefully over the favored branch.

Dad got right out of the car and instead of heading to our new front door, he veered into the Orwig's front yard to help. Burnham Wilson Orwig was skinny, but tall for his age, so he looked older than he was. I'm pretty sure Dad was afraid the rock was going to land on someone's head, so he dashed over and offered to help Burnie. He quickly came back to our overloaded automobile and grabbed a hammer from his tool box in the trunk.

"A hammer will be much easier to control when we throw it, son," said Dad. "and it will be easier to attach to the rope. A lot easier."

Burnie looked relieved to have a grown man there to help out. His dad was not back from work yet and he wanted to get the job done so he could surprise him. The hammer went over the branch on the first throw, and Bernie was obviously impressed.

"That throw sure was the bee's knees, sir," admired Burnie. "I'll get the old tire out of the garage if you would be willing to help me tie it on."

Dad smiled and got the tire securely tied on in a jiffy. Rosie was swinging, Burnie was happy, and Dad had introduced himself to our new neighbors as a good guy. I was the good guy's daughter.

Dad had decided to leave Steamboat Rock, give up the welding and blacksmith shop he had on the north side of town near our house. He was fascinated by all the tall steel buildings going up all over the country and decided to move us to Des Moines, where he was closer to the trains that would take him to places like Chicago, Houston, and Dallas. They were building skyscrapers in those growing towns and he now made good money as an iron worker. He might be gone for weeks at a time; once he was gone for three months, but he always sent money to keep the house paid and food in the cupboards. When he was home, we were inseparable. As an only child, I was probably a little spoiled in some ways, but both Mother and Dad were strict when it came to me being taught manners and respect for adults.

Today, Burnie would be on his back porch, in the afternoon shade, sorting through his most recently acquired sports cards. He had his favorite players and I had mine, but since my dad did not smoke or chew, I had no opportunities to collect any cards. Burnie had at least fifty or sixty, and I was envious of his cigar box full of them. His favorite was a pitcher named Dazzy Vance, who was born in Orient, Iowa. Burnie was a pitcher on our North High Polar Bears team, so that made sense.

He loved to tell about how in 1924, Dazzy struck out three batters on nine pitches in the second inning of a 6–5 win over the Chicago Cubs. My Chicago Cubs. Dazzy didn't play for Burnie's beloved Yankees; he played for the National League Brooklyn Robins, but if they were beating my Cubs, that was enough to keep Burnie's incessant needling of me and my Cubs going. He was still my best buddy. I knew my Cubs would come through with a string of wins very soon.

"Hey, Burnie, it's time for those baskets we talked about yesterday! Are you ready to get clobbered again?" I teased.

"OK, Mable Hall, I guess I can take a few minutes out of my busy afternoon to give you a chance to beat me. But you can just forget that baloney about clobbering me." Burnie always started out confident, but the truth is, his only game was baseball. He had some great pitches, but very few basketball moves. I started out letting him get ahead a little bit like I always did, but then finished him off and won 10-7. Our shooting contests always ended with a similar score. And we were always still best friends.

The Lincoln

Harley felt both dread and delightful anticipation on the milk route days. What did he dread? That would be the back-breaking toting of the milk crates, the lurching stops and jolting starts of the milk truck, and the cranky, demanding notes left by those town-type housewives in their front porch insulated milk delivery boxes. The anticipation? Another look at that 1933 Lincoln L Dual Cowl "DC" Phaeton 4-door convertible.

Harley had never seen another car even close to the beauty of that one. He knew better than to tell his mother or father about his obsession with it and he was pretty sure they suspected nothing. He also tried to hide his fascination from Uncle Lynn when they drove past the mansion on Waterbury Circle, south of Grand Avenue on the west side of Des Moines. It was at the very eastern edge of their milk route. Most of the deliveries from Uncle Lynn's dairy were in Valley Junction, but he had a few really good customers in the Waterbury neighborhood. They were extremely wealthy customers and he was particular to give them exactly what they wanted, when they wanted it. His uncle had told him that he sometimes made special deliveries to them on days that were not on the schedule. They always gave good tips and were very generous at Christmas, also. Harley always received a part of those tips, so he did everything Uncle Lynn told him to do.

So, this early summer Saturday, he loaded all the crates of heavy glass bottles, filled with milk, into the back of Uncle Lynn's 1924 Model T panel body truck. Lynn had bought it used, without the panels, and fixed it up out on his farm. It managed to make it through the milk route every Tuesday and Saturday, year around. It was a reliable little truck, but it was ugly to Harley. It had a big wooden case in the back, lined with ice to keep the milk cold. That truck had a purpose, and it did what it needed to do.

That Lincoln, though, was a magnificent car. It was amazingly shiny and exquisitely black. He managed to get a good look at it every time they made a delivery. Seeing the buff-colored convertible top and the luxurious leather seats made Harley feel like he was dreaming. The Lincoln convertible sat in front of that huge home, looking perfectly in place near the tall white columns on the front portico.

Right there, Harley made the decision that he would have a Lincoln. He didn't know when and he didn't know how, but he would find a way. He might have a nice house, he might live in town, although that was not really what he wanted to do. Harley was a farm boy and the city did not appeal to him at all. He just wanted a Lincoln; that's all he knew for sure. Every time he drove past it, he was even more certain.

Sometimes Lena would question the big smile on his face when he came home from Uncle Lynn's. He would hand his mother the day's tips and tell her it was just a really nice day with his uncle. That seemed to satisfy her. That was a good thing, Harley decided. Someday he would surprise his parents and drive a brand-new Lincoln up to their front door and take them for a ride. He would pay off all their debts and fix up the house. There would be indoor plumbing and any other thing they needed. He loved his parents with all his heart, but he was not going to be poor.

The whole country was going through what was being called The Great Depression. Harley knew his family was in trouble, but he was sure they could pull through it together. The banks had closed for a while after the big stock market crash. Prices for farm equipment and supplies went sky high. The prices they could get for their livestock and harvested crops were ridiculously low. Their savings account was nearly empty. There had been a farm strike, where some farmers in the area had tried to prevent milk and eggs and other farm produce from getting to the town people. They were trying to get them to pay higher prices, but unfortunately, not enough farmers joined in to make it work. At least they still had Harley's milk route income, and a few cattle left to sell.

At times, it seemed like it would be better to move into town and have everyone try to get a job, but there really weren't jobs to be had. Most of the time, it was definitely better staying on the farm. Lena could can and preserve the enormous bounty of her large garden. The horses had been sold to help with expenses, but the goat gave milk, the chickens laid eggs and also provided an occasional Sunday dinner treat. The man who owned the meat locker in Grimes butchered one of the cattle, took a share of it for his fee, and Lena traded some of the rest of it for butter, flour and sugar at Dolan's grocery in nearby Grimes. Since she started baking her own bread again, both Charley and Harley had put on a few pounds. Harley picked mulberries for jam in the spring and Charley climbed as high as he could in the giant pear tree in the fall, for fruit for all of them. They felt like they could make it through these hard, hard times, if they could just keep working together and hang on.

It was starting to get cooler at night, and Lena decided she wanted the whole house cleaned before winter set in. A traveling salesman had come to the farm with a trunk of cleaning supplies, but Lena was not easily sold frivolous household supplies. The man did have, however, a special oil that he said was imported from Africa and it was supposed to be the best thing for restoring old furniture so it would look like new. Lena bought it. She had her special stash of change in the back of the cupboard, and she just splurged and bought it for herself. She had been thinking about how hard it had been for her parents and her grandparents to haul that big walnut chest all over the Midwest for all those years. She felt a little guilty for letting her only real family heirloom fall into dusty disrepair, so the next day after breakfast she asked her two men to take the chest down the steps and into the front yard. Her plan was to use that oil and see if she could make it look like new.

It was a good plan. Lena decided go out and see what she could do with it after lunch. The men did their barnyard chores and just before they went in to eat their sandwiches and soup, they even had time to put a fresh coat of paint on the outhouse. Lena had already eaten her lunch before they came in; she was in a hurry to get out there with that oil and as the salesman said, "work a miracle" on that darkened walnut.

She worked all afternoon. It had always been the largest piece of furniture in their house, but Lena found out exactly how large that day. It took her most of the afternoon to do the front, both sides and the top. She stood back and looked at it. The dull walnut chest of drawers was much brighter and it looked like it was somehow happier. So that made her happier, too. She wasn't quite sure what to do with the back. It wasn't really finished like the front. It had rougher wooden slats that had never been stained or varnished. Some of the slats had been repaired or replaced; she couldn't tell for sure, and it just wasn't pretty at all. Lena realized she didn't want to do anything to the back. It would be a reminder of the use and service that the old chest of drawers had given her family, her parents, her grandparents, and her great-grandparents.

 Out of nowhere came the thought that she wished she had asked her grandmother more about it. Lena might have been able to hand this down to Harley with a family story. All she knew was that her Grandma Kessel's father made it in 1830, so that would make the dresser 100 years old. She had plenty of other family stories, but none had an actual family treasure like this to go with them.

Hollering down towards the barn to get the attention of Charley and Harley, she started gathering up the rags she had used. Lena's grand plan for them was to eventually burn them, but first she would use them to polish up the dusty coal furnace in the basement. Then they would be ready to burn for sure. She wanted the men to move the chest over on the bricks by the back door. The sun would finish drying it off and then they could move the now-beautiful chest back into the bedroom, looking like new.

"Golly," Harley was actually whining, "This thing must weigh two tons, Mom."

"Well, you know it don't weigh that much, but it's even heavier on my end if you don't lift your end a little more, son," grunted Charley.

Harley took more of the weight of it on himself, not wanting to have his father get the most part of it.

"Scooch it as far from the house as you can and still have it on the bricks, please," Lena asked. "I want the sun on it this afternoon as long as possible. I surely am thankful for my two strong men."

The two men followed instructions, then headed back down to the barn to finish their farm work; Lena went in to start dinner. She wanted to get a pie in the oven as a surprise thank-you for their help. They would settle for cookies, but the dresser was so beautiful now, she wanted a suitable reward for them.

The sun got low and they sat down for dinner, all prepared to relax and enjoy their family time together. Lena had some thoughts to share with them around the table. "You two know how old that chest of drawers is, right? You know it was made about a hundred years ago? I'm pretty sure Grandma Kessel's father made it, but I aim to ask my mother more about it later this week. Maybe Sunday we could go over there for a visit after church. It's been since July fourth, and I want to see that she's feeling fit still." Lena looked around the table for a response.

Charley offered, "I'll be happy to take ya down there to Valley Junction, Lena. Maybe Lynn and Alice can come too. You two ladies could pack a lunch and we could have a picnic in the back yard at yer mother's place. Tell Alice to make them homemade rolls like she does, huh?"

Lena nodded in agreement and added, "I was also thinking that maybe Mother would like to take a trip back up to South Dakota next summer, if she's able. I would like to go see the old homestead. I could maybe get some extra mending or sewing jobs this winter and save up a little trip money. I have always wondered if there is any trace of the old soddie we built."

Harley's ears picked up a new word. "Soddie? What's a soddie?" His mother had taught him to be curious about every new word he heard or read. She always told him that he would never learn anything new if he didn't ask questions.

"You never heard me and your mom talk about soddies, son?" Charley looked at him squarely, but doubtfully.

"Not that I recall. What's a soddie?"

Lena smiled and patted her son's hand. "A soddie is a sod house, boy . It's a house built with bricks of sod. We cut it deep on the prairie up there in the Dakotas. The roots went way down and some of those bricks were twelve inches thick. We stacked them up; the houses were usually built into the side of the hill if there was a hill around. They were as warm as any other kind of shelter in those long, cold winters, and stayed nice and cool on the hot summer days that would scorch the grass up there."

"You lived in a house made of dirt?"

"Made from sod, Harley. That's a natural building material; just as good as wood, but cheaper. And easier to find up there in the northern parts of the plains," added Charley. Then he remembered, having mentioned wood, about the chest, which was still outside. "Are we bringing that chest of drawers back in tonight, Lena?"

"No, Charley. I checked on it earlier, and the finish still feels a bit sticky. I put an old sheet over it and we can bring it inside tomorrow. You can't see anything of it from the road, so it will be safe out there," Lena assured him.

Harley looked relieved and excused himself from the table. He cleared his plate and his parents' plates also. "I'm going to read now, if that's okay with you two. Mother, where is that new Reader's Digest? May I start it tonight?" queried the hopeful young man.

"It's on the stairs up to your attic, Harley. Make sure you read the Word Power section first. I know there are some new ones in there that you don't know yet. We'll go over them tomorrow night at dinner," Lena replied. "Enjoy yourself!"

Harley always enjoyed himself when he was reading. The Word Power was always the section he read first, after he skimmed through the pages for a Lincoln advertisement! He headed up the stairs, grabbing the magazine as he took the steps two at a time.

Lena and Charley smiled at each other and got up to start the dishes together.

NORTH DES MOINES HIGH SCHOOL   B T CO. NO. 103

Shakeup at the Oracle

I could spend hours talking to my dad about sports. He taught me so much about baseball, football, basketball, and even boxing. Dad had taken me to a few major league games. We went to a Cubs game in Chicago; we went to a Cardinals game in St. Louis, and once we went back to Chicago for a Bears game. Mostly, we attended many Des Moines Demon baseball games with Burnie every summer.

Dad also taught me how to swim at Pine Lake when we lived in Steamboat Rock. I think he wanted to make certain I was safe around water, but I don't think Dad ever expected me to take swimming to the level I had now that I was a high school swimming champion. I had been a diver, too, but gave that up because it was damaging my already significant hearing loss. That was something that started after I got the mumps when I was little.

Not being able to hear very well was the one thing that made high school hard for me at times. It was most difficult to hear in crowds of people, where there were a lot of people talking at once. I mostly pretended to be listening at the tables of girls during lunch, or sometimes I would go sit with some of the fellas I knew. I was able to hear lower pitched sounds better than higher pitched sounds, so it

17

was always much easier for me to have conversations with boys. They had lower voices, and they didn't all talk at once or gossip. They mostly talked about sports, so I learned pretty much everything about all kinds of sports. Most of my good friends all through middle school and high school were boys. I guess you could call me a tomboy. Sure, I liked boys, and had a few dates, but I was so busy with sports and keeping my grades up, that there wasn't a lot of time for a real boyfriend. That was fine with my parents. They were both pretty keen on me meeting my future husband in college, not in high school.

When school started again in the fall of my senior year, I was not surprised to see that Miss Hawn, the teacher who coached the high school newspaper staff, had not changed a bit over the summer. She obviously had not spent any time outside, because she was as pale as she was last spring. She looked healthy enough, I guess, but not fit. I mean she wasn't a beanpole, but she wasn't tubby either. She had the kind of curves a woman should have, my mother said. She was an excellent teacher and she had golden blonde hair, which I envied. Old-fashioned is the best word to describe her. I say this because I got the feeling at times that she thought a girl should not be as interested in sports as I was and certainly not as good at sports as I was. Even with that drawback, she was one of my favorite teachers because she encouraged me in my writing.

I was on the girls' basketball, volleyball, field hockey, tennis, and swim teams. I had earned varsity athletic letters as a junior and was looking forward to more my senior year. Some kids were saying that I had already accumulated more athletic letters than any other girl had ever earned at North High. That sounded like it might be right, but I had little interest in trying to find out if it was true. I just liked to play, and I really liked to win! I had goals, but not all of them were athletic. I wanted to study journalism at the University of Iowa, so Miss Hawn was a stepping stone in my plan to achieve that goal. However, I wanted to be a sportswriter, which was unheard of for women, so Miss Hawn was also a potential obstacle to my plan to achieve that goal.

After several summers of lifeguarding and teaching swimming lessons, I had managed to save some money for my first year of tuition next year, but not even half of what I would need. Mother and Dad had promised to pay for my room and board, which was really generous of them. We were not well-off; no "putting on the Ritz" for us, but they were determined that their only child would be a college graduate. That goal did not seem to completely jive with my mother's declared desire that I meet my future husband and father of her grandchildren in Iowa City. How was I supposed to stay home, cooking and cleaning house for a husband and several children, if I was going to be a reporter covering all the most hotly contested sporting events around the country?

Mother and Miss Hawn were living in the last century. This was the 1930s! Girls and women had a lot more freedom. We could even vote! I'm the girl who was named Mable Bertha Woodrow Hall; Mother wanted to honor my grandmother Bertha and President Woodrow Wilson. I was not trying to be a floozy Flapper, and I was no dumb Dora either. I just wanted to write about sports and I knew that I was already really good at it. Miss Hawn, if she would let me be Sports Editor of our North High Oracle, would know it, too. That would be the feather in my cap that could get me a journalism scholarship. Maybe it would even be enough money to take the pressure off my parents to help pay for the rest of my education. Finally, the first day of my senior year come!

"Miss Hall, I saw your name on the sign-up sheet for Sports Editor. Did someone put it there as a prank?" Miss Hawn could barely conceal her amusement.

"No, ma'am," I said as calmly as I could. "I am the one who wrote my name there. I am the best person in this class for that job." I was confident that was a fact, and I had to make sure I did not appear even a tiny bit doubtful, but she made me nervous as she looked around the room, checking for reactions from my classmates.

"There are three other names on the list, Miss Hall. What shall I tell those young men, if I assign that job to you?"

I needed to choose my words carefully. Two of those boys were my friends, and the other was Robert Dodd, but I had to have the job. I looked at the three of them, trying to read their faces for any sign of what they were thinking. None of those cowardly pikers would even look me in the eye. They were afraid Miss Hawn was actually going to make me the new Sports Editor! They apparently did not know her as well as I did. Last year she had all the others girls in our journalism class doing school surveys, writing about dances, interviewing new teachers, and other fluffy news articles. When I kept writing articles about the different sports teams, she would give them to one of those boys to read to make sure I knew what I was talking about. None of them ever changed even one word of what I had written. Those three fellas knew perfectly well that I deserved the honor, and they knew I could do the job better than they could.

Last year's sports editor, Johnny, had graduated in May and the top candidate this semester was my nemesis, Robert. He thought he knew everything about sports and that he was a shoo-in for the job this year, but I had different plans. Robert Dodd was going to be working for me! The fact that he wouldn't even look at me now gave me even more confidence.

"Well, Miss Hawn, I think you should tell them that you know they would want you to pick me, because they read all of the sports articles that I wrote last year,

and given an opportunity to edit them, they changed nothing. You should tell them that I had more sports bylines in the Oracle than any of them had last year. And I would like you to tell them that I think they would make an excellent sports staff. They are all smart fellas and together we will make this year's sports pages the very best ever!"

Golly! Where did that moxey come from? I was wishing that Burnie was there to back me up, but I suddenly realized that planning this takeover with him had given me this extra confidence. We had talked about this moment many times last summer on his back porch.

Miss Hawn was not so easily convinced. "Mable, swim season has already begun and you are practicing every night. There is a full schedule of swim meets."

She also had her arguments ready ahead of time, I'm sure, from the minute she saw my name on the sign-up sheet.

Miss Hawn continued. "I'm trying to picture you going to school all day, going to practice or a meet, and then trying to find time to follow all that is going on with the football team, going to the games, and then catching up with the players and coaches. All the coordination an editor has to do takes a great amount of time. Then there are all the other fall and winter sports which need to be reported on: girls' swimming, cross country, field hockey." She took a short breath and kept going. "In addition to all that, the sports editor has to be looking ahead and be able to preview the winter sports; boys and girls basketball, wrestling, boys swimming. You participate in so many sports, Miss Hall. How are you ever going to have time for everything that's involved with being sports editor?" She then directed her focus to the other contenders for the job.

"Even these young men who want the job will be running in circles to get all the news and features we will need." She gestured towards them with one of her pale arms, and they all seemed to immediately shrink away from her, trying to look invisible now, like they were the ones she had been trying to talk out of the job. With her grueling description of the task ahead, she had managed to eliminate my competition for me! I saw my first real chance to convince her.

"My old German grandmother always said, "Busy people get things done." and that is what I have always done. You know I worked hard on the Oracle all last year, and the year before, Miss Hawn. At the same time, I was earning my athletic letters and setting state records in the pool. I will continue to do that. I have some great ideas that will make our sports reporting the best North High has ever seen. I know I can make it the best of any of the schools in the city! Sports and writing are my dream. I love them both, and that makes me perfect for the job. I know I am a girl, and that you are having a hard time thinking I can do this, but if you

look over all the work I have done the past two years, you have to know I will be a great sports editor."

She looked unsure of what to say next for just a second. She glanced over at the three ever-shrinking boys again and asked them, "Do any of the rest of you want to say anything? I'm ready to listen to anyone else's reasons for having this job."

Everyone in the class was looking at me, not at Miss Hawn. They were silent. She saw this and finally just threw up her arms.

"Well, I suppose we are going to have a female sports editor. It appears you have convinced your classmates, so I am willing to give you a chance, Miss Hall. Please remember that if you run into difficulty and want to quit at any time, no one will think less of you. If that happens, I feel like Mr. Dodd will be able to do the job. I am making him your assistant sports editor; Herbert and Bill will make up the rest of the sports staff."

I had to bite my tongue. I wanted to tell her thank you but felt that I had earned this more than she had done me a favor, so I simply said, "I will not disappoint anyone. I can't wait to get started."

I looked at the dumbfounded boys and announced, "Sports staff, we will meet tomorrow morning, right here, at 7:00 A.M., to start planning our coverage for the first issue of the Oracle."

I could not wait to get out of school, finish swim practice, and then run home to tell Dad and Mother; and of course, tell Burnie, too. Mom and Dad would be shocked and very proud of me, but Burnie wouldn't be surprised at all. I was closer to my college scholarship and Dad would be busting his buttons!

Rags and Ruin

No one really knows how it started. It most certainly involved the chemical-soaked cleaning rags, but what ignited them will always be a mystery. Maybe it was a spark from the small coal fire Charley had started in the furnace right before bedtime. It was just a little one, to take off the early autumn chill. Whatever it was, corncob husk, errant coal ember, who knows?

Harley heard his name. His father was screaming at him.

"Harley! Harley! Run, run outside! Get up and run outside!" Charley was yelling up the stairway to the attic and pounding on the plaster wall. Harley smelled the smoke; then he saw the smoke. He looked out the window and black smoke was billowing out the back door. Then he heard the roar. Fire! He sprang up, grabbed his work jacket from the headboard of his bed and leaped down the stairs.

He saw his mother run in front of him, racing through the kitchen to the back door. She immediately turned around and slammed into him from the other direction.

"We can't get out that way!" she cried. "The fire is in the cellar. It's coming up the stairs and blasting right out the back door. Run to the front!"

Harley grabbed her hand and dragged her out of the kitchen, across the hall and through the living room. It seemed like it only took one second, and they were standing in the front yard. He could see through the windows that the fire had raced up the stairs and was already in the kitchen. It was a small house. In just a moment the living room curtains would surely be in flames…whoosh…there they went!

"Where is your father?" Lena shrieked over the blazing roar. "Where is your father?" She tried to pull away from Harley, but he held her fast.

"He went out the back door before the fire came up the cellar steps! I saw him run out the back door right after he woke me up and I came into the kitchen. He must have been right in front of you, mother. You didn't see him?" Harley asked.

"Are you sure he's out? Are you sure he's not in there? Where is he? Where is he?" She was panicking and it frightened Harley. He had never seen his mother like this.

"Let's go look on the back side. Maybe he doesn't know we are over here."

As they ran towards the back, Charley was running towards the front. They met at the cement blocks over the top of where the well was. Lena ran into Charley's arms, sobbing. "Our house, our house! Our house will be gone!" He just held her, and then he reached with one strong, long arm for his son.

"Come over here, Harley. Comfort your mother. I have something to finish." Harley wrapped his jacket over his mother's shoulders and put his arms around her.

Charley charged around the back of the house again; Lena and Harley followed him at a distance. Then they saw what he was doing. He had turned over the old chest of drawers and was pushing it across the bricks, onto the grass. He was pushing it as far away from the house as he could. He was saving Lena's chest of drawers, her family treasure.

Suddenly, Lena's tears just gushed out. It seemed so strange; his mother crying tears of joy as their house burned to the ground. He understood and once again wrapped his arms around her. Charley joined them in their family embrace, as the Monahan family came running across the road. Lena saw Jim and Betty's truck coming from a ways down, also. The wood frame farmhouse where Charley had been born would be a total loss. There was no fire department that could get there fast enough to save even a piece of it, especially at this time of night; whatever time it was, she did not know. To Lena, it didn't matter what time it was. She just knew that when her rooster crowed, as the sun came up tomorrow, there would only be a pile of ashes and a crumbling brick chimney left. The coal furnace would be sitting by itself in the middle of the block basement. The sole survivor. Well, there was also the walnut chest.

The flames were shooting out of the attic windows now and the roar of the fire was quite loud. Glass was breaking in the bedroom windows and the smoke started to blow towards the west, towards the hen house. She hoped the hens wouldn't suffocate. She had seen other houses burn and knew exactly what they would have left…nothing.

They would have to begin again. Charley, Harley, Lena, and the chest of drawers. She sobbed into the sleeve of Harley's work jacket.

Charley and his family spent the rest of the night across the road in the Monahan's parlor. Their neighbors, who were even poorer that they were, had offered them their beds. Lena would not hear of it, but gladly accepted the davenport and the loveseat for herself and Harley. Charley laid his long limbs across Jim Monahan's overstuffed leather chair, sort of reclining and sort of sitting back. It wasn't comfortable, but it was a warm, safe place to keep his family for the night.

As the sun rose, and that old rooster started his crowing, it seemed like they all awoke at the same time. From their various reclining places, they could view the wisps of smoke smoldering up from what remained of their home. Their first instinct was to go do the chores for the animals and make sure they were not too smoked or too spooked by the fire. The out buildings were far enough away from the house that they were never in danger of igniting from the fire, but they were down the hill from the house, and plenty of smoke could have settled in them.

The men got up and went to their animals. Lena went to the Monahan kitchen and started a pot of coffee. Seemed like the neighborly thing to do. Maybe she would have a few minutes to herself for thinking, and for praying. One of Lena's younger brothers was in seminary, and she felt like she should always be praying and going to church more. Somehow, she had the feeling she would be saying a lot of prayers in the near future. She and Charley had a lot of planning to do, and she knew they would need the Lord's help for sure!

Mable In Charge

"We think you are one crazy gal, Mable. You standing up to Miss Hawn like that was something ziggy to watch!" Robert seemed to be speaking for all my new sports staff; after all, he did say, "We think." I was relieved we could still all be friends. This was our senior year and I wanted us to all have a good time wowing the whole school with our sports articles. North High had some promising teams and we were going to have great fun doing nifty writing and giving our school newspaper complete coverage of all the sports. It was going to be hectic, like Miss Hawn said. There were many games to attend and many players and coaches to catch up with for an interview.

"Thanks, guys. This meeting is to help us get organized and decide who is going to do what this fall. I went home yesterday and wrote down how we might be able to get everything done and not let the Oracle down."

Robert had settled down in one of the desks by the windows facing east and looked out at a bright sunrise. There were still leaves left on the trees, but the gleam of the state capitol building's gold dome looked spectacular shining through them. Despite his initially encouraging words, Robert looked a little bit dejected; maybe he was disappointed, after all, that he had not fought to get the sports editor job a little harder. I had something up my sleeve that would make him a little happier.

I spoke quietly and a little bit slower than usual. I didn't want to come off as some brassy girl. My mother warned me about that once in a while when she heard me getting bossy.

"Here's what I want to do, Robert. I want Herb and Bill to get all the pre-season interviews going. Talking to the coaches and the players about how they think the season will go will keep you two busy as heck." Herb and Bill were nodding and started writing in their notebooks already. That's what I wanted to see!

"Robert, I am going to put you in charge of everything to do with our Homecoming game against Roosevelt. Everything. And after you are rested up from that, I want you to take the lead on any post-season and playoff games that we hopefully get to play in. Herb and Bill will have to pitch in on that, and help out with Homecoming, too. But, I will leave their assignments for Homecoming and post-season completely up to you."

Robert looked shocked that I was so organized. You'd think he had not worked with me on the Oracle the past two years. That's how I do things. I think about what needs to be done, I get my plan organized, and then I get busy! He would get used to it.

We went on to discuss some details, like assigning specific game coverage to each of us. We either had to write the articles right before the games, or right after them. Timing was important, and we needed to get the stories in quickly. I had the final read on all of them, so I wanted plenty of time to do a good job. Miss Hawn would be watching me very closely!

Making Hard Plans

The first decision Charley and Lena had to make was where they were going to live. There was no money to rebuild the house and Lena's sewing machine was gone, so the only extra income they would have was Harley's milk route money. Charley was firmly set against borrowing any money from anyone, so they planned to sell the cattle and the goat. Mrs. Monahan agreed to take care of the chickens. The dog would go with Charley and Lena, wherever they went, and the cats could be fed over at Jim and Betty's until they could get back on their own place again.

It was so uncertain when that might be, that Harley felt completely bereft. Not like an orphan, but like a kid without a home, for sure. His books and his Reader's Digests were ashes blowing around the eighty acres, like so much fertilizer for the crops. Jim would help Charley harvest the corn and bean fields in the fall. Harley, it was decided, could go live with Uncle Lynn and Aunt Alice for a bit, while Lena and Charley got a cheap boarding room until they could maybe find a Valley Junction house to rent.

The bank could get paid from the sale of the livestock as well as take all the crop money. Lena would be able to harvest her garden and use Betty's kitchen for the preserving work. Her canning jars were all destroyed in the fire, but maybe the ladies' circle at church could each contribute a few that she could use, and she could help store up food for her family that way. Charley and Lena talked and brainstormed and plotted and schemed every way they could think of to make the best of this. Uncle Lynn was proud to give the old walnut chest of drawers a place to rest in his home for a while. Lena said a little prayer of thanks every time she thought of the fortunate decision to buy that wood cleaner from the traveling salesman. Those oily rags may have been the cause of their house being destroyed, but there was nothing to be done about it now. She just knew she still had the chest and that seemed to be all that she had left to hang ono; the chest, and her two men.

You know how things never seem to go quite the way you plan? Well, some things did go as planned for Lena and Charley, and some didn't. The animals did get sold, and the crops were growing well. The garden's bounty was canned and safely stored in Betty's cellar, waiting for Lena to get a house rented. Harley kept doing his milk route with Lynn as the school year approached, but he went to live with Lena's mother in Valley Junction. He would start his senior year at Roosevelt High School in Des Moines from there, and graduate with the Class of 1934. His grandmother's house was closer to town than Lynn's farm. Some neighbors out by Charley's farm offered to let Harley live with them for the school year, so he could finish at North Walnut School where he had been going. This included Maxine Findley's parents, but he wanted to stay closer to his family. His mother had raised him well.

The bank was given every cent the family could scrape together. Other farmers around them were going bankrupt because of high operating costs and low crop prices. Family farms were turning up vacant almost every week in Polk County, and some of the closing auctions were pretty rowdy; people were mad. It was also sad. The most populated county in Iowa was feeling the economic pinch wherever you looked, and farmers were hit especially hard.

Lena took a part-time job as a secretary at a law firm, thanks to a connection with her younger brother Mark, who was an attorney in Osage, Iowa. She also found another part-time job working at a little grocery store in Commerce. The homeless farm couple was also staying with Lena's mother, but would be moving to a small rented house soon. Charley was feeling pressure from no one but himself, but it was there. He knew Lena did not want to hear about him hitting the rails to go west to work the wheat harvest, but there seemed no other way to get Lena into a rental house and to start saving for rebuilding at the farm. As harvest-time neared, Charley knew he had to make a decision soon, so he went to the co-op in Adel to inquire. Lena was furious when she found out.

"Those rail-riders are ruffians and rowdies! You know all the violence there has been? It's in all the newspapers. They all fight and some get killed, and I won't hear of it, Charley! I won't hear of it!" He could tell Lena was serious, but in spite of that, he had made up his mind to do it.

"Can't get nowhere sittin' here, sweetheart. And you know they don't all fight. Them newspaper folks only write about the ones that's fightin'. They get all the attention. You know I don't fight nobody about nothin'. If they was all fightin', how would they get all that wheat harvested and make all that money? Don't be worryin'!"

"I won't have it, Charley!"

"What you won't have is a farm and a house to live in. You know we ain't got a pot to pee in, and I aim to get us a pot and a house, and to keep my farm! I done made up my mind. Quit yer fussin', honey. Jest quit yer fussin'. I'm leaving Monday." Charley looked her square in the eye, so she knew the discussion was over.

"Monday? This coming Monday? Why so soon?" She was thoughtful; not sure why he had picked that date.

"Well, two reasons. First of all, I checked with the co-op in Adel, and a train is going through there on Monday, headed for Kearney. I can git on it when it heads out. Second, it will give us the weekend to go see Jim and Betty. Maybe Alice and Lynn, too."

"Harley will be so upset. He'll probably want to go with you. We can't have that!" Lena warned.

"Of course, we can't, and we won't! That boy is finishing high school this year and going to college, jest like his mother," Charley insisted. "I can make enough by myself. I ain't that old and feeble that I need a boy to help me. I can earn my way through those fields. I'm jest gonna miss you, something awful…jest simply gonna be so lonesome. Ya better write me every day!" Charley pulled out his adorable two-eyed wink and threw it her way,

"Oh, my Lord, Charley!" Lena gave him a little smile, but no laugh this time. "What am I going to do with you?"

"You are gonna give me lots of hugs and kisses between now and next Monday. And you are going to get Monday off from the office and the store, so you can drive me out to Adel." Charley winked again, "And then you are comin' home and write me a letter!"

The wink did not work this time and she continued to fuss at him. "Where on earth would I even send a letter? You're going to be roaming all over the Midwest!"

Lena didn't appreciate having this plan of her husband's just pop up like this. The last time they had talked about it, she thought it had been settled that he was not going to leave the family. Times were already bad enough, so how could their situation get made any better by her husband leaving? She felt frustration welling up inside her, but did not want it to spill out. She loved Charley so much and she knew he felt worthless with no part in making money for the family. It had been his dad's farm, and she knew he would do whatever needed to be done to keep it.

"I guess I'd better get some stamps at the post office," Lena sighed, and made a mental note to get Monday off.

Football with Dad

"I do not want you to go to the football game with wet hair, Mable. I mean it!"
My mother was convinced that wet hair could make me sick. I had wet hair every
day of my life; I was a swimmer. Shower, pool, shower, pool; it never ended. I
was rarely sick, but she was sure I was going to die of wet hair someday.

"Yes, Mother, I will towel it completely and then come and sit in front of the
stove. Dad is still not home from work. I have plenty of time. You know he is going
to want to eat dinner before we leave, so my hair has more than enough time to
dry."

What I wanted to do was to go early and have Dad catch up with me later at the
game, but I knew Mother was not going to let me leave with wet hair. Burnie had
already left because the band was practicing before the game. He played the
trumpet and played it well. Only boys could be in the marching band, and the
director only picked what he called "the best boys", so you know Burnie had to
be a really good trumpeter. He was also in the concert band and was always in
the first chair. That was another honor for the best players of each instrument.
Burnie always supported me at all my meets and games, so I would have gone to
the football games even if I wasn't an enormous football fan. Dad went for the
football; I went for the football and for Burnie's band.

Finally, Dad got home from his construction job. Sometimes he worked nights at the city water plant; in Des Moines, they call it the Water Works. He never worked on Friday nights, though. He had no trouble with just grabbing a quick dinner and then taking me to the games after working all day. Being a blacksmith, and now a high-rise steel worker, he was in good shape. Dad was older than most of the dads of my friends, but he sure could keep up with them. Of course, after working all day and then taking me to a football game, he was always ready to sleep heavy after all that.

"I'm done eating, Mable," Dad called to me from the dining room. "Is your hair finally dry? Mother's not letting us out of the house until it is, you know!"

"I know, Dad. It's been dry for about thirty minutes. I want to get there in time to see Burnie before the game, so let's hurry. I need to check on those sportswriters of mine, too. They did a great job on pre-season and tonight's Homecoming game. I can't let them start goldbricking as we get closer to the end of the season."

Mother heard that comment. "Don't you go getting brassy on us, Mable. You stay sweet and polite with those boys."

"Yes, Mother, I was just joking," I reassured her, "We are all working swell together; even Miss Hawn says so." With that, I grabbed Dad's hand and we dashed out the door.

I treasured the time that I had alone with Dad. He was a kind, strong father, but he was also like a teenager sometimes. He would get so excited about sports, and he taught me how to enjoy them by appreciating the athletic efforts of individual players. I don't think there was another man in Des Moines who knew more about sports, except maybe for Ted Ashby or Sec Taylor. They were incredible sportswriters for the Register and Tribune, so it was their job to know more. Dad was right up there with them!

We had not had much time to talk lately, with his work schedule and with all my fall activities, and he started to question me, "So, honey, how is the swim season treating you? Are you keeping up with all your schoolwork and with the newspaper?"

"The swim team is winning meets like gangbusters, Dad. We have the best relay teams in the city in the medley, breaststroke, and freestyle. My backstroke is getting even smoother and faster. I've set a goal to break the city record in the 100-yard backstroke in the next meet. Then we have the state meet. I'm shooting for that record, too. It's getting close to the end, Dad. I hope you can make it to

our last home meet in three weeks. It will be my last high school competition, except for the state meet."

Dad got quiet all of a sudden, and maybe looked a little sad. I couldn't quite tell. I did not like that look and he noticed.

"I will be there, honey, don't worry. I know I have been working a lot, but I'm kind of like the squirrels you see running around in all the trees right now. They are hustling to gather up enough nuts and food to get them through the winter that is coming. Your mother and I are trying to save up enough money to get us through the winter. Pretty much all of the outside jobs at the Water Works and other construction places disappear over the winter. If I don't want to have to head south to Texas over Christmas, we need to have a bundle of cash saved up. I can make plenty of money in Dallas or Houston; they both have big new skyscrapers going up, but I would rather be here to watch all your senior year sports, kiddo." He was the best dad ever. I loved him so much.

I realized it wasn't fatigue or sadness I saw on his face, it was worry. He was worried about money again. Times were so hard for many people now, and I knew Dad worked hard to make sure our family did not end up in the dire straights that hit many families in this Great Depression. We were more fortunate than most, for sure. His worry was deep, however.

"Well, are you going to fill me in on the newspaper and your grades, too? Life does not revolve around swimming, you know? Unless you're Johnny Weissmuller, of course! Five gold medals in the last two Olympics. There's a swimmer for you, and it got him into the moving pictures, too!"

"Or Sybil Bauer! Wow, she really showed the whole world in the 1924 Paris Olympics, didn't she, Dad? She totally clobbered everyone in that 100-meter race. She won by FOUR seconds! Who does that? Boy, oh boy, would I like to do that! I am going to do that someday, Dad. Wait until I get to the University. I am going to set national records, Dad. I know I can. Maybe I can even swim in the Olympics!"

He gave me a patient smile. "I'll bet you can do anything you set your mind to, darling daughter, but first let's get you graduated from high school. Your mom graduated back there in Steamboat Rock, but I didn't, and you know how much it means to us that you get that diploma."

"Dad, you know I am going to graduate. And then I'm going to college, and I'm going to get a degree in journalism." I winked at him and gave him an elbow as we walked along. "And then I am going to be a sportswriter for a big newspaper and put everything you have taught me about sports to use! That stuff is better

than everything I've learned in my classes!" I stopped him right where we were and gave him a little bear hug! He gave me one of his great big bear hugs back. He really was a very strong man! And he was the best dad in the whole world.

"We'd better get a move on if we are going to get to talk to Burnie before the game, little girl," Dad reminded me as we started walking faster, hand in hand.

Burnie was on the edge of the football field, right next to the opening in the fence that went around it. He saw us coming and waved at us to hurry up. He could see over the heads of all the band members, even with their high hats on. With all the height he had, I never could understand why he didn't play basketball. Actually, I did know why; he showed me regularly on his driveway. The kid had no moves. He could pitch some real zingers with a baseball, but a basketball was unmanageable in his hands.

"I'm so glad you could make it in time, Mr. Hall. You, too, Mable. The band has worked up a keen version of John Phillip Sousa's The Gallant Seventh to march onto the field with for the Star-Spangled Banner before the game. Then at half-time, we are going to do a whole marching routine with that and a couple of his other marches." Burnie barely stopped for breath. "You are going to love it! It is so exciting!"

"We're here now, Burnie. Mable made sure we got here in time. I barely had time to put down my lunchbox when I got to the house after work." Dad added, looking Burnie right in the eye, "I want you to know that I am very proud of you for making the band, Burnie. I know your director only lets in the very best young men, and even though you never learned know how to get a rope over a branch for a tire swing, you sure have learned how to make that trumpet sing. Good job, young man."

"Gee whiz, thanks so much Mr. Hall. You know, I have been teasing your daughter ever since she got that sports editor job, that maybe she was going to try to be the first girl in the marching band, too." Burnie and Dad both laughed out loud at that comment.

"Very unfunny. Very, very unfunny, fellas." I was about to start defending myself when the director waved to Burnie and he had to go line up with his band mates.

"It was funny, Mable," Dad said, "but you know Burnie and I are both proud of you and the work you are doing on the Oracle and on the swim team. Your hard work has been impressive. You never answered me, though, on how your grades are going."

Dad was satisfied to hear I had all As and Bs. We were not even to the nine-week mid-point of the semester, and everything I had spent the summer planning was happening just the way I wanted it to. My senior year was going perfectly. Homecoming was tonight, my dad was my date for the game, and Robert Dodd had to do all the work on writing this one up for the Oracle. I started thinking that he and the other two fellas had done a respectable job as my sports writing staff so far this year. None of them was Grantland Rice, though, that was for sure.

It just popped into my head! "Dad, I just thought about that article Grantland Rice had in that New York paper last week, about the Notre Dame football team. Remember that? You read it to me, I cut it out, and I have it pasted inside my journalism notebook. That is the most amazing sports writing I have ever read. The words he used were not football terms. It was a lollapalooza! I want to write stuff like that!"

I couldn't stop. "Miss Hawn said it was too much and not really sports news, but I think it's the best I ever read. It would make anyone love football. I wish I could have been at that game! I would have loved to see it like he described it; 'Outlined against a blue-gray October sky, the Four Horsemen rode again.' I wish I could've been one of the 55,000 people who were there. That would be like if half of all the people in Des Moines showed up at one of our games. Half of Des Moines, Dad, half!"

"Calm down, Mable. It was a wonderful description, and I am sure someday you will write spectacular lines like that. Until then, be a good girl and spread out this blanket on the bleachers so we can sit down and watch Burnie. I love reading Mr. Rice's articles as much as you do. Remember the one I read to you a couple of years ago, about Babe Ruth?"

"Mr. Rice loves sports and he loves athletes. I wonder if he will write about me when I set Olympic records. I would love to have him write about me. He wrote about Babe Didrikson, so I know he likes women athletes. What if I became a sports writer, and I got to meet him…like after he had written about me. We could be friends, and he could teach me how to write better. Maybe I could meet him if I go to the National Telegraphic Swimming Meet when I am in college. Do you think he would be there, Dad? Dad? Dad?"

Dad had gotten up and walked over to the fence again, so he could see Burnie better. I guess I had been talking too much. It was okay though, because as soon as the game started, all Dad and I did was talk football, calling plays like we were the coach, and cheering for our North High Polar Bears.

After the Star-Spangled Banner, Burnie joined us on the rickety bleachers until half-time, like he always did. It was getting cooler, so I sat between my two favorite fellas, and stayed warm for the whole game. We cheered, we jumped up and down, and we had all the rowdy fun that good fans whose team is winning always have. A few times I saw Robert and his assistants on the sidelines of the field. They were taking notes, which is what they were supposed to be doing. This Sports Editor job was not nearly as difficult as Miss Hawn had tried to portray it.

The march that Burnie and the band played was outstanding. That old Sousa guy really knew how to write a rousing march! The sousaphones in our band played the loudest, but Burnie had a trumpet solo right in the middle of the march. I was really glad that Dad and I were there to see it. Burnie's dad almost always worked late and usually did not get to his marching band performances. It didn't seem to be as important to him as Burnie's baseball games. Mr. Orwig was always at those and cheered really loud...a little bit too loud sometimes, if you know what I mean.

When the game ended, our wonderfully burly Polar Bears were victorious once again. There was nothing quite as thrilling as winning the Homecoming game your senior year. Except maybe meeting Mr. Grantland Rice and having him write an article about you breaking an Olympic backstroke record, with the giant headline 'Marvelous Mable!' Well, I could always dream.

Leaving Time

Charley wanted to get to Adel early, so he and Lena got up while it was still dark. The crickets were cacophonous as the farm couple made their way to the car with the kerosene lantern. Lena sat close to Charley in the front seat, but she was missing him already. She had packed a few sandwiches and put several apples in his duffle. He had a clean blanket and a change of clothes. The migrant wheat workers her husband was about to join traveled light. Charley wouldn't need much, but he had his razor, of course. At first, he thought he might grow himself a beard while he was gone. Lena put her foot down about that. No man she was married to was going to have facial hair and she told him that last night.

"Men with beards look like the rear end of a rooster, Charley. You won't be looking like that! It doesn't matter if you are near me or far away, that doesn't change! No hair on that handsome face of yours, do you understand?" Lena was adamant, and Charley had absolutely no choice but to agree with her on this point.

She made him promise, too. Not just agree, but promise. Promises were a really important commodity between them. They both held honesty and loyalty in the highest esteem. That's why they had such a strong marriage. They promised each other, and they kept all their promises.

The road to Adel was long, and Charley had lots of advice for Lena as he drove. "Take your paychecks to the bank the day you get them. Don't take out no cash. Write checks for everything, so you know where every penny goes. Do the same with the money Harley makes. Don't buy no more crazy things from them traveling salesmen," he went on and on. Finally, Lena caught him between breaths, and cut in.

"Charley, will you give me a chance to talk? I have some things I want to tell you, too," Lena pleaded.

"Ya do?" Charley was sincerely surprised.

"Yes, I do. Send your paychecks to me the minute you get them, I put some envelopes and stamps in your bag. I also put a little bottle of kerosene in there, in case some of these wheat bums have lice. That will kill them if you get them on you. And I put a pad of paper in there, so you can write me back. Do not leave your bag anywhere. Take it with you everywhere you go. There are probably a lot of thieves in that bunch. Don't trust anyone. And remember how much I love you." Lena stopped to take a breath. She had more to say, but her husband thought she was done.

"I'll do all of that, Sweetheart. It's all good advice. Thank you very much."

"Well, there's more, you big lug! I have been reading the newspaper, and I know all kinds of things go on that I don't want you to have any part in."

"Like what?" Charley asked.

"Like going to town, and drinking, and gambling. And like the women who follow those camps and get money for doing sinful things." She just blurted it all out at once. Then she waited, hands folded in her lap.

"Oh

 my word, Lena. Tell me you ain't really worried about all that? Ya know I hate town. Ya know I drink milk and coffee. Ya know you are the only woman on the whole earth for me. We done promised. Ya remember that? You was there. Remember?" Charley laughed out loud. Lena hrumphed. Charley laughed some more.

"I'm sorry. You are lookin' kinda silly here, little woman. Please don't be worryin' about that kind of silliness. I'm your man and nobody else's. Now look at me!"

Lena turned her head as Charley squeezed her shoulder. He gave her that goofy two-eyed wink of his, and she had to laugh, too. Laughing while her heart was sinking. She knew she had the best man ever, and she was going to miss him so much.

Arriving in Adel, they drove to the far south side of town, where the railroad tracks were running east and west. There was a train due about 4:45 a.m., and that was the one Charley wanted to get on. The manager at the farmers' co-op had told him that the "bulls" who were hired by the railroad, to try to keep the hobos from jumping on the freights, usually did not show up until the 6:00 A.M. train. Jumping on in the dark might be more dangerous, but for an athletic man like Charley, it would be easier than for most. There were many men who jumped wrong and ended up losing their legs or their lives under the moving trains. Charley did not mention that to Lena. If Lena already knew, she did not mention it to Charley.

"I'm gonna get out here, Lena, and wait over by that big ol' tree for the train to come in," Charley informed her, as he carefully pulled the car up next to an old corn bin. "I'll be fine here, and you can get home in time to get over to the Commerce store to open it up for business." Then he leaned over to kiss her.

Lena was shaking a little bit and was surprised by how hard Charley kissed her. It was a wonderful kiss, and she kissed him back, but did not want to let him go. He wrestled away a little, saying, "Ain't got time for that now, girlie, but I'll be back as quick as I can. You know that. Ya drive careful, hear me?"

With that, he was out of the car, facing her from the other side of the door. "Slide on over here behind the wheel and take this car home," he commanded, reaching in and patting the driver's seat. She slid over; Charley stuck his head through the open window and planted another kiss on her cheek. Lena turned her head and got one more while she could. Her heart ached, literally, her whole body hurt. She didn't want to leave, but she certainly didn't want to wait around and watch her husband leave on the train. Without a ticket, he would have to find a car to hide in, climb up in it, and hope there wasn't already some creepy or criminal type in there already. Lena had to leave now. Her plan was to drive as far as the county courthouse in the Adel town square and wait there until she heard the train blast its departing whistle. She felt like crying, so she probably shouldn't be driving anyway.

So she said to him, "I love you, Charley," and put the car in gear.

"I love you, too, sweetheart," Charley declared as he turned and strode away. He headed toward the big tree, where he would wait until the train pulled in.

Lena circled around the big lot of the co-op and drove to the court house. She did sit there and cry, and she also prayed. After staying until she heard the early train's departing whistle, as the tiniest bit of daylight creeped up the horizon, she headed east, back towards home. Well, it really wasn't home, but it was the only place she had to go. She knew there were folks in these terrible times who had so much less than she had, so she let the Lord know how grateful she was for what she had, praying while she drove. Lena sang a little, too. She couldn't explain to herself why she felt like singing, but she did; it just made her feel better.

Charley was gone to the wheat circuit. He'd be working, and sleeping, eating, riding the rails, and associating with all sorts of men. Some would be good men, like him, who were just trying to earn some money for their family. Others might be really bad, evil men, who wanted to take advantage of others who might be in a desperate situation. Charley was smart, and Lena knew he wouldn't get swindled. She just didn't want him to get hurt.

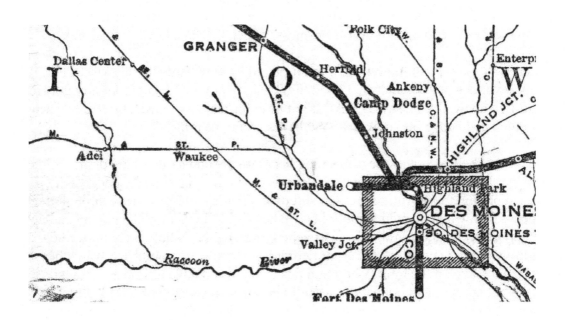

Bad News for Daddy's Girl

Mother and Dad were in the parlor. I could hear their voices. They hardly ever sat in there in the afternoon, and I felt like I interrupted a discussion they didn't want me to hear. I had come home early from swim practice because the coach wanted us to rest and think about the state meet this coming weekend. Coach said we should go home, do our homework, and have a nice dinner. That sounded good to me, except I also planned on shooting a few baskets with Burnie if he had his after-school chores done. He wasn't very busy after the marching band was done with football season. He had a few weeks before concert band started their winter practices after school.

I came in the house before going to Burnie's because I was a little bit hungry and hoped mom had made little cinnamon rolls out of the extra pie crust, like she usually does. I knew she had made an apple pie today, because I could smell it from the street! Sometimes I wished I had a brother or a sister, but when Mother made those little cinnamon rolls, I was very glad to be an only child; I didn't have to share them with anyone else!

I heard Mother say, "Mable's home early. Hush!"

I heard Dad say, "When are we going to tell her?"

Mother answered, "After dinner. I'm going to see if she wants a snack. I made those cinnamon rolls she likes."

I dashed into the kitchen as quickly as I could. I was sitting on the little red stool by the back door when Mother came in.

Pretending I hadn't heard them in the parlor, I asked, "Are there cinnamon rolls in my future? I smelled apple pie from the sidewalk."

"There sure are, Sweetie. I know what makes my girl happy." She handed me a small pink plate with four miniature cinnamon rolls on it. She had even made a little powdered sugar frosting for them. She had never done that before.

All I could think was that they must have had some really bad news to tell me. I had no idea what it could be. I mean, they weren't even going to tell me during dinner; they were waiting until after dinner. I slowly chewed the rolls, worrying more by the minute. They did not even have a taste. Well, I guess they did taste... like trouble.

"You should have your homework done before dinner, Mable," Mother said over her shoulder as she began taking some vegetables out of the ice box. "It will be ready in about an hour."

I knew the best thing to do was to go straight to the dining room table and get my math and science done. Those were about the only subjects I ever had homework in. Math and science did not get along very well with me, so I had to work extra hard to make sure they didn't ruin my GPA. Just having athletic skill was not enough to get me into college; I also had to have the good grades. Of course, now the homework was the last thing on my mind. I did finish it quickly, though, and then all I just sat there and drew the little cubes I liked to doodle, while I wondered what on earth the bad news was going to be. Shooting baskets with Burnie was going to have to happen later.

After what was an extremely elongated hour, Mother called from the kitchen, "Please clean up your homework, Mable, and get the table set for dinner. Please use the brown placemats and the cloth napkins. Then you can come out here and help me put this food on the table. Thank you. You're a good girl, the very best girl a mother could have."

Whoa, horsey! My mother was a loving parent, but that kind of talk was over the dam. All I could think now was that someone must have died or something. I hoped my grandmother in Steamboat Rock was not ill, or something worse. As I quickly set the table, I braced myself for a quick and silent dinner.

Dad was trying really hard to make it a nice meal. "These pork chops sure are delicious, Henrietta. Did you get these at Gapinski's Butcher Shop?"

Mother played the game with him. "Yes, I did, dear. Do you like the carrots? They are that last bunch from the garden, except, of course, for the ones I put in the root cellar."

"Would you please pass the Jell-O salad, Mable? I'm glad you made pie for dessert, Henrietta, but I'm afraid I'll have to save it for later. The rest of this meal really filled me up. It's not like it was when I was a teenager, like Burnie. I could eat all day, and never fill up."

After what seemed to be an eternity, Dad thanked Mother for a delicious meal and she cleared the table. I thought maybe I would at least try it, so I asked, as I usually do, "May I please be excused, Dad?"

"No, Mable," Dad said solemnly, "Just give Mother a minute to clear the dishes. We need to have a little conversation with you."

"Daddy, is Grandma okay?" I just had to know right away. The suspense seemed cruel.

"Oh, Mable. Grandma is just fine. You are actually going to be getting to spend some more time with her. She is coming for a visit."

"So that's what you wanted to tell me? Is that all? That Grandma is coming to visit?" Gee whiz, was I relieved!

Mom came rushing out of the kitchen. I could tell she was not wanting to miss any of our conversation. "John Henry, could you just wait a minute until I can sit back down, please?" She sounded a little peeved.

"Sorry, dear, but Mable started asking questions right after you left. She was afraid something was wrong with your mother. I had to reassure her. Really, Mable, Grandma is just fine and she will be here to visit soon."

"Oh honey, that is so sweet, to be worried about Grandma," Mother said as she patted my shoulder. "I'm so sorry if we frightened you. I told Dad we had to talk to you really soon." Mom looked at Dad with a sad glance. Then she turned

towards me and tried to smile. I could tell she knew I had seen the same look on Dad's face. She looked away from me again.

"Whatever you have to tell me, please just say it," I begged.

Dad cleared his throat. He shifted his chair a little and it scraped on the wood floor. Leaning towards me, he said, "Mable, I

need to go down to Texas for a while. A long trip this time. I got a telephone call the other day, and your mother and I have been discussing it. I have a chance to go work on a couple of buildings in Texas, and we really cannot pass up the money I can make. Hours that I can get paid for at the Water Works in the wintertime are pretty skimpy. We need to get through the winter with enough coal for the furnace and enough money to be sure that you have everything you need to get to college next year."

I hated it. Really, I just hated it when Dad had to go away for a couple of weeks. At least this time, Grandma would be here and we could spend more time together. I wondered why they were making such a big deal out of it, so I asked.

"So, at least you'll be back in time for Thanksgiving, right? That's no big shakes, Dad. Mom and I will have fun with Grandma. And the state swim meet is in five days, so you will here for my last swim meet."

"Well, that's why it's a big deal, darling daughter. They want me there by Friday. I need to leave tomorrow morning if I am going to make it. Some of the men they had down there in Houston were making trouble and they fired them. They are way behind on completing their building. My friend down there has talked to the foreman and he wants me to get down there pronto. This is a chance to make money that we cannot afford to pass up or even procrastinate on." He said it with such finality, there was no discussing it or bargaining, I was sure.

After what seemed like an unnaturally long silence, I choked out the question. "You mean you're going to miss my final state meet? Just miss it altogether? Not be in the state, even? Just gone, not there at all?"

Dad stood up and came over next to my chair. He knelt down and put his construction-man strong arm around me. "The Tellepsen Builders in Houston need me to be up on the high ironwork for a month or two and the PacBell Company in San Francisco needs me for another month. Same deal. This will give me and Mother an opportunity to keep this house warm all winter and to make sure we have the money you need to start college in Iowa City next fall. The basketball season will still be going when I get back, so I will get to see some of your games. I have been going to all your swim meets, and I will come watch you swim next year in Iowa City. I am really looking forward to that. I'm going to miss you and Mother terribly, but Grandma will be here, and you will have a great time at Thanksgiving and Christmas. I went early Christmas shopping yesterday.

"You're not going to be here for Christmas?" I howled. "They're going to make you work on Christmas?"

"No, Mable. I won't be working on Christmas. Usually when I go on these work trips, I spend the weekend at the home of one of the workers. I'm sure that's what I will be doing on Christmas. Texas and California are just too far away to come back for a day or two. It's not like when I worked over in Chicago. That was a day's drive and I came home for your birthday two years ago. Remember? This is much farther. I'm really sorry, honey, but Dad's got to be gone."

I was on the verge of tears. This was not fair. It was my senior year. Burnie's dad didn't have to leave Des Moines to make a living. Why couldn't my dad work in an office? Or why couldn't Des Moines build a skyscraper? I broke down; I just gave in to the idea of Dad missing my state swim meet, of him missing our Thanksgiving, of not having him here for our family Christmas celebrations. My heart felt like it was crumbling.

"I understand, Daddy, I really do," I sobbed. "It's...it's just that I had my senior year all planned. You were supposed to come to ALL my meets and games. This ruins everything!"

"It will be fine, Mable. I will call you on the telephone after every meet and every game and you can tell me all the details. You need to have that guy on the Oracle staff, the one with the camera, you need to have him get busy and make sure your old Dad has stacks of photographs of his champion daughter, okay?"

"I'm trying not to cry, Dad, but this is just so unfair," I tried to explain, but I started feeling like I didn't want to talk to my parents anymore tonight. I wanted to talk to Burnie. There wasn't anything he could do about this, but he would know what to say to make me feel better.

"I'm not trying to be impolite, Daddy, but I think I just need some time to get used to the idea of this. I know you are doing what you think is the very best thing to help me and Mother. I truly do appreciate how hard you work and I know you wish you could stay here."

The more I talked right to Dad, who was still kneeling next to me, the better I felt. His being right there with his arm around me gave me strength, but I had to go over to Burnie's and let him know that my senior year was falling apart.

Dad knew what I was thinking. That is what made him the most incredible dad on earth.

"Why don't you go over and shoot those baskets with Burnie now, Mable? It will give you some time to work this out in your pretty little head."

Dad knew exactly what to say most of the time, and this was one of those times. He knew I just had to have some time to get things figured out.

However, what he didn't know was the idea I had wanted to talk with him about when I came home today. I had mentioned it once to Burnie, but at that time, I think he assumed I was just joking. I don't joke about sports or journalism. I would think Burnie would know that much about me. With this new development of Dad leaving, I only had one day left to talk to him about it, so I was going to have to go next door right now and talk to my best friend about it first. I was hoping and praying that Burnie would understand and be able to give me the moral support I would need to talk to Dad about it.

I knocked on the Orwig's front door, hoping they were finished with their dinner. Burnie peeked out the big front window in their living room. He made a goofy face at me and motioned that he would be right out. He had no idea that the wheels were falling off my perfect senior year.

Becoming A Bum

Charley crouched by the tree. The grass was damp and either a possum or a coon was rustling around in the branches above him. It was pretty dark out still, but hopefully it would get a little lighter before a train came along. He figured there had to be a first time for everything, and that this was going to be his first time hoboing on a train. Charley also imagined that a farmer like him was big enough and strong enough to handle whatever came his way. The farm life was all he had known. City ways were unfamiliar, and Charley had absolutely no experience with the hobo existence. Soon this farmer was going to find out first-hand about the vagabond life he had only read about in newspaper stories.

While Charley waited and kept an eye out all around, he got to thinking. Remembering his good fortune to have a strong family, he realized that he'd probably run into some fellas who didn't have nobody, so staying quiet about his family might be a good idea. He didn't want anyone getting jealous. Charley would have to find private places to write to Lena, and a secret place to keep her letters. Not too many of these guys would be getting much mail, so keeping his put away would be best. Work, sleep, and eat, that would be his life in the wheat fields. Making friends was not the purpose for this journey. Charley's purpose was to earn money to keep from losing his farm on the auction block like so many others in these desperate times. And, of course, money to rebuild the farmhouse.

Then he heard it. The hum, the rattle, the whistle. A train was coming in from the east. Lena had probably driven past it going the opposite way. Highway 6 ran right along the rails on the way back to Des Moines. The time was here to put his plan into action. Lena would be fine on her own; he had to get going and do his part. He stood up, gathering all his things. Lena had gone to a great deal of trouble to pack each item where he could easily find it.

There he went again, thinking about Lena when he should have been figuring out how to get on that train that was coming! That's when he saw a pair of shadows walking toward him. He put down his pack and stood tall.

"Hey, there," one said.

"Hey," Charley replied.

"Goin' on the train?" asked the other shadow.

"I'm gonna give it a go, I'm aimin' to get to Kearney. Heard this train goes straight there." Charley wondered if he was giving them too much talk.

"We're goin' there, too. Ya reckon to ride with us? We ain't no drinkers or bums. We's brothers from St. Paul. Tryin' to help our folks out."

Charley knew that these guys could just be making up a sob story to get him alone. He decided to give them a test.

"I'll go in with you two fellas, if you can tell me what the good Lord made on the fifth day of creation."

"What?"

"If ya know yer Bible, I'll throw in with ya. If ya don't, be on yer way. I don't want no trouble," Charley tried to sound calm. He was getting nervous wasting this time talking, when he should be seeing about getting on the train that was getting closer and closer. "Well, do ya know or not? Don't be wasting time I ain't got."

The shorter shadow said, "That would be the critters. God made the goats and pigs and elephants, that's what he done made on day five. Is ya satisfied now? We ain't got all day to git on that train, ya know."

Charley was surprised but relieved they had the right answer. As they stepped closer, the two appeared to be not much older than Harley.

"Well, let's go then," he said. "Did you two get here on a train? How's this work? I ain't never done it, and I ain't aimin' to get kilt doin' it," Charley admitted. "I'm a whole bunch older than you two boys, but I'm pretty fit from years on the farm. Heck, I got a boy at home about yer age, and I don't have no trouble doin' the same as him. Just lead the way and I'll keep up, don't worry!"

So, the two younger men led the way. Charley followed them to the far side of a little tar-paper shack on the other side of the tracks. They explained that they had to jump up on the side of the train that was opposite of the station. They would be less likely to be seen by the stationmaster, or the men loading and unloading freight.

"This early in the morning, at most trains, there ain't no bulls around. That's what they call the toughs that the stationmasters hire to chase us away. They must not like to git up early like us hobos," ventured the tallest boy. He seemed to be the older of the two.

"I know about the bulls, but do we get on the train when it stops, or do we get on it after it gits a goin'?" asked Charley.

"It depends," said the younger brother. "If they are unloading something, we have to wait until they get done, and sometimes after they start the train moving. Too many people around to take the chances. Those bulls have nearly beat some men to death, from what we hear, so we sure don't want to cross paths with them."

"So," Charley asked, "we are just gonna hide behind this shack, wait 'til the coast is clear, and jump on a car?"

"That's 'bout it."

They stood behind the shack, each one taking turns watching what was going on. The train was not too long, only about twenty cars or so. Most were boxcars, a few others were empty grain cars, and three or four were flatbeds with cargo strapped down on them. All of the unloading was taking place on the station side of the train, so the St. Paul boys were right about that part. There were very few men who came over on the side where they were watching. Charley started to figure this wasn't near as hard as people made it out to be.

One of the boys said, "Looks like there's still a passle of them over there by the train. We is probably gonna have to wait until the dang thing starts rollin'."

They all went around the back of the shack again, and the two boys explained to Charley how it was going to work. They would start now and begin walking towards the front of the train, but stay in the shadows. They would wait close to the few front cars, looking for ones they thought would be easy to get on, and better to stay in. If they got on the wrong car, they might have to climb up on top of it, and ride there. That would be bad. It would be uncomfortable and they would be more easily seen unless they laid down the whole time. It got mighty windy and pretty cool up there once the train got going full speed.

Charley was going to get to the wheat fields no matter what it took, so he readied himself for anything. As the three men were standing up close to the front, the men who had been loading started leaving from the other side of the train. He could tell because he couldn't see their legs anymore. It got real quiet. Then someone on the station platform, way back there, yelled.

The train started rolling. The boys started running. Charley followed. They were fast, but he kept up pretty good. His packages were bouncing and he had to keep tossing the straps back over his shoulder, but he stayed with them. The train was moving faster, but he knew he could get on it if he got close enough.

"That car, the one with the open door, about three cars back! Go for it when it gets up to us!" yelled the tall brother. In a short second, the tall brother threw his tote in the car and grabbed the edge. The short brother ran up next and his brother grabbed his arm and yanked him up. Charley pushed harder but the train was going faster, too. This was it! He took his bag off his back and tossed it at the brothers. The little one caught it and the big one reached out his whole arm.

"Come on, old man…come on! You are comin' with us!"

Charley lurched at the boy's arm and felt a vise-like grip on his forearm. The younger brother grabbed his other arm, and they pulled him off the ground.

"Kick one leg up! Kick one leg up!" they hollered in unison.

He kicked one leg up. Charley was on the train. He was a wheat hobo, on his way to Nebraska to earn enough money to keep his farm and build a new home for his family.

One More Talk with Dad

I sat on the steps of Burnie's front porch with my elbows on my knees. He bounced out the door, singing my most despised rhyme, "Mable, Mable, strong and able, get your elbows off the table!"

He stopped after one verse, when he saw that I wasn't laughing the fake laugh I always gave him when he started up with that silly song.

"What's wrong, Mable? Did Coach Rollins put you swimmers through the wringer at practice tonight? I thought I smelled an apple pie over at your place when I came home from school. That should have cheered you up!"

"Darn it! I didn't even get a slice of pie after dinner," I whined. "I'll bet Mother will let me have one before I go to bed, though, after the horrible news they gave me." I almost started to cry again, but I didn't want to, not in front of Burnie.

"Whoa! There really is something wrong. I was just joking around! Sorry. What's going on?" Burnie plopped down next to me and became the concerned best friend he could now tell that I needed him to be. He was the nicest fella in Des

Moines. He asked me again, "What's the matter? You look like someone just died. Is your grandmother okay?"

"Grandma Von Dornum is fine." I could feel a large waterfall of words coming. I hoped Burnie was ready.

I let it all spill out, "What died is my perfect senior year. My dad has to leave for Texas and California to work on a couple of stupid skyscrapers. He's leaving tomorrow morning, and he's not coming back until after Christmas! He'll miss the state swim finals and at least half of my basketball games! Plus, I wanted to talk to him about what I want to really do instead of basketball, but I haven't even had time to talk to you about it, plus now I am so confused and it just makes me so sad! What am I going to do, Burnie?" I put my head down in my lap and just folded myself in half.

"Good grief, Mable. Pull yourself together. This sounds really bad, but you're completely out of control. I don't think I understand at all what you just said about basketball. I'm sorry about your dad, but what do you think you are going to do instead of basketball?"

"You know what I want to do. We talked about it last Saturday when we were raking leaves. You just laughed at me, but I was serious. I wanted to talk to you about it before I talked to Dad, but now there are only a few hours left, and everything is a big bunch of hooey. I was sitting pretty for the rest of this year, and now I am completely stymied about what to do. Burnie, you have to help me!"

"I'll help you, but first you have to help me remember what I was laughing about. You make me laugh about a whole pile of things!"

I was done crying. This was a mess, but Burnie was my only chance to fix it. I had to do this quickly. By "fix it," I mean how was I going to get Burnie on my side about what I was going to do, when he couldn't even remember me telling him about it earlier? Then, how and when was I going to talk to Dad about it? I had to tell Dad about it before he left tomorrow morning. He was at home right then, packing his trunk.

I just dove right in, "Don't you remember what I told you I wanted to try to do last week? I was going to try a different sport this winter instead of basketball?"

Now Burnie looked completely confused. "Another winter sport? All there is, you goof-ball, is basketball and boys' swim team." Then, as he let what he had just said soak in, his face turned white and he asked, "You want to be on the boys' swim team? Are you crazy? It's all boys. Coach Johnson isn't going to let you be on the team with all boys."

"Miss Hawn let me be Sports Editor; all my assistants are boys and I'm doing a good job. No, I'm doing a fantastic job. Anyway, I can swim faster than every boy on that team. Why wouldn't Coach Johnson want me?" I demanded.

Burnie answered me slowly, like he thought I needed a very simple explanation. It annoyed me when he did that. He knew I was at least as smart as he was, and he still said it really slow. "He probably would not let you on the boys' team because you do swim faster than every boy on it, and... You... are... not... a... boy."

"Exactly! I'm faster! That's dumb! And ridiculous! That's what I just said! I thought you would think this is a good idea. It gives me a whole new season to prepare for the University of Iowa. Competing against boys will help me. They don't swim as fast as I do, but they swim better than the girls. I need to keep swimming!" I was a little miffed at Burnie for not supporting me.

"That all sounds good, Mable, but I guarantee you they are not going to let you on the team. Even if Coach Johnson wanted to try it, I know the boys on the team would not have any part of it. They might even all quit. How would that work? It's not a good idea at all. Just go out for basketball. Find out if you can use the pool for your own practice when no one else is using it. Trying to get on the boys' team is a waste of your time. It's not going to happen." Burnie folded his arms across his chest, like he had just decided everything and solved some big problem for me.

I was sad about Dad leaving and now I had no support from my best friend. Maybe I could just break a leg and then my life would be a three-way disaster! I instantly scolded myself for thinking about something as awful as that.

"Well, I can see that I am getting no support from my best friend, so I am going to leave now and go speak with my dad. Maybe he will think it is a good idea. He wants me to swim!" I blasted the last words over my shoulder as I marched back toward our front yard.

I heard Burnie mutter under his breath, "Crazy girl!" as I reached our porch.

I flung back at him, "You just wait and see how crazy I am!" I still had time to talk to Dad before bed. I stormed into the house and slammed the front door. I must have slammed it a little bit too hard, though, because Mother came running out of the kitchen.

She saw me. "Heavens to Betsy, Mable! What's going on?"

I immediately pasted a repentant look on my face. "Sorry, Mother. I was just in a hurry to see Dad. Is he packing for his trip?"

"Yes, he's upstairs, honey. You'd better hope you didn't break that door, slamming it like that," Mother warned me. "Dad won't have time to fix it before he leaves and I'll have to pay someone to do it."

I gave her a hug and said, "I am really sorry, Mother. I just have something important to talk to Dad about and I'm in a hurry." I went back to the door to open and close it several times. It seemed good to me. "It's not broken, Mother. I won't ever do that again, I promise. May I go talk to Dad now?"

"Of course, dear. You could always talk to me, too, you know." Mom looked a little hurt, like I was leaving her out.

"It's about sports, Mother. We will have plenty of time to talk when Dad is gone. I'll come back down and say goodnight to you before I go to bed, okay?"

With that reassurance, I bounded up the stairs. Mother didn't like it when I skipped steps, but Dad said it was good for my strength and flexibility.

I knocked on the bedroom door and called to Dad, "It's me, Dad. You were right. Shooting some baskets and talking to Burnie helped me straighten all this out a little bit."

Dad smiled and said, "Did you come up to help me pack? I'm not very good at folding shirts. Mom is packing me some food for the trip. You'll be at school when I get on the train tomorrow morning. I'm sorry, but this is going to help us out when we really need it. You'll be thanking me when you are at the university next fall."

"You're probably right, Dad. In fact, I'm sure you are. It is just happening so fast," I said as I sat down on the bed. His trunk was on the floor at the foot of the bed. He had packed it about half full so far. I had to get over him leaving for a couple of months and get over it really fast. I suddenly realized, sitting there talking to him, that I had to focus on my new goal. That would make those months seem like minutes and would make Dad even more proud of me.

"Dad, I've got to talk to you about something else right now. I was going to wait, but now that you are leaving tomorrow, we have to talk about it tonight. It's a sports thing; actually, it's a big sports thing."

"Is it about swimming, or is it about basketball? Swimming is coming to an end here pretty darn soon, and it's looking like you girls are going to have a great basketball season starting up in about two weeks. What's this big sports thing?" Dad closed the lid of the trunk and plopped down on it, facing me; looking right at me and waiting for me to tell him something "big."

"Okay, Dad, you know how I wanted to be the sports editor of the Oracle, and Miss Hawn thought I couldn't because I'm a girl? I knew I was the best person for the job. I convinced her that I could do it better than the boys, and I've proven that I was right. The sports section of the Oracle has never been better. Being a girl did not stop me on the Oracle, and I'm not going to let it stop me now," I pronounced, perhaps a little too adamantly.

"Stop you now?" asked Dad, "Stop you from what?"

"Dad, I'm trying to tell you that I'm going to ask Coach Johnson if I can swim on the boys' team. I'm not going to go out for girls' basketball. I'm going to try out for the boys' swim team." There, I said it.

Silence. Dad said nothing. I was pretty sure he had no idea what he should say.

I was wrong. He knew exactly what to say. His voice was strong.

"Mable, I think it sounds like you have thought about this for a while. You certainly have done an excellent job with the Oracle. You are a champion swimmer. I hope Coach Johnson decides you would be a real asset for his swim team. I wish I could be here in person to support you, but you know how I feel. You are a very special girl, a very special athlete, and a very special daughter."

He stood up and motioned for me to stand up, too. We had one of those great big bear hugs, then he stepped back and put his hands on my shoulders, saying, "You go and get on that team, little girl. I won't be here, but your mother and Burnie will back you up."

I felt so much stronger than when I stepped into that bedroom. I was not quite as sure as Dad was about Mother and Burnie backing me up, but even if I had to do it all by myself, I was going to try out for the boys' swim team. Dad thought it was a great idea, and that was all I needed to hear.

"Dad, do you think you could talk to Mother about it tonight? I mean, after I go to bed? She's busy in the kitchen now, and you're busy packing. Please tell her it's a great idea. I really need you to tell her what you told me. Then when you're gone tomorrow night at dinner, I will talk to her about it." Suddenly, I had a plan in mind.

Deciding to share the plan with Dad, I continued, "Swim tryouts with Coach Johnson are not until a week from Thursday. Our final girls' swim meet is this weekend, so I'll have a few days after that to decide when to go talk to him and what to say. I can't just show up at the tryouts. The boys and Coach would be shocked if a girl just showed up with no warning. I would never do that. I have to convince Coach to want me to try out." This was beginning to sound possible. I'd show that old Burnie!

Dad seemed to think all that was a good idea. "You go ahead, finish your homework and get ready for bed, Mable, and I will take care of Mother knowing about this scheme of yours."

"Dad, this is not a scheme! This is a game plan! I'm very serious about being on the boys' team and being able to compete with them. And I finished my homework before dinner!"

"Sorry, sweetie. I didn't mean to say scheme, I like your plan. If any girl can make this work, it will be you. Go down and kiss your mother goodnight. Scram!" he laughed and pointed to the door. "Then get yourself to bed, young lady! You have school again tomorrow."

Missing Lena and Finding Work

The three men turned to walk to the back end of the boxcar. There were a few crates at one end, so they headed for cover there. They could sit behind the wooden boxes and remain unseen if anyone looked in at a station farther down the line. This train went straight to Kearney, but there might be a stop or two on the way, like in Omaha.

Charley stepped behind the crate and felt something move next to him, on the floor of the car.

"Hey, watch yerself, buster!" said a scratchy voice.

It was dark and he couldn't see anyone, but there was someone there, for sure.

"Sorry, didn't see ya; it's pretty dark in here. Is there room for three of us back here?" Charley asked, in what was probably a too-polite tone.

"Well, if there's three of ya, I can't stop ya. Hang on here and I'll move my bindle. I'm Joe."

So, Charley and the brothers settled in and made acquaintance with the older bum. He said he wasn't going anywhere in particular: he was "just goin', that's all." Said he had no family. His wife had passed and they had no children. He'd lost his job and the bank took his house. Joe had a typical story for those times. He was homeless, unemployed, and grubbing the towns on the railroad lines for food handouts and maybe some odd jobs.

The boys shared some of their family story, too. The taller older brother was Henry, and the shorter and younger one was Mel. Their parents had owned a leather goods store in St. Paul. After the stock market crash and the bank failures, their business got slower and slower. Folks didn't have much money for leather luxury items. People in this depression had to get new soles on their old shoes, not buy expensive new ones. The store closed and the bank foreclosed on the building. Then, the bank foreclosed on their house. Henry and Mel's parents were offered a room in the basement of a kind neighbor, but there was no room there for the two sons. Their parents were totally against it, but the boys jumped on a train one day.

They found a little work at a blanket mill in Faribault, Minnesota, which unfortunately was closed down shortly after they were hired. They sent all the money they made back to St. Paul and moved on. Then they heard about the work in the wheat fields. People told them they were hiring thousands of men out there for a few months, and paying decent wages.

Being city boys, Henry and Mel had never harvested or shocked wheat before, but they were young and figured they would learn fast. So they were on their way, and Mel even said he was sure God had sent them Charley, who was a farmer and could teach them what they needed to know.

As they told their stories and the train clattered along towards the west, Charley started thinking about what he should tell them about himself. Them boys was nice young fellas, but that poor ol' Joe was a sad case. Maybe Charley didn't need to tell the others anything, but they seemed nice enough. He was pretty certain he could trust 'em. He didn't have to get real personal 'bout it, just tell 'em about the house fire, and his wife and son workin' so hard. Sure, that couldn't hurt nothin', he thought.

The brothers finished up their tale and the three men looked at Charley.

"What's your story, farmer?" asked Mel.

"Dang, I ain't as bad off as you kids or Joe, but I got a family to support. Our farmhouse burnt down a while back and we had to move to town in a dingy little room. My wife is workin' two part-time jobs and my son...he's seventeen...he's workin' a milk route with my wife's brother. He ain't livin' with us; he's with my wife's ma. We ain't got room. I got land, but I don't know how long I'll have it. The bank is auctioning off places all around me. I'm not aimin' to lose my place, so I got to get enough money to build us a little house out there again so I can work my fields and take care of the animals. A neighbor cousin of mine is helpin' us with it right now, but I can't 'spect that to go on forever." Charley took a deep breath.

"I'll work as hard as I need to for the money they pay…'til I gets enough to start a little house. I don't care if it's got dirt floors, but I am determined as all blazes to get back on my land. That's all I know." He crossed his arms tight across his chest. "That's all I know."

"Well, God bless you and your family, Charley," Henry said.

"Amen," said Mel.

Charley smiled for just a flash. "Thanks, and God bless all three of you, too."

It was bright daylight outside now and the western Iowa farmland was flying past them. They sat in silence for about ten minutes and then they felt the train starting to slow a little bit.

"Are we fixin' to stop, do ya think?" asked Charley.

"I believe we is coming up to Omaha," Joe said. "Been here a few times. They might throw a few more crates in this car. We need to get these ones arranged so they can't shove them in here and crush us."

Henry stood up and looked over the crates that were there. "We can make a little space back here and stack these crates around us. If they push more against us, we can push back with our feet and they will think there is a crate here."

Charley jumped up and said, "Let's get it done. That'll work. We sure don't want 'em to find us here. Won't none of us get to where we want to go if we get caught."

Henry and Mel started moving the crates while Charley and Joe moved all their belongings and made sure there was room for the four of them back there. Then the brothers climbed in and each man figured out where he was going to push if he needed to. The train stopped and sure enough, Joe had correctly predicted what was going to happen.

The four freeloading riders laid low and men piled crate after crate into their boxcar. Their plan worked. Just the right amount of pressure at the right time and their safe spot was preserved.

As the train started forward again, Charley asked, "Ain't we about halfway to Kearney, Joe?"

"Yep, not that far to go. About three hours and we'll be in wheat country."

Charley really got quiet then. He had some thinkin' and plannin' to do, at least as best he could. He went inside his head, pretending to be asleep. First, he thought about Lena. He'd not really been able to do that since he jumped on the train. Getting' to know these fellas and tryin' to keep hidden had taken up most of his time.

With his eyes closed, Charley could see Lena. He could see her peach-colored house dress and her blond wavy hair. Not a lot of curl in it, just a little. It was pretty. She wasn't very tall, but she had a big personality. He felt lucky just to have her. She was the kind of woman who really didn't need a man; she was self-confident and knew how to do a lot of different things that most women didn't even try to do. Lena could fix a wire fence, and plaster over the lathe on a hole in the wall. She built their henhouse all by herself! She could replace broken pane of glass in a window, and she was a formidable cook. Her food was always the best Charley had ever tasted. Other women was always askin' Lena for her recipes. She jest had 'em all in her head!

Charley missed Lena somethin' awful already, and it wasn't even noon yet. When he got himself settled in a wheat camp, first thing he was gonna do was write her a long letter. It was way too bumpy and jumpy on the train to even think about writin' her.

His mind turned to Harley. He was so proud of that son of his, he felt like bustin' out of his overalls. The kid never complained and did everything his parents asked him to do. He was work smart and book smart. He knew how to work hard to earn a dollar and he knew how to figger out all sorts of big math problems. Thanks to Lena gettin' that Reader's Digest magazine, Harley was a kid who loved words and loved to read. Charley's son was darn smart and handsome, too!

When Harley finished high school next spring, Charley and Lena wanted him to go to college. Harley really wanted to go too, but so far not a dime could be saved for his education. If Charley could just earn enough shockin' wheat, maybe Harley could get to college after he graduated next year. Charley didn't know exactly what his son wanted to be, but he knew Harley didn't want to be no farmer. Charley didn't understand that, and Harley couldn't explain it. Harley only knew he didn't want to be poor. Charley woulda felt poorly when Harley told him that, if it hadn't been the truth. There just weren't no rich farmers anywhere around them in these terrible times.

Charley knew there musta been rich farmers somewhere; he just didn't know any of 'em. Harley didn't want to be no doctor or lawyer; he said he wanted to own his own business. That always puzzled Charley. What kind of business? He sure hoped, for Lena's sake, that he would own his own business in Iowa. She refused to discuss it, but she warned her husband that he'd better find a way to keep their grown son in close proximity of them, or Charley would be wishin' that he lived with the devil.

He must have fallen asleep thinking about his family; then he awoke, feeling the train starting to slow down again.

"Are we comin' into Kearney now?" Charley asked as he jolted himself awake and sat upright.

"Yep," said Joe. "And we gotta have a plan to get you three offa here without gettin' arrested by the Kearney bulls. They is as mean as they come. When they open the door and move these crates, we are sittin' ducks, so here's the plan: First of all, don't worry 'bout me at all. I'm goin' to jail and get a free meal. I'll be out in three days with a full stomach, clean clothes, and a shower."

"What in blazes is you talkin' about?" demanded Charley. "I don't want to go to no jail!"

"You ain't goin' to jail, I am! I'll get out on the station side, where the bulls will be waitin'. They mob me and snatch me up right away. While they're all distracted and such, you three will jump out the backside of the car and run like crazy. Head south and you'll find the co-op in about two miles. Big ol' grain bins. You can sign up for the wheat fields there." Joe explained it as though he had been through this many times before.

"You *want* to go to jail?" asked Mel.

"It's usually the hottest meal in town, for free anyway. I start out in the jail of almost any city I gets to. That way I'm always washed up and fed when I start lookin' for work."

"You are pretty smart for a bum, Joe. Sure am glad we met up with ya," offered Henry.

Charley just shook his head. Joe was a different kind of guy than he'd ever known. That man couldn't wait to get to jail! It made Charley even more grateful for his small, but loving, family.

Joe's time-proven plan worked perfectly. The bulls swarmed him just like he'd predicted.

Charley wasn't sure whether it was harder to get on or get off the train, but he was trying to get all set for jumping off. The train was stopped, so it had to be easier to get off than it was to run and climb on. That had been very scary and hard. The brothers were right behind him, so he would have to be the first to jump. Henry reached to give him a little shove, as he teetered over the edge. He wasn't even sure he could do it, but he knew that he had to, so over the edge he went! Curled himself up in a ball and rolled out like a brand-new hallway carpet.

The hobo farmer got to his feet quickly and took off in a jog, hugging his pack and bindle. Joe had told him that's what the hobos called their bedrolls. He didn't know why, they just did, so Charley did, too. He didn't want to stick out too much as different, so he would try to fit in by talking like them. Pretty soon after he started running, the brothers caught up with him. They didn't have time to look back. They heard a few shouts behind them, but couldn't tell whether it was the bulls hollering at Joe or bulls chasing after them.

The three of them ran for a little bit and then walked the rest of the way to the co-op. It was the middle of the afternoon when they got there. Charley had never traveled so many miles, from Des Moines to Kearney, in so little time. He'd never been on a train before, and they sure was faster that cars. He guessed that was why so many people liked to ride 'em; they sure got ya where you was goin' in a hurry!

The men straightened themselves up before they walked into the co-op office. Charley led the way, since he looked most like a farmer and not a like a hobo.

"Howdy," said the man at the desk, who was wearing a seed cap just like Charley's.

"Howdy back at you, sir," Charley replied. "We three is lookin' to get on a wheat team that might be leaving out of here. I heard about it over in Iowa a couple of days ago. Ya know what I'm talkin' about?"

"Sure do. They are going in trucks tomorrow to a couple thousand acres west and south of here. If you wanna sign up, you need some identification; so you can get paid proper. Got some identification?" he asked as he looked at the two brothers doubtfully.

"Sure, we have some," said Mel. "Who don't?" he added rather defensively.

Don't get all riled," the man said. "We get a lot of no good free-loading bums in here, who try to sign up just to get a meal that night and then take off before the truck leaves in the morning. Just show me your identification and sign up. Didn't mean no offense, honest."

"It's okay," Charley rushed to assure the man at the desk. "We came here to work, that's for sure."

They showed their identification and each signed a contract for two weeks. After that their jobs would be from week to week, if they proved themselves to be hardworking. This was exciting. Charley would have his first batch of money in only fourteen days! He really had somethin' to write to Lena about tonight.

"Looks like everything is straight and good here, men. You can head on down to the blacksmith shop. It's at the end of town, just a little over a quarter mile from here. Head south. There will be about a dozen other men sleeping in the barn behind the shop with you tonight. A truck will pull up at dawn tomorrow morning, so don't be thinkin' about carousin' all night in town. If ya miss the truck, they ain't comin' back to get you later. You won't be working for us. Don't bother to come back and sign up for another crew. If you'd rather hug a whiskey bottle that a shock of wheat, we don't want ya. Understand?"

"We ain't drinkers, we work. We'll head over there now and be ready bright and early," Charley assured him.

The three new friends left the co-op and took off towards the blacksmith shop. They had their bindles, but they were getting hungry. Since they would be eating at the wheat camps starting tomorrow, Charley decided to offer the brothers some of the food Lena had packed for him. They stopped in a small woods, started a quick fire, and set up some logs so they could sit down for a while. Charley opened his pack and dug through all the food Lena had carefully packed. There was some dried beef, some bread, a big bag of cookies, and some canned chicken parts. Nothing they needed to heat up, but the fire felt good after a day of being crammed together in the freight car. Charley made up some sandwiches with the beef and the chicken parts.

Henry and Mel ate heartily and thanked Charley many times. They told him the worst part of riding the rails was begging for food at the back doors of farmhouses. They knew the farmers were poor, too, and they hated to ask for any of their food, especially if they saw kids around the place.

Charley kicked dirt on the fire to put it out and said, "Let's get goin'. Don't know how crowded that blacksmith's barn is gonna be and I don't want to be sleepin' outside tonight."

Three of them approached the blacksmith's shop and the barn. They stayed on the backside of the main street just to make sure they didn't bother anyone. There was plenty of room in the barn; there were only about five other men there when they arrived. Shortly after it got dark, more men trickled in, most of them by themselves but a few groups of three or four. By the time the blacksmith came by to count them and close up the barn for the night, there were maybe twenty men in there. Most of them did not try to look anybody in the eye, which made Charley suspicious.

"I think we ought to sleep close to the door," Charley told the boys, "in case anything goes wrong. We could get out of here fast." He continued, "Some of these dogs don't look very honest."

"I'm with you. I don't like bein' in a group this big. If somebody was to start a fight or something, we could get hurt. Let's move now before someone else puts their bindles down over there," said Henry.

So they moved closer to the main door and as it turned out, there were no fights. No drunks. No problems. These men, after all, were just as worn out and tired as they were. Most just laid down where they were, rolled over a few times getting kind of comfortable, and went to sleep. Riding the rails was exhausting. Charley was relieved and fell asleep quickly himself.

Burnie Comes for Dinner

I got to see Dad before I left for school. We had breakfast together. Neither Dad nor Mother said anything about boys' swimming but Dad winked at me a couple of times when Mother had her back turned, so I think he was trying to tell me everything was okay with her. After I finished eating, Dad and I had lots of hugs and then I headed over to Burnie's house so we could walk to school together, like always. Burnie was still speaking to me but we did not talk about boys' swimming. I was pretty sure that was an off-limits topic.

Burnie broke our silent walk a couple of minutes after we started down the sidewalk toward North High.

"Sorry about being so stupid last night, Mable. I still don't think it is going to happen, even though I think it should. I don't want you to be disappointed. I mean, it all went so well with Miss Hawn, but she knows you from working on the Oracle the last couple of years. Coach Johnson's job is to put together a swim team of boys. Those boys are on the team to represent North High. Coach Johnson certainly knows who you are, and he knows you are not a boy."

I immediately set him straight with, "He also knows I can swim better than any of the boys on his team. He was one of the first coaches I interviewed for the winter sports preview for the Oracle. I told him about the records I had from last year,

65

and that I was going to be setting more records this year. He was very impressed and wished me lots of luck."

"But did he invite you to join the boys swim team?" Burnie countered.

"Not exactly, but he said he wished he had a boy who could swim that fast! That's practically the same thing and you know it!"

"But he didn't invite you to be on the team, right? How do you think the boys on that team are going to feel to be swimming against a girl who they know can beat them?"

Oh boy, I already had an answer of that one. This conversation was going to be good practice for me, preparing me for the arguments Coach Johnson would probably throw at me!

"Burnie," I said calmly, "One of the best ways to improve in any sport is to play the game against a team that is better than you. You know that from baseball last summer. Remember when our North team played against the East High School team? You played them several different times and they always beat you, but every time you played them, you played a little better. The first game you lost 16-2. The last game was lost 5-4, but in extra innings. You can't help but build your skills when you are playing against a strong opponent. I'll be doing those fellas on the swim team a favor by beating them!"

"That sounds a bit extreme. Mable. No one is going to thank a girl for showing them up. A fella's got to have his pride," Burnie said with a fake whimper in his voice.

"What's that supposed to mean? From the way you said it, you aren't going to feel bad for any of them if I beat them. You think it would be funny, don't you?" I was definitely surprised by Burnie's hypothetical betrayal of his own kind.

As we walked up the steps at school, Burnie just smiled at me. We wished each other a good day and I thanked my buddy for a very interesting and informative conversation.

I had a little trouble concentrating during first and second hour classes. I was watching the clock and when it got to 9:00 A.M., I pictured Dad getting on the train with his big trunk. It was like a dividing line. Dad was here; Dad was gone. I had to take care of this swimming business by myself. First, I had to shine at the state meet this Saturday and then I had to show some more of that Mable moxey and have a serious talk with Coach Johnson next week. I put all that in the back of my mind so the rest of the school day would pass quickly.

Swim practice was tough. Tuesdays before meets were always like that. After warm-ups, Coach Mortenson put us in groups based on our times for the last meet. We swam timed races in groups of three. After everyone had raced she took the top four swimmers in each event and had them race again. The top two in each of those races would be competing in individual events at the state meet on Saturday. The bottom two would be on the relay teams with the top two in each of the events. Only the fastest girls swam in the state meet. There was, fortunately, the chance to swim in multiple events, if your times were the fastest. Coach felt no obligation to be fair and let everyone compete. It was an earned privilege. The North High Polar Bears girls' swim team had a reputation to defend! Based on this selection process at practice, I was going to be swimming in the individual 40 yard and 100-yard backstroke, and I was also the backstroke lap in the 400-yard medley. Perfect. There had to be at least two state records in there; we had a whole team of strong swimmers.

When I got home, Mother was on the telephone with Aunt Helen in Steamboat Rock. They were speaking in German. I was wondering why she had not waited until the night phone rates started. Calling during the day was much more costly. She didn't talk more than a minute after I came in the door; I was just opening the cupboard where she kept my snacks, when she was already back in the kitchen.

She started with the questions right away. "How did practice go today? Dad wants me to ask every day. What events will you be swimming on Saturday? Are you and Burnie speaking again?"

"Mother, practice was great. I'm swimming the 40 yard and 100-yard backstroke and then in one of the relays, and Burnie and I are speaking again. He's really on my side on this boys' swim team plan."

Mother looked surprised at that last revelation. She tilted her head a bit to the side, looking bewildered. "After the way you stomped in here last night and slammed that front door, I am really surprised to hear that! Surprised, but happy for you it's worked out so soon between you two. You are like sister and brother. It's hard to stand by and watch a disagreement like that. Are you having a peanut butter sandwich and some milk?"

"Yes, that would be just what I need, Mother. Are there any cookies?" I added, knowing she would not give me cookies before dinner.

"No, there are no cookies. You still have to help finish that apple pie. Your dad is gone. Who is going to eat all of that big pie? Do you want to see if Burnie has had dinner yet? Eat your sandwich and this piece of pie, and then why don't you go over and ask if he would like to join us for dinner in about an hour? Tell him six o'clock, please."

Sandwich and pie? Golly, I think Mother was going a little overboard trying to make up for Dad being gone but I was not going to argue.

"That's a wonderful idea, Mother. Thank you. Dinner with you and Burnie will be the bee's knees!"

"Better get a wiggle on with that snack then, dear. You need to catch Burnie before he eats at home."

Mother liked to have guests for dinner. Dad always joked that he was surprised she didn't go drag a bum in off the street to feed. Somehow, I never thought that was very funny. Dad used to also joke that he really wouldn't care if she actually did that some night, but that she'd better make sure whichever bum she brought home wasn't a 'harp'. That's what they called Irish fellas. That kind of confused me because I know Dad had some Irish in him; after all, he had a lot of red in his hair! Sometimes I could not figure out my parents.

I wolfed down my sandwich and pie, then dashed next door. Burnie said his mother was going to be serving leftover kidney pie, so my mother's beef croquettes were an easy choice. His mother was as good a cook as my mother was. I knew that because I had eaten there many times, but kidney pie was not appealing to either of us kids, no matter who made it. Burnie told his mother that he would come home after dinner and help her with the dishes.

Later, when we sat down to dinner at our table, I realized I was smiling quite broadly. It was hard to believe I could be so happy when Dad had just left and was going to be gone so long. It was awfully quiet at the table for about the first five or ten minutes. Bernie and I were eagerly digging into the croquettes, potatoes with gravy, Jell-O salad, and string beans.

"So, Mother, what did Aunt Helen have to say this afternoon? When is Grandma coming and how is she going to get here? Dad can't go pick her up this time."

She had an easy answer. "Your Uncle Albert is bringing Aunt Helen to Des Moines to see a doctor for her stomach troubles. She has an appointment on Monday. They will be arriving Sunday afternoon and bringing Grandma with them. Pretty late, but in time for Sunday supper," she informed me. "I suppose the next thing you are going to ask about is the sugar cookies? Don't worry. As her one and only niece, you are sitting pretty. She is bringing us a giant tin of her sugar cookies. Now that the weather is getting cooler, it's not a problem for her to do more baking in that old wood stove she has in her kitchen."

"That's swell, Mother," I said excitedly. "That means I have until Sunday to eat the rest of that pie!"

"There's apple pie left?" queried Burnie. "Hot diggety! Your croquettes are delicious and now there is pie for dessert?"

Mother was pleased to hear him raving about her cooking. "It's a pleasure to have you over to eat, Burnie. You have quite an appetite. Are you sure you'll have room for pie?"

"Yes, I will, Mrs. Hall. Apple pie is my favorite. I smelled it yesterday when you made it. I sure have been hoping to have a piece, please?"

I knew exactly what the answer to that was going to be, and true to form, Mother commanded him, "Well then, young man, you had better clean your plate. Don't you waste any of those string beans. Do you need any more potatoes to go with that gravy on your plate?"

It would be a miracle if he didn't explode before he had time to get to the pie. Mother was stuffing him with food. It was as if, since Dad was gone now, she needed another man around to eat all the food she had prepared and Burnie sure was the right man for that job!

Barnham Orwig

Mable W. Hall

Day One in the Wheat

The truck pulled up and someone leaned on the horn for a solid minute. If they intended to wake up every single soul in the whole town, that would have been the way to do it. Men were hustling around like crazy people, trying to make sure they didn't leave anything behind and make sure they didn't get themselves left behind. Apparently, the guy at the co-op had given everyone the same lecture about missing the truck and not getting on the crew.

Charley and the boys piled into the truck and found three of the last seats along the side. Anyone who got on after them would be standing up for the duration of the trip. Charley made a mental note to make sure he got on the truck early every time. He didn't want to have to be standin' up in the back of a truck for the Lord only knows how long. That wheat shockin' was going to be back-breaking work enough.

A short stocky fella jumped up on the back of the truck. He pushed back the canvas dust flap so everyone could see him.

"Listen to me, men! My name is Walt; my dad owns this truck and runs this crew. Hope ya'll can learn to get along back here, 'cause then we'll get more wheat work done and then you all make more money! If ya ain't strong enough to work hard all day long, get off this truck right now 'cause we ain't givin' no rides back if you change your mind!"

"How much we gonna make a day?" hollered someone from the back.

"If you work all day, dollar and a half a day, Monday through Saturday; but only paid at the end of the week. Not payin' anyone for part of a week. Any more questions to waste our time or can we roll outta here and shock some wheat?" Walt didn't wait for any more questions. He just jumped down off the back of the truck. The men heard the tailgate of the truck slam shut and they lurched forward, toward the wheat harvest.

The roads the truck took were smooth at first, but after about thirty minutes, they got a lot rougher and dustier. Charley sure was glad he was sitting down, although there were times when he was lifted off the bench where he sat. There was a cloud of dust hanging in the back of the truck; it got so bad he finally got his handkerchief out of his pocket and put it over his mouth and nose. The boys had their shirts unbuttoned and the shirttails pulled up over their faces. Charley was pretty hungry and hopin' for a chance to get some more of Lena's bread out of his duffle. It was too crowded and dusty in the truck, but as soon as they got where they were goin', he was going to dig in.

They did finally stop, the cab door slammed shut again, and Walt appeared, lifting up the canvas flap at the rear of the truck, hollering, "Everybody out! Head over to the tent and grab a quick cup of coffee and some flapjacks." He pointed to his left. "When you're done eating, throw any gear you have on one of the cots in that big tent over there. We'll be gone all day. Be back in the truck in fifteen minutes. I'll honk the horn in ten minutes. Don't be late or I will leave you behind and you can walk back to town."

Of course, all the men who were standing up in the truck were able to get off first. Charley could tell by the look on the faces of the two brothers that they were hungry and eager to eat their share of the flapjacks.

"There better be some left when we get there, man. I'm starvin'!" said Mel.

There were plenty of flapjacks and piles of bacon to go with them. Charley was astounded at the amount of food on the table in this food tent. There were only two farm gals cooking and serving, but they did the work of eight people. Breakfast was flying off the griddles behind the cook table. Charley and the brothers sat down and ate quickly, not wanting to miss the truck to the fields. They were one of the last ones on the truck, however, and were standing when the truck started up and rolled out again.

It was only about a ten-minute ride to the field. There were wheat fields clear to the horizon, in all directions. It looked like an ocean of wheat. When they got out of the truck the men were divided into teams of four. Charley had already explained to the brothers what had to be done, so all that was left to do was to actually show them how to do it. They motioned over to middle-aged guy, who looked like he was in pretty good shape and was actually wearing overalls like Charley's, to be on their team. He introduced himself as Al and the four men all went to the front of the truck like they had been told to do.

Walt assigned them to one of the waiting tractors and the new crew told to wait next to it. Turned out Al was a farmer like Charley, but he had already lost his farm.

"I lost my land and my soul, I believe," Al supposed. "Everything in my life went sour all at once."

His wife left him for the banker who had foreclosed on their land. Fortunately, Al told them, he didn't have any children, so he just up and left. He planned to start someplace new when he got a stake saved up. Charley immediately counted his blessing of his strong marriage to Lena. He couldn't imagine life without her, or without Harley. He vowed to himself, at that moment, to be certain that no amount of financial hardship would ever cause that kind of damage to his family.

An additional bonus of choosing Al was that he knew how to shock wheat, so Henry and Mel would each have a partner to show them what to do. They were lucky and showed their appreciation by just listening and learning while the two farmers swapped stories. They didn't have but a few minutes, though, before the crew boss hollered at them to start following the tractor with cutting blades down its path in the field.

Shocking was a two-step process. There was a tractor with a large cutting scythe on the back. It would cut an eight-foot wide swath of wheat. The shockers would walk behind in pairs. The front pair would each pick up an armful of wheat off the ground, squeeze it together in the middle, and twist a few stalks of the wheat around it like a piece of twine. Then they would stand it up by the cut end and gather another bundle; over and over again. The second pair would come along, gather up ten of the smaller bundles and stack them up together into a larger shock, one in the middle and nine around the outside. All the smaller shocks had to lean in so the whole stack would remain upright for drying for a couple of weeks. Then they would place two more of the smaller shocks across the top, for a total of twelve. The top two shocks served to help keep all the rest of them dry and held them together on windy days.

The team of four would move as quickly as they could behind the tractor. If they got too far behind, more pairs would come over and help them. It was a lot of bending over and walking. Demanding as it was, Charley could hear men whistling, joking, and swapping stories. The crew bosses said they didn't care about that, but they better work hard, or "we can take ya back to town and bring back some real men!" They worked until about one o'clock in the afternoon this first day, and then a wagon showed up to bring them lunch.

Charley assumed they would take the ten-minute drive back to camp, but the crew boss said that would use up a good half hour for a round trip, and they weren't getting paid for lunch, so they should eat quickly. "You make more money that way," he explained, but since Charley had been told that he would be paid by the day, not the hour, he decided the crew boss must think they were all stupid or something. It didn't matter, as long as Charley had some water, he never did eat much at lunch. He liked breakfast…Lena's breakfasts, and he liked Lena's dinners. This evening, he reminded himself, he'd need to write to Lena.

The chow wagon pulled up with their lunch on it…it was cooked cabbage and ham. The men lined up for a plate of it and everyone dug in. From the looks of them, about half of the men were younger than Charley and about half were older. The younger ones definitely ate the most food. The bread they served with lunch was nearly as tasty as Lena's, but not quite. Walt told Charley that the bread was baked by a widow, named Mary Lynn, who roomed at their farm and helped cook for her keep. She must have had Lena's recipe, Charley thought. He felt like he could have skipped the cabbage and meat, and just lunched on that bread!

Al noticed that Charley was pretty quiet and asked him, "Whatcha thinkin' about?"

"My wife's cookin'. This bread ain't as good as hers, but it's close."

"Well," Al supposed, "there's nothin' like home cookin'. Some nice woman prob'ly worked hard fixin' all this chow but it weren't for her family. Maybe if it was she would cook better."

Charley had a hard time following that line of thinking, because Lena always tried to cook her best for other folks, to impress 'em. That Mary Lynn gal, who cooked this lunch, might not have been out to impress the wheat crew; that's what Charley decided. Lunch was short enough, for sure. Walt rang a big bell on the chow wagon and hollered at everyone to bring their plates and cups back, then get back to work. Their tractor started moving again and Charley followed it back to the wheat fields with the brothers from St. Paul and his new farmer friend, Al.

The sun was hot for an early September day, but not any more so than September in Iowa. Charley didn't mind sweating, until he started wondering about the bathing situation. He sure hoped they had a good place to shower at night. He was a meticulously groomed man for a farmer. Lena loved that about him. She had commented about how she "never could have married a dirty man." Throughout the whole day, he frequently found himself thinking about his little blond wife. He realized that missing her might be the hardest part of the whole wheat crew experience. His comfort came in knowing that Harley was taking good care of her.

It was peculiar to him when he realized he wasn't missing his son that much, until he realized that the two brothers were most likely helping with that. They goofed around with each other and made jokes like Harley did with his friends. Maybe if Harley had been a younger boy, Charley would have felt differently about leaving him behind. With Charley's brother-in-law Lynn having Harley help him with the milk route, his son had a grown-up man there if he needed anything. Charley kept up with the pace of the shocking, comforted by the knowledge that his family was doing fine without him, at least for the ten weeks or so that he expected to be gone. His focus was getting money to rebuild his house. Silently picking up another armful of cut wheat, Charley reaffirmed his commitment to do whatever it took.

State Records and Mr. Ashby

It was terribly early to get up. I mean, I didn't mind getting up early on school days, but 3:00 A.M. on a Saturday was awful. I had to be in Iowa City at 8:00 A.M. The Iowa High School Girls State Swim Meet started at 9:00 A.M. in the new University of Iowa Field House. It was exciting to be competing in such a magnificent pool. Built in 1927, it was the largest indoor swimming pool in the whole United States; some said even in the world. A more perfect place for me to set some girls' swimming records was unimaginable.

Burnie's father had bought a Ford Model T Sedan last summer, so he offered to take us there. It was a real fancy car. It had three foot pedals; there were two forward speeds and one reverse speed. Burnie told me his father spent almost $700.00 for it. I guess he could make that kind of money working all those long hours at the Bankers Life Insurance Company. The Orwigs knew it would save us the train fare and the cost of staying overnight. Burnie had such a kind family and they never made us feel like they were giving us charity. They knew Dad was working very hard.

It worked out well that I was not diving any more. The diving part of the state meet was held on Friday, and the girls got out of school for the day. If I had still been a diver, we would have had to stay overnight in Iowa City and probably not been able to afford that expense. I had been competing in diving and swimming my freshman year at North. I practiced all the time on the high-dive platform at the Birdland pool, which was close to our house. Then, I began having more and more trouble with my hearing. The doctor told my parents that I had to give up diving. He was certain it was making my hearing worse. None of us wanted that to happen. My hearing aid was costly and I was not going to make it so my parents had to buy me a new one. The doctor said I could keep swimming, but only in the backstroke because the starting position in that event is in the pool. I didn't have to dive into the pool to compete in the backstroke.

Iowa City was 115 miles east of Des Moines. Mr. Orwig said he wanted to allow three and a half to four hours for the drive - if everything went well. He had already taken the car out west to Omaha, which was about the same distance as Iowa City. He reassured us that it was an easy trip and there was a lot of beautiful scenery. The weather had been quite dry, so mud and ruts would not be problems. There were more and more cars on the roads all the time and the state was trying to get the routes all marked with highway markers. Communities between all the stops on the roads were taking better care of them and service stations where you could buy gasoline were popping up in the towns along the way.

This car was big, shiny, and black. The weather was crisp and cool when we got out of the house and into the back seat. There were seats for five people, so with me, Burnie, Mother, and Mr. and Mrs. Orwig in the car, it was full.

There were three possible routes between Des Moines and Iowa City. We could take either Whiteway-7-Highway, the Detroit-Lincoln-Denver Highway, or the River to River Route. Mr. Orwig chose the River-to-River route.

He said, "If it was good enough for the military during the Big War, it's good enough for me."

It kind of made me feel patriotic driving on it. However, leaving at 4:00 A.M. in the morning made me feel less than energetic for the swim races ahead of me. It was dark but later we would be driving into the sunrise. Mother told me to close my eyes and try to sleep a little. She and Mrs. Orwig even brought pillows. Mother was sitting between me and Burnie in the back seat, so each of us had a window to lean on. I don't know who went to sleep first, but I know we both slept until we got to the turn-off for Cedar Rapids. We were almost to Iowa City!

"You packed my swim bag, right Mother?"

"Yes, dear. If you remember, we packed the car last night before dark, just to be sure we would not forget anything so early in the morning."

I was waking up fast and replied, "Oh sure, I remember now. Boy, I'd better focus and get ready to swim!"

Burnie chimed in, "You'd better focus and get ready to WIN, Mable! Right, everyone?"

Mrs. Orwig turned around a bit in the front seat and answered over her shoulder, "You will have us all cheering for you, and for the other North girls, Mable. We are all so proud of you."

"Thank you, Mrs. Orwig. And thank you, Mr. Orwig, for taking your whole Saturday driving us all the way over here." I took a brave deep breath and added, "The only thing that would make it better would be if Burnie was going on the tour with us. I know you went to Purdue and so Burnie wants to go to Purdue, too, but Indiana is so far away! Maybe he could go to Iowa State instead. I asked the counselor at North and he said Iowa State has a really good engineering program. It sure is a lot closer."

Both Burnie and his father smiled, but there was no verbal response, so I dropped that subject. At least I had tried!

For the next ten minutes, the Orwigs talked on and on about how great Purdue was, and Burnie kept saying he was so excited to go there. The Purdue baseball coach had written the North High coach a letter about Burnie's pitching and had come to watch him pitch last spring. I realized it was way too late to stop Burnie from leaving the state to go to college, so I was just going to have to decide to be happy for him, like a best friend should.

It meant a lot, though, when Burnie added, "You know, Mable, the reason I became interested in engineering in the first place was all the conversations I had with your dad over the past couple of years, about all the buildings he works on. I learned all about different kinds of engineering, and now I've decided to be a chemical engineer. No insurance business for me, like my dad does. It's engineering that has my attention, thanks to your dad."

It felt good to have Burnie respect my dad. We were getting close to campus and I had to start to think only about the races, but there was so much more to the day that just swimming. I was entering my future.

It was going to be a busy day. All the races were supposed to be done by three o'clock. My last race, the medley, was scheduled for two o'clock. The meets were usually not run completely on time, but I was hoping this one was close, because we had an appointment to take a campus tour at four o'clock. The swimming coach and leader of the Seals Club, Miss Camp, was going to come along with a person from the Admissions Office on the tour. We would be seeing the dormitories, journalism building, Memorial Union, and the Old Capitol. I would have already seen the gym and pool. I was really hoping Miss Camp and the Athletic Director would see at least one of my races. This was all so exciting; the more I thought about how important it all was, the more I started missing Dad.

When we got to the pool every thought I had about anything else was gone. It was all about swimming then. The meet started with a flag ceremony and the national anthem, and then the racing began. I had to stay warmed up between the different heats and races, so I had no time at all to go visit with Mother or Burnie and his parents. They were good fans; I could see them in the balcony that was over the pool, cheering for all the girls from North in every race.

The individual event qualifying heats were first, then the relays and medleys. The preliminaries were in the morning and the finals started at noon. There was a lot of swimming to pack into the one-day meet, so they did not even take a lunch break. We just had to grab a bite to eat between our races. I didn't feel like eating much anyway, but I went up to the balcony one time to grab half of one of the sandwiches that Mrs. Orwig had packed. The large balcony circled all the way around the upper level of the pool area. They had a perfect view of all the action.

In the morning, I had the fastest time in the 40-yard backstroke preliminaries and in the 100-yard backstroke preliminaries as well. I was in great shape to try for some state record times in the afternoon. Just as the announcer was calling for the finalists in the 40-yard backstroke finals to report, I glanced up at Burnie and my parents. Burnie was making exaggerated pointing gestures to the section to the right of where they were sitting. The Athletic Director and the Seals Club coach were both sitting over there! That was really going to give me an edge in the race. Here was my chance to prove I had the goods and deserved some scholarship money from the university.

"Go, Mable. Go!" I thought I could hear Burnie cheering, even without my hearing aids. I'm sure he was yelling louder than it sounded to me, but it felt swell. The starter gun went off, I pushed hard away from the edge of the pool and flew backwards down my lane. I won easily with a time of 27.3 seconds. It was a state record! The girls on the team swarmed around me as I got out of the pool. I looked up at the time on the race clock on the wall and realized I had achieved the first of my goals for the day. How proud my dad would be was the next thought that came to me.

The 100-yard finals were a carbon copy of the first race. Fans cheering from the balcony, and I could hear Burnie's voice above them all. The University of Iowa folks were still in the stands to see this race, and I set another state record, with a time of 1 minute 22 seconds. I could hardly wait to tell Dad!

One of the last events was the 400-yard medley. We won but did not set a state record. Still, Coach Mortenson was pleased and proud of our team's performance for the whole day. We had a few other first place races, as well as several second and third places; we won the over-all state meet title by eight points. It was an exceptional season for the North High Girls Swim Team!

Right after the presentation of the championship trophy to our team, a man with a Des Moines Tribune lapel button came over to me. He said he was Ted Ashby! I started to tell him I had read and enjoyed so many of his baseball articles, but he stopped me and asked, "So, are you the little lady sports editor who is after Sec Taylor's job?"

Sec Taylor had been Sports Editor of the Register for the past ten years, and I would never think of trying to take his job! I just wanted to be a great sportswriter. That's what I told Mr. Ashby.

He replied, "Well, little girl, if you can write as well as you can swim, you might just be able to make that happen. I wanted to interview you, but Coach Mortensen says you have to rush to a tour of campus right away. I'm sure Sec would want me to write up something we could put on the front page of the Tribune. You really showed everyone some top-notch swimming today! Maybe I can call you next week and set up a time?"

I had to tell him, "Yes sir. I'm on my way to take a tour of the campus right now. The Seals Club coach and a man from the Admissions Office are waiting at Memorial Union for my mother and me. I really have to hurry."

"I understand," he said quickly. "You go on ahead to your tour and I will try to catch up with you Monday in Des Moines."

"Well, now that girls' swimming is over, I will be free right after school. My sports writers will be working on the Oracle article for this state meet, but those fellas won't need me. They're really good." With that, we agreed he would telephone me on Monday, and he went over to interview Coach Mortensen.

After meeting up with us at the Memorial Union, Miss Camp and the admissions director, Mr. Cookman, gave all of us a quick tour of the campus. We didn't have a lot of time to go to all the buildings, and all I really wanted to see were the dorms and the Daily Iowan office, anyway. They seemed impressed that I was the Sports Editor of the North High Oracle, but they kept asking football and basketball questions of me to see if I really knew my sports stuff. Burnie was doing a little bit of laughing at them, behind their backs, because every time they seemed so surprised that I could answer all their questions. One time I saw his mother frown at him for it, but his father was smiling, too. I think they were finally satisfied that I knew what I was talking about when the admissions fella said, "Miss Camp, I think this girl really knows her onions." Again, I could not wait to tell Dad about that!

The tour was finished, and we walked back to the Admissions Office. Mr. Cookman told Miss Camp that he would let her know when I had finished my application for entrance and then she could talk to the Athletic Director about what kind of financial assistance they could offer me. They were both happy with my grades, too. He kept saying I was going to make a "great Hawkeye," and even tried a couple of times to convince Burnie not to go to Purdue, but he didn't have any better luck with that than I did.

We piled back in the car for the drive back to Des Moines. It was going to take a little longer to get home, because Mr. Orwig insisted on stopping along the way at a restaurant to buy us all a celebratory dinner. We did not get home until nearly eleven o'clock that night. It was too late to expect Dad to call like he promised. We probably missed his call. I just hoped he wasn't worried about us, but I knew he would call tomorrow morning. The phone rates would be lower on Sunday, anyway, so we could talk a few more minutes. I couldn't wait to hear his voice.

A Most Difficult Day

The men shocked wheat until after six o'clock. Their grumbling about when they were going to eat dinner got pretty loud and some even stopped working without being told. Walt came around and told them to keep working 'til seven o'clock; "weren't nobody gonna starve to death." Cursing ensued and Walt offered them a ride back to town in the morning. The complaining and swearing stopped. Every man who was there realized they needed to be grateful for the work and probably remembered their personal reasons for being out there in the middle of nowhere shocking wheat all day and into the evening. Charley and his crew never stopped. They were silent inspirations to each other.

When they did get back to the tents, Charley hopped out of the truck and looked around.

"The creek is down the hill over northwest of the tent, men, if ya wanna wash up!" shouted Walt. "Dinner will be here in ten minutes."

Charley didn't even speak to the other three; he grabbed his bag from the tent and headed down the hill. Hanging his clothes bag from a limb on an old walnut tree, he grabbed a clean shirt and pants out of it, along with the big bar of soap Lena had packed. Some clean BVDs, too. Hanging them on the branch, he then hiked the rest of the way down to the water. Removing only his work boots and socks,

Charley jumped in the creek with his clothes on. The creek water wasn't unbearably cold, and it was running pretty smooth and fast.

He took off his shirt and used it to soak and get soapy. Starting at his head and working down, he scrubbed hard and quick. Stripping his pants off in front of the other men wasn't as hard as he thought it would be, because they were all doing the same thing. Some of them must've been in the Great War and bathed with other soldiers, 'cause it sure didn't bother them a bit. When he was all washed, Charley tied his shirt around his waist, retrieved his shoes and socks off the bank, and went back to the tree where his clean clothes were still hanging. He got dressed and wrung the water out of his soaked clothes, which were now clean. The plan was to hang them up in the tent to dry and wear them another day in the fields.

Charley guessed that would work; he'd wear the same clothes in the field every day and use these same clean clothes to eat and sleep in each night. He had more clean clothes in his bag but figured he might as well save them until he needed them. Lena had done a great job of packing.

As he rubbed his hand over his chin, Charley was hoping he might have time to shave; he was not a man who liked to have facial hair but doubted there would be time to shave before they rang the dinner bell. As dark as it was getting, there would probably not be enough light to shave by after dinner. The clean-cut farmer resigned himself to a scruffy, unshaven look for the next day. Lena would be disappointed if she saw him now but would understand. He would shave before he bathed tomorrow.

There was a stew for dinner…kind of a goulash with some noodles in it, and some delicious homemade rolls. The food needed a lot more salt, or something, but Charley realized his wife was not going to be cooking for him for a long time yet, so he'd better get used to eatin' different tasting meals.

The four men had found cots next to each other in one corner of the huge tent. Some of the shockers went out to sit around a couple of campfires and drink some more coffee, but Charley decided, at his age, he had better go to bed. It was completely dark now, and morning would come soon enough. He needed to sleep. The two brothers wanted to hear some good stories, so they went to the campfires. Al agreed with Charley and headed to bed. There were other men, mostly older ones, who had enough sense to get to bed at a decent time, so soon the tent was a busily snoring place. The sun came up suddenly, it seemed.

When they awoke, the air was heavy and damp. It didn't appear as if it had rained, but it was bound to. If it didn't, Charley knew that the high humidity would make the shocking work today pretty much insufferable. And if it did decide to rain, the wheat work would continue, but the cut wheat would be heavy and the work would be harder on his back. Whatever developed though, he knew he would do what had to be done.

Al and the brothers were not complaining about the state of the weather, like many of the other men. Charley thought that most of them must not be farmers, because farmers know there is no use in complaining about the heat or the cold or anything else that Mother Nature delivered. Didn't do no good, ever. Weather was what ya got whether ya liked it or not, and the smart man just learned to make the best of it. Charley said a silent prayer to let God know he was thankful for a job and for his friends. He said his "Amen," and climbed up into the truck.

It did start to rain about ten o'clock that morning, but the rain was spotty and light. Then the hot sun came out again and the air became dreadfully steamy. Men removed their shirts and kept cutting, tying, bunching, stacking, leaning, walking. The sun beat down all during lunch, which was left-over goulash with bread and butter sandwiches. This time, instead of water, they brought big buckets of lemonade. That really surprised Charley, as fruit was quite a luxury item. Walt explained that a fruit truck from California had stopped in town and a whole crate of lemons was traded for a tire patch at the co-op. Walt's brother just happened to be in there when it happened and bought the whole crate from the co-op for a dollar. The lemonade wasn't cold, but it was refreshing. The blistering heat weighed all the men down. Every one of them was moving in slow-motion, even Walt; but the work had to be done.

They tramped, soaked with sweat and getting weaker in the knees, through the fields. The sky gradually got darker and the wind picked up. Out westward, Charley could see towering thunderheads of clouds that were coal black on the bottom.

"There's gonna be a big storm, fellas," he warned his immediate crew. The guy driving the tractor in front of them hollered back to them, something about if they saw any lightning, to let him know. That made Charley feel better, as he and Al exchanged knowing nods. They were glad that they were working for folks who weren't so stupid as to stay out in an open field during a lightning storm. Al told the brothers that their plan in case of lightning was for the four of them to run for cover in the nearest side ditch of the road. Nebraska is just plain flat, so unfortunately, they were all out in the middle of a centered 160-acre plot, and the nearest ditch was a good third of a mile away. The brothers said they weren't worried, having been good runners all their life. Charley and Al nodded at each other again, knowing the brothers would be having a bit of a boasting challenge as to which one of them got to the ditch first. They were right, 'cause Henry and Mel immediately began making informal wagers with each other about the impending footrace to safety.

Charley kept as close an eye as he could on the horizon. One of his steers was killed by a lightning strike once and it was a frightening sight. Remembering the stench of the burned flesh, he knew sure as heck that he didn't want to see that happen to a man, especially him! No bolts appeared anywhere around them, but the wind got stronger and stronger. The mid-afternoon air got more and more dark, but the clouds started turning a strange yellowish color, and then an ominous green. The clouds sank so close to the ground, it seemed like if they were over his farm, they would have touched the top of the windmill. It was hard to judge out here in this unfamiliar flat land. The wind swirled so hard now that it started to cool off a little, but the heaviness in the air remained.

Then the shout came. It was faint and came from the back of the pickup that was barreling across the field. Walt was driving and there was another guy standing in the back, hanging on to save his life! "Twister, look south, twister," he yelled, over and over. "Twister, twister, run for cover!"

They all looked south and started running east to the ditch at the same time. Over his right shoulder, Charley could see it coming through the darkness. It was loud, and there was cut grain starting to fly off the ground and spin up into the sky. The twister was about a half-mile away, as far as he could judge. Henry and Mel were in front of him and Al was right next to him. Charley was running as fast as he could, but the rotating beast was getting closer.

Praying as he ran, Charley shouted to Al, "We ain't gonna make it to the ditch, Al! I'm goin' for under that tractor over there!" he hollered, pointing to a red Chamberlain with a scythe attached, that was about 100 yards from the road. They both adjusted their path, and as he and Al slid in between the big back wheels of the tractor, he saw the two brothers dive into the ditch. The twister was bearing down on them.

It wasn't a direct hit, but darn close. Hail about the size of walnuts pelted the field; the rain poured down in sheets. The tractor shook and vibrated, literally inching along the ground, but never going airborne. Charley was still praying like crazy, but with one eye on the ditch. Them boys was probably gettin' pelted with the hail and would have some bruises to show for it, for sure. He was trying to keep his head low and make sure the tires didn't roll over his legs. That tractor stayed on the ground, but it had moved at least ten feet, as near as he could figure it. He scooted along on his belly, managing to keep up with it. The twister seemed to be just getting past them, when he remembered Al. He looked around and there he was, behind the rear end of the tractor. Al had ended up under the scythe.

"Charley, I been cut by the scythe! I been cut bad! Get me outta here!" Al hollered. "I'm a bleedin' like a stuck pig!"

Charley scrambled out of where he was and crawled over to where Al was. Oh, it was bad alright. Really bad. The kind of bad that would last only minutes. He looked into Al's eyes, and he saw that Al knew it, too.

Farmers learn things about anatomy without all that formal schooling. Between dressing deer, butchering livestock, and farming accidents, they know when there's been a fatal blow struck. That slice the scythe blade had made into Al's groin was fatal. Charley and Al both knew that there is a big blood vessel there that can't be stopped with any amount of pressure, or a tourniquet, or anything. Al's blood was pouring out onto that field at a rate that would only give him a few minutes left on earth.

"Don't try to move me, Charley, just leave me here and pray with me." Al looked at Charley with a look that showed he knew and had accepted his fate just that quick. The brothers were running back, and Charley waved them over, but hushed them before they got there.

"Al's been cut and killed. Well, he ain't dead yet, but Death is on his way to get him right soon. You two boys kneel down and pray with me right now. That's what Al wants."

Charley began The Lord's Prayer, "Our Father, who art in Heaven, hallowed be Thy name." The brothers joined in and all three prayed together, "Thy kingdom come, Thy will be done, on earth as it is in Heaven. Give us this day our daily bread and forgive us our trespasses as we forgive those who trespass against us. Lead us not into temptation, but deliver us from evil, for Thine is the kingdom, and the power, and the glory forever and ever, Amen."

He looked up, and again, his eyes met Al's. "Pray, Charley, pray!" Al urged weakly. "Pray like a tent preacher, until I'm gone."

"We's doin' the 23rd Psalm, boys. I know ya knows it!" Charley said, but began reciting it before he even saw the brothers nod. The three of them spoke it together for the dying man. "The Lord is my shepherd; I shall not want. He makes me to lie down in green pastures; He leads me beside the still waters. He restores my soul; He leads me in the paths of righteousness for His name's sake. Yea, though I walk through the valley of the shadow of death, I will fear no evil,"

Al let out a moan.

Charley prayed on, "for Thou art with me; Thy rod and Thy staff, they comfort me. Thou preparest a table before me in the presence of mine enemies. Thou anointest my head with oil. My cup runneth over." Al groped around for Charley's hand and put it in a vise-like grip. Charley looked up at the young men.

Tears were streaming down their faces; faces twisted in horror at the dying man lying at their feet.

Charley finished by himself, "Surely goodness and mercy shall follow me all the days of my life; and I will dwell in the house of the Lord forever. Amen."

There was a crimson pool of blood in the golden wheat under Al, and his spirit slipped away. Al had been wrong; he was not a lost soul. He'd lost his farm and his wife, but his soul was with the Lord. Charley shook his head, removed his cap, and removed Al's cap, too. He placed it over Al's face.

Out of nowhere, there was a crowd of the men around the tractor when Charley stood up. "Al's done bled to death, fellas. The scythe cut a big blood vessel in his leg, and he's gone. It was quick. Can somebody flag down Walt and the truck?"

 The men rearranged themselves around the scythe so they could see what happened, while Charley sat back down on the ground, exhausted. The work that day had been hard enough with the heavy air and wet wheat; Al dying like that was unexpected and Charley didn't know what to think, or what to do. Walt could figure that out.

Walt did come with the truck and two of the men pulled Al's body from under the tractor. They gently wrapped him up, using the canvas curtain that had hung from the back of the transport truck. Walt said they would take Al into town and the preacher there would see that he got buried, what with him not really having a family that anyone knew about. It's all they could do in times like these; all the men agreed. Charley and the brothers would have liked to have been there for the burial, but they knew it wasn't possible.

"We prayed over him when he really needed it, boys, so we'll jest have to let the preacher do his job," Charley reassured them. They were so young and not used to death like Charley and the older men were. Charley wondered how much more of life, and death, those boys would see before they got back home to St. Paul.

The twister had missed the farmhouse and the workers' tent. None of the farming equipment had been damaged, so the harvest would continue the next day. There were about three hours left to shock wheat when Al died, but Walt had all the men taken back to camp early. It had been an especially difficult day.

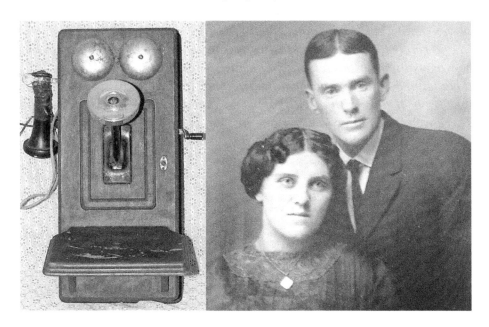

John Henry Calls Home

I woke up about eight-thirty Sunday morning and Saturday seemed like a dream. The huge pool, the cheering fans, the beautiful Old Capitol building, meeting Ted Ashby, and the long, long automobile trip; what a day. I wanted to take a hot soak in the bathtub, but I didn't want to miss Dad's phone call. I put on my green chenille bathrobe and ran down the stairs to let Mother know I was awake. She was in the kitchen drinking coffee and I smelled coffee cake in the oven.

"Good morning, Mother. Do you think I have time to take a bath before Dad calls us? My legs and bottom are still a little stiff after all that swimming, and then sitting in the car for so long."

She answered easily, "You go ahead, darling daughter. I already had my soak. Your father said he would be calling before Sunday dinner, and the coffee cake has only been in the oven about five minutes. You have plenty of time for a good soak."

I was so glad we had indoor plumbing in Des Moines. Back in Steamboat Rock, they still had to use the outhouses and well pump at Uncle Albert's house and at Grandma's house, too. Our tub with running water was wonderful! It was especially nice in the winter. I headed to the back of the house, to the room just off the back porch. There was a tub and a heater right next to it. It took a while for the water to warm up, but eventually I was clean and comfortable.

Mother was getting a little anxious when I finally arrived in the kitchen again, all dressed and ready for a late breakfast. It was a minute or two past ten o'clock and she was waiting for the telephone to ring. It was hard for both of us. We missed Dad and couldn't wait any longer to hear his voice. Just a minute later the telephone rang. It rang with three short rings. On our party line, that was our ring. There were four other families on our line, but the receiver was only picked up if it was our ring. Polite folks never listened in on other people's telephone calls.

Mom answered it on the second three rings. "Hello? Is it you, John Henry?"

"Yes, it is, my dear Henrietta. This is your John Henry, calling from Houston. Are you and Mable doing okay? Is she up already this morning?"

Boy, he had a lot of questions. I know Mother would want to talk to him first, and last, but that she would let me be the one to tell him about yesterday.

"Yes, she's up. Already had herself a nice bath and is ready for some coffee cake. She wants to tell you all about yesterday, of course," Mother replied.

"In a minute, Henrietta," Dad answered. "She can tell me all about the state meet and campus tour, but first, I want to hear from you about the house and how your travels yesterday went."

"Well, the house is fine. The yard got raked Friday afternoon by those two young Erickson boys and I gave them each a dime. One did the front yard and one did the back yard. It only took them about an hour. They dumped all the leaves in the burn pile back by the alley, and we will burn them before they blow around, probably this afternoon if the wind stays calm. The trip on the River-to-River route was long, but pleasant in Mr. Orwig's new car. There was plenty of room for all of us. On the way back, he stopped at a restaurant and bought us all dinner. It was a delightful and exciting day. We both wish you could have been here, but we know you are doing the best thing for us, John Henry. I love you and miss you."

"I love you, too, Henrietta. I know you can take good care of everything. I'll be sending some money up there every Friday. Just keep the bills paid and save the rest. When is your mother coming?"

"Albert and Helen are arriving this afternoon, hopefully in time for dinner," Mother answered. "Here's Mable. She can hardly stand still waiting to talk to you. She has an awful lot to tell you. Bye for now, John Henry."

Mother handed me the receiver. It was hard not to grab it out of her hand, but I was certainly raised better than that. I just had to tell Dad everything!

"Hello, Dad? I set two state records! Two, do you hear me?" I shouted into the receiver.

"Whoa, little girl!" Dad answered. I could tell he was excited to hear that, but I guess I was a little too loud. "I want to hear all the details, but you had better calm down or it won't come out right like it needs to. Please, we don't have all day, so give me the good news so I can understand it."

I took a really deep breath. "Sorry, Daddy. I swam so well. All the practice and everything was worth it. I won the preliminary heats and then I won in the finals of the 40-yard and 100-yard backstroke. I set state records in both. In both! Our medley team came in second, but we ended up winning the Iowa State Championship trophy by eight team points. All the girls swam really well. It was the most fun!"

"Whoa, again, darling daughter; one thing at a time. That is wonderful, and I am so proud of you. Did the people from the university come and watch? How did the tour go? Are they going to help with your tuition? What did they say?"

"Dad, they were really swell to all of us. The Old Capitol was so elegant. I loved the journalism program and I got to see where they print the Daily Iowan and where they work on the Old Gold yearbook, too. The swim coach is Miss Camp and she brought the Athletic Director to watch me swim. Miss Camp is waiting to hear from the Admissions Director about receiving my application and then they will let me know what they can do to help with my tuition and other expenses. Everything is going just like we hoped. Don't worry." I think I said that all in one breath; I was so eager to tell him. I added, "I sure wish you could have come with us."

"I'm where I belong right now, Mable. It's so good to hear that the meet and tour went so fine. I have always been proud of you, no matter what; win or lose. I am even more proud of you now. I will always be proud of you. You know how to work hard. You know how to go after what you want and how to get it. You are going to shine even brighter at the university. I will be home after Christmas; probably around the middle of January. You make a strong finish with your grades this semester, okay?"

"Okay, Dad. You know I will," I replied.

"And, darling daughter, have you had a chance to talk to that boys' swim team coach yet?"

"No, Dad. I wanted to wait until our swim season was over and until I had the records at the state meet. I'll talk to him this week, though, I promise."

He asked me to give the phone back to Mother. I did.

At first, she just listened for a minute. I don't know what he was saying, but she said, "I don't like the sound of that, John Henry. You get yourself to a doctor tomorrow, you promise? Promise me?"

Dad answered her with, "I don't know if I can get there tomorrow," and Mom frowned.

"Okay, then some other day this week, and you call us up on the telephone again next Sunday. But you'd better be able to tell me what that doctor says." Then Dad talked some more and finally Mother said, "Goodbye for now, John Henry. I love you, too." She put the receiver back on the wall.

She turned to me and reported, "You father said he was feeling kinda poorly and had to miss a day of work. You know how strong he is and he's never been sick a day. So, I told him to get to a doctor tomorrow. He probably picked up one of those germ things on the train. Who knows what kind of people were riding with him. Those trains are so closed up and you are just sitting there with a whole car full of strangers. Who knows?" She continued, "He promised he would go. We'll hear from him again next Sunday. We'll just put him in our prayers, Mable, like we always do."

"Is that all he said, Mother?"

"Well, you know he added that he really believed in you, and that I should give you all my support for this boys' swim team problem. I'm not sure I agree with the two of you, but I will support you just like Dad would. I believe in you, Mable, just like your father does. You are a remarkable daughter, and both of us love you more than you will ever understand." Mother was starting to get a few tears in her eyes, and so was I.

I had the most wonderful parents in the world. I was such a blessed girl. We did not go to church much; usually only at Christmas and Easter, but we prayed and we loved God. He had been good to all three of us. All I could answer her with was, "I love you both, more that I can ever tell you."

We had a big long hug. It wasn't a bear hug like Dad could give. We both knew it, but it was a strong hug; like there should be between a mother and daughter.

1911 Polk County Baseball Champions

Going Where the Wheat Is

From then on, from the day Al died, Charley and the brothers worked as a threesome. Walt kept saying that someone was goin' into Kearney to get one more worker to replace Al, but it never happened. Maybe, Charley thought, word had got around town that a man died in the wheat harvest, and superstition kept anyone from stepping forward to replace him. It was hard to believe, in these slim-pickins time for work, that anyone would let that stop them. He ended up just figurin' that Walt didn't want to spend the gas money to go all that way to pick up one man. Everyone else in the crew seemed to be toleratin' the work well.

The weather stayed warm during the day, but it was getting cooler at night and they continued to move north. This spread was enormous. Charley guessed that it was at least a thousand acres. He was afraid to ask because he didn't want anyone to think he was getting tired or that he wanted to quit. It would sound like a little kid in the back of the buggy askin' his folks, "How much longer 'til we get there?" He had kept track of the days in a black notebook that Lena had packed in his bag. On the twelfth day, he realized he had not yet written to Lena.

She was probably worried sick and working her way up to bein' angry. Charley knew he had to write her, but by the time they got back from the field every day, he shaved, got washed up in the creek, and ate dinner, he was all tuckered out. He shoulda written last Sunday afternoon, but he had fallen asleep after the outdoor prayin' and singin' service. Some preacher's son had come over to the camp from the small town nearby to put it on for the men. A good number of them was pretty religious and really appreciated it. But most also took naps afterward. Some of the young ones played horseshoes or cards.

That twelfth day, after dinner, Charley forced himself to stay awake until he got a letter written. He told Lena all about meeting the brothers and about the rail bulls catching the bum they rode in the boxcar with. He told her about Al, of course. He purposely had not thought about it much since it happened, but writing Lena brought it all back. It had truly been the worst thing he had ever gone through, except for the house fire. Charley told Lena, however, that he really had nothing to complain about. He knew that it just as well could have been him lying down back there at the scythe end of the tractor, and Al could have been safe up there under the wheels. He thanked God every day for that.

Charley also described the beautiful golden wheat fields that ran all the way to the horizon in every direction. Charley had never seen an ocean, but he imagined it would be like that - the same in every direction if you was in the middle of it. He was pretty sure Lena would have enjoyed the sunsets, too.

Then, of course, he got around to the main part of his letter which was how much he missed her, missed her face, her hugs, and her pretty blond hair. How much he missed her cookin' and pies and bread. How the lady who prepared meals for them was a fair cook, but Charley doubted she had ever heard of salt, or pepper for that matter. He told her that what he missed most, except for spoonin' with her every night, was her chicken 'n noodles and her lemon poke cake.

Charley didn't even try to be fancy with his writin' because he knew he was no match for his wife's way with words, but he wrote from his heart and he knew Lena would like that. When he was done he had two big pages on both sides. The lines wasn't so straight, but he made sure Lena could read every word. He looked it over before he put it in the envelope and proudly realized it was the most he had written since his final essay in fifth grade. That would help make up for his first letter to her being written so late, he hoped. Charley told her that he wanted to give her a big squeeze, and that was just what he was gonna do first when he saw her again!

He wrote his Grimes address on the envelope. Lena had already put a stamp on it. For a return address, he was going to have to ask Walt if there was a place Lena could write so Charley could get a letter back from her.

Charley closed his eyes, tipped back his head and tried to picture Lena walking from the house down the short steep drive to the mailbox. This time of year, the milkweed and goldenrod in the ditch would be starting to mature. The monarch butterflies would be thick, and the hawks would be soaring around the front of the property, on the lookout for a ground squirrel snack. Then he remembered; she wasn't at the farm and the house was gone, but he knew she would be checking the mailbox.

He started wondering about what was going on with Lena's jobs and with Harley. Charley was savin' his money and hoped she was doin' the same. He wrote in the letter that he was getting paid in cash and wasn't going to take the chance of sending that in a letter. Harley was probably getting itchy for school to start, but first he would have to help Jim harvest his farm and Charley's farm as well. He knew Harley could do the work, but he wished he could be there to help, too.

Wishin' was something Charley did a lot of lately. He even wished he could quit wishin'. He was used to making things happen. If he wanted something done, well, he just went and seen that it got done. Shocking wheat wasn't like that. Nothing ever got done! One enormous field simply blended into the next one. Maybe there was a fence or two, but usually not. Just hundreds and hundreds of acres of grain; and men sweeping across them. On foot, bending over, standing up, and bending over again. Move along, follow the scythe.

Charley hated the sight of that scythe, but there it was in front of him every day. He decided to start thinking that every swipe of that scythe was bringing him a little closer to being home. If he didn't, these months away from home would maybe kill him. Or at least kill his spirit. He wanted to return to his family as the same ol' Charley, just with money to build his new home.

Henry and Mel had the two of them earning money for their family. They was able to save twice as much money as Charley had. He tried to be happy for them. They was helpin' out their parents, like Harley was helpin' his folks. All three boys was givin' up some of their wonderful young years workin' as hard as grown men. They shoulda been out huntin' and fishin' with their friends or playin' baseball like Charley did when he was their age. He had been the catcher on the Polk County champion baseball team in 1911.

But, these Depression days were not normal times. Very few families, in town or country, were unaffected. Husbands and wives were forced apart depending on where there was work. Children lost their childhood. Many families lost their homes. He had heard of people driving all the way out to California and living in their cars, or in tents by the side of the road. He was living in a tent, but still had no complaints. He had blessings to count and he knew it.

Charley had three squares a day, a place to wash his clothes, and steady pay. There were people unable to feed their families. His family had a huge garden; they would always have food to eat. He just wanted to sit down at the table with Lena and Harley and have a meal together.

Charley realized he was falling asleep, but he wasn't in his own bed. He had scooted over to the edge of the tent to get the last bit of daylight to write Lena's letter. He rolled back over and stood up. The brothers were just coming back from the campfire and a card game. They realized Charley was still awake, even upright, and were obviously surprised.

"Hey, old man," Henry hollered, "What you up so late fer?'

"I been writin' that letter I told ya about. Don't want my wife worryin' no more," Charley replied.

"Well, ya better let us tuck you in. We got a real long day tomorrow. We gotta pull up this tent before we hit the fields. They's movin' us up farther north tomorrow night," Mel offered.

Charley didn't know what to say. That was a huge surprise. No one had mentioned that. "That's a new one to me. When did they decide that?"

"Don't know," answered Mel, "but we were tryin' to decide how long to stay. We done made a lot of money. We been talking about it and think maybe we'll only stay another two weeks."

Charley hardly knew what to say, but he knew he didn't want those boys to leave. They was the best Christians in the camp. No drinkin' or carousin' for them. They was darn good clean company for Charley to have, and good workers to boot!

"I don't see how you could have enough money to really get your folks back on their feet, even with yer two salaries. Ya maybe got enough to make sure your family has a place to live and some food for a month or two, but you kids are gonna have to stick it out here in these fields until winter kicks us out, don't you know that?" Charley asked.

"That's what I tol' the little whelp," Henry said. He's the one who wants to go home. Misses his gal and is sick of all this work. I tol' him he's jest being a big fat sissy!"

Mel gave Henry a hard shove, sending him to the dirt floor of the tent. "What'd I tell you I was gonna do if you called me a sissy again?" he demanded.

Henry bounced right back up and socked his little brother in the jaw. Men all around them, readying their beds for the night, started jeering. "Fight! Fight! Them two is fixin' to fight!"

"No, they ain't!" hollered Charley above the din of the workers' shouts. "They ain't fightin, or they'll be fightin' me!" He pushed himself between them and grabbed both their shirt fronts and pushed them in opposite directions backwards. They landed in the dirt again and Charley stood there with his arms crossed on his chest. He had not yelled like that for a long time.

"Cut it out! You boys is acting like heathens! Heathens, I tell you!" Then he realized how loud he was being. Lowering his voice, he spoke directly to Henry, "You can't fight your little brother. I'll betcha yer mama told you to take care of him. Is that what this is? Huh, it that what this is?"

The boys were still mad, but they were also obviously shamed. Charley was right about their ma. She had told them to watch out for each other, and here they were trying to beat each other up. They still looked pretty steamed at each other, so Charley moved his cot between their cots for the night. They got themselves settled down silently, and Charley told 'em that their bedtime prayers darn well better include each other and a whole lot about forgiveness. He heard a 'hrumph' from each of them, but he knew all would be fine by morning, and it was. Mel probably didn't like thinking he had to listen to Henry, but he knew Charley was right about them havin' to stay longer. He didn't like it at all, but he knew it was gonna be that way.

Takin' that tent down in the morning reminded Charley of the time a big ol' circus came to Des Moines, over by Fort Des Moines. Half of the show was watchin' them put up the giant tent and then take it down again before they left town. The circus had elephants to help with it, but the wheat shockers only had a few horses. Walt kept yelling directions, and they finally got it down and loaded on a long trailer.

They started about six in the morning and finished around ten o'clock. Now they were going to ride another hour in the back of the transport truck, have a lunch of sandwiches, and then work until dark in a new field. Some of the men would stay back in the new camp so they could get the tent put up for sleepin' in again.

So, this is how it would go. It would be another month or more before Charley could have enough money saved to take home to Lena and Harley. He might as well stay as long as he could. He knew his cousins and neighbors could help him get his house built pretty quick. If they got the outside done, he could finish the inside when winter hit.

The three men shocked wheat until each field was clean. Then they moved on to the next field. Town to town, county to county, Nebraska, Kansas, South Dakota; wherever there was wheat, that's where they went. Charley and the boys hung in there, going through it all together.

Family Comes to Visit

The rest of the morning and into a little bit of the afternoon, Mother and I were bustling around getting the house ready for our family. Burnie came over right after Sunday dinner at their house and Mother put him to work. He was happy to help us out, by sweeping the front porch and the sidewalk out to the street. He knew how excited I was to see Uncle Albert and Aunt Helen again, and my Grandma Von Dornum. I was pretty sure Burnie was also thinking about the big tin of sugar cookies that Aunt Helen was supposed to be bringing. Food was always on his mind.

I made certain the guest bedroom was ready. Grandma would be sleeping with Mother, because we had only one extra bedroom, and that was where Uncle

Albert and Aunt Helen would stay. Albert was Mother's younger brother. I think he was about four years younger that she was. There was another brother, Wiard, who was born between them, but he was kicked in the head by a horse and killed when he was seventeen years old. His grave was up in Steamboat Rock, next to Grandma's husband, Klaas. There was a plot there for Grandma, but I prayed she would live for a long time yet.

Grandma Von Dornum had a difficult childhood and took an extraordinary path to come to the United States of America. She was born Bertha Wilhelmina Fank in Berlin, Germany in 1861. Her mother died when she was a baby; her father was in the army and could not care for her or her siblings. Although her brothers and sisters were sent to live with various relatives, Bertha was cared for by a neighbor for a while but was then placed in an orphanage until she was seven years old. She was taken out of the orphanage by a local man, to work for him in his household, but he did not send her to school like he agreed to. He used her to herd sheep on his huge farm. She had two flannel dresses, a shawl for the winter, and no shoes. In the evening, she had to peel potatoes for the large household. If she peeled them too thick, that was all Bertha got to eat the next day; a stack of boiled potato peelings, as were fed to the hogs. She was twelve when authorities discovered that she had never been to school.

The man was charged in court and had to pay a huge fine; he became quite angry. He got drunk and beat Bertha severely. She began to lose her hearing after this beating. At the school attendance hearing in Berlin, Bertha's uncle, who was caring for one of her sisters, asked to take Bertha to live with him. The judge refused and she was returned to the man who beat her. When he realized Bertha was starting to go deaf, he did not want her and took Bertha to her uncle. The police found out and went to search the uncle's house. Bertha was hidden in a rain barrel partially filled with cold water, as plans had already been made to send her to live with her oldest brother, August, who had gone to America. When Bertha arrived at Ellis Island, she was ill and she was rapidly losing all her hearing, probably from the beating and from being in the rain barrel. She was held at Ellis for a year, during which time she helped with babies and made herself useful with other immigrants. She was so useful that her brother, waiting for her in Iowa, had to go to Ellis Island to get her.

Young Bertha Fank was able to help her brother's family by working in a dry goods store in Eldora, Iowa, which is just on the other side of Pine Lake from Steamboat Rock. Even with her deafness, she worked hard and earned love and respect from the customers in town. She met a young man, Klaas Von Dornum, in Eldora; they married and moved to Steamboat Rock. Bertha kept working in the store for a little while, but then Klaas bought a farm and they moved out to the country. They started a family and raised their children on the farm. Taking care of four children and helping her husband with work around their acreage was a hard, physical life, but she loved living in the country and caring for her family. Grandma was now in her seventies and frail, because being a farm wife had not been easy. I thought her life was so unpleasant in Germany, it was probably better that she did not remember much of it. Grandma told Mother that she felt like her life here was a dream; she was happy and had made a good family with her husband Klaas.

Klaas and Grandma had four children. My mother, Henrietta, was the oldest, then Wiard. Their third child was Uncle Albert and then Hazel, who was the youngest. Uncle Albert married Aunt Helen and moved to a house on the east edge of Steamboat Rock. Mother and Dad married, then we lived in Steamboat Rock until I was in sixth grade. At that time we moved to Des Moines.

Mother's younger sister, Aunt Hazel, was living in Eldora and teaching school before the Great War. She met a soldier fella at a church social in Iowa Falls and fell madly in love. They got engaged and then he went off to Europe to fight. Sadly, he did not return. He was killed in France. Aunt Hazel was so heartbroken that she vowed she would never love anyone else and never marry. She moved to Chicago to teach. That was twelve years ago, and she's still not married. Mother told me that Hazel was always a very sensitive and emotional child, and Mother now believed that her little sister never would marry. That always made me feel badly, especially when I saw how happy my parents were. I wanted Aunt Hazel to be that happy, too.

I was so excited for our guests to arrive. Finally, as I was sitting on the deacon's bench in our entryway, I heard the car pull up. I ran out the front door and didn't even close it. Mother came behind me, but she closed it.

"Grandma! Grandma! Welcome to Des Moines!" I yelled. I know she couldn't hear me, but I was sure she could tell how glad I was to see her. The last time I saw her was Christmas, so it had been almost a year.

Uncle Albert helped Aunt Helen get out of the old car right after Grandma. Grandma was walking like her legs were stiff. I knew just how she felt, after that trip we took to Iowa City and back yesterday. I ran out to hold her arm, but first she had to give me a sweet little hug and kiss. "Oh, meine süße kleine Enkelin! Ich habe dich so sehr vermisst. Du bist so groß geworden!" I kissed her back and took her suitcase for her. I didn't speak German, but I knew she had given me a loving greeting. She also motioned with her hand above her head, so I knew she was also commenting on my height. She was so sweet!

Uncle Albert called to me, "Please take that suitcase into the house for

Grandmother, Mable, then come back out here and get this extra box she packed. It's not too heavy, but she has it all tied up with string like it's a big secret. She said it was for you."

I hurried back into the house with the suitcase, ran to the upstairs hall with it, and dashed back out to the car. I wanted to see what was in the box, but Grandma figured out what was going on in my head, and warned, "Berühre nicht die Soirte dieser Box. Es ist für dich, aber noch nicht. Du wirst es bekommen, wenn du graduierst."

Aunt Helen said, "Grandma says you don't get to see that until your graduation!"

That seemed like a long time to wait, but I knew it would be worth it. A thought ran through my head; maybe it was the makings of one of Grandma's beautiful quilts! She couldn't hear, but she was an artist with fabric. Her quilts were ab-so-lute-ly exquisite. Mother hated it when I said ab-so-lute-ly, but everyone was pronouncing it like that lately, and I just picked it up. I never said it when I was around her, but I frequently thought it.

When I went around to the back of the car to get that box, I saw something else I had been anticipating! The tin of cookies! I'll bet Aunt Helen had to put that tin in the back of the car so that Uncle Albert wouldn't eat them all on the trip down to Des Moines.

I called out to Mother, who was still hugging her mother and brother, "Mother, I found the tin of cookies!"

"Keep the lid on and take it into the pantry, Mable," she said to me. Then turning to Aunt Helen, she asked, "No cookies until after dinner, right, Helen?"

"Let her have one. Well, maybe two. She's waited a long time," was the generous response of Aunt Helen. I loved her! I was a spoiled niece, in addition to being an only child.

I knew I had better help with unpacking the car before I opened that tin, so I grabbed as much I could carry. I deposited everything of Uncle Albert's and Aunt Helen's in the spare bedroom and moved Grandma's suitcase to Mother's bedroom. There really wasn't much except for Grandma's secret box and her big steamer trunk. She was going to be staying for two months; so that trunk was too heavy for me. I knocked on Burnie's door and he helped Uncle Albert carry it up the stairs.

Grandma, Mother, Uncle Albert, and Aunt Helen all went into the parlor. Mother sent me into the kitchen to make some tea and to put a stack of those delicious sugar cookies on a tray for everyone. She had just been teasing me about waiting until after dinner! Burnie, of course, tagged along to the kitchen because he was also interested in the sugar cookies. He labored to make a symmetrical stack of cookies on the tray, like it was an engineering project, while I heated the water for the tea. Burnie reached up to the top shelf of the pantry for me to get down the good tea service, and the tea tin, also. I scooped the tea into the tea strainer like Mother had taught me and poured the steaming water into the pot. I carried out the tea tray and Burnie followed me with the plate of cookies. We both showed remarkable restraint and did not take any of the cookies to eat while we were in the kitchen. That's just the way we were raised.

Mother was pleased with the way we prepared and served the tea. She taught me well; I did what I was supposed to do and Burnie really just followed my lead. I was supposed to serve the oldest guest first, so that was Grandma. Then the next oldest. Between Aunt Helen and Uncle Albert, I wasn't sure who was older, so I was taught to serve the lady first, then the gentleman. Lastly, I was to serve the hostess and then the host. I poured the tea for each person and Burnie dutifully followed me around the room, serving the cookies. We were quite proper. I had done this with the ladies from Mother's neighborhood club when it was her turn to host the third Saturday afternoon tea that they held every month. I had gotten fairly adept at it, and Mother smiled approvingly at me as we went around the room. It felt a little awkward using this manner of serving tea to my relatives; I felt like we should just all be sitting around the table in the kitchen, laughing and catching up. I wondered if Mother was trying to look more formal because Burnie was here, or if she wanted to impress Grandma. Neither one of those was necessary. I would wait until later and ask her about it, but right now, it was the kids' turn to get some tea and eat some cookies! Burnie and I finished off the plate of cookies, and Mother was still smiling.

"So how was the trip to Des Moines?" asked Mother, looking at Uncle Albert.

"It was a pretty easy trip. The only place we stopped was Ames. We got a little gasoline and went on our way again. Most of the crops are all in from the fields. The farmers seem pretty satisfied with what they got done this year," he answered. It was a farmer's answer.

Aunt Helen added, "That's the truth. All the farm women are coming into Eldora and spending crop money on things they are going to need to get them through the winter. Warm socks for their kids, hats, mittens, and salt, of course."

"How do you know that. Helen?" my mother asked. "Mother doesn't work at the dry goods store anymore. Who's telling you things like that, about who is buying what?"

"Oh, Henrietta, that young Mr. Hahn who took over the dry goods store from his father is still so nice to your mother. He came by her house the other day while I was there and brought a big box of men's suiting samples; it was a full of little squares of wool that are outdated. He knows Bertha loves to make quilts, and he thought she could make good use of them. So, he filled me in on all that shopping gossip!"

Burnie burst into the conversation with his own question, "What do they need salt for in the winter? I mean, so they need more salt in the winter than they do in the summer?"

Mother laughed. "Oh Burnie, you are such a city boy! The farm women need salt for all the preserving of food that they do. Salt for the pork and beef, salt for the cabbage to make it into sauerkraut, salt for all sorts of things. They need to make the harvest last all through the winter, so they use the salt to keep the food from getting spoiled."

"Thanks, Mrs. Hall, that isn't anything I knew about before. Sounds very thrifty and smart. I don't suppose it is easy for those farm women to get to town all the time in the winter."

Mother replied, "No, it isn't. We used to be stuck on the farm the whole winter. When we were small children, I don't know how mother kept her sanity through those long winters."

I had the perfect answer for that. "Grandma was deaf. She kept her sanity because she couldn't hear all the fussing you kids probably did."

Everyone laughed heartily at that comment. I offered to refill their tea, and Burnie dashed out to the kitchen to get a few more cookies.

We all had long visit with a lot of old-time reminiscing about Steamboat Rock, as well as Mother giving my aunt and uncle a complete recounting of my state swim meet victories. Mother made me go upstairs and get my medals, so Grandma could see them. Mother spoke enough German to help Grandma keep up with most of what we were talking about, but I wondered if being left out of a lot of the conversation bothered my grandmother or not. It bothered me at school, especially in places like the cafeteria, the locker room, or the gym. Large groups of people all talking at the same time made it nearly impossible to understand what anyone was saying, even if they were speaking directly to me. I was getting better at reading lips all the time, but often it was difficult to join in on the conversations.

Burnie headed back to his house about four o'clock. Mother put me to work setting the dining room table for dinner. She kept going back and forth between the kitchen and the dining room, planning what serving dishes she would need and who was going to sit where at the table. Our houseguests had gone up to their rooms to freshen up and rest a little.

This gave me a chance to ask Mother about why she entertained in the front parlor today, instead of just having everyone come into the kitchen and get comfortable around the big table in there.

"Mable, I think you will be mature enough to understand why I did that. One thing I wanted to do was let your aunt, your uncle, and your grandmother have a chance to see what a gracious hostess you have learned to be. Also, none of them thought it was a good idea for your father and me to move to Des Moines. They thought we would end up poor. This is only the third time since you were in sixth grade they have come down here to see us. If you recall, we are the ones who always do the traveling to visit them up in Hardin County. The last time they came down here was about three years ago, and we were still struggling financially. We were still fixing up this place. I entertained them in the parlor today so they could see how hard your father has worked to make a nice home for us. Your father has skills that people will pay for, and that has kept us above water in these hard times. Does that answer your question?" She looked right into my eyes.

I looked back, not even blinking, and said, "I am so proud to be your and Dad's daughter. I love you so very much."

We hugged again, just like we did this morning after Dad called.

I went upstairs, as Mother asked me to, about fifteen minutes before dinner, to let the others know we would be eating soon. First, I told my aunt and uncle, then I went to Mother's room to let Grandma know. I wasn't quite sure how I was going to tell her, because I didn't speak German. As I knocked on the door, I realized how silly it was to worry about that. Grandma was deaf. She couldn't hear knocking and she couldn't hear German any better than she could hear English. I was probably going to have to use gestures. I wished I had be able to spend more time around her, but we only went up to Steamboat Rock twice a year. We would always go on Decoration Day at the end of May, to put flowers on Grandpa Von Dornum's and Wiard's graves. Then we would either go up on Christmas or Thanksgiving. If the weather was bad for those days, we would wait until Easter to drive up there. I felt a little jealous of Burnie. His grandparents lived on the south side of Des Moines. He saw them all the time.

I opened the door slowly since knocking wouldn't really help. I didn't want to surprise Grandma or frighten her by just dashing in. She was sitting on the bed, surrounded by piles of the most luxurious looking fabric I had ever seen! It was silk velvet. I could tell it was silk by the shimmer coming off of it. There was gold, crimson, teal, cinnamon, peach, bronze, ivory, black, deep green, and navy. I didn't know they made that many colors of velvet. When she saw me, she tried to throw the bed covers over the piles of fabric, like she didn't want me to see them. Oh dear, I thought, she is going to be upset and I don't know what to say.

"Bei Donner!" she yelled out. "Sollte das deine Abschlussüberraschung sein, kleine Schnüffelnde Maus." She called out to Aunt Helen, "Komm schnell her, Helen!"

Aunt Helen quickly darted across the hall and exclaimed, "Oh dear, Mable, Grandma wanted to surprise you with this velvet quilt for graduation. That's why she yelled. She's not angry."

I felt so bad. I think Grandma saw the look on my face, because she stood up and gave me a hug around my waist. She was so tiny, almost like a little girl.

She said, "Du wirst überrascht sein, meine süße Mable. Es wir schön sein, genau wie du."

Aunt Helen told me what she had said, and I felt so much better. As I gave her another gentle hug, I remembered why I was sent upstairs. "Aunt Helen, would you please tell Grandma that dinner is in fifteen minutes?"

Aunt Helen said, "Bertha, Henrietta hat Mable hier heraufgeschickt, um dir zu sagen, dass das Abendessen in fünfzehn Minuten ist." She motioned downstairs, used a gesture for eating, and flashed her five fingers at Grandma three times.

I sure was glad Aunt Helen and Uncle Albert could speak German, even though Grandma could barely hear them. It was respectful that they still spoke to her, and that they had learned how to let her know what was going on. Grandma nodded and started packing the velvet back into the box. She motioned with a couple flips of her fingers for me to scoot out of the room. I gave her a little wave and left, smiling as I thought of what a beautiful quilt I was going to be taking to college. Or maybe she meant it for my hope chest? Either way, I thought about what it would feel like to wrap myself up in its satiny softness. What a wonderful grandmother I had.

Dinner was interesting. Some of the conversation was in German and I liked hearing Mother speaking German. Uncle Albert would correct her now and then, and she didn't really mind. I know she liked Aunt Helen, but she probably would not like it if her sister-in-law corrected her German grammar, because Aunt Helen never did that. I think she knew better.

Apparently, Aunt Helen as having some stomach problems. The doctors in Eldora thought she might have ulcers, whatever those were. I didn't follow that part of the conversation very well. I thought talking about your stomach at the dinner table was not very polite, but we were all family, and the grownups probably would not be interested in what I thought about it anyway.

Uncle Albert was taking her to a doctor downtown in the morning, and they were hoping to drive back to Steamboat Rock in the afternoon. It was not as far away as Iowa City, and they could get home before it was too dark.

I had no homework left to do, so I decided to go to bed early. No basketball with Burnie tonight. It was getting pretty cold out now, too. If I couldn't go to sleep right away, I could spend time planning how I was going to approach Coach Johnson about trying out for the boys' swim team this week.

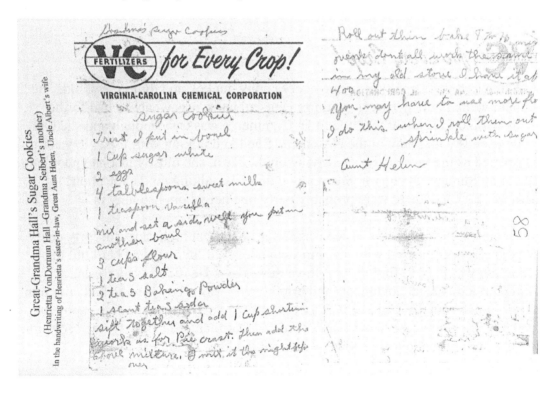

Great-Grandma Hall's Sugar Cookies
(Henrietta VonDornum Hall –Grandma Seibert's mother)
In the handwriting of Henrietta's sister-in-law, Great Aunt Helen, Uncle Albert's wife

Lena Gets a Letter

At home in Iowa, Lena was saving every penny, nickel, and dime she could. About twenty hours per week, at thirty cents an hour, was what she had for her main income. Her job at the grocery in Commerce was easy enough and she had made friends with many of the customers. She liked talking with folks; it wasn't as isolated as the farm had been. Living on the farm, she mostly just had people to talk to on Sundays at church. She really didn't like talking on the telephone because she knew there were probably party line neighbors listening in.

Lena's job at the attorney's office was fewer hours, but higher pay, at forty cents an hour. He was pleased with her impressive level of literacy, and her kind of schooling was hard to find in rural Iowa those days. He didn't want mistakes going out in his legal documents and briefs. Lena was pretty sure he had ambition to be a judge someday, and he was a very nice young man, so she was happy to lend him a leg up in the "letters and words" department. She only worked for him twice a week, for about five hours a day, but it added up in the bank.

Harley was taking the milk route on his own some days. Uncle Lynn had hurt his back when he got thrown off a horse, so he was pretty uncomfortable riding in that bumpy old truck. Harley didn't mind at all because he got to keep all the tips those days, and he could take almost as long as he wanted to look over that Lincoln. One day, he caught himself thinking maybe he had developed an obsession with that car. He thought, "If you look up the word obsession in the dictionary, there is probably a picture of me staring at this car." He had heard his mother use a version of that joke when she was talking to Uncle Lynn about his hired hand, Jack. Only the word next to Jack's picture would have been "lazy." Harley thought that was a clever way to call a person a name.

But mostly, Harley thought about the Lincoln. Mr. Ford really outdid himself when he created that car! For sure, even without knowing how or when, Harley would have one. He would buy it with cash, drive it to his parent's farm, and give them a ride. Heck, he'd even let his dad drive it to Grimes. Harley imagined taking his folks for a Sunday drive to Des Moines, driving in luxury, all the way over to the Iowa State Capitol grounds. They could have a picnic and watch the sunset shimmer off the towering gold leaf dome. College first, then his own business, then his Lincoln; Harley had his dream.

The closer it got to school starting, the more anxious Harley became. He worried because they had not heard from Charley. Lena tried not to appear concerned or upset, but Harley knew. His parents were the closest-together married couple he'd ever seen. True, he hadn't seen many other families besides his relatives, but he could just tell. Lena mentioned her husband every day. Only once did Harley hear her scold an imaginary Charley for not writing yet. She was washing some clothes in the washtub and he thought she was almost going to tear those clothes apart, the way she was scrubbing and scolding so hard! They were the cleanest clothes he had ever seen, for sure.

Harley also picked up handyman jobs for folks in Valley Junction, Commerce, and sometimes for the farmers out by Grimes. He'd go right up to the house or meet a man out in his own front yard and just ask the fella outright if he had any jobs that a strong young man could do to help out his mother, who was all by herself. That line always got him a little sympathy and usually a job that he would get paid a dime or a quarter for. All those little coins went into Lena's account and hardly anything ever came out of it.

Harley was also working the milk route and helping his grandmother around her house and yard. He kept doing odd jobs for neighbors so he could tuck away some money for school shoes and books, as well as trying to keep up on his reading. It wasn't a good day at all if he ran out of time to read. He walked the two miles to his mother's rented house a couple of nights a week to eat dinner with her and give her news of Grandma and of Uncle Lynn and Aunt Alice.

While he was at his mother's, he would get a chance to read his beloved Reader's Digest. Lena would not let it leave the house. She had lost all her other copies in the fire, so the new copies, as they arrived in the mail every week, were put in a special place near the back porch, where she could grab them if there happened to be another house fire.

Lena had taught Harley well. Hard work and thrift were the lessons. Borrowing was the last resort. Just save up for what you need. Don't go into debt. Pay all your bills on time. If it's broken, fix it; don't go get a new one. Buy used, if you can. Wear it out, use it up. Go without. Yea, go without was a big rule these days. Of course, Harley had everything he needed. The only thing he wanted was… well, the only *two* things he wanted and didn't have were a Lincoln and his father at home. He was reminded frequently by his mother how blessed he was, and he knew it was true. But even that knowledge could not cool the burning he had inside to be successful enough to pay cash for a Lincoln. Someday.

Harley kept his eye on that Lincoln convertible. Having never told his parents about it and concealing his fascination with it from his uncle was the easy part. Wanting one like it so badly was the hard part. He had no doubt, in his mind, that he would have one someday. Not knowing for sure how he would earn the money to buy one was part of his unsettling frustration. If he only had a plan, that would make it easier to wait. He knew he would have to go to college. He knew that wealth doesn't ever really just happen overnight. He knew that whatever he did, it would take hard work, and lots of it.

"Shoulder to the wheel," his dad would say. His mother liked to quote the well-known British writer, Richard Whately. "He said," Lena would remind him, *"A man who gives his children a habit of industry provides for them more than by giving them fortune."* Then she would add on to it, "So get out there and show me some industry! Get on out there and get those chores done right quick!" Then she would laugh and give him a hug, as she pushed him out the back door. He had proven over his growing up years on the farm that he had industry. He was just so anxious to put his industry into some task that could earn him enough money to buy a Lincoln! School would he starting in the middle of September. He wanted to have his clothes and transportation to school all lined up. From Grandma Burt's house he could ride the street car to Roosevelt. It was the farthest west high school in Des Moines. It was one of the largest high schools in Des Moines; only Lincoln had more students enrolled.

Kids who went to school at Roosevelt dressed differently than the ones at his country school. If Harley was going to go to school in town, he felt like he should try to dress the same as they dressed, so he didn't stand out and wasn't called a "farmer boy." He was going to need some shirts with collars and some new shoes, for sure. Only poor kids wore shoes that were canvas, and not leather. Lena kept telling him that he was worrying about the wrong things. She rightly insisted that he needed to be more concerned about studying and learning than he did about shoes. Harley knew his mother was right, and he told her so every time she gave that lecture.

It didn't help that Harley found another advertisement for a Lincoln in the Reader's Digest one week. He looked at that picture for a long time before he turned to the Increase Your Word Power section. He wanted to cut out the photograph and keep it, but he knew his mother would be asking about it and then she would know something he didn't want her to know. Lena would probably think that her son was unhappy with his life, but he certainly wasn't. Harley loved the life they had on the farm. Even after several months in town, he felt awkward walking on sidewalks. Just didn't seem right, when there was perfectly good grass right there next to it. He didn't mind getting his shoes wet or having a little dirt or mud on them. Seemed like a waste of good concrete to him. He'd rather use the cement for a real floor in their garage.

That was Charley's practical side coming out in Harley. He was a good son and he respected his father. He missed his father, also. Harley prayed every night that his father was safe. Stories were all over in the newspaper about fights among men who were riding the rails. There were unions getting involved and immigrants. Harley had to trust that Charley could take care of himself. They had to have money to rebuild the farmhouse, so Lena and Harley just waited and worried.

Finally, the first letter came from Charley. It had been over a month since he left. Rural Free Delivery seemed to take forever. Lena knew they got mail four times a week most weeks, which was better than the rural delivery twenty years ago, but the wait had been exhausting. Surely, there had to be a way to speed up the mail. She was grateful she didn't have to go to Grimes to pick it up at the post office. They brought it right to a cavernous country mailbox on the old wooden post by the driveway. She had Betty check it every day, and finally she received a call that there was a letter from her beloved Charley.

The attorney she worked for let Harley drive Lena in his car out to Grimes to get the letter. He knew how torturous her wait had been. She was an important asset in his office, so it was the least he could do. Lena wasn't just anxious to get the letter, she wanted a return address also! She had been writing a little bit of news to Charley every day. Sometimes it was just a couple of sentences, especially if she was tired, but she wanted to be ready to answer him whenever he sent her a way to reach him. She had several pages ready to go. So, it was surprising to Harley when she just held the letter in her lap. He had thought she would be tearing it open like a madwoman.

"Mother, open it up. What's he got to say? Is he okay? What was the rail riding like? Open it up!" Harley urged Lena, as she sat peculiarly upright in the seat of the car.

"I'm going to wait until I am home. I want to read it by myself, son. I'm sorry, I just need to read it alone first. I will answer your questions as soon as I get home and get it read. That'll be soon enough. Just hurry now and drive on back to town." Her voice was forcefully calm. Intentionally. He could tell she wanted to tear it open, but her self-discipline had gotten them this far and he was going to have to do as she said.

"Okay, Mother. Home it is." With that, Harley headed back out of Betty's driveway and sped towards town. He knew his mother wanted to tell him to slow down, mostly because it was not their car and she didn't want them to have an accident. Harley also knew she really did want him to hurry up and get her home so she could read Charley's letter. The ordeal of waiting and wondering was over.

Once back in town, Harley slowed down a bit, but not much. There was more traffic, of course, and Lena didn't want any of the lawyer's friends to see his car barreling through Valley Junction, with a teenage boy behind the wheel. He parked in front of the house, and then he couldn't believe his ears.

"Harley, please take the car back to the attorney's office and then walk back home. I'll be done with your father's letter by then. We'll sit down and talk things over. Go now, please. I'm going inside and read this," she said as she stepped out of the car. His mouth fell open, and his mother must have seen it.

Lena added, "I'm sure you want to know all about your father's adventure, but we must return the car before something happens to it. You've waited over a month; another thirty minutes isn't going to hurt." She shut the car door and walked directly into the house, never even looking back to see his still-gaping mouth. Surely, she was able to feel his deep disappointment. Then again, maybe she couldn't. His mother had no one to share her feelings with since Charley left; Harley noticed she had pretty much just cut her emotions off. She still showed him motherly affection, but there were no highs or lows of normal living. She was always the same. With Charley around, Lena could be mad, happy, sad, or plum crazy. There was none of that since he left to ride the rails. The only emotion Harley ever saw from his mother lately was worry.

As Harley drove to the attorney's office, he hoped his father's letter would help alleviate that worry. When he arrived, he handed the keys to his mother's employer and thanked the man generously. "Mother was very pleased to be able to go out and get the letter. She's at home reading it right now. She thanks you sincerely, sir."

"I admire your parents tremendously, Harley. They are both making extreme sacrifices in an unfortunate situation." He paused and then added, "These are trying times for everyone, but with your house fire and your father out working the wheat, your family is being tested with extraordinarily difficult circumstances. You come from sturdy stock and I am sure you will be a success in whatever you do when you grow up."

Harley was surprised by this tribute from a man he barely knew. "Thank you, sir," was all he could think of to say in response.

"I am going to run home now and see what was in Father's letter," Harley blurted out. With that, he turned and ran out the door and down that blasted silly concrete sidewalk. Running on grass would have felt better, but the folks in Valley Junction were particular about their front yards, so Harley knew better than take shortcuts.

He raced himself home. Lena was on the front porch. The little house had a tiny porch, but there was just enough room for one wooden chair on each side of the simple front door.

"What does he say, Mother? May I read it? Tell me everything, please!"

"It's a letter with things in it for just me, Harley, but I shall read all the parts that will answer your questions. Actually, you may read both sides of the first sheet; it tells all about how he got out there and some pleasant people he has made acquaintances with. There's also a very unfortunate incident with one gentleman. I'll let you read it for yourself. Here, dear." With that introduction, Lena handed him the first page. Harley was surprised at how rugged his father's handwriting was. He thought a second and realized he had never seen his father write anything but his own name. On the other hand, Lena was always writing. She'd write lists of things to do and grocery lists. She'd write down things she wanted to remember from the preacher's sermon on Sundays in a little black notebook she kept in her gigantic purse. Quotes she read in books or magazines would go in the notebook also, as well as every new word she heard.

So, Harley took the first page from his mother, who was holding the letter like it was a golden treasure. "Be careful with it," she said.

"I'll be careful, Mother. Thanks for letting me read it myself."

The letter was printed and easy to read. It was a little rugged; obviously a man's handwriting. Harley read both sides twice. He was satisfied that riding the rails was as exciting as he thought it would be. Imagine having to hide from a thug the railroads hired. His father was amazing. He had lived through a tornado that actually killed a man lying not more than ten feet away from him! As he read more, it dawned on him that he could have or maybe should have gone with Charley. Those brothers from St. Paul weren't very much older than he was! He should have been out there working with his father!

His mother's voice came, as if she had been reading his mind, "I know what you are thinking, Harley, and you can stop it right this minute. You are staying here, you are doing your milk route, and going to school; you are not riding the rails west. Don't even think about it!"

"But, Mother..." Harley started to defend the possibility.

"No, absolutely not. Your father left you here with me, and that's where he wants you to stay. Did you read something I didn't read in that letter? Did your father ask you to come out there? No. Just plain no," Lena said with a finality that told Harley it would be pointless to pursue her approval of the idea. He hated it when she was right, but how was he going to ever have his Lincoln if he never got off the farm? Harley wished this was over and that his father was home again.

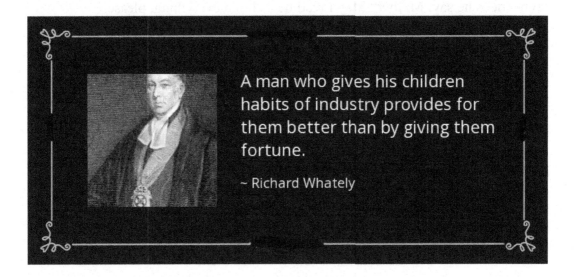

A man who gives his children habits of industry provides for them better than by giving them fortune.

~ Richard Whately

Coach Johnson

Mable Talks to Coach Johnson

I left for school early. After making myself a piece of toast, I left Mother a note. I think both she and Grandma were pretty tired from yesterday. Uncle Albert and Aunt Helen were just starting to come down to the kitchen as I went out the front door.

I told them, "I need to get an early start today. Good luck at the doctor and have a safe trip home. Love you!"

They really didn't have a chance to answer. I needed to get out of there and have a nice quiet walk to school without any distractions. It was barely light out. I knew Mother would make me wait until the sun came up a little higher, and I was a bit afraid that my aunt and uncle might try the same "It's not safe" argument on me. Our Oak Park area was very safe. Sure, there were a few gangsters and bootleggers in Des Moines, but not in our neighborhood!

I knew Coach Johnson would be in his classroom early. He also taught anatomy and biology classes. He would be in his room doing all the planning for his classes before school started in the morning.

I knocked on the door of his classroom and through the window in the door, I saw him look up. He was obviously busy with papers stacked all over his desk, so I knew I would have to be quick with my request. He motioned for me to come in, and with a big smile he said, "Well, if it isn't our state champion, Miss Mable Hall. Congratulations, young lady. You and that girls' swim team really showed the whole state how to swim! I can't wait to see that new trophy in the trophy case."

I think I blushed a little, but managed to press forward with my mission, saying, "Thanks, Coach Johnson. We had a good time. Now that the season is finished, there is something I want to talk to you about, if I may?"

"Certainly, Miss Hall, what's on your mind?"

Golly, this was happening faster than I thought it would. I had to get right to the point. I was mentally kicking myself in the pants for not giving the details of this plan more thought. I started with, "Coach, you know I love to swim, and you know I am really fast, right?"

"Yes, Miss Hall."

I was having a hard time looking at him, so I pretended to be picking something off the sleeve of my sweater and continued, "I have been thinking about this for quite a while; since the beginning of the school year, actually."

"Thinking about how fast you are?" Coach asked, sounding unsure of where I was heading.

"No sir," I started stammering, "I have been thinking. . . that I . . . would be a great . . .addition. . . to your swim team." There, I said it. I rapidly added, "You know I can beat almost every boy on your team!"

"Whoa, little lady!" he cautioned, "How do you know that?"

This part I had thought about a lot. "I know that because I know their times. You know their times, too. You know I can beat them."

"Miss Hall, it's a boys' team. It is for young men. Not for young ladies. Your swim season is over and it's time for you to go out for basketball."

"Please, Coach? I'd rather be swimming, and you know I could help you win more swim meets. Maybe even a state title, like the girls' team."

I realized there was a begging tone to my words, so I stopped right there. If he was a good coach, he would want the best people on his team. I was not going to beg. My intention was to persuade. Obviously, he was going to have to be persuaded. Perhaps this morning was not the right time for that.

I stood there, and he was looking down at the papers on his desk. I decided it would be best if I left soon and let him get back to work. He also might need some time to think about what I said. I tried to think of what I should say next.

He finally looked up and said, "I have a lot to do right now, but our practices start soon. I will need to speak with the principal and the boys on the team. I will need to check the state rules and see if there is anything that applies to this situation. Right now, I don't see how you being on the boys' team would work well at all. I appreciate your enthusiasm and you are a fine young lady, but it is a boys' swim team. Please excuse me now. I don't mean to be short with you, but we will have to finish this discussion later. Come and see me during lunch today,"

That sounded almost like a big 'no' to me, but he really didn't say the word, and he had asked me to come back and talk to him at lunchtime. 'Maybe' was better than 'no'. My plan could still happen.

I knew this particular discussion was over, though, so I offered, "I can talk to you about this later. I understand you are busy and need to check on the rules. Thank you for talking to me."

I backed out the door, and left him with, "I hope you have a good day of classes, sir."

I fell back against the lockers right outside his room. That conversation was a whole lot harder than I thought it would be. I had to be better prepared next time. What I needed to figure out was the best strategy to use to convince him. I needed to talk to Burnie. I needed to talk to Dad.

It was still pretty early to be at school. As I walked past the classrooms up there on second floor, it seemed like only about half of the teachers were there yet. I headed downstairs to the front office, hoping to find another early student to talk to. There stood Burnie! Right in front of the principal's office.

"You left without me this morning, kiddo. Why didn't you knock on my door before you walked over here?" Burnie asked.

"I had to get over here to talk to Coach Johnson, alone, before school. I wasn't going to wait for a whole crowd of kids to be up there. I'm sorry I didn't tell you. I needed to get it done. Boys' swim practice starts soon."

"Well," Burnie offered, "so does girls' basketball practice. Which one are you going to?"

"I'm not sure yet. He asked me to come back during lunch. Coach said he had to check on some things, like talk to the principal and look up some of the rules. He didn't sound very positive, Burnie. I'm a little discouraged, but I'm not going to give up."

Burnie nearly snorted through his nose trying to laugh and talk at the same time. "Oh, I know that, Mable. You are definitely not going to give up! I'm feeling sorry for Coach Johnson right now. With you trying to convince him to let you on the boys' team, he's got a real tiger by the tail!"

I gave him a sweet little smile and said, "I'm going to take that as a compliment, Burnie. Thanks."

Other students were starting to arrive now. The debate team had their meeting before school, so did the Student Council and Future Teachers Club. Mother thought for a short time that I would be a teacher, but by middle school, she had given up on that idea. Dad had me excited about sports, and I was already proving to be a skilled writer by seventh grade. That was when I made my decision to be a sports writer.

Dad was very happy and proud about that; Mother was wondering "what will become of her?" I thought it was a funny question, and Dad did also, but he never said so in front of Mother. He kept assuring her that if I knew enough about sports and if I was an excellent writer, some newspaper or magazine would hire me.

That never satisfied Mother, though. Then she started asking, "How can she be a sports writer and get married? Or have a family?"

That's when I would leave the room. Dad always defended me with comebacks like, "She'll find the time, I'm sure. All good things happen in their time. I think you are worried, Henrietta, that she is going to become a flapper. We have raised her better than that. She does not have time for that sort of thing." Dad sure was right about that. I just wanted to swim and write.

The halls were becoming filled with students now and getting louder, so it was getting hard to have a conversation with Burnie. We had to get to our lockers and to our first class.

"I'll see you at lunch, Mable. Need to get going now. The bell is about to ring," Burnie said as he turned and stepped out into the river of students hurrying to class.

"I can't eat lunch with you," I hollered after him, "I need to go see Coach Johnson again."

I think he answered with "good luck," but he was drowned out by all the other students and their chatter. I would have to tell him after school.

My three morning classes went extremely slowly. I was sitting up, paying attention, taking notes, answering teacher questions, but I might as well have been home, lying on my bedspread, daydreaming. All I could think about was being on that boys' swim team. I could think of nothing else. I was visualizing myself swimming against the boys, beating the boys, being the star of the boys' team. I kept telling myself, "this could happen." The morning lasted ab-so-lute-ly forever!

The bell rang for the end of class and the beginning of lunch. I had my third class on the first floor, so I had to run up the stairs to Coach Johnson's room. Students were still leaving the classroom when I got there. Casually leaning against the lockers, I waited. Coach followed the last student out and then stood next to me at the lockers while the hall emptied.

It was hard to tell his decision by the look on his face. It looked pleasant enough; I was hoping he had the answer I wanted.

He began with, "I had time to talk with the principal and time to telephone the Athletic Commissioner for high school athletics, Mable. They have never had such a request before."

He paused, and his face became more serious. "I wish I could give you a better answer, but they don't think I should allow it. It's not against any rule, but neither man thought it was a good idea at all."

That still wasn't a "no!"

Since it seemed like he was done talking, I jumped in with, "Well then, if there is no rule against it, I think you should give me a try at it!"

"What I'm trying to tell you, Miss Hall, is that I'm not sure it's a good idea, either. I think I need to talk to your girls' swim coach, and maybe a couple of other boys' swim coaches in the city. And I especially need to talk with the boys on the team, too. This is just so different than anything else."

I bounced back with, "That doesn't mean it's bad, just because it's different. Miss Hawn didn't think a girl sports editor was a good idea either, and now she's really glad she gave me a chance. This is the same thing."

He shook his head. "It's not really the same, Miss Hall. There are other girls on the newspaper staff. There are no girls on any boys' swim team."

"But, Coach," I pleaded, "the girls are on the newspaper staff because they are good writers. I would be on the boys' swim team because I am a good swimmer. It is the same!"

He looked right at me. "For now, the answer is no. I need to talk to the other coaches and to the boys on the team. I will let you know if I change my mind. You should go get some lunch now."

I could see the conversation was over, but I was not going to accept this as a final answer. "How about this, Coach Johnson, may I come back and talk to you in a week? That will give you more time to hear from other people. Just remember, I'm the best swimmer in this school. In the whole city. Actually, I'm the best backstroke swimmer in the state of Iowa. You could use me on your team!"

He let out a very deep sigh. "This is hard, Miss Hall, because I can tell you are very serious about this, and I know you are a terrific swimmer. I need time. Next week, okay?"

I knew that was about as much of a commitment as I was going to get for now. I didn't want to let it go, but I had made up my mind I was not going to beg. "Okay, Coach. Thank you."

"You're welcome, Miss Hall. And again, congratulations on your state records."

"Thanks again, Coach. I'll see you next week." I turned and walked away, trying not to look discouraged and trying not to be discouraged. Dad would not want me to give up.

Cashing Out

It was hot enough to pop the popcorn right on the stalks; unusually hot for South Dakota in late August. Charley always worried about another twister whenever it got this warm and sticky. Tornadoes weren't that common in this state in the summer, but he didn't ever want to go through another one close up like that one in Kearney.

He felt as strong as he had ever felt in his life. Not having Lena's wonderful cooking, combined with laboring all day in the fields, had brought him back to almost the same physique he had as a young man. And those two Minnesota boys had matured from the same experience; they both appeared heftier and more muscular. Charley was also sure they had each grown taller over the summer. The three wheat shockers had taken care of each other in every situation they had found themselves over the past few months. Charley felt as if the two brothers were his own sons; he regularly settled their sibling rivalries and gave them advice about life. They certainly admired his maturity and good common sense. All three of them felt a close bond with their prayers and support for each other as they lived apart from their loved ones.

Charley missed Lena all day, every day. He wrote her on Sunday afternoons. Only two letters from her had arrived for him in three months. The first was a really long one, and a second one caught up with him about three weeks later. Since then the crew had moved so many times, so it was understandable how letters would get waylaid. It was disappointing, but Charley kept writing to her anyway.

He didn't want Lena to worry about him. It got more difficult with every letter to tell her again how much he wanted to give her a big hug and kiss her, but not be able to do it. But he always told himself that he was doing whatever was necessary to keep his farm and build a new house for his family.

The best thing that had happened with the harvest was that the farther north the shocking crew went, the larger the farms got. Some were hundreds and thousands of acres. This improved the work, because the farmers had more money, were willing to pay the workers more, and they had an extra machine, called a binder. This gadget scooped up the grain as it was cut and wrapped twine around each shock. All the men had to do was stand up the shocks in clusters and throw two more shocks across the top. The whole harvesting process went much faster. There wasn't so much bending over and twisting involved. All the men were happier.

Charley had started in Nebraska, then worked the wheat fields through Kansas and South Dakota. He and the brothers from St. Paul had ridden the rails with bums, avoided railroad bulls, slept in tents as well as under the stars, and shared philosophies of life around dim campfires. They had survived a twister, shocked thousands of acres of wheat, and watched a man bleed to death.

He was going home soon. He planned to have $250.00 his pocket. If Lena had saved her money good, they could put it all together and get a place put up on the farm before winter set in. He hoped his neighbors would help. Heck, he knew his neighbors would help; most of them were his cousins! Except for Campbells, Findleys, and Monahans, everyone within miles of his farm was cousins. And there were many more cousins living in the town of Grimes. Wheat harvest would be over in about ten days. Even if it wasn't over, he'd made up his mind that he was leaving.

The nearest town was Huron. A rail line went through there and he was gonna jump on it. Both brothers were heading home also, so they would all go as far as Minneapolis together. Charley could get back to Iowa from there. The bull situation at the railyards had gotten worse over the summer, he heard, but nothing was going to stop him from getting home. He would stick out his thumb and hitchhike if he had to. The weather was decent, so there shouldn't be any problems, but even if there was, nothing was gonna keep him away from Lena and Harley any longer. He had his money in his shoe, and if somebody wanted to steal it, they would have to be takin' shoes off a dead man, he was sure of that.

The next ten days seemed like a dream. He didn't really think about what he was doing, nor did he have to. After this summer, Charley knew he could shock wheat in his sleep. His movements were automatic and he really didn't feel up to the usual conversation that went back and forth among the men all day long in the field.

He imagined what it would be like to see the green corn in Iowa; at least he hoped it would still be green. They had been going through a dry spell and sometimes the corn leaves curled in on themselves to preserve moisture, but he was pretty sure it wasn't hot or dry enough to turn it prematurely brown. That would be bad. He preferred to daydream about it being that late summer dark green that he remembered. He had not seen much green in the past few months Wheat is brown, but the wheat farmers call it "golden." Charley preferred green over golden or brown.

His mind also kept seeing Lena. In his vision, she was wearing her favorite peach-colored dress, sitting on the porch, the sun making her blond waves look even more blond. He wondered if she was still pale, having had two indoor jobs all summer and not being able to get outside much. Well, maybe she got some sun goin' out to the farm to tend the garden. In her first letter, she said Harley was takin' her out there two or three times a week. Thank goodness they had a well that hadn't dried up; at least the last he heard from Lena it hadn't. Some folks had wells that were only about thirty feet deep. Those dried up fast in hot summers. Monahan's had a shallow well, and out of her kindness, Lena had told them they could use her well until they got the new house built. Charley's well was dug ninety feet deep and had never dried up. He had a flash of how deep his love for Lena was…kinda like that well, it would never dry up.

Harley was on his mind also, out there in that wheat field. Charley tried to visualize how much taller and stronger his son had become over the summer. He would probably be surprised to be seein' his father looking so strong. Maybe Charley had a chance in a footrace with him now; he thought for a moment, but then realized that was foolish. That boy of his was a fast one. Charley still didn't have a prayer of winning the race.

The summer had gone slowly, but the last few days went by very quickly. Charley and the boys stood in line to get their last pay envelope and then piled on the truck heading to Huron. It wasn't far and Charley was glad. The truck was moving, but he was sitting down, so it didn't feel like he was getting any closer to home. He was going to be very short on patience from now on. Every minute sitting still was a minute he couldn't be with his family. He wasn't going to waste any time getting home.

The farmer refused to drop them off at the railroad station; the railroad people would have none of that. So, the men were dropped about a half mile outside of town. They would have to find their own way to the rails. Charley scanned the horizon and located the local farmers' co-op grain bins. Those were usually close to the railroad tracks.

He pointed. "Over there, you two! Let's move out quick. Ain't no train gonna wait on us."

Huron was sparsely populated, so it was unlikely that there was any more than one bull at the station. They would get close enough to see what was going on and then decide what to do. As it turned out, most of the other men who had been shocking wheat on that last farm with them decided to stay in town for a night and spend some of their paycheck on whiskey and such. That was okay with Charley because it meant there would be fewer men trying to hop a freight and attracting attention down at the railyard.

The brothers and Charley worked their way toward the caboose end of a train headed east. The sun had just gone down, but it was still light enough to find a car with the door open. Hopefully, they could get on while the train was sitting still. He knew it was mighty dangerous to jump on a moving train. If you didn't hang on tight and have enough strength to pull yourself up, you would be certain to go under the train. He had not gone through all those weeks harvesting to lose a leg or his life. Charley had spoken with plenty of the men he had worked with in the fields, who had witnessed it personally. He never wanted to see that and prayed it would not be his fate, or the fate of Henry or Mel. He told them on the way into town that if he ever had a chance to meet their parents, he would tell them what upright young men they had for sons. Charley had no plans, of course, of stopping in St. Paul to meet their parents. He was on his way home to Lena, and no one or nothing could slow him down!

Fortunately, there were several doors open on cars and there was no one around guarding them. Henry and Mel were suspicious that it might be a trap, since they figured the whole town knew that the wheat harvest was done and all the bums would be leaving town. Charley let them in on what he had learned as they passed the co-op. He saw a big ol' poster for a big harvest dinner and dance that was being held that night. Most of the folks in town would be there, he explained. No one was gonna be carin' any about the bums gettin' on the train for that one night. So, they took their time and picked out the cleanest of three cars they found open. They settled in one end of the car with their bindles and began to relax.

That train sat there for what seemed like hours. Charley was sure it was midnight before they felt the first lurch of the car. The brothers had fallen asleep, but he couldn't. He was so anxious to get moving. He woke up the brothers.

"Here we go, boys," he informed them, giving them each a firm shoulder shaking. "Rise and shine, we are on the road home!"

"Huh? Huh?" was the only response from the two young men.

"I said," Charley repeated, "we are heading home. We're moving!"

"Uh huh, we hears ya," came back a mumble.

"Well, we got outta town without a fuss and we are headin' east. If this train goes all the way though without more than one or two short stops, you boys will be home before noon tomorrow," Charley informed them. "Just thought you might be interested."

"Charley, we are interested, but we are so tuckered out. Even on this hard old train, we are gonna sleep until we get home. Our ma will be pretty angry if we show up lookin' sickly," Henry said. "You don't want to see our ma angry. For a fine Christian woman, she does a mean imitation of a wet polecat!"

"Okay then," Charley replied, "I'll be lettin' you two sleep all ya want. Don't want you to go home to no wet polecat ma!" Charley laughed out loud and then chuckled a little longer under his breath, as the boys went back to sleep. He had his own son, so knew how much those boys' mother must have loved them. She would have her sons back soon, and he let them sleep.

That train only made one stop, about ninety miles west of Minneapolis, in some farm town named Litchfield. So, it was about eleven the next morning when they rolled into the enormous St. Paul railyard. He had never seen a place like that. They had more roundhouses than he could count, and what seemed like hundreds of rail cars and lines of track. They went out in every direction. His first thought was wondering how he was going to figure out which train to take to go south to Iowa. He would have to ask the boys.

"You're home, you two rails bums!" Charley let them know along with another big shoulder shake. They were so sound asleep he thought they might be dead. He had to give them both a gentle boot in the rear. They woke up and truly took a few minutes to even realize where they were. It occurred to Charley that they all had been so used to sleeping on the cots in their bindles, that waking up in the rail car must have been confusing. He had only had a few short naps on this trip east, so he never lost track of the reality of it like the boys apparently had.

"I said, yer home, ya two rail bums. Get up and go home to yer folks! G'wan, git outta here!" He yanked Mel up by the arm and started shoving all his belongings into his arms. "Here, take yer stuff and go!"

"Whoa, Charley, let us get our bearings here," said Mel. "Lemme get my eyes open for a few minutes. This train just got here; it ain't goin' anywhere that fast."

"Besides," added Henry, "we ain't had a chance for a proper goodbye for you, old man."

"I don't need none of that sentimental baloney," Charley said, scowling a little bit too hard. "That's for the womenfolk. Jest git goin'!"

"We are gonna shake your hand and wish you well. We ain't talkin' about hugs and kisses, ya old fool," Henry assured him.

"You sure ain't!" Charley scoffed. "Then get over here an' shake my hand, both of ya! Then get off my train and go home!"

Both young men gathered up their belongings and rolled up their bindles. "May as well keep these, in case we want to go campin' sometime," Mel said.

Charley repeated, "May as well." He stuck out his right hand. First, Henry shook his hand and jumped out of the car in one big hop to the ground. As he watched him land, Charley felt two strong arms wrap around him from behind.

"Gonna miss ya somethin' terrible, old man. Good luck to you with your house and your farm. God bless your family." Mel released him and leaped down to join his brother.

"God bless your family, too," Charley said, and the boys turned and ran to the east, in the direction of St. Paul.

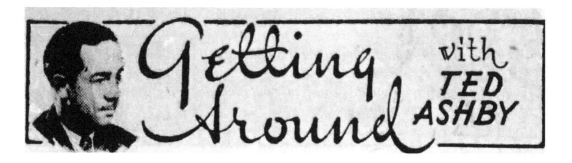

Mr. Ashby Calls

When I opened the front door, our telephone was ringing. It was only Monday, so I knew it wasn't going to be Dad. Mom was in the kitchen this time of day, so I figured she would answer it. She did, and then called out, "Mable, don't head upstairs just yet; you have a phone call."

I did not get many telephone calls. I was difficult for me to hear on the telephone. Men's voices, since they were lower pitched, were easiest for me to hear, so that's why I could hear Dad so well last Sunday. I headed over to the kitchen, having no idea who might be calling me.

"Hello?" That seemed like a safe opening since I didn't know who was on the other end.

It was a man's voice. "Miss Mable Hall?"

"Yes?"

"Miss Hall, my name is Ted Ashby. I write for the sports department of the Des Moines Tribune. I spoke with you on Saturday, remember?"

Mother was staring at me strangely and wanted to know who it was.

"Yes, Mr. Ashby, I know who you are. I read the sports page every day." Now, Mother's mouth fell open. I had forgotten to tell her that he talked to me after the meet on Saturday.

"I'm not surprised," he continued, "and I am tracking you down like I said I would, so you can sit down for an interview with me. Are you going to attend the University of Iowa next fall?"

Golly, he was trying to "track me down" for an interview!

I told him, "Yes, sir. I am trying to get a scholarship there."

"Well," Mr. Ashby continued, "You really put on a show for us over there. Those two state records were amazing."

"So, is that what you want to interview me about?" I asked.

"That's part of it," he replied. "The other part is that I have been told you are actually the sports editor of your North High student newspaper. Is that true?"

"Yes, sir. It's true. I ab-so-lute-ly love sports!"

Saying that made Mother give me an unhappy glare. I mouthed "Sorry!" to her.

"When would you be available for an interview?"

"Any time, after school, of course," I said excitedly. This was the cat's pajamas!

"Would it be okay if I came over to your house tomorrow after school? Will your mother be home?"

"Yes, sir. Well, let me ask Mother really quick."

"Mother," I whispered, "Mr. Ashby wants to come and interview me tomorrow after school. Is that okay?"

She nodded. She had such a big smile on her face. I wanted to call Dad the minute I hung up, but I knew we would wait until Sunday to have Dad call us. It was too much money to spend.

"My mother says that would be nice, Mr. Ashby. I should be home by three-thirty."

"Then I will see you tomorrow. Thank you."

"Thank you, Mr. Ashby."

I hung up the receiver and leaped toward the door to go tell Burnie.

"Where do you think you are going?" asked Mother.

"I need to go tell Burnie! Mother, Ted Ashby is an important writer for the Des Moines Tribune and he is coming to interview me tomorrow. I have to tell Burnie right now!"

"Would you please come right back right away? Will fifteen minutes be enough to talk with Burnie for now? I really want you to spend some time with Grandma, and I want your homework done before dinner."

"When am I going to have time to really talk to Burnie about it and about what happened at school today?" I asked.

"Well, if you have your homework done before dinner, you can go over there after dinner. Grandma and I will do the dishes. What happened at school today that is so important?"

I guess she had forgotten that I was going to talk to Coach Johnson about the boys' swim team today, so I gave her a brief summary of it.

"I went to talk to Coach Johnson today and asked him if I could try out for the boys' team. He said he would check with the principal and with the head of some student athletic group in the state. I went back at lunch and he said it was not against any rules, but that he wanted to talk to some more people about it."

"What other people?" Mother demanded.

"Other coaches in the city, other coaches at school, and he wants to ask the boys on the swim team what they think. I think asking everybody in the whole world is just him stalling me and not wanting to tell me 'No'. I'm a little bit mad about it," I confessed.

"So, when is he going to tell you his decision?" Mother sounded a little bit mad, too.

"I told him I would come back and talk to him next Monday. He said that would be good. I just have the feeling that he's only putting off giving me a final answer. What he said today was a 'no', but he said he still wanted to talk to those other people. I can wait. If he makes his final answer 'no', then I will just go out for basketball. I will only be a week late. May I go over a tell Burnie? I'll be right back," I promised.

Mom sighed, "You go ahead, Mable. See what Burnie has to say and then get back here and do your homework. Grandma is busy with your graduation quilt right now, anyway."

Out the front door I sailed, making sure it didn't slam. I waved at Grandma sitting in the parlor as I raced past, but I don't think she even looked up from the quilt pieces she had in her lap. Grandma didn't use a sewing machine to make her quilts; she made every single stitch in them by hand.

I saw Burnie walk around the corner of his house and go into the backyard when I jumped off our porch. I hollered, "Hey, Burnie, wait up!"

I don't think he heard me or saw me, because he didn't answer or reappear around the corner. I walked back there to see what he was doing. When I got around the back corner, I saw him beating rugs on the clothesline. There wasn't much dirt flying around, probably because his mother was such a neat housekeeper.

Both his mother and my mother were second generation Germans, and those women really knew how to keep a house clean. My mother told me that young girls back in Germany actually had to take classes in school about how to clean a house and how to take care of children. Grandma taught Mother how to clean, and Mother always tried to teach me. I had managed to avoid much of the housecleaning because of all the after-school sports and other activities I participated in.

"Hey, Burnie! Can I talk to you while you do that? I talked with Coach Johnson again at lunch today."

He stopped beating the rugs right away. He spun around and asked, "Really? What did he decide? Are you going to try out?"

"He said I have to wait. He tried to say no, but then when he talked to the principal and some state high school sports guy, they said it wasn't against any rule. So now, he wants to talk to other coaches and ask the boys on the team what they think. What I think is that he doesn't want me to, but he's just stalling and putting off telling me "no" for a final answer."

Burnie knew I was unhappy. "I'm sorry, kiddo. It's a shame. All you want to do is keep swimming and competing. It would really help you out. I wonder if he would let you practice with them, but not compete in meets? That way, you could keep swimming and getting better times."

"That wouldn't be such a bad idea, Burnie, if I wasn't able to actually beat all the boys, but I can. It sounds like being satisfied with getting second place, and that never satisfies me. If I can't actually be on the team and compete for them in meets, I'll just go out for basketball. I'm the tallest girl in school, so the basketball coach will be happy to see me, even if I'm a week late."

"What do you mean, a week late?"

"Girls basketball practice started after school today. Coach Johnson said to come and talk to him again next Monday. So, if he tells me no then, I will go to basketball practice that afternoon."

"I see," said Burnie. "I'd better get these rugs finished now."

"Okay, I have to go do my homework anyway. Can we shoot baskets after dinner?"

"Sure! There's always time for that. Sorry he's making it tough, Mable. I think he's full of baloney!"

"Thanks," I said as I started to walk back over to my yard, "See you later."

I picked up my books off the hallway table where I had left them when the telephone call from Ted Ashby came. I always did my homework at one end of the dining room table. When I sat at the far end, Mother could keep an eye on me from the kitchen, and Dad could keep an eye on me from the parlor, where he usually read the afternoon Tribune every night. Mother was in the kitchen, but Dad was not in the parlor. Grandma was there quilting, but not in Dad's chair. It was empty, and she was sitting on the davenport by the big front window. The light was probably better there for quilting, and when the sun went down, there was a big floor lamp next to the davenport she could turn on.

It had been a crazy day at school, but it was nice to be home and feeling mostly happy as I settled in to do my homework. Tomorrow would be a better day, and then I would get to meet Mr. Ashby!

Charley Heads Home!

Charley walked around for a while in the sunny warmth of the railyard, not believing that he was not being harassed or even questioned by anyone. In the air was the familiar smell of hot machinery. As a farmer, he loved that smell. It was somewhat different from the aroma of the farm but he figured machines was machines.

He worked his way down to what he could tell was the far south side of the railyard. There he sighted a cluster of about six rail bums, sitting under a tree that was just starting to turn its fall color. That cloud of green leaves that was beginning to yellow a bit around the edges reminded him that it was definitely time to get on home for the winter. Of course, the trees would be changing up north here much sooner than they would in central Iowa, so he had plenty of time to get that house built before it snowed. Especially when he got his neighbors and family to help like he planned.

The hobos in the group were sitting quite still and at first, it seemed like they weren't going anywhere soon. As he got closer, he heard them in an intense conversation, figuring out ways to get themselves arrested so they could spend the frigid Minnesota winter in jail, where it was nice and warm, with three hot meals a day. Charley could hardly believe his ears. They were scheming to do crimes that were bad enough for county jail time, but not so bad as to end them up in state prison. They just wanted to be out of the cold for about four months. A hundred and twenty days. His jaw dropped even farther as they actually got up and started off to do their deeds. They were sayin' to each other that they hoped to see the other ones soon, "in the tank." Not one bum even glanced at him as he stood a short distance away.

Charley was appalled to think how low those men had to be on dignity and how high their desperation had to be *to plan* on going to jail. He wanted to talk them out of it, but then he remembered he had his money in his shoe. These men might like to have a nice, warm pair of work boots for the winter. He kept his distance and decided to wait until they were all gone to try to find the right tracks for heading south. If he pushed his luck in his hurry to get home, it could be the cause of him not getting home…like if he was waylaid by these lazy, no-good bums. At least he had been a working bum. In his mind, there was a difference, a big difference.

So, Charley waited in the shadow of a train that was one set of rails away from them. The lazy bums crawled out of a hole in the bottom of the railyard fence, and soon they were all gone. He headed over to the tree they had been gathered around and found a clean place to sit. It wasn't long until a few more darkly dressed men made their way to the tree. One by one, they came out of the boxcars and around the back of the roundhouses. Charley was leery of all of them, and decided when he saw the first one that he would not be the first to speak. They were a mix of young men and older men, but not of them looked like they had been working outside in the fields. To be as pale as they were at the end of a hot summer, he knew these men were not farm workers. He wasn't sure what they were. He put his bindle across the top of his shoes, not wanting to give anyone a reason to be jealous of his boots. He thought about standing up but didn't want to appear aggressive. He was about as uncomfortable as he had been in the whole time since he left Adel that first night.

"Where ya been, farmer?" asked an older man with a crusty white beard.

Charley looked up at the man and slowly replied, "I been in South Dakota." He still wasn't sure if he should stand up, but he decided he'd better. The guy was so close that he could have kicked Charley in the head if he felt like it. He stood and added, "Been shockin' wheat."

"Well, then you really is a farmer! Ain't that somethin'!" the old guy exclaimed. "I could tell you been out in the sun a while."

Charley didn't really feel like talking with this guy, but he thought he'd better hold his ground, so he asked, "Where you been?"

"Oh, I just came in from Chicago. Promised an old friend I'd meet him here tomorrow; we was here together way last May. Think we're gonna head south. He's been up in northern Minnesota looking for work in the iron ore country up there." He scratched his beard and Charley backed up a little bit, hoping there weren't any lice on the man. "I hope he's got some kind of a stake for us to live on, 'cause I sure didn't make no dough in Chicago."

Charley didn't want to talk about money with this bum, but the craggy man kept after him, "Make good money in them wheat fields?"

Now Charley knew he'd better make up a good ol' lie, or he was about to get rolled for his money. "I made a fair amount, but I got a bad gamblin' habit. That's why my wife left me last year. I done gambled every dime away. I just been sittin' here tryin' to think of a way to get myself arrested for the winter." Then he thought he should add, "Got any ideas?"

The old bum bought his story; his face went blank and he was no longer interested in a conversation. As long as he thought Charley had nothin', he would leave him alone. Realizing he had just talked his way out of a dangerous situation, Charley turned and quickly worked his way across several tracks and found a boxcar with Rock Island Line printed on the side. He knew that the Rock Island Line went through Des Moines, so he decided to take a chance. He threw his bindle in and hopped up into the car. He moved way to the back and wedged himself in between some large crates. He just wanted to get away from the other bums who were milling around. Charley did not want to get robbed. He wanted to get home. He slid down on his haunches and fell asleep, praying.

Charley was more exhausted than he realized, because when he woke up, the train was nearly at full speed. He looked around, and there was no one else in his boxcar. Hardly believing his luck at getting away from that hardcore bum, he said another prayer. He had to do some thinking about how he felt like God must have been watching over him all these past months.

First, though, he wanted to figure out which direction he was headed. He remembered going to sleep, praying that this boxcar was going to be heading south towards Des Moines. Someone had closed the doors of the boxcar. There was some afternoon light coming in through splits in the floor, but Charley couldn't see out the sides. How was he going to figure out where he was?

He looked all around the four walls of the boxcar. He was not able to find one crack he could see out of; then he looked up. There was a vent on the top of the car. He could see the shadows, he could tell the sun was coming in, and it appeared as though the sun was on his right, as he faced the direction the train was traveling. That meant the train was going south! He was headed back to Iowa!

"Thank you, Lord," sprang out of his mouth! He added, "Hallelujah, Lena, I'm comin' home today!"

Sitting down on the crate behind him, really just falling backwards with relief, Charley let out a huge sigh. He had been kept safe through all his travels and work in the fields. As far as he knew, his family was safe and healthy. He was still exhausted but was feeling blessed. He was just hours from giving Lena that big squeeze he'd promised her in all his letters.

All Charley really needed right now, he realized, was some more sleep. He had been awake almost all the way from Huron, while the two brothers had slept. Crawling back behind the biggest crate where he had been before, Charley gathered up his bindle. He wedged it in behind him, where he had been sitting on the crate below the vent in the roof. If the sunrays ever managed to reach inside that boxcar, he wanted to be right there where they would land on him. It wasn't chilly, but he longed to feel the warmth on his skin. He had spent so much time outside this summer that it felt strange to be out of the sun's reach. He couldn't wait to get back to the farm. Charley wanted to be on his tractor all day, and with Lena all night.

Now, he knew he had to pray again. Charley thanked the Lord for keeping him safe in his travels, but also prayed for it to all be over soon. He thanked Him for sending those two brothers, and even that old Joe bum who helped them escape the railroad bulls that first time getting off the train. Charley prayed for Joe's continued safety. He was thankful, even for binder machines and for women who don't use enough salt when they cook. A considerable amount of time was spent being grateful for Al and praying that his soul had been received in Heaven. He prayed again for the brothers and their parents. Then Charley thanked God for Jim and Betty, who were helping Harley and Lena take care of the farm. Finally, as he leaned back with his head resting on the crate behind him, Charley fell asleep.

As the train rolled into a station; the jerky de-escalation awakened him. Charley waited until the train stopped, taking an enormous risk that there would be some railroad bulls waiting. He listened carefully and heard a lot of voices on one side of the train. He figured that was the side facing the station, so he pried open the door on the other side. The midday sun was bright! Especially bright was the gleaming golden dome of the Iowa State Capitol building. He was in Des Moines...his prayers had been heard!

Jumping down onto the gray shale alongside the tracks seemed easy, and he began running west. It was a bit of a stiff-legged jog because he had been in the boxcar for a long time. If he could get over to Grand Avenue, he could hop onto the streetcar out to Valley Junction. Granted, he would be a strange site to the other streetcar passengers, especially going past all the wealthy homes that were constructed on the south side of Grand, west of downtown. He didn't care. He hadn't shaved in three days, but he couldn't think of anywhere to go except a barber shop to get shaved before he saw Lena. He sure didn't want her to see him with his whiskers like this, but it couldn't be helped. Well, maybe if he saw a barber shop on the way, he could get a shave. Otherwise, he'd be givin' her that big ol' squeeze, whiskers and all! Still, he knew he probably wasn't gonna get any kisses until he got shaved and cleaned up, but he knew he was gonna get that hug!

He did get stares, starting with the streetcar conductor. It was Saturday, he found out. There was a bunch of ladies who must have been downtown shopping. They had handfuls of department store packages and bags. A few of them stared and the rest of them made a big show of intentionally not looking at him. He was sure he did look out of place, but he didn't feel out of place that much. He didn't have much occasion to ride the streetcar previously, mostly just when the family went to the State Fair over on the east side of Des Moines, but it didn't matter what those other people thought. Soon he would be exactly where he belonged. That's all that mattered. Some of the folks on the streetcar looked at him like they had never seen a farmer before. Then he realized that he didn't look like a farmer to them; he looked like a bum. He still didn't care. Charley knew he was a farmer. He straightened up in his seat and smiled. Most of the passengers looked away when he did that.

The streetcar ran right to Railroad and 5th Street in Valley Junction. That's where it ended, turned around, and headed back to Des Moines. It was a little bit west of the end of town, but it was the closest point to Commerce. He thought about going to their rental house first, thinking maybe Harley might be there, but he couldn't wait to see Lena. He figured Lena would be at the store in Commerce. Charley was going straight there.

Stepping down from the streetcar, he started to jog again. He felt like he did when he first met Lena. Joyful. Young. Bursting with energy. He had money in his shoe for his new house. He was going to be sleeping in his own bed. Harley would be making his coffee every morning. In these hard times, Charley had every reason to be happy, although by most standards, he was one of the hardest hit. He smiled as he ran.

Down the hill and around the curve to the Commerce Grocery he ran. He stopped for just a minute, about a hundred yards away. Taking out his handkerchief, Charley wiped his face. He was not even breathing very hard, but he was sweaty. Lena didn't like hugging him when he was sweaty. He fanned himself a little with his hand. It was about seventy degrees out, so it wasn't too difficult to cool down. He straightened his hat, then he decided to take it off. Charley ran his fingers over his flat top haircut. It felt neat enough.

He really did not want to alarm Lena by looking like such a rail bum when she finally saw him. His whiskers were a problem, but it was too late to do anything about it now. Then he realized that he'd had the same clothes on for three days. No, that would never do.

Charley walked into the woods next to the road. He went deep into them, about fifty yards, so there was no way anyone passing by could see him. He did a 360-degree turn-around to be sure no one was within sight from any direction, and then he dug into his pack for a set of clean clothes. What had he been thinking? Lena might have screamed, seeing him in those grimy overalls! He pulled out a clean denim shirt that he had always worn on Sundays for church, along with a white t-shirt, and a crisp pair of denim blue jeans. He even changed his socks. He transferred the money from his shoe to his wallet at the same time; it was ready to show Lena what his months away had earned him. There, now he was ready to walk into that store!

Back on the road, a few cars passed him by, going both directions. No stares from those folks. He looked more like a regular fella than a bum now. More confident that his appearance would please Lena, Charley found himself in front of the Commerce store. He needed an entrance plan. He wanted to make it special. Lena would like that. He had looked for some wildflowers alongside the road but had only seen goldenrod and milkweed. He wasn't gonna give a fistful of weeds to Lena.

Then he got the idea...make it more private. He lowered his voice a little to disguise it and spoke towards the screen front door, "Any shop lady in there to give me a hand out here?" He waited.

"I'll be right out," came Lena's voice.

"Hurry up, please, I need somethin' right now!" he said, a little more urgently.

The door swung open and there was Lena. She had on her peach-colored dress! His favorite, the one in his daydreams; he hoped he wasn't dreaming this! His arms opened wide and she was in them instantly. Neither one spoke. It was a silent embrace, except for a little breath that came out of her when he squeezed her so tightly. He felt his arms around her waist, and her arms around his neck. Lena's sweet face was pressed against his scruffy whiskers, and she didn't seem to care at all. It felt like time was standing still. Neither one moved, even a bit. He opened his eyes and looked down on her beautiful hair. She tipped her head back and looked at him.

"That's quite a face full of whiskers you have there, Charles Frederick." Whenever she called him that, he knew he was in trouble.

"I couldn't wait to stop and shave somewhere, sweetheart. When I got downtown, I made a bee line for you. I'm sorry."

"You are not in trouble, honey! I'm just teasing you. Oh my word, it is so good to have you home. Come here!"

She reached up again and grabbed him around the neck. This hug lasted even longer. He was home, in Lena's arms. Everything would be okay now.

The Interview

When the last bell rang, I left school as quickly as I could, not even going to my locker to put away the books I didn't need for homework. Taking all the books from my afternoon classes, I high-tailed it home. About a block away, I saw there was a car parked on the street in front of our house, and a man was just stepping up to the front porch. It had to be Ted Ashby. I was excited about this all day at school, but suddenly, nerves took over. This guy was one of my heroes!

Deciding to give Mother time to get him comfortable in the parlor, I slowed down my walk. I wondered if she had made some sort of special after-school snack. Most days I ate graham cracker sandwiches with her homemade powdered sugar frosting in the middle. That possibility was quickly dismissed as I got closer to the house. I smelled pie again! My pace quickened until I had my foot on the top step of the porch. I paused, then opened the front door.

"I'm home! Is that Mr. Ashby's car?"

"Come into the parlor, Mable. Mr. Ashby is right here. Why don't you leave your books on the table in the hall?" Mother suggested. She probably didn't want the parlor to look messy when we had company.

Mother introduced me to Mr. Ashby saying, "Mr. Ashby, I'd like to introduce you to my daughter, Mable. Mable, this is Mr. Ashby." It was the exact way she had taught me to introduce two people to each other. Mother and Dad taught me manners from the time I was really small. It was very important to them. So, I knew what I was supposed to say next.

"How do you do, Mr. Ashby? It's very nice to meet you."

Mother was beaming.

Mr. Ashby replied, "I'm really pleased to meet you, Miss Hall, and I want to thank you for taking time to meet with me today. Shall we sit down and talk a little bit? I have a lot of questions I'd like to ask you. Where are you going to sit? I'd like to start by getting a picture of you to go with the story, if that's okay with you, Mrs. Hall?"

Mother had already moved toward the entry hall and was probably on her way to the kitchen. She turned, walked back a few steps and said, "Certainly, Mr. Ashby. A picture would be nice. Would you like to sit in Dad's chair, dear? Or would you like her to be standing up?"

"Standing up is better, Mrs. Hall. Let's have you stand right by the doorway, Mable. It will be a simple background and the doorframe will let people see how tall you are. You are taller than most young ladies, Miss Hall. How tall are you?"

"I'm five feet, eight inches tall, sir," I replied. "I'm the tallest girl in my class."

He went to his case on the floor by the davenport and produced a camera. It was a Leica, the newest camera on the market. I saw one advertised in Life magazine last summer. Miss Hawn had said it wouldn't be long before all newspapers and magazines would be using them because they were small, very portable, and took exceptionally clear photographs. It was beautiful.

"That's a brand-new camera isn't it, Mr. Ashby?" I asked. "I saw an advertisement for one like that in Life magazine last summer. Did you just get it?"

"That's a good observation, Miss Hall. I got it two weeks ago. It takes remarkably sharp pictures. Maybe I will let you try it out. Are you a photographer, too?" he asked.

I explained, "No, not really. There is one boy at school who takes most of our sports pictures. He has to use a big, old camera that the school has had for a long time, and the photographs he takes are okay for our high school newspaper. He complains about it being too hard to take everywhere, but he gets pretty darn good pictures with it."

He directed me to stand up straight and smile, as his camera clicked. He took about five pictures of me, so I hoped there would be at least one flattering shot he could use.

We sat back down, and as he tucked the camera back in the bag, he started asking me questions. The camera went in the bag and he reached deep into a side pocket of the bag, pulling out a note pad. I saw that he had his pencil behind his ear. It was funny and pretty cliché. I was surprised with myself that I didn't notice that when we were introduced. A good reporter has to notice details; I felt somewhat disappointed in myself, but shrugged it off as Mr. Ashby kept talking to me.

"Like I said on the telephone yesterday, Miss Hall, when I saw you swim in Iowa City last weekend, you put on quite a display. How long have you been swimming?"

"I was probably four or five when my Dad took me to Pine Lake, up by Steamboat Rock and Eldora. Do you know where that is?" I asked.

"Sure, I do. There's a nice park around that lake. So that's where you learned to swim?"

"There, and in the Iowa River. The river there is pretty wide and not too deep. Then we moved to Des Moines when I was in sixth grade, and it was wonderful to have the city swimming pools to go to in the summer. That's when I started diving, too," I added.

"You dive?" he asked. "Why didn't I see you diving over in Iowa City?"

Golly, he wanted every detail of my swimming! "I gave up diving because it was bad for my hearing." I pointed to the hearing aid that I wore tucked just inside my top. He apparently had not noticed the wire that ran from inside my blouse, up to the earpiece. "I haven't been able to hear very well since I had a bad case of the mumps when I was little."

"Never would have known that, Miss Hall. It sure doesn't affect your swimming. Tell me about setting those two state records. What did that feel like? Is that what you were aiming for?"

That was an easy question. I had guessed his questions would be hard to answer, but then when I thought about it, he was only asking me to talk about myself. I should be able to do that!

"I have wanted to set a state record since I started high school. That has always been my goal. I give swimming lessons in the summer, but almost all the rest of the time, I am swimming and practicing." I also offered some extra information. "I do the backstroke because I don't have to dive into the pool. The doctor says any diving will make my hearing worse."

"Well then, you had better listen to the doctor," he advised. "I know when you started swimming and that you used to dive. Let's talk about the University of Iowa for a minute. How did your tour of campus go?"

"I had a lot of fun. Their journalism program is really nifty. I'm filling out my application this week, and when they get it, they are going to let me know about what scholarship help I might get this fall."

"Journalism department? Is that why you are Sports Editor of the Oracle?" he asked.

"Oh yes! I want to be write about sports, just like you do. I want to meet Grantland Rice. Meeting Sec Taylor would be wonderful, too," I bubbled.

"So, you like all sports, not just swimming?"

"My dad taught me everything about all kinds of sports, Mr. Ashby. I love football, basketball, volleyball, baseball, golf, and even boxing!" I said enthusiastically.

Mr. Ashby put his pen and notepad down. We started visiting about good players, great games, incredible plays, and our favorite teams and players. I told him that my favorite sports heroes were Johnny Weissmuller and Babe Ruth. He told me a little about the most exciting sporting events he had covered. Mother brought in pie and tea, but neither one of us touched them. Ii was almost as much fun as talking with Dad about sports. We talked for about an hour, and then Mother came in and mentioned that this was a school night and that I had homework to do.

"I'm sorry to stay this long, Mrs. Hall, but your daughter knows an awful lot about sports. She is amazing. You and your husband must be very proud of her."

Mother beamed again, "Yes, we are, Mr. Ashby. We are looking forward to seeing this article about Mable you are writing. When do you think it might be in the Tribune?"

He explained, "This is Tuesday, so by the time I get it written and turned in to the copy editors, it should be ready for the Sunday edition. I'd say this story is worth being on the front sports page of the Register's Sunday paper. I can't promise that, but I'm going to write it like that's where it belongs."

"Really?" I exclaimed. "My picture on the front page of the Big Peach?"

That's what the newspaper called their thick Sunday sports section. It was even printed on peach-colored newsprint.

"Of course. I think I have all the information I need, Miss Hall, so I will say goodbye and wish you and your mother a good evening," he said, rising from the davenport and picking up his camera bag.

"Wait one more minute, please," Mother said suddenly. "I went up to Mable's closet and got her varsity letters to show you." She handed him my tennis and volleyball letters.

"These are impressive, Mable. Well done. Are there any sports you haven't tried?" he asked.

I smiled a little sheepishly, "I guess I forgot to mention the boys' swim team."

"Boys' swim team? You are on the boys' swimming team?" He was astonished.

"Well, not yet, exactly. I spoke with Coach Johnson about it yesterday, and he found out that it's not against the rules. He said he still wants to talk with some other coaches and with the boys on the team about it. He's going to let me know next Monday," I explained.

"May I mention this in the article? You really won't know for sure until after it comes out, will you?" asked Mr. Ashby.

"Go ahead. I don't think it will matter at all. I really hope he will let me swim with them. It will give me a great opportunity to keep swimming this winter and keep improving my times," I added. "If he won't let me try out for the team, I am just going to play basketball. Either way, I'll be doing some sport. I'd prefer swimming, that's all."

"I certainly wish you luck with this, Miss Hall. I am going to be on my way now."

Mr. Ashby turned to my mother. "It has been a pleasant and interesting visit to your lovely home, Mrs. Hall." He concluded with, "Thank you for your hospitality." As he reached the door, he turned and smiled at me. "Your parents are completely justified in being so proud of you. Don't ever quit your sports or your writing. Goodbye, now."

As the door closed behind him, Mother and I looked at each other. She said, "What a nice man."

I replied, "He knows so much about sports. I really want to be just like him someday, Mother."

"I think you might even be able to be better, Mable. You don't just write about sports, you play them!"

Well, she was right about that. I just had to keep hoping for good news next Monday. I got my little bit of homework done and went to bed early. The past two days had been a really hectic beginning to the week, and I was exhausted.

A New Home

The reunited family sat down at the kitchen table in the Valley Junction rental. Charley put his $250.00 in the center, Lena put her $78.00 on top of it, and Harley placed his $42.75 down. They had $370.75. That would be enough for a simple house. Four or five room houses could be purchased for $2,000-$2,500 in town, but they had basements and garages. With his family and friends helping, he could get the materials for the cash they had. They could buy supplies at the Grimes lumber yard. They sold plans there and would have everything: lumber, nails, windows and doors, shingles and pipes. Yes, he told Lena, pipes. Charley was going to put water in the kitchen. It wouldn't be a fancy place with an indoor toilet yet, but Lena would not have to go to the well for water any more. It would be almost the size of the old house, except for the basement. They were going to have to put in a half basement, just big enough for the furnace and the coal, and maybe a small root cellar/storm shelter. There wasn't going to be time to dig a full basement. Half would do. Lena didn't object; it would be home and that's all she wanted.

Charley had all his tools in the shed, and his family, friends, and neighbors would bring theirs. Lena had recruited folks the past few weeks when she had heard from Charley about when he could be expected home. They would have Pastor

Schlenker at St. John's Lutheran in Grimes make the announcement in church tomorrow; the house would be started next Saturday. Eight o'clock in the morning. As soon as everyone got their own chores done, they would be over at Charley and Lena's farm. Betty agreed to cook the lunch. Lena was so grateful. Mrs. Monahan said she would help cook and serve, too. Harvest would be starting soon, but the farmers had some time before that. It would be just enough time to build a house.

Saturday came and the load of lumber was ready. Charley and Harley had gotten the basement dug with the help of the co-op's crew. The bricks from Grimes Brick had been laid. The cement was dry, so the framing began. By noon, the men had the basement reinforced with framing and the above-ground walls were done. Lunch was filling, but brief. Charley had to cut some corners with his limited funds, so it was decided that the two bedrooms would go over the basement; it would keep them warmer in the winter. There would be no second story or attic, just a crawl space below the roof. The kitchen would not have a framed floor. It might have to be dirt; Lena wasn't too sure about that, but Harley stepped forward and said he had an idea for making that work and assured his mother that it would be clean and pretty when he was finished. Lena was dubious without knowing all the details, but she had no choice. Tight as the money was, she was going to be happy just to have a roof of their own over their heads before the snow started flying.

No one worked on Sunday, but on Monday morning after that, the men came again. Betty cooked again, and Mrs. Monahan made pies. All week, the crew was various sizes, but by Friday, it was clear that only one more Saturday would be needed. Lena couldn't remember being so happy since the day she and Charley married.

Lena had picked out a used cook stove at the hardware store in Grimes, and it was installed. Charley and Harley found a really good sink at the dry goods store in Valley Junction and traded the owner with some of the leftover lumber. Lena was so excited to have running water in her kitchen. She still did not like the dirt floor in her kitchen, but the floors in the bedrooms, hallway, and living room were sturdy and warm. The stove would help heat the kitchen, and the warmth would flow into the rest of the house throughout the day. Charley said he thought that as long as his bedroom was warm, he would be happy, and that's what Lena really cared about. Charley had sacrificed months of comfort and convenience, risked his health and his life, and braved the dangers of riding the rails to provide a home for them. She loved, admired, and appreciated him more than ever. She was going to make this a wonderful home for him. Farming was a hard life. Her ambition was to make it less hard. Charley's ambition was to just make it. Harley's goal was to make it out and own a Lincoln. But for now, he was going to finish high school and find a way to go to college.

The weather cooperated that last day. The roof went on and the windows went in. The interior was unfinished, but Lena knew how to paint and caulk. She could sand and varnish. She could hang a door, and if they were short on doors, she knew how to hang a curtain across it. Whatever needed to be done inside the house, she would do it. She was, however, still worried about her kitchen floor.

Harley assured her he had a great solution. She could sweep it, mop it, and it wouldn't be dirt. She could even wax it, if she wanted to. He kept his plan such a mystery, it was starting to drive Lena crazy. Finally, she gave him a deadline.

"I need it in by the day before school starts. That gives you two weeks, Harley. Two weeks. Now that the house is done, your father needs you to help in the field, so whatever your plan is, it'll be dark when you are doing it, you understand?" Lena was visibly upset, and she continued to go on about the floor not being done. "I don't know what you have up your sleeve, son, but I cannot abide this dirt floor in my kitchen much longer. You understand, this is where the term 'dirt poor' comes from, right? It means you are so poor, you have dirt floors in your house. I have no intention of giving anyone cause to call this family 'dirt poor'."

"I understand, Mother. It will be done. It is a nighttime project anyway. I will not let you down, I promise." Harley still sounded confident, so Lena let it drop for now, but she did not stop worrying about the dirt floor.

Charley and Harley had to focus on the harvest now. The son kept up with his early morning milk route and helped his father and Jim with getting the corn in. Lena got the last of the vegetables out of the garden and began putting them in the jars the ladies at church had given her. Using the well water in the garden all summer, she had a generous harvest. She even donated some to church for them to give to some of the less fortunate town folks in Grimes. Charley was impressed by that, but Lena did it because she had been raised that way. Even in tight, hard times, she had learned, share what you have with others who need it.

Harley was making trips to Granger at night after dark. He would return with a large crate of "something" every evening. He carried it immediately to the basement. She saw him bring in a large ball of baling wire and the wire cutters from the shed. She had no idea what was going on. She asked Charley if he knew what Harley was doing down there.

"Charley, do you know what Harley's plans are for the dirt floor? He's making all those trips to Granger and being mighty mysterious about what is going on in the basement. He won't let me go down there. He's been making all the trips to the put the food in the root cellar for me, even. Mighty mysterious," Lena said.

"I do know, but I ain't tellin' ya. It's fun watchin' you squirm and fret!" He laughed heartily. "You'll find out Sunday," he assured her.

"What's going on Sunday?"

"Well, Sugar, after church I am takin' you to your mother's house. We are spending the afternoon visiting with her and Lynn and Alice. Harley tells me that when we get home for supper, he will have the floor done."

"Is it going to be a nice floor, Charley?" she asked. "I don't need anything fancy…well, I know it isn't going to be fancy, but I want something nice," Lena declared.

"Relax, Sweetheart, it's gonna be real nice, and pretty, and colorful, and sturdy, and different than anything you have ever seen. Just relax," he repeated. "Harley is doing his best for his ma. You know he loves you," Charley reminded her.

So, she let it go again. Harley was a wonderful son, and he did try to please his mother in everything he did, so she had to trust him.

Sunday came, church was over. Charley and Lena dropped Harley off at the foot of their driveway and headed off to a fried chicken dinner at her mother's house. Harley was going to heat up some leftover bean soup at home and get busy on the new floor.

'New' wasn't exactly accurate. It was a 'used' floor if he wanted to be truthful. One of the men who helped build their house had a junkyard up in Granger. He had hundreds of old cars, not running, that he was selling for parts. City-folk and farmers alike would haul their old, non-running cars and trucks over there, and he would give them cash. Then he would sell the parts. The man, named Russ Law, said it was a business that didn't exist twenty years ago and he was right. Harley thought the guy was pretty creative, having found a way to make a living off of other folk's junk cars. Harley was still thinking about careers that could afford him his new Lincoln eventually. He didn't think owning a junkyard would fit the bill. He'd keep looking. But, Russ was nice to him, and generous. He offered Harley another creative idea. He could use the old license plates for the floor of his mother's kitchen.

They were colorful. They were sturdy. They were easy to clean. Perfect for a floor, but they were small pieces. Harley looked at a few license plates that Russ brought when he came to work on the house one day. They had little holes in each corner. He could patch them together with bailing wire. He had promised his mother a pretty, sturdy, washable floor, so he made several trips to the junkyard, to remove the old plates from the junked cars. When she came home Sunday evening, Lena's floor would be done.

Harley had pieced the floor together in sections that he could carry up the stairs, put down on the floor, and then wire all the edges together. The biggest section he had was about six feet by six feet. He also had two smaller pieces wired together. The small kitchen with a tiny dining area was ten feet by twelve feet. He would fold up the sections he had and carry them up the stairs. After wiring them together in place, he would add on individual plates to fit them to the walls.

First, he moved the table and chairs into the hallway. After laying down a sheet of tar-treated felt that he had let Uncle Lynn help him buy, he dragged the sections of the floor up the stairs and started placing them where they fit the best. Harley had measured pretty well and was relieved to confirm that he had enough extra license plates to complete the whole dirt part of the floor. Because he had waxed them all individually while wiring them together, the floor was as colorful and shiny as he had hoped. It was also as pretty and practical as he had promised his mother it would be.

Harley was mildly surprised by the pleasure he felt in flooring the dirt part of their home. He realized he had actually contributed to the house in a way no one else did. He wasn't a house framer, or a roofer, or a plumber, but he was the floor man. It really felt wonderful. After putting the table and chairs back, Harley admired the floor, walking around on it, packing it down more level in a few spots, and generally making sure all the corners were good and secure. When he heard his father's truck come up the short driveway, he was ready. This was it!

He ran outside, waving hello to his parents. Charley could tell by the look on his son's face that the floor was done. Up until now, Charley had thought it sounded like an interesting possibility, but really did not know what to expect. From the look on Harley's face, though, he could tell it turned out well.

Harley was so anxious to have his mother see it, that he didn't make any grand plan for having her close her eyes or anything like that. He whisked her across the side door threshold and fairly pushed her into the kitchen entryway.

"Oh! My goodness!" Lena cried. "Look at this. Just look at this! I have never seen anything like this…this…this…floor. It's amazing!" She moved her weight from foot to foot, shifting to check the floor. It was sturdy and practical, and so unusual. She walked across the kitchen, making a pass in front of the ice box and the stove. Harley had lined up the license plates to fit perfectly against the planks where the wood floor for the hallway started. Lena was truly impressed.

"Well done, son," said Charley. He was very proud and looked at Lena. She was beaming but was definitely having a hard time expressing herself. It was obvious from the look on her face. She couldn't stop smiling. Her eyes were sparkling; actually, a little moist. She shook her head when she looked at Harley.

She finally found a few words, "This floor is wonderful, and you are incredible, Harley. I love you so much. I know this took you a long time; many hours and a lot of effort. I will absolutely treasure this floor."

Harley had his speech planned. It was almost like a dedication for the floor, or even for the whole house. "Mother, and Father. Our family has struggled since the old house burned down. We still don't have a lot, but we have our new home, and we still have the farm. I wanted to make sure no one could call us dirt poor, so I covered it up, with the prettiest license plates I could find. We are now officially license plate poor, and I don't think that is poor at all, do you?"

Tears slid down Lena's face, as the late-afternoon sun shone through the west kitchen window. Charley put his arm around her shoulder and she leaned into him. Harley stepped up beside her and put his arm around her also, just on top of his father's arm.

"No, Harley. We are not even the slightest bit poor," Lena whispered. "We are richly blessed. God has blessed us all."

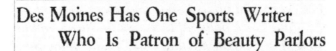

Des Moines Has One Sports Writer Who Is Patron of Beauty Parlors

It's Miss Mabel Hall of North High, and Does She Know Athletics?

BY TED ASHBY.

According to a substantiated disclosure Tuesday, Des Moines has the only sports editor who wears rouge and sings soprano—the only recorder of athletic events who embroiders pillow slips after the final edition goes to press.

As a general thing, sports writers omit spit curls from tonsorial requisitions and extend their hand for assistance only when payday is three days distant. But this unusual individual gets a seat on a crowded street car while fatigued laborers dangle from ceiling straps.

The first and second paragraphs have referred to Miss Mable Hall, sports editor of the North High school Oracle.

Knows Her Passes.

Never having been confronted with a feminine sports writer, your interviewer assumed that her knowledge of athletics and athletes consisted of a firm belief that a forward pass is a dining table relay that works the tomatoes toward the end zone. Not so with Miss Mable Hall, sports editor of the North High Oracle.

Miss Hall rattled off definitions of football plays that sent the interviewer into a huddle with his 1936 gridiron guide. For instance, she knows that

Continued on Page Four.

MABLE HALL.
She Knows a Forward Pass Isn't a Dining Table Relay.

On the Front Page

Grandma was down in the kitchen before I left for school the next morning. She and Mother were visiting, and Mother was able to include me, by doing some translating, with a little writing, some gestures, and our loud voices. Our family was a loud family, with two of us so hard of hearing! From Mother, Grandma had learned about the interview with Mr. Ashby yesterday. My grandmother didn't understand why I didn't come home right after school every day and help with the cleaning, maybe do some needlework or tatting. She said she would be willing to teach me how to tat. I told her that I thought the tatting she did was beautiful, but I really did prefer to be involved in athletics. Mother explained to her that my sports were going to help pay for my college education. Then Grandma decided that my sports were okay because no one in the family had ever graduated from college. I was her only granddaughter, and she certainly wanted that for me. Grandma was so understanding and sweet. Her artistic talent with the quilting and her kindness to everyone made her a special grandmother.

The rest of the week crept past on its hands and knees; it went so slowly. A few things that kept me going were being able to talk to Burnie about all of this and looking forward to telling Dad all the news on the telephone Sunday. And of course, my nightly visits with Mother and Grandma Von Dornum.

One night, we started talking about all the quilts Grandma had created. Mother showed me the quilts she had in a cedar chest in the attic; Grandma had made them over the years. There was a Texas Star, a Flower Garden, a Log Cabin, a Flying Geese, and the first heavy wool quilt that Grandma had made out of the men's suiting sample fabric square from the dry goods store. Not one square of fabric was the same as any other. The man who owned the dry goods store now is the son of the man Grandma originally worked for. Whenever suit samples were discontinued, he brought them to Grandma and she added them to the quilt. It would fit a big double bed and was really heavy and warm. She was thinking about making another one like it, as he brought her more samples.

The other quilts were so beautifully designed, they looked like works of art. Grandma was a true artist with fabric. I was so excited to have her making me that velvet quilt for graduation. She was very careful, though, not to ever let me see her working on it.

Grandma had so many stories about raising Mother and her siblings on the farm near Iowa Falls, but of course, Mother had to be the translator for all of them. Some were funny, and others were quite sad, like when Uncle Wiard died.

Those stories made the evenings of this long week go faster. Nothing had been able to make school days go faster. Burnie was somewhat helpful, shooting baskets with me, but it was getting rather cold outside for that. Saturday finally came and there was just one day left before Dad would be calling. Finally! Mother kept hoping Sunday would come sooner, too. She wanted to see that picture of her daughter on the front page of the Big Peach in the Sunday Tribune, and she wanted to be able to send a copy of it to Dad; I just wanted to talk to him! It seemed like a month, but it had only been one week since our last conversation.

Finally, it was Sunday morning. Three short rings! I ran for the phone and blurted, "Dad! I love you! I'm going to be in the paper today! Maybe on the front page of the Big Peach!"

Silence. Then, "Golly, Mable, do I even get a 'hello'? Settle down a little bit up there. I think I need an explanation. Weren't the results of the state swim meet in last Sunday's paper?"

"This article isn't about the state swim meet, Dad. It's just about me. You won't believe this. Well, maybe you will. Ted Ashby called me on Monday."

Dad interrupted with, "Ted Ashby of the Tribune. The sports writer?"

"Yes, Dad. Let me finish. He called me on Monday and wanted to interview me. He saw me swim at the state meet, but I couldn't talk with him because we had to go on that campus tour. So he promised to call me Monday at home, after school."

"So, when did he interview you? Was it at school or at the house?"

"He called me like he said he would and then he came by the house after school on Tuesday. Mom made another apple pie, but we were talking so much that we didn't even have time to eat it. It was almost like talking to you about sports. He knows so much! He stayed almost until dinner time. I barely had time to get my homework done, but don't worry, I got it all done."

"And it's going to be on the front page of the Big Peach today? All this because of your two records?" Dad asked.

"Not really. He found out from Coach Mortenson that I'm the sports editor for the Oracle, and he thought it was strange for a girl to be able to do that, so he wanted to find out about me. Good reporters are curious, you know. I told you Miss Hawn always tells us that, right? Well, he was really curious!"

"I'm so proud of you, darling daughter. I hope you will send me a copy of the article. What else is going on? Any news about the boys' swim team?"

"I'll tell you about that in a minute, Dad. First, I want you to know he took my picture, too. It's going to be with the article. He had one of those brand-new Leica cameras. It was so shiny! I can't wait to see how the photograph of me turned out."

"Then send me the article and the picture, dear. What did Coach Johnson say about the boys' swim team?" Dad prodded me.

I went ahead and told Dad about how Coach Johnson had asked the principal and the other man from the state athletic group. I told him about how I met with him during lunch, and he put me off for a week; how he was going to talk to the other coaches and to the fellas on the team. Dad agreed with me that Coach was probably going to tell me 'no'. He said that I could stay in shape playing basketball and that my records were plenty incentive for the University of Iowa to give me some help with the tuition or room and board. Even if they didn't, Dad said he was going to make plenty of money up there on those high steel skyscraper beams, and I did not have to worry; I was going to college in the fall, no matter what. Finally, Dad asked to talk to Mother. The phone call was going to get pretty expensive if we weren't careful.

Mother filled Dad in on how Grandma was doing and what the doctors found out about Aunt Helen's stomach. It wasn't too serious yet. She was just going to have to be more careful about what she eats and drink a cup of buttermilk before each meal. Dad also told Mother that he had not gone to the doctor yet, but he had an appointment for the next Friday. They said their 'I love you' stuff, then Mother said she would write him and that I would send the article. He gave Mother the address where he was staying, and the phone call was over.

Now, I just had to wait for the Sunday paper to come.

About thirty minutes later, I heard the paper hit the front porch. I was down the stairs in a flash, but Mother was already coming in the front door with the paper in her hand.

"What were you doing, Mother, sitting on the front porch?" I asked.

"No, silly Mable. I was just in the kitchen starting the coffee and a coffee cake. I thought you would be upstairs, but now that I think about how excited you were when you spoke to Dad, I'm surprised you weren't sitting on the front steps."

"Let's see it. Where is the sports section?" I asked eagerly.

"Right here, Mable. Stay calm. Oh look, it is right here on the front page. A big picture of you, it is! Humph, looks like they changed the background. Didn't like the way my house looked?" Mother spoke a bit indignantly.

"It's fine, Mother. The parlor looked perfect. It just must have not looked good in the picture. Perhaps the wallpaper background was too busy. I have a pattered dress on, see? It would not have looked good at all. That's what photo editors do; they decide what pictures look good, and then change what they need to. They didn't do it to hurt your feelings, I promise."

"It certainly is a beautiful picture of you, Mable. You are standing up so straight and tall." Mother walked into the parlor and took a seat, saying, "Here, sit down next to me and we will read it together."

The headline said, "Des Moines Has One Sportswriter Who Is a Patron of Beauty Parlors." *Then there was a subtitle of* "It's Mabel Hall of North High, and Does She Know Athletics?"

"Mother, he spelled my first name wrong!"

"It's okay Mable. People will know it's you."

"I'm a bit disappointed in Mr. Ashby, Mother. That's his byline right at the top of the article, and if information is not accurate, it's his fault. Reporters are supposed to be accurate!"

Mother calmed me with, "Let's just read the article, dear. Everyone makes a mistake now and then. Mr. Ashby is a very nice man and you already know he is a good reporter."

The article read, "According to a substantiated disclosure Tuesday, Des Moines has the only sports editor who wears rouge and sings soprano – the only recorder of athletic events who embroiders pillow slips after the final edition goes to press.

As a general thing, sports writers omit spit curls from their tonsorial requisitions and extend their hand for assistance only when payday is three days distant. But this unusual individual gets a seat on a crowded street car while fatigued laborers dangle from the ceiling straps.

The first and second paragraphs have referred to Miss Mable Hall, sports editor of the North High School Oracle.

Knows Her Passes

Never having been confronted with a feminine sports writer, your interviewer assumed that her knowledge of athletics and athletes consisted of a firm belief that a forward pass was a dining table relay that works the tomatoes toward the end zone. Not so with Miss Mable Hall, sports editor of the North High Oracle.

Miss Hall rattled off definitions of football plays that sent the interviewer into a huddle with his 1932 gridiron guide. For instance, she knows that the Star of Bethlehem wasn't a triple threat man. And she is aware, too, that all linemen don't work for the telephone company.

Won Two Letters

Miss Hall has won two letters at North and is the only girl in school who has qualified in golf, tennis, volleyball, and other girls' sports to this extent. Just now she is pleading with Coach Johnny Johnson to include her on the North High swimming team, composed entirely of boys.

She has a thorough understanding of football, baseball, and basketball and 'covers' for the school publication all of North's athletic contests. Miss Hall has two assistants, both boys. She's 17 and a junior."

Under the photograph, it said, "She Knows a Forward Pass Isn't a Dining Table Relay." And he spelled my name right under the picture, but I'm a senior, not a junior. He got everything else right, I guess.

"Well," said Mother. "What do you think of that, Mable?"

"Mother, I'm really proud it's on the front page. You know what that means, right? Everyone is going to see it, because everyone at least looks at the front page of the sports section. That makes me happy."

"If it makes you happy, it makes me happy, Mable. You know your father and I have always been proud of you. Sports editor or not, you are our darling daughter." Mother smiled at me with that sunbeam smile of hers, and I got up, bent over her and gave her such a big hug.

"Are you going to be able to translate the article for Grandma, Mother?"

"Not word-for-word, but I can explain all about what it says and let her know how important it is. I have to shout so loud, so I will need to keep it short. She already knows what a special girl you are."

"Thank you, Mother. I have the best parents in the world." I really meant that. My parents really believed in me. I think it was hard for Mother sometimes that I wasn't as girly as some of her friends' daughters, but she always supported me. Dad was one-of-a-kind. He taught me everything he knew about sports and still treated me like a girl. Sometimes Burnie teased me about being 'Daddy's boy' like I was trying to be athletic like a boy, to make up for being an only child who happened to be a girl. He assumed that parents always want boys. How would that work? No girls in the world? If all fathers got all boys for children? That would be the end of the human race. Mother and Dad were not like that. I wore dresses, I knew how to sew and how to cook. I was a girl, who was a good athlete. They let me be me, to do the activities that I enjoyed and that I was good at. They were wonderful parents and I loved them both so very much.

So, after Mother filled Grandma in and showed her the picture on the front page of the sports section, Mother carefully cut out the article and put it in an envelope for Dad. I was going to mail it on the way to school Monday. There was a big post box down at the corner.

At school on Monday, I went upstairs to talk to Coach Johnson during lunch, and he was in the room waiting for me. He had Raymond with him. Raymond was the captain of the boys' swim team. When I saw him, I suspected what the answer would be, and I was right. Not one of the coaches in the whole city and not one of the fellas on the team thought there should be a girl on the team.

They repeated over and over, "It's not because you are such a good swimmer, Mable; it's because you are a girl." I wanted to ask them if they saw the article in the paper yesterday, but I didn't. I knew they had seen it. There was no chance they had not seen it, and they didn't mention it either. How could they? If they said, "Nice article; way to go, Mable" they would be admitting that not letting me on the boy's team was different than letting me be sports editor.

But, they knew it wasn't any different, so they didn't dare say anything. I was smiling and nodding, and I told them, "I understand."

What I wanted to say was, "You are a bunch of 'fraidy cats and I hope you lose all your swim meets." I know that was mean and wrong, but they were the ones who were being mean, and they were the ones who were definitely wrong. I know if Dad was here, he would tell me, "There's nothing you can do about it, darling daughter. This is the 1930s, and the ladies have the right to vote now. That took a lot of work and a lot of years. Everything else that may follow is going to take a lot more years, and a lot more work. I want you to just be patient and do your best."

Dad always had such good advice. I was so glad I could hear his voice in my head and that I was able to imagine what he might tell me. Otherwise, I might have been tempted to bop ol' Raymond in the nose. I thanked the coach for all his time that he had put in checking and deciding. I didn't say anything to Raymond.

I went to basketball practice after school and all the girls there were happy to see me. They talked all about the article they saw in the paper and made me feel good about it all. They said it was the boys' swim team loss and the girls' basketball team gain. That really made me feel swell. On my way home, I stopped at Burnie's and told him the news. Then I went up to my room and wrote a letter to Dad about it. It was done, and I was going to get on with my senior basketball season.

Another Stroke of Bad Luck

Charley and Harley had to focus on the harvest now, and Harley had to get ready for school. The family had decided he was going to stay with Lena's mother in Valley Junction and attend Roosevelt High School for his senior year. Charley could do the morning chores, since they didn't have all the cattle and horses back yet. Harley would stay on the farm for the weekends and help his father; then he would go to church with them on Sunday, and back to Grandma Burt's house on Sunday night.

Lena paused from her household chores to gaze out the kitchen window. She really liked the way Charley had put windows on the west wall and on the north wall of her new kitchen, as she had asked him to. She enjoyed being able to see him as he worked in the fields on the forty acres just north of our house. The old house had only one window on the west wall, and all she could see was the old outhouse. She delighted in watching her husband working his own land again and smiled to herself. They might not have much as far as money or possessions go, but they had each other and they had a fine son. She was so happy to have Charley back home. He had risked his life in those wheat fields and riding those rails, to save his family, to build them a home, and to preserve their land. He was a wonderful father, and a loving husband. Once in a while, her husband would put his foot down about some topic or other, by giving her that stern stare, but she had never known him to become cross or angry. Charley had never raised his voice to her, or his hand either, For Harley, he had been a firm but fair father. Lena had never served Charley a meal that he had not thanked her for. Even in the middle of this horrible economic mess, Lena felt satisfied and fulfilled with her family.

Her kitchen floor rattled under her feet a little as she moved towards the sink to finish the dishes, but she was still grateful. The license plates were better than dirt; they were pretty and colorful. Harley had gone to the dump and the car heap dealer to gather them all and clean them up. Lena was so grateful, and so proud of her son's hard work and initiative.

Harley was going to graduate in May and Lena had tried to get him to talk about his plans. He kept hinting that if he was going to go to college like she expected, he would not be coming back to make his living as a farmer. He wanted to own his own business, be his own boss, and make a lot of money. Every now and then he would talk to Lena about being rich and generous, like he was going to come back driving a big fancy car and have a fat bank account. Harley promised he was going to pay off all their loans and build them a large Sears catalogue farmhouse. Lena would really like that. As long as Harley made his money in an honest job, she would be proud of anything he accomplished.

Lena glanced out the north window to spy on Charley again. She waited, thinking he would pass around the field again. She waited some more, and then got impatient. As she was walking down the stairs from the kitchen to the back door, she paused to take off her house slippers and put on the boots she used when she fed the chickens. Who knows, she might have to walk halfway down to the barn before she could catch sight of him. Lena went back to the kitchen and got a glass of lemonade out of the icebox. He might be thirsty, riding in that dusty field all afternoon. She didn't mind if she had to walk clear across the forty to get it to him, because it was a beautiful fall day. Sunny, with a little breeze. Just sun and the quiet whirring of the windmill in the feed lot. Walking out the back door, it was only the windmill that she heard.

She realized there was no chugging tractor sound. No scraping and scooping sound of a combine. That was strange. Charley usually didn't take breaks. He just worked and worked until the job was done, or until it got too dark to see where he was going. Lena started walking a little faster down the drive that curved towards the barn. Harley was working in the barn on the cattle pens, removing some of the older boards that needed replacing. Charley hoped to be able to get back to raising some cattle after the harvest came in.

"Harley, where's your father? I came to bring him a lemonade, but I don't hear or see the tractor anywhere." Her tone was anxious; rising with a bit of concern.

"I'll go check, Mother, I'll go check. He may have had some trouble with the tractor over in the northeast corner. It's a long walk back over here to get some tools. I'll get the tool box and go check on him. He might just be taking a break," Harley reassured her.

"Please just go. Forget the tool box…just get on out there. I want to know what's going on. This just isn't right. Harley," Lena persisted.

So, Harley set out at a good-paced trot. His mother's voice was too urgent for him to walk. Even with his long strides, walking would not be acceptable.

As he ran, his eyes scanned the horizontal plane of the bean field. There was not tractor in sight. He started to share his mother's concern. It just didn't seem normal. He kept running, but a bit faster now. Where was his father? He heard his mother yelling, "Do you see him? Do you see him?"

Then Harley saw him. The tractor was tipped sideways, run up against the fence, and it looked like Charley was pinned between the tractor and one of the fence posts. The machinery was all tangled up.

He turned back towards the barn. Hollering as loudly and plainly as possible, he shouted at his mother, "Go up to the house! Get the operator to call the sheriff! Dad needs help! The tractor's on him."

Lena ran as fast as she could in her "chicken boots." The phone line was open so she didn't have to kick anybody off the party line to get to the operator. Lena tried to stay calm so she could talk, but her heart was pounding with panic and her head was swirling with sheer terror. She knew Marlys, the phone operator, would get the sheriff as quickly as possible, so she started back out to the field. Before she ran out of the house, she grabbed a couple of clean dish towels, not knowing why, but wanting to be prepared. Then she dashed out the door.

Harley got to his father and realized he was stuck, but not tightly pinned, between the tractor and the post. He tried to wake Charley, as it appeared he was unconscious. "Dad, Dad, are you awake? Are you okay?"

Charley did not move. His eyes opened. He mumbled, but Harley could not understand what he said. His body looked very limp and Harley was relieved to see his father's eyes open.

"Mother went to call the sheriff, Dad. Are you in pain? What happened?" There was no response, but his father's eyes were still open. That's when he noticed one eye was wide open, while the other one looked droopy. Harley was trying so hard to stay calm, but inside he was terrified that his father would not be okay. He didn't know what to do. A helpless feeling began to engulf him. He looked around and saw his mother coming toward him, moving faster in her boots than he ever thought she could.

"He's alive mom, he's alive! Is the sheriff coming?" Harley wanted to run out and meet his mother, but he did not want to leave his father. "Hurry, he has his eyes open."

Lena was there beside Charley in the next instant. She had to climb across one of the dirt-caked metal tractor wheels to get to him, tearing her house dress in the process.

"Charles! Charles! What happened?" she coaxed as she took his gloved hand. "I'm going to take off his work gloves, Harley. That will be okay, won't it?"

"He's going to need a doctor, Mother. Did you ask the sheriff to get Doc Templeton out here? Dad's face looks funny. It doesn't look like he's in pain or that anything's broken, but he just doesn't look right."

"I told Marlys to call the doctor, too. I am taking off your father's gloves. One of his hands…well, his whole right arm...it is just floppy, like he is asleep; but he is awake. I don't know what's wrong," she sighed and moaned at the same time. "Oh, dear Lord, please let my Charley live!" Charley tried to mumble something again, but she didn't understand at all. "We are getting help, Sweetheart," she said. "We are getting help." She took the dish towel and gently wiped his face.

"Mother, here they come! Down the road, look!" Harley yelled, as he ran to the fence to wave them down. "Over here, over here," he screamed as he waved his arms frantically.

The sheriff's car ground to a noisy and dusty halt on the gravel road. A swirling cloud of dust gathered around it, as the doctor and the sheriff jumped out and ran down into the ditch to get to the fence.

"Is he pinned down?" the sheriff asked.

"Not so bad. He's not pinched in there. I think he's just twisted up under the tractor a little, just next to the fence. He isn't bleeding anywhere I can tell," Harley explained.

"Well, I had the operator call Jim and tell him to bring his tractor over here. Probably need to get Charley out from under there before we can do much," the sheriff said, and then he turned to Doc Templeton. "Can you get over that fence and check him out, Doc? Move back, Lena, and let the doc get in there for a look-see."

Lena said nothing but climbed back over to the other side of the huge wheel. She was beginning to get even more frightened because Charley just looked so different, and he couldn't speak. If she stretched out her arm, she could still touch Charley's back.

Harley and the sheriff started to look things over so they could figure out how to hook up Jim's tractor when he got there. Charley's tractor had basically just run sideways into the fence and then tipped over when the front wheel got jammed in the wire. They decided to have Jim put his chain around the back tire that was up in the air and pull the tractor back to an upright position, and that should free Charley without injuring him more.

They heard Jim's tractor chugging across Charley's field and turned to look; it was in high gear and the tractor was bouncing up and down like crazy. It looked like he was riding a bull at the rodeo. Jim swung out, made a big circle, and then backed it up to the up-ended tractor of Charley's.

Lena's focus was entirely on her husband. "Doc, what's wrong with Charley? Can you tell what's wrong? How could this happen?" Her questions came so rapidly, Doc did not even try to answer them in order.

"Appears to me like Charley's had a stroke, Lena. It won't kill him and luckily, having the tractor tip over didn't kill him either. Probably had the stroke first and then he lost control of the tractor. It doesn't look like he has any broken bones, but he's definitely lost some feeling and some control on his right side. We are going to have to get him to the hospital."

Lena had no more questions. She simply nodded.

"Let's move out of the way now so they can get this tractor moved," Doc Templeton said, as he gently guided Lena away from Charley's side.

Jim and Harley cut through the fence so they could carry Charley across the ditch and lay him down in the back seat of the sheriff's car. It took all four men to carry him. Charley was a tall, strong man before this, and it was quite a challenge to get him through the fence, down into the ditch, and then back up out of it again. They accomplished it as carefully as they could. Lena sat in the back with her husband's head in her lap. She spoke softly to him all the way to town, except for when she cried for a few minutes. That seemed to upset him, although he still couldn't speak with any plain words, so she only succumbed to her tears that once.

The ride to town was uneventful and at the hospital, the doctors told Lena there really wasn't much they could do for him. As strokes went, it was what they called a "medium" one. Given time, Charley would probably recover his speech and some strength on his right side. For right now, however, he would have to be in a wheelchair. Bed rest was the best medicine they could offer. It would just take time.

The sheriff had to leave, but Jim drove into town in his car and stayed with Lena at the hospital; after all, Charley was his cousin. Harley went to the café down the block from the hospital and got them some sandwiches. Charley was going to have to have his food mashed for a while, until he got some control of his jaw muscles again. The doctor started explaining all the things that her husband would not be able to do, and the more he spoke, the more discouraged Lena became. Besides not being able to chew, Charley would not be able to walk, drive a car, or go to the bathroom by himself. He would need a lot of help to get dressed and undressed, a someone would have to bathe him. It might be weeks or even months before he could be able to sit up at the dining room table or in his favorite chair, but for right now, Charley was ordered to stay in bed and rest. Put a coffee can under the bed; that was the doctor's advice. Then her husband could sit on the edge of the bed, with some help, and relieve himself. That would save her trying to get him to the outhouse. Lena was left speechless with this new reality.

That morning, she had a strong, healthy man at her side. This evening, she had an invalid who was going to need help doing the most simple tasks for himself. Lena's thoughts raced but had nowhere to go. What would happen to their farm now? They had just started to rebuild. It seemed like all of the responsibility was going to be on her shoulders. And Harley's.

Charley slept a long time in the emergency room bed. How was she going to get him home? Harley would have to come home to stay now; or maybe she could handle this by herself. Harley had to finish high school this year. She wanted him to stay in town with her mother. Roosevelt was the best school in Des Moines. Charley would want him to stay in town. Lena decided one thing after only a few minutes of thinking about this; Harley would stay in town, and Lena would find a way to take care of her husband by herself. Her son's future would not be detoured by this despicable stroke. Lena's mother would agree, and so would Charley; she was sure of that.

Harley didn't like the idea. He was so loyal to his father. He tried to insist, tried to say that he was going to be the man of the house now.

"I don't know where you heard foolishness like that, son, but your father is still the man of this house. You will need to go to college and get your own house to be head of; but your father is not dead, he's just hurt, and he's going to get better soon. You need to just go about your business, which is finishing your education. And, we are done talking about this matter. It is settled!" With that said, Lena gave her son a long stern look, like the ones he sometimes got from Charley, and Harley knew the discussion was finished.

Lena did everything the doctors said to do. Fortunately, their friends and neighbors got the rest of the harvest done, shipped, and sold. They would have enough money to get through the winter. After that, when spring came and the crops had to be planted, they would just have to see. Lena had never driven a tractor, but she was sure she could learn quickly. She would do whatever it took to keep the farm going until Charley was ready to farm again, because she was certain he would be farming again.

His left side was just fine. He was already doing an amazing job of recovering on the right side. It was slow like the hospital said it would be, but he was hoping he would soon be able to use the crutches the hospital gave him. She did not mind what Charley called his 'pee can', which he kept under his bed. He said he wanted to make it to the outhouse with his crutches, so Lena kept the path shoveled in the winter, but he never felt like he could make it.

Lena did all the chores during the week. It really wasn't that hard. Without Harley to cook for, it took less time to prepare meals for just the two of them. First thing every morning, she fed the chickens, the cats, and the dog. Then she got breakfast for Charley, gave him a sponge bath, and helped him get dressed for the day. He had figured out a way to shave himself. Even though his right side was affected by the stroke, Charley was pretty good with his left side. He probably started out to be left-handed as a kid, but the teachers at school made him write right-handed. He got a lot of sharp raps on the knuckles of his left hand and learned to be right-handed. Now, he was back to being a lefty.

Charley was lucky to have Lena. She did not just take him home to slowly recover. She took an active role in his rehabilitation. Lena's mother had been widowed for about ten years, but remarried. Lena's step-father, Dr. Burt, was a physician in Valley Junction. He and her mother, Grandma Burt, were the ones who had taken Harley in so he could attend Roosevelt. Dr. Burt had been very generous with his advice and had even sought opinions about Charley's condition from several doctor friends of his in Chicago and St. Louis. He learned there were some therapies that could help Charley recover more quickly. He paid for a nurse to come to the farm twice a week to work Charley's right side. It was making a real difference. Lena at least had hope that he would be able to farm again someday.

Settling Into Senior Year

Thanksgiving was really special because Grandma was living with us in Des Moines. The only way it could have been better would be to have Dad there. Uncle Albert and Aunt Helen telephoned us on Thanksgiving Day, and we had a short but loving exchange with them about all the events going on with me and the news we were hearing from Houston. Dad's visit to the doctor was inconclusive. The doctor told him he may have been working too many hours for a man his age, so Dad told the boss that he needed to stop getting overtime hours on Saturdays. My parents were a lot older than the parents of my friends; Mother was thirty-nine years old when I was born, but Dad seemed like a pretty active and healthy fella and my mother had no serious health problems. All I know is that my parents did not seem old to me.

Dad told us that he expected to be in Houston for another month, and then he would be going to San Francisco to work on a skyscraper there. Those big cities out west were really growing and booming. I found myself wishing I could go visit Dad when he went to California. I knew it was just a fantasy, but I missed him so much. We spoke with him every Sunday, but it was not enough. Sometimes those phone calls only made me miss him more. Mother and I started doing some Christmas shopping for him. We had to get a package in the mail soon, so he would get it in time for December 25th.

Thinking about Christmas also made me wonder about how Grandma Von Dornum's quilt was coming. Recalling all those gorgeous pieces of silk velvet I saw spread out on the bed when she was unpacking was exciting. To think that she was making something that beautiful, and then giving it away was a staggering concept for me. If I made something like that, it would be hard for me to give away. It said a lot about how much Grandma loved me. I know that makes me sound selfish, but I couldn't help it. It was so glorious. Then I remembered she had said there would also be "a surprise" in addition to the quilt.

I admired people who could think up surprises for other people. It seems like such a thoughtful thing to do. Many times, I got so absorbed in what I was trying to accomplish that I didn't take any time to think about other people. I had made that my New Year's Eve resolution last year, to be more thoughtful. Maybe that would have to be my resolution again this year because I certainly had not kept it last year. I would just have to keep trying, and I was blessed to have a role model like my old German grandmother to inspire me.

Mother and I went downtown to Woolworth's and bought three new pairs of work socks for Dad. I also helped her pick out a new denim work shirt for him, and a package of white men's handkerchiefs. We didn't have a lot of money to spend, so our gifts had to be practical; something he needed. I told Mother I would make a card for him and we could wrap them all up together. I wanted to bake some chocolate chip cookies to send to him also, but Mother said the chips might melt, so we decided I would make peanut butter cookies and snickerdoodles. Neither of those had much anything that would melt in them. Mother was right, of course, because although it was freezing cold and snowing a couple of times a week in Iowa at the beginning of December, it was warm in Texas. We didn't want Dad to get a melted mess, as Mother called it.

As the end of first semester came closer, Mother was inquiring about my grades. My grades mid-semester had been all A's and B's, which satisfied Mother and Dad. I assured Mother the grades were still where they needed to be. I wasn't going to tell her that I really didn't think it mattered that much if one or two grades went down. After all, I had received my letter of acceptance from the University of Iowa. They also notified us they were going to pay half of the year's tuition, each year, as long as I was on the swim team there.

I asked my parents if Dad would be able to come home for Christmas, since half my tuition would be paid, but they said he had made the commitment to those companies to work through February, and he needed to keep his word. They could build up a savings account to use in emergencies. I didn't like that answer. It didn't make sense to me. I missed Dad, Mom missed Dad, and Dad missed us. So why not just have him come home and let us all be together again? The adults made things so difficult sometimes.

Basketball was going well. We had won all our games so far, except for the East High game. Those girls weren't as tall as we were, but they sure were scrappy. The rules didn't allow players to touch other players to get the ball away, but those East girls were very adept at getting the ball the very second we let go of it. They would steal the ball when we dribbled and intercept our passes. They scrambled for rebounds. 'Hustlers' is what our coach called them and he said we should try to play more like them.

"You girls have to WANT the ball more than they do," he'd tell us. He even put up a sign in the girls' locker room that said, "Move with alacrity!" That sent us all scrambling for the dictionary! I found out that 'alacrity' means speed or quickness. If he wanted us to move faster, why didn't he just say so?

While the girls' basketball team was winning nearly all our games, the boys' swim team was losing most of their meets. I went to some of them that were home meets, but Robert Dodd covered most of them. I was writing the girls' basketball articles for the Oracle, Robert was writing swimming, Herbert was covering boys' basketball, and Bill was writing the wrestling articles. The fellas on my staff were very easy to work with. They knew exactly what to do. I think all three of them were wishing they had not given up the sports editor job so easily. They never said that, but at some point, I know they all realized the difference between the reporters and the editor was that I get to delegate the assignments to them, and for that I got the title Sports Editor. I was going to get a separate picture in the yearbook. It was like being captain of the football team, only not sweaty.

Soon the first semester would be over. Basketball season went through March, so at least Dad would be able to see some of my games when he returned from California. I would just keep playing basketball, writing sports articles, and studying my books until Dad got home.

Plans for College

Dr. and Grandma Burt were wonderful to Harley. She was the only grandmother he knew. Charley's parents had passed away before Harley was born. Grandma Burt bought Harley new clothes for his senior year. He decided not to play sports at Roosevelt, although he was a very good basketball player. Dr. Burt had been involved in Golden Gloves boxing and he encouraged Harley to try that. Harley did start going to the boxing gym on 5th Street in Valley Junction and he became a skilled pugilist in a very short period of time. He actually won enough matches to get him into the local Golden Gloves tournament, and he won that. Charley and Lena were so proud of their son, who apparently was a natural athlete.

Harley's grades at Roosevelt were exceptional also. His education at the local one-room Walnut School has prepared him well for the city schools. All his teachers praised him highly and he was on the honor roll every grading period.

Even though Harley did not participate in Roosevelt sports, he became good friends with some of the athletes. There was a young man on the basketball team named Mike McMichael. He was Catholic, and Harley's parents, as older German Lutherans, were prejudiced against Catholics. Harley never told his folks that his best friend was Catholic, so he was allowed to bring Mike out to the farm to visit for several weekends. Mike really enjoyed trying out the country life, and both Charley and Lena were impressed with his work ethic. They found out that Mike was planning on attending the University of Iowa, and that their Harley was thinking that might be a good place for him to attend also. College! That is exactly what they wanted for their only son! Mike's religious affiliation never came up for discussion. Harley loved his parents, but he let his friend know that it was just the way they had been brought up in the old days. He told Mike he thought he was a good friend and that it didn't matter at all what his religion was.

The school year was going so well. Harley had been able to save a little bit more college money from his milk route since the new house was all paid for now and Grandma Burt had bought his school clothes. That Lincoln on the route had been replaced, by a new Lincoln! Harley loved the new one even more than the old one and imagined having enough money to buy a new Lincoln every year. The more he visualized that, the more determined he became. Harley knew he would make it happen someday. All he had to do was go to college, graduate, and start his own business. He wasn't sure about exactly how all that would happen, but his mind was made up. Mike's father was wealthy; he earned his money selling insurance. That didn't sound like a good job to Harley. It sounded like a desk job. Harley wanted to find something that was more active, he was sure of that.

The harvest money from the farm was mostly going to purchase coal and food. Corn prices had gone down so far, some farmers were burning the corn for fuel, because it was cheaper than coal. Why sell the corn and then pay more per pound for coal? It was not a good time to be a farmer. Charley, still hoping he could get back to full-time farming, kept making progress and was to the point where he could walk down the hall and back with his crutches.

It was difficult for Harley to see his father like this. Charley had come back from his wheat shocking as a very strong, vital man. Even though he was becoming more mobile, slowly but surely, Charley was obviously never going to be completely recovered. Lena would never admit to this obvious fact, so she and Harley quit talking about it. However, not discussing it did not change it. A small share of the savings Harley had from his milk route money had to go to pay for food for the livestock. Charley refused to take any money from Dr. and Grandma Burt. They were already supporting Harley; that was appreciated, but it was all the assistance the proud farmer would accept.

All around the Midwest, farmers who could not pay the bank for their land or loans were having their farms auctioned right from underneath their feet. Harley was terrified that would happen to his parents. Lena would have gone back to work at the lawyer's office or at the Commerce store, but there was no one who could take care of Charley. Besides that, the gasoline back and forth would have used up her wages. The Depression weighed heavily on Harley's family, just like it did the rest of the country.

Then, when Harley was sure nothing worse could happen, it did. Dr. Burt died in an auto accident. He had been called to a home in southwestern Des Moines, making a late-night house call to an elderly woman with pneumonia. It happened just after Thanksgiving and there was a thin layer of freezing ice on everything. It proved to be a deadly layer. His car slid off the bridge going over the Des Moines River and his car plunged into the freezing water.

Grandma Burt was devastated. She had now lost two husbands. To make it worse, it came to light that Dr. Burt had a lot of debt. He had treated many patients without collecting payment, because he was the kind of man who often helped people who had no money. After his death and without his income, his wife was unable to pay all the bills. She was able to keep the house that was paid for, but their savings account was used up to settle the debts that she could. There was nothing left. It was another heavy blow to the family that was already burdened in these dire economic times.

Grandma Burt needed help now, so Harley started a job after school. He spent his afternoons working at a furniture store in Valley Junction. He swept floors, stoked the coal furnace, kept the storeroom straightened, and made deliveries. His pay was small, but it was better than nothing. His parents insisted he give the money to Grandma Burt and not to them. This made it possible for her to keep him at her house and keep him fed, so he could graduate from Roosevelt as planned.

Working at the furniture store was enjoyable for Harley. He liked it when people would ask him to help them pick out furniture, or match colors. It was really different than any job he had done before. He discovered that he was good at talking to people, listening to them, and he discovered that he truly enjoyed helping them. It was a learning process for him, and he became a good student of people.

As graduation grew closer, Lena and Charley both noticed Harley becoming increasingly more quiet and withdrawn on the weekends. Earlier in the school year, when he would bring Mike out for the weekends, he could be boisterous and rowdy. The house was filled with the two boys' horseplay and energy. In the final spring of his high school year, however, he was more silent and thoughtful. Lena suspected something hard was on his mind, so she decided to ask him what was going on.

"Harley, can you come out here so we can talk a bit?" Lena asked as she tapped on his bedroom door. It was Saturday night; Charley was in bed so he could get up to have visitors on Sunday, and Harley was done closing up the barn for the night.

"What's going through your head, son?" Lena asked. "You seem so serious and introspective lately, so I'm thinking something is weighing heavily on your mind. Am I right?"

"Yes, you're right, mother. I have been trying to figure out how I am going to get to college in the fall, and I have no idea where the money is coming from. I just don't know. Dr. Burt was going to help, and that's not going to happen now. I had a small bit in savings but had to give most of that to Grandma Burt, so she could buy food for me. The University of Iowa isn't an expensive place to attend, but I'll need tuition, books, room and board. I can work once I get over there, but I need some money to get enrolled. I have practically nothing!"

"I'm so sorry, Harley. You know how much your college means to me, and I know how much it means to you. It's your ticket off the farm. Your father knows it, too. He'll always live on the land, but he wants you to find your own path. We have talked about this and we have prayed about this, but we have no answers. We have no money. You have all our love and all our prayers, always." Lena had tears welling in her eyes, and Harley hated that.

"I don't want you to worry at all. You have taught me to work hard. I will find a way. I haven't given up. I haven't even started to think about giving up. I will be at the University of Iowa this fall. I don't know how, but I will make it happen," Harley insisted. His tone shocked his mother out of her sadness.

"Well, with determination like that, I believe you. I don't know how it will happen either, but if it is what God wants and if you are willing to work hard at it, I believe it will happen!" Lena felt so encouraged, and she reached out to squeeze her son's hand. Harley reached for her and gave her a big bear hug.

"I love you, Mother, and I love Father, too. I will make you proud."

"We are already proud, Harley." Lena squeezed him back. He let his mother go and she turned to leave, starting her evening prayers before she even got the door closed.

Weeks passed, and Harley seemed more positive, more talkative and relaxed than before his talk with his mother. What he had done, but did not tell his parents about, was write a letter to his mother's oldest brother, Gene, who lived in Washington State. Gene had an enormous sheep ranch and apple production operation there. Harley asked his uncle if he could come out there to work for the summer, so he could earn money for college in the fall. He waited for a reply.

One day in early April, a letter from Gene came to the farm's big, white rural mailbox. It was addressed to Harley, so Lena didn't open it, but she phoned Harley to tell him he had a letter from his Uncle Gene. Harley told her he would open it on Friday night, when he came out for the weekend. Lena waited. It was difficult not to read a letter from her brother, but it was not addressed to her, so she waited. It was probably an early graduation present, Lena thought. Hopefully, money Harley could use for college. She'd just have to wait two days to find out. Maybe it could be the start of his college fund.

Friday afternoon came and Lena sat on the front steps, watching down the gravel road for Mike McMichael's gray Ford sedan.

Finally, here it came, in its usual cloud of gray dust. It was hard to tell the dust from Mike's car. She had the letter from Uncle Gene in her apron pocket, ready to hand to Harley. She didn't want to seem too anxious, but she didn't write to her own brother that often, so it seemed odd for Harley to have a letter from him, just out of the blue.

Harley leaped out of the car, ran to Lena, and held out his hand.

"Where is the letter, Mother?"

She pulled it out of her pocket and thrust it towards him. It was hard to tell who was more anxious, Lena or Harley. "Here, open it!"

He looked at it briefly, turned it over a few times, then tore off a short end. He blew into the envelope and took out two pages of paper. He unfolded them and glanced up to see a look of disappointment on his mother's face.

"No cash or check?" she queried. "I hoped he had sent you an early graduation gift."

"No money, Mother. I hope the news will be better than money."

Lena was puzzled and looked like it. "I don't understand. What you need for college is money, not news."

"Let me read it, Mother, then we will know for sure what's good news or not. Just give me a minute to read it."

Harley started to sit down on the semi-circle front steps where his mother had been seated before his arrival. The concrete had been cheaply home-made and little rocks were already settling out of it, so he brushed a few pebbles out from underneath himself before he sat down. First, he read the front of the first page, then he turned it over. Then he read the front of the next page, and then turned that over. Uncle Gene's handwriting was beautiful and large, so the letter was not really long, despite there being four pages.

This silent letter reading was about to make Lena go insane. "What's Gene say, Harley...what's Gene say?"

Harley looked his mother straight in the eye. "He says he has a job for me, Mother. He says I can come out there after next month and work with his sheep and in his apple orchard all summer. He says I can live with him and earn all the money I need to get started at the university. I'm going to college, Mother!"

Mike slapped his friend on the back. "Congratulations, Harley! What a wonderful uncle you have! Here we come, Iowa City!" He shook Harley's hand heartily and slapped his back again. "Gotta run now. Pick you up Sunday night?"

"Yes, thanks, Mike. See you Sunday."

Harley turned to his mother, as Mike headed down the driveway and back to town. Lena had sat down on the steps and was sitting quite still. She didn't look as happy as Harley thought she should. "What's the matter, Mother? This is wonderful news!"

"Wonderful news? What are you talking about? How did this idea come up? Did you write to your uncle?" Lena's tone was changing from shocked and moving towards angry.

"Well, yes, I did. I told you I would think of something, Mother. Do you remember that talk we had earlier this winter? I told you I would find a way."

"Not this way, son, not this way! That's too far to go. How are you going to get there? Is he going to send you money for a ticket?" Lena's questions were the right ones, but Harley knew she was not going to like the answer he had for her.

"Mother, I am going to ride the rails out there."

"No!"

"Yes, Mother. I am going to ride the rails out there. There are so many boys my age doing it. I will have plenty of good company." Harley's voice brightened a bit, to give his mother some encouragement towards liking the idea.

Lena stood up. She turned her back to Harley for a moment and he could tell she was preparing to have a verbal battle with him. It was the way she stood up as tall as she could and set her shoulders back. She slowly turned around in front of him. She had that stern look in her eyes. "No. It doesn't matter how many other boys are doing it. Those are desperate boys. You don't know if they're good company. They are most likely very bad company. I forbid you from riding the trains!"

Harley matched his mother's stare for the first time ever. "I am a desperate boy, Mother. Desperate for college, for an education, for a better life. It's my only chance."

"No," was Lena's only answer. "No."

"Uncle Gene says he has hired young men off the rails and nearly every one of them is a good boy. Some are my age, and some are even younger, like sixteen, or even fifteen. Their families couldn't feed them, so they took to the rails." Harley took his mother's shoulder. "I will be fine. I promise."

Lena shook her head, sadly. "No one can promise you will be 'fine'. The only place your father and I can be sure you are fine is if you stay right here. Then, you will be fine."

"I can't stay here, Mother. You know I can't. If I stay here, it will be years before I get to college, and I may never get there. This is the only way to do it right now. It's not the best way, but it is the only way. I don't want to get in a big argument about this, and I know you are going to worry like always, but perhaps it will be better if you just pray for me instead." He was still matching his mother's stare, but he added a slight smile now.

Lena had nothing else to say. She had no way to stop her son from riding the rails out to the west coast and she knew it. She had no idea how she would tell her husband. Charley had been making so much progress, but he was still not going to be able to get on a tractor again in a month and plant their fields.

Harley saw she was done with her arguments, and knew he was going to leave when school was out. He guessed what his mother was thinking about now. "You are wondering who is going to work the fields, right? Well, I am going to get the planting done before I leave, I promise. And, I am going to teach Mike how to till and do the rest. You know he really loves coming out here, and he'll be me for the summer. He said he would like to help Uncle Lynn with the milk route, too. "

A hesitant "What?" was all Lena could manage at this point.

"Mike wants to learn how to do the jobs on the farm, Mother. He won't let you down, I promise."

"We love Mike, son, you know we do," said Lena, "but you know we can't pay him any wages. You know that, right?"

"Of course, I know that," Harley assured her, "and Mike doesn't want any wages. He doesn't need the money and thinks it will be great fun to be a farmer for a summer before he goes off to college. He is always saying he is so jealous of me because I get to do 'city' and 'country'. He wants to try it. He won't let us down, because he knows him helping you out here is the only way we will be get go to the university together this fall. It's perfect, Mother!"

"No, Harley, it's not perfect. It's nowhere near perfect. What would be perfect about you getting killed on the rails? Would it be perfect with you getting sick or something so far away from home? A whole summer of worry for me and your father? That's not perfect."

Harley looked his mother square in the face again. He had a kind, understanding look on his young face. "It's perfect because it will get me to college. It will let me out of the comfortable place where I have lived my whole life. It will be my time to grow up, before I actually do grow up. I cannot live at home with you and Father forever. I have to do this. I will be safe."

"I have no idea how to tell your father this," Lena confessed.

"I will tell him, Mother, I will let you pick the time, and I will tell him. That is my responsibility. He will be responsible for helping me teach Mike how to be a farmer over the next month or so before planting starts, so I should tell him soon. I don't expect you to tell him anything about this."

Lena's head was spinning. She couldn't imagine her son riding the rails. She barely survived Charley doing it out to the wheat and back. It didn't seem to matter to her that he would be staying with her oldest brother, or that there were even younger men than he riding the rails. Harley was her only child. She sat down on the steps again, head in her hands.

Harley was trying to conceal his total delight with the news from Uncle Gene. He had to tell his father first. Then he could spread the news to his friends. One step at a time. And perhaps his father could give him some rules for rail riding and how to stay safer. For now, he could go inside, sit down in his room, and write Uncle Gene a thank-you letter for this golden opportunity.

Harley returned from walking his thank-you letter to his uncle down to the mailbox at the foot of the driveway. He tipped up the red metal flag on the side, so the postman would get it from the mailbox tomorrow. He felt like his journey was finally beginning. He had a lot to plan. As he looked back up the rutted drive towards the yellow house, he noticed his mother had stepped out onto the bricks by the side door on the north side of the house. She had finished the dinner dishes and was drying her hands on a blue flowered apron she had made from some scraps of Mrs. Monahan's old living room drapes. His mother's motto ran through his head, "Use it up, wear it out, fix it. Don't waste anything." It was a saying for the hard times they were in. Harley was not going to waste the opportunity Uncle Gene was giving him.

"Harley, your father is waiting to hear from you. He's rested and fed, but don't get him upset. I told him you had something important to talk to him about, man to man." His mother gave him that direct look she had, and he nodded agreeably.

"I'll talk to him, Mother. I won't upset him, I promise."

Harley headed down the short hallway towards his parent's bedroom. He cautiously opened the door, knocking gently on it. "It's me, Father. I need to talk to you."

Charley waved him in and turned slightly in his bed to face his son.

Harley began, "I need to talk to you about college, Father. I have a great plan to earn the money for this fall."

"Harley, I heard you and yer mother talking. Every word. This house ain't that big and the windows are all open. Sounds like ya got yer mind made up and like yer ma can't talk you out of it," Charley said matter-of-factly.

Surprised by this, Harley stood silent for a moment, trying to read his father's face for his reaction. Was he going to try to talk him out of it, also? Harley figured and hoped he could ask his father for advice on riding the rails and just avoid another argument, so he said, "I am hoping you can give me some good advice about how to get there in one piece. You know, what to do and what not to do?"

"Well, son, pull up that ol' chair over here, next to me. I'll do what I can. A lot of it is luck and keepin' your yap shut, to start with. Don't join up with more than about two or three other men. Use your common sense. Don't tell about yer private life, like your parents or goin' to college plans. Keep clean. Take a bath or shower any chance you get. Watch out for lice. They itch like crazy and are just plain hell to get rid of. Don't tell yer mother I said hell."

"What? Did you get lice?" asked a surprised Harley.

"Nah, and if I did, I sure wouldn't of told Lena. She hates 'em more than mice in her pantry. Goes crazy just hearing the word. Be careful and sleep by the fire, but not too close to any other bum's bedding."

"I'll be careful, I promise. Anything else?"

"Don't get maimed or kilt getting on and off those trains. Watch how the other fellas do it and leave yourself plenty of room. Don't take no chances. There will always be another train along. Listen, Harley, I'm gettin' a little tired. You go make sure your mother is okay. I'll talk to her later tonight."

"A question. What are you going to tell her?" asked Harley anxiously.

"I'm going to tell her you'll be just fine, son. You'll be fine."

News from Texas

December 15th started out like any Sunday. I awakened, got dressed, and headed down to the kitchen to have coffee cake with Mother and read the paper while we waited for Dad to telephone us.

Except Mother wasn't in the kitchen. She was sitting in the parlor. She was sitting across the room from Aunt Helen. What was Aunt Helen doing here? How did she get here? When did she get here? Those reporter- type questions came so naturally. 'How curious of a development,' I thought to myself. Something strange was up. Was Uncle Albert here somewhere, too?

"Hello, Aunt Helen. Good morning, Mother. Is Uncle Albert around here also?"

I was getting more curious by the minute. Aunt Helen looked at Mother, and Mother looked at Aunt Helen. Neither one of them was looking at me or answering even one of my questions.

Mother finally spoke to me, saying, "Please come in here and sit down, Mable. We have the coffee cake in the oven already."

I went in and sat down, uneasily, because Mother's voice did not sound right.

Mother continued, *"Aunt Helen is here because something terrible has happened. We need to tell you about it, so she came to be with us."* Her voice was shaking more with each word that she spoke.

"Oh dear," I said, my own voice was starting to shake. *"Has something happened to Uncle Albert, Mother?"*

"No, Mable, nothing is wrong with Uncle Albert. He just went over to the church this morning. He'll be back later."

Aunt Helen spoke next. *"Mable, I'm here because something has happened to your father. He won't be calling this morning."*

"What? Did he get hurt? Is he in the hospital?" I pleaded for information. *"Is he going to be okay? Is he coming home?"*

"He was in the hospital, dear," Aunt Helen said. Mother had her head buried in her hands. Aunt Helen continued, *"He passed away yesterday. Late yesterday. He had a massive heart attack."*

Mother was sobbing now. Aunt Helen went over to the davenport and sat next to her, with her arms around Mother.

I stood up and wailed, *"Oh, Mother! Daddy's dead? It can't be true!"*

I sank back into the nearest chair and slumped over the arm of it. This was not possible. Dad was healthy. He was working on skyscrapers. He was coming home in January or February. He couldn't be . . . dead.

Now Aunt Helen and Mother had their arms around me. Aunt Helen was saying, *"Just go ahead and cry, Mable. Just go ahead and cry, Henrietta. We'll stay here and hug each other as long as we need to."*

I kept crying. I wanted my daddy. I wanted a bear hug. I wanted to talk baseball and football with him. I wanted him to see me graduate. I wanted him to see me swim. I wanted him . . . to come home, but not come home dead.

Aunt Helen, Mother, and I hugged and cried until Uncle Albert came back in the front door.

"I've talked to the minister. I caught him before church started. Some church ladies will come over later this afternoon to help you gals with arrangements." He added, *"I'm so sorry Henrietta and Mable. John Henry was a wonderful man. He's gone way too soon. Only, what was he? Fifty-six?"*

"Hush now, Albert," said Aunt Helen. "Not now. Let these gals be. Maybe you could take that coffee cake out of the oven? I'm sure it's about to burn. We might feel like eating later on."

Uncle Albert replied, "Sure, Helen. I'm sorry. Then I think I'll go over and let the neighbors know, if you think that's a good idea?"

"That would be fine, Albert. Thank you. Also, someone has to tell Grandma. Maybe you should go upstairs and tell your mother before you go next door."

"That's true. I'll do just that. See you in a bit," he said as he went into the kitchen.

I heard him take the coffee cake out of the oven. Then I heard him go up the stairs. I couldn't bear to open my eyes. I just wanted to go back upstairs, get back in bed, and start the day over, like this terrible morning never happened. Mother was still moaning and crying. She was kind of lying on the davenport, and Aunt Helen had gotten a throw to put over her.

I looked up at Aunt Helen and asked her, "When did you get here? How did you know?"

She explained, "The company called us last night. About midnight. They tried your telephone first, but there was no answer. You were probably all in bed and didn't hear it ring. Your father had also put our telephone number down in case of emergency, so they called us." She paused, and then continued, "I told Uncle Albert that we had to come right down here and be with you two. We got in the car and drove all night. I did not want those people to tell Henrietta on the telephone. I wanted her to hear it from us. I got here as your mother was waking up and putting the coffee cake in the oven. We will stay and make sure your father gets back to Iowa and has a good funeral. That's what family is for, Mable."

From upstairs, I heard Grandma exclaim, "Vat Thunder!" Then there was a lot more German, and she kept calling Henrietta's name. My mother went to the stairs and started to slowly climb up them. "I need to go see Mama," she said sadly. I knew her Mama would give her hugs and try to comfort her, too.

Aunt Helen came back to me and put her arm around me again. "I am so very sorry, Mable. Your Dad was such a good husband and father. We will help you and your mother. You can count on that."

"Aunt Helen, this just can't be true. Are you sure? What happened? Daddy was fine!" I argued.

She tried explaining, "You know he had not been feeling well, Mable. He went to the doctor again about two weeks ago. They couldn't find anything wrong. He was getting ready to go to bed for the evening at the boss's house, and just keeled over. They took him to the hospital, but they couldn't get his heart going again."

I didn't hear much of that. I had to cry. My head and body ached and my heart hurt. Daddy was gone. I loved him so much. What was to become of me and Mother? How could we get along? It was too much. It was too hard.

Uncle Albert came back downstairs and started out the front door to go to tell the Orwigs. They were like us; they mostly went to church on Christmas and Easter, so they would be home. I thought for a minute that I should go tell Burnie about Dad, but I knew it would be too much. I felt like I could stay in that one chair in the parlor all day, all curled up, and just keep crying. Uncle Albert could tell them. I knew Burnie would understand how terribly sad I was. He was like a son to Dad, and like a brother to me.

I eventually went back up to my room. Mother and Grandma were in Mother and Dad's room. Aunt Helen was answering the door and the telephone. Friends and neighbors were calling, and bringing over salads, and sandwiches, and desserts. Mrs. Orwig was there helping make tea for people. Mother would go downstairs once or twice an hour to visit with the people who came to the house. No one stayed very long. They just wanted to say they were sorry and make an offer to help in some way.

I never realized my parents had so many friends. There were the neighborhood ladies, of course. Many people who worked for the city over at the Waterworks and Street Department also came. Folks from church came, and some of my friends' parents. Miss Hawn came and so did my girls' swim coach. I wondered how the news traveled so fast. I'll bet we had at least twenty-five or thirty people stop by our house before it got dark on Sunday. It still didn't seem real.

At one point, Uncle Albert had gone down to the railroad station. He had to make arrangements to have my father's casket sent back to Iowa. An undertaker in Houston was doing all the arrangements on that end. Not surprisingly, I found it impossible to picture what that might involve. I knew it was going to cost money, because I heard Mother ask Uncle Albert about that. I was so relieved when he told Mother that the owner of the construction company was going to pay for those expenses, and she burst into tears. That made my tears start coming again. It was about time for me to start getting ready for bed, when I heard Mother calling me from downstairs. I went down, and Burnie was standing in the entry way. He looked so sad. I took the clean handkerchief that Mother held out to me and followed Burnie into the parlor. We sat down on the davenport together.

"I was waiting until other people were done going in and out," Burnie spoke softly. "I wanted to come earlier, but my mom and dad said to wait. I'm so sorry, Mable. Being so sudden and all, this is just awful. I don't know what to say. I'm just so sorry."

"It's okay, Burnie. I can't believe this. I've been crying all day," I started crying again, and Burnie put his arm around me.

"My mom said you would be crying, and that it's good for you. This is so sad and, well, just awful. Your dad was the nicest, smartest fella I knew. I don't know what else to say. I'm so sorry. I'll do anything I can for you and your mother, Mable."

"There's nothing anyone can do, Burnie. My dad is gone and it hurts so much. I just ache all over. It's the worst thing ever," I said quietly. Then I just buried my face in the handkerchief Mother gave me, and sat there, not really crying; just sighing.

We sat there for at least thirty minutes. I kept my face buried and prayed this would all be a bad dream. I prayed for my dad to make the telephone ring and talk to me. I prayed the most that Mother and I would be okay. Burnie sat there with me. When I took my face out of the handkerchief and finally looked at him, it looked like he had been crying some also, and his forehead was all wrinkled, and he looked. . . so sad. He said goodnight and went home, slowly closing our front door behind him. I watched him cross my yard and his yard, and then go up his steps. I don't think I had ever seen him walk so slow. Burnie was such a good friend. I knew we would be friends for the rest of our lives.

Aunt Helen and Uncle Albert had calmed Grandma down. She was worried about Mother, and how she was going to pay for the funeral and pay all the bills. However, just like he was paying for Dad's trip home, the owner of the construction business was going to pay for the funeral, also. At least we had a burial plot up in Steamboat Rock, where Grandpa Von Dornum and Uncle Wiard were buried. There was plenty of room for Dad up there. Mother got a telephone call from the Rock Island Line, as well as a telegram from the construction company owner, telling her that Dad's casket would be arriving on the 21st of December. Our pastor was helping Mother and Aunt Helen plan the funeral for December 23rd.

If there was anything good about all of this, it was that I was going to get to see Aunt Hazel for the first time since I was seven years old. She was coming to be there with Mother. Mother told her that she didn't have to come, but Aunt Hazel insisted that since it was Christmas vacation in the Chicago schools, she had plenty of time. On the phone, she told Mother that she was looking forward to seeing the whole family and would help in any way she could. She was arriving on the train the afternoon of the 20th, so Mother made arrangements for her to stay in the Orwig's spare bedroom.

I was not looking forward to the funeral, but Mother was. She wanted to see Dad again. I did also, but I did not want to see him in his casket. I was afraid it would just be too hard. Aunt Helen said that Dad was at peace now, in Heaven, with Jesus, but that was little comfort to me. I wanted Dad in the parlor, with me, reading the sports page.

Graduation and Mr. Flynn

Mike regularly came out to the farm and started driving the tractor up and down the road. He learned how to drive with Harley standing on the back, giving directions. He took right to it. Soon he was practicing making turns in the field, without tangling up in the fence. Then they practiced having him drive some straight rows with the planter, but there were no seeds in it. He did a great job. That part of the plan was going to work out beautifully.

Harley and Mike also readied themselves for graduation. It would be on the western portico at Roosevelt. Baccalaureate, where there was a minister, would be first. His parents were both there, and Grandma Burt. Uncle Lynn and Aunt Alice came, also. After that, there was the graduation ceremony. Many of his friends were in the band and the choir, so they had to run back and forth from their seats with the graduates to perform with their groups. Harley just stayed put. Mike stayed put, too. They were all seated alphabetically, and it worked out that Harley was sitting almost directly behind Mike. Mike kept turning around to make a comment or tell Harley a joke about what was going on.

The speaker for the commencement was the owner of one of the biggest dairy companies in Des Moines. He had been a Roosevelt student years before and was one of their most successful graduates. Harley listened carefully to his whole speech because he wanted to be a successful business owner, too. The man, Mr.

Flynn, gave the graduates a long list of good advice. Work hard. Be honest. Help your employees be better people. Listen to your customers. Help the community. He said it did not matter that there was a terrible depression going on. He told them that customer service, giving back to the community, and showing respect for everyone would make any business successful.

Harley was spellbound. Then, the man started talking about the benefits of being rich. He did not want to make anyone feel less important, but he was proud that he had been successful and told how he grew up as a poor farm boy, worked hard to get to college, and finally came back to Des Moines to start his own business. He decided on a dairy, because of his farm background. He was able to buy a big house south of Grand Avenue. Harley knew that area because it was where he delivered milk with Uncle Lynn. Mr. Flynn said he was able to buy a new car every year, even in these bad times. Then he told them he just bought a brand-new Lincoln! That's when Harley realized that Mr. Flynn was the customer who had been so inspiring to him all this time! He knew he had to meet this man after graduation today.

Mike knew about Harley's dream, and turned around and rapped him on knee, when he also realized that Mr. Flynn was the "Lincoln guy." It was really swell having a friend like Mike, who cared about Harley's hopes and dreams as much as Harley did.

After the speech, it was time to award the diplomas. Harley caught his father's eye just before he took the last step up to the stage. He could tell Charley was proud of him. Even if Harley did not go to college, just graduating from high school would have been plenty for Charley, with his fifth-grade education. Lena had her hanky out, of course, as did Aunt Alice and Grandma Burt. Aunt Alice had to give Uncle Lynn a little elbow to wake him up, so he didn't miss Harley walking across the stage to shake hands with that very rich man.

As Harley approached the principal, to be given his diploma, he put out his hand for the administrator to shake, but he was already focused on the dairy owner whose hand he would shake next. He readied his quick request, and as he shook Mr. Flynn's hand, he whispered, "I deliver your milk. May I stop in and see you tomorrow afternoon?"

"Yes," was the rich man's reply. "Come by about four o'clock," he said as he gave Harley's hand an extra shake.

Graduation was on a Sunday afternoon, so Harley would be going to see Mr. Flynn on Monday at four o'clock. He could go over there after he got done at the furniture store. The street car went right from the corner where the Valley Junction furniture store was, over to Grand Avenue. It would work perfectly.

Harley's plan was to inform Mr. Flynn what an inspiration he had been to Harley already. That was all. He wanted to thank the man. Well, that, and maybe Mr. Flynn would have some more excellent advice for Harley. Harley was a complete sponge for advice at this point. He was also curious as to why a man who owned a large dairy company bought his milk from a small dairy farmer like Uncle Lynn.

Everyone went to Grandma Burt's house after graduation. She had a delicious luncheon set up and had baked a real graduation cake. She had put out her fancy punch set. It made Harley feel special. She had even arranged a table where Grandma Burt told him to set his diploma out for everyone to admire. Lena had also brought his Golden Gloves boxing trophy to put on the table, along with his senior picture.

After they got done with the late lunch at Grandma Burt's, Uncle Lynn took Charley back home so he could rest. Lena and Harley left for the reception that St. Peter Lutheran church in Grimes was having for their graduates. It started at five o'clock, and they made it there right on time. Harley put his diploma on a special table there, also. It was the only one from Des Moines schools. All the rest were from Grimes, Granger, Johnston Station, or Dallas Center schools. Every little town around there had their own school.

All the other graduating seniors wanted to see what Harley's big-city diploma looked like. They discovered that it looked almost exactly like theirs. In talking to them about all their plans, he discovered that every single one of them was done with their formal education. None of them planned on going to college. One girl was going to beauty school so she could work in Younker's hair salon downtown. All the rest were boys who were going to work on their father's farms or girls who were going to work in the city, for an insurance company, bank, or department store. How they thought they were going to get a job in these difficult times, Harley had no idea. A few of the girls talked about finding a husband. Harley stayed away from them, although there was one girl who appeared to be following him wherever he went. He just kept moving, until it was time to leave. He had no time for girls. Not yet, anyway.

It had been a long day for Charley and for Lena, so when Harley got home he made sure his father was comfortable in bed and then helped Lena prepare dinner. The evening chores did not take long at all, and he even had time to read a few pages in the new Reader's Digest. For graduation, his mother told him she was going to get him his own subscription to the magazine, but she would wait until he got settled over in Iowa City. He was not going to be reading it this summer on Uncle Gene's ranch, that was for sure.

Harley finished all his jobs early at the furniture store on Monday, to be certain that he caught the right street car to get to Mr. Flynn's house on time. He certainly did not want to be late, and he wasn't. It was Mrs. Flynn who answered the door. She led Harley into the parlor, where Mr. Flynn sat in a large leather chair. He gestured towards a matching chair on the other side of an ornate oak side table and said to Harley, "Have a seat, young man. Thank you for asking to speak with me today."

Harley was immediately puzzled. "Oh no, I need to thank you, sir, for taking time to see me today."

"Phooey," said Mr. Flynn. "I appreciate knowing that at least one of you young people was actually listening to my speech. Many graduates do not have their mind focused at graduation. They are only thinking of their presents and their party, not what they are going to do with the rest of their lives. Do you know what you want to do?"

"Not exactly, sir, but I have already been working on it. I have two jobs right now. I deliver your milk and I work at the furniture store in Valley Junction."

Mr. Flynn frowned a little. Harley did not like to see that. Then he asked Harley, "Is that your future, having a 'job'?"

"No sir!" Harley exclaimed. "I want to own my own business. I just don't know what it will be yet. After I work this summer, I will have enough money to start at the University of Iowa, and I will study business there."

Mr. Flynn laughed, "You aren't going to start another dairy, are you? And try to put me out of business?"

Harley laughed now also. "No. I really don't know what kind of business. But I do know that I don't want to work at a desk, I know that for sure. I have to keep busy. I cannot just sit around. I am riding the rails out to Washington State later this week to work for my uncle on his sheep ranch and he has a large apple business. I'll be out there all summer."

The business man got serious again. "That is very dangerous! Do your parents approve of this plan? Do they even know about this plan?"

"Yes, they do, sir. My mother is not happy about it, but it is her brother who offered me the job. My father had a stroke early last spring and is not able to work our farm yet. We have a small farm and one of my best friends is going to help them while I am gone." Harley tried to give him the important details, since Mr. Flynn really seemed interested in his plans.

"That riding the rails part is what I think your parents would not like, son."

"Well, my mother doesn't. My father rode the rails out west last summer to harvest wheat, so he knows what can happen. I have heard many stories from him and he has warned me about all kinds of things not to do, sir."

"Harley, I admire your ambition and your spunk."

Harley replied, "I admire you, sir. I admired you even before I heard you speak yesterday at graduation. I have been delivering your milk twice a week for about two years."

 Harley paused, then asked another question, "I need to know, Mr. Flynn, why you buy your milk from my uncle's small dairy farm? You own a huge dairy business. Why don't you just buy your own products?"

"Good question, young man. I'll tell you, it's an important part of giving back to the community. It's about helping others succeed. I patronize your uncle so he can keep his farm and his dairy herd; I help him be successful, and his prospering helps the whole community. Does that make sense to you?" Mr. Flynn was so sincere, and now Harley was even more impressed with him.

"Yes, I understand sir. I never thought of it like that. It's so true, and makes sense, just like everything you said yesterday!"

Mr. Flynn nodded. "So, tell me about the rest of your plans, please."

Harley explained, "When I first saw the Lincoln in your driveway last year, I made up my mind that I was going to have one for myself. Not now, but someday. I have been thinking about getting my education, about going to college, about what kind of business I want to have…all kinds of things in the past year or so. I'm working for a furniture store right now and I like working with people. I'm good with my hands. I know how to work hard. I know I can do anything I put my mind to. I want to be able to buy a new Lincoln every year, just like you! That's all."

"That's a lot of ambition, Harley. I believe you will be successful. Is there something I can do to help?" Mr. Flynn asked.

"That is generous of you, sir, but I need to do this on my own. It won't mean anything if I don't have to work for it myself." Harley continued, "I think you have already done what I needed you to do. You just said you believe in me, Mr. Flynn. That's what I need you to do…to believe in me. I can do the rest on my own."

Mr. Flynn shook his head. "I believe you can do it, Harley, but you need to be very careful on the rails. Will you allow me buy you a train ticket to Washington?"

"Thank you very much, sir, but I am going to ride the rails just like my father did. I think of it as an adventure. I'm a boxer. I won the Polk County Golden Gloves tournament, and I'm a farm boy. I can take care of myself." Harley stood up and reached out his hand. "I really appreciate you taking the time to talk to me, but I need to get home now and help my mother."

Mr. Flynn stood up, too. He smiled at Harley and shook his outstretched hand, saying, "You are a very interesting young man, Harley. I think you are going to have a great adventure, and I am certain you will be successful. You know where I live. Please come back and see me again sometime, son."

Harley smiled back and Mr. Flynn and he walked to the front door. Suddenly, Mr. Flynn stopped. He said, "Harley, would you like to drive the Lincoln once?"

"Wh…wh…what? You would let me drive it?" Harley stammered.

"Sure. Hop in the driver's side. I'll go get the key." Mr. Flynn ran inside and was back in less than a minute. Harley was waiting in the driver's seat. Mr. Flynn got in the passenger's side of the car and handed Harley the key.

"Start it up, farm boy. I hear farm boys can drive anything! Is that true?"

"I think I can, sir. How's this fancy ignition work? Just turn the key?" Harley asked.

Mr. Flynn pointed to a black button at the bottom far left side of the instrument panel. "Go ahead and turn the key; that unlocks the ignition and the steering gear. Then, press that black button, and the engine fires up. It's a beautiful sound!"

"Oh, yes sir!" Harley said. The key turned so easily, then he pushed the button and the engine purred. Harley backed up the luxury car carefully. He didn't even ask Mr. Flynn where he should go. He just drove the neighborhood milk route.

Neither one of them spoke a single word. When he got to the last house where he usually delivered milk, Harley backed the Lincoln up and turned around, heading back to Mr. Flynn's house. He pulled the beautiful car back where it belonged in the driveway, turned off the ignition, and let out a deep sigh.

"That was swell, Mr. Flynn. Thank you very much," Harley said, handing him the keys.

"You are very welcome, Harley. I wish you well. Promise me that you will let me know if I can do anything at all to help you."

"I will, sir. Thank you again."

The two got out of the car, and Harley left for the farm. Mr. Flynn went back in his house. Both smiled broadly, knowing they had each just met an exceptional man.

John Henry's Funeral

Walking up the sidewalk to the church was awful. I could barely stand up. Burnie was on my left side and his mother was on my right side. I wouldn't say they had to drag me, but my body felt so heavy, it seemed like they were almost carrying me.

Dad had on a new suit and tie. Mother said they put it on him in Houston. He had not taken a suit with him because he went there to work on construction. It had been almost ten days since he died, but this somehow did not seem completely real. I was at my father's funeral.

I stood by his casket. Burnie and his mother backed up a little bit to leave me alone with my Dad. I wanted to touch him, but I didn't want to be disrespectful or have anyone think I was crazy. The urge was overwhelming, so I reached out and touched his tie. I just ran my hand a couple of inches down it. I heard Burnie's mother let out a little gasp. I heard Burnie tell her it was okay. As my hand was resting on his tie, I told Dad I loved him. Then, I moved my hand away, and walked slowly over to sit next to Mother. Burnie and his mother sat behind me and he put his hand on my shoulder as I sat there.

Aunt Hazel sat on the other side of me, and Uncle Albert sat on the other side of Mother. Aunt Helen sat next to him. The people attending Dad's service were the same ones who came to the house right after we found out about Dad. They all had kind things to say to us. We sang the songs that Mother had picked out and the minister read Dad's favorite scripture; Philippians 4:6. When the church choir director, Mr. Western, sang The Lord's Prayer, I began crying again. This time it was just tears rolling silently down my cheeks. I was saying goodbye to my father; the man who taught me everything about sports, encouraged me to be the best writer I could be, and who completely loved and supported me in everything. I was lost.

Christmas was lost. We gave Dad's Christmas gifts to Uncle Albert. It was interesting getting to know Aunt Hazel, though. She was a loving person and I could see how she could have completely given her heart away to her fiancé. When he died in the Great War, she simply never got her heart back. She was pleasant, but I got the feeling that she would never be able to be truly happy. From the time we spent together, I knew that she was a good and caring teacher. Aunt Hazel said that she loved kids, but that she would never have any of her own.

After Christmas, Mother and I went with back up to Steamboat Rock with Aunt Helen, Uncle Albert, and Grandma Von Dornum. Grandma was going back to her house for the rest of the winter. If she had any problems, Aunt Helen and Uncle Albert could help her. She didn't want to be a burden to Mother. Their minister up there did a quiet graveside service for Dad, and he was buried in the cemetery there, right next to Wiard. Mother was going to have a gravestone made that would have Dad's name and her name on it, with the year they were each born and the year they each died. I didn't even want to think about it; Mother dying, that is.

Burnie came over and walked me to school the first day we were due back at school in January. Mother had given him a hat and scarf she knitted for a Christmas present. He was wearing them and looked quite dapper in them.

Most of my teachers knew that my dad had passed away and each took the time, either before or after class, to pull me aside and tell me how sorry they were. That was nice for them to do, but I had decided to just do the best I could at school and try not to think about how much I missed Dad. I did find it a lot harder to concentrate, and my grades slipped a little, even with Burnie studying with me a couple of nights a week.

One weekend when we were in the kitchen, Mother mentioned it. "Mable, what on earth is going on with your schoolwork? I saw the papers you left here on the kitchen table yesterday morning, and they didn't look like your usual fine work. What is your report card going to look like?"

"Mother, I am trying. It's been hard to concentrate. I keep thinking about how much I miss Dad." I could tell she was genuinely concerned. I hated the thought of causing her worry.

I continued, "I worry about not swimming. I am tired from basketball. I can't seem to keep up. I keep forgetting something I am supposed to do every week. This week it was the health report. Last week was the test in math and before that I missed a project deadline in science." I slumped down in the chair at the kitchen table and added, "I am so sorry, Mother."

"I'm not angry, Mable. I am worried and disappointed." She added, "Your senior year should be fun. Losing your father was a terrible thing. Terrible for both of us, but I am so afraid you're going to let your grades slip and the university will change their mind." It looked like she might cry.

"Mother, I am so very, very sorry. Perhaps I should quit basketball. Maybe then I could keep up with everything." The second I heard myself say that, I couldn't believe it.

Mother spoke quickly. "What? What are you talking about? I didn't say anything about quitting basketball. Is that what you think I mean?"

Now I was the one who felt like crying. First, I have her worried about my grades, and now I have upset her about basketball. This was a mess, and it was getting worse.

I offered, "I don't know what to say, Mother. Basketball is going great. I think the problem is that I keep worrying about everything."

"Everything?" she asked. "What do you mean by everything?"

I didn't know what I meant by everything. School had never been hard for me. Sports had never been hard for me. Even keeping up with a busy schedule of both school and sports had never been hard, either. I had just slacked off at my schoolwork. I was goldbricking; something I had never done before. The time I was wasting, when I should have been studying, was being spent worrying about . . . I don't know what. It was difficult to explain to Mother.

She was upset and had plenty to say. "I don't know what you are worrying about, because there is nothing you can do about anything, except do your schoolwork and play your sports. Your father would never want you to quit basketball. I can't believe you would even consider that. That's the worst thing you could do. I really don't think you meant that and I don't want to hear one more word about it!"

I sat there with my elbows on the kitchen table and my face buried in my hands. I couldn't even look at her. "I don't want to quit. I will get my grades back up where they belong, I promise."

"Mable, I am going to tell you what I think your Dad would have told you. Don't waste time worrying. You should never worry. What you need to do is take action. It's one of the first things I learned from him after we were married." She took a deep breath and continued," If there is something wrong and you can DO something about it, then DO it. But, if it is something over which you have no control, then do not worry about it. Let it go. Worrying accomplishes nothing."

I was listening. I let that soak in.

She kept going, "I want you to focus on keeping your grades up. On basketball. On the Oracle. You have a lot of senior activities coming up this spring, and you need to plan for those. Concentrate on school and your activities. Those are the only things right now that you can control. Do you understand?"

"Now I do, Mother. I think I am worrying about Dad missing all my games. I think I am worrying about money for the university."

She pounced on that with, "See, those are two perfect examples of things you should not worry about, because you can do nothing about them. Dad is gone and cannot come to your games. I understand how you miss him but worrying will not bring him back."

"I know," I murmured.

"Then there is the money for school next fall. With your swim team scholarship, there is enough. Do not worry about that. You can make more money this summer, like you did last summer with swimming lessons and lifeguarding. There will be enough money for you for school. It's nothing you should worry about. Stop."

"I'll try, Mother. I truly will try," I promised.

"Please do, Mable. Just concentrate on school and basketball for right now." She paused and looked right at me, saying, "I promise I will try to come to more of your basketball games, okay?"

"Okay, Mother," I agreed, "that would be nifty."

She leaned over and gave me a hug. It was a tender hug and she felt so warm after standing over the stove.

She had one more thing to add, "Your dad was very proud of you, darling daughter. I still am very proud of you. I'm certain your father knows how you are continuing to work hard, and just like he would never want you to quit, he would not want you to waste any time worrying, either. Go to school, have fun, and you will continue to make both of us happy; if you are happy."

I stood up and gave her a kiss on the cheek. She smiled and said, "Why don't you head over to Burnie's and see how he's doing today. Maybe you could let him win, just once, in one of your little basketball games over there." She winked at me and turned back to her kitchen work.

Mike Helps Harley Leave

Harley had explained to his parents what he was going to do. He assured them both that he would take all precautions to keep himself safe. No one except he and Mike knew when Harley planned to leave, but Lena thought she would be driving him to Adel, like she had driven Charley. Charley thought he had convinced Harley to go up to Granger to hop on the line that went up through Perry, and on into South Dakota, through northwestern Iowa. That was so, Charley explained, he would not have to ride through Denver with all the old wheat bums and the crazy young kids trying to get to California to find their fortune. They were both wrong. Harley wanted to see the Rocky Mountains, so Denver was exactly where Harley wanted to go. He put his plan into action.

After church on Sunday, Harley told his parents he was going to go shoot baskets at Mike's house; that he had been invited over there for one last Sunday dinner. That part was true. He gave both his parents a big hug and a kiss when he left them at the farmhouse around noon on Sunday. He told them that he would be back later; they had no way of knowing that he meant later that summer.

He did go to the McMichael's house for Sunday dinner. Then Mike took him down to the Rock Island station. It was more crowded than Harley expected it to be. The train that was there was a passenger train. That wouldn't work at all.

Mike suggested they go drive around the Iowa Capitol building and the park over by the river while they figured out what to do. They got out and acted like little kids on the swings at the park. There were some men playing baseball in an open field and the boys watched them for several innings, then Harley had Mike drive him farther over on the east side of town. There were packing plants on the southeast side, with tracks running right past them.

As a farmer, Harley had no problem riding with raw refrigerated meat. When he thought about it, and he and Mike talked about it, it made good sense. The other bums, if they were from cities, might be upset at the idea of riding in the boxcars with the raw meat. It made no difference to farm boy Harley. Mike tried to help Harley reconnoiter the best place to hop on. The train might not be moving, or it might be going slowly. Either way, Harley was sure he'd have no problems getting on the train. His dad had told him the best way to do it and not get hurt or killed.

What Harley didn't reckon was that it was Sunday, and the meat packing plant was closed. There would be no trains loading there and leaving until tomorrow! Mike tried to talk him into going back to his house and staying the night. Harley didn't want to do that because when his parents called the McMichaels to find out why he did not come home Sunday night, he could not ask Mike's parents or even Mike to lie for him. That would never do!

"I'm just going to camp out here for the night, Mike," he told his doubtful looking friend. "I have my pack and bindle in the back of the car. I'll take it out, you can tell your dad I have left town, and he can help you take my parent's truck back to the farm. Sound good?"

Mike was not ready to be that flexible. This was not the plan. "This sounds crazy, Harley! Really, why would you sleep outside when you could just sleep at my house? Or you could just go home, and I could bring you down here tomorrow night. Who knows what kind of awful bums hang out over here on the east side at night?" Mike questioned him.

"Are you really serious? That is funny, Mike. Do you realize I am going to be sleeping outside for at least a week? It is going to take me that long or maybe longer to get to my uncle's farm in Washington. There are going to be questionable people around me all day and all night. My dad told me what to watch out for. And besides that, I have my hooks and jabs from boxing, remember? I can take care of myself; don't worry," Harley reassured him.

"Hooks and jabs won't do much if some bum comes at you with a knife, Harley," his friend warned him.

"I have a knife in my bindle. Actually, I have two of them. My dad gave them to me. He insisted I have one in my pack and one in my boot. He rode the rails last summer, remember? I told you all about it. I'm ready for anything, honest."

Mike shook his head, "You sound so sure, Harley. I'm gonna be sayin' a bunch of Hail Marys for you, if that's okay?"

"Sure, Mike. Prayers never hurt anybody!"

"Oh, hey," Mike blurted out, "I almost forgot. I brought you a lucky charm…well, it's a saint, but it's the saint that protects travelers, St. Joseph. Just put him in your pocket, okay?" Mike shoved a little figure of a man into Harley's shirt pocket. The thing looked a little like Jesus to Harley. It was only about two inches tall.

"I have plenty of room for a little guy like him, Mike. Thanks," replied Harley, as he reached out to shake Mike's hand. With a sly smile, he added, "You'd better be getting home. No telling what kind of unsavory fella you might run into over here on the east side."

"Wait, where are you going to go now? Maybe I should stay with you until it gets dark. Don't you think?" Mike asked.

"No, I am going over by that shed next to the gate. I will just hunker down in the corner where the shed meets the fence. No one can sneak up behind me, and I will wake up right away when they open the plant in the morning. You had better scram. Now, get out of here!" Harley shooed his friend away with his hands and turned to walk to the shed. "Get going! Take my folks' truck back. Tell them I've already left town, and that you couldn't stop me."

Harley got to the corner where he was going to spend the night and turned to see Mike pulling away. They exchanged waves, and then Harley was alone as the shadows on that side of the packing plant got longer and longer. The night turned out to be uneventful, except for the late spring chill that brought shivers to Harley's whole body. He decided not to pack much of a blanket because summer was right around the corner. It was the end of May and he didn't figure he would want to drag a heavy blanket around all June, July, and August.

Covering himself with almost everything in his pack and throwing his bindle on top of all of that, Harley crouched down in the corner and slept off and on. It was quite dark around the packing plant and it did not smell good at all. It smelled like…well…like dead animals. Not the kind of dead animals that laid out in the road for a couple of days, but like a lot of old dried blood, and like burned animal bones. He was pretty sure they didn't burn bones at the packing plant, but he knew they must have done something horrible with them to make that odor. He had heard the west-side kids at Roosevelt making jokes about how stinky the east-side smelled because of the packing plants, but he had never smelled it before. They were right; it was really foul. He tried to cover up his nose while he slept, but would wake himself up, not able to breathe clearly because of the clothing he had put over his face.

He was pretty sure he heard his father's voice, telling him, "Ya better toughen up, son. You ain't even started yet and you is already actin' like a weak kitten." He knew he must have dreamed that, but it seemed so real. Charley was right, even if it really wasn't his voice; Harley was acting like a baby, not like an independent young man ready to ride the rails with grown men and bums.

Suddenly, as he was awakening for what seemed like the tenth time, he saw car headlights coming around the corner. He shrank back against the fence, as far as he could, gathering up his stuff that he had spread over himself for warmth. The car drove past. That is when he decided to pack up and go wait somewhere besides right next to the gate. After filling up his pack and moving the bindle to his back, he started to walk around the whole building. It took up most of an entire city block.

Most of the back of the packing plant had fencing around it, but then he found a dock where they probably unloaded the animals. He wondered if they only slaughtered cattle, or if they only slaughtered pigs, or maybe they did both. Figuring he would find out as soon as trucks started pulling in, he moved around the building to the opposite side from where he had been sleeping. He was now at the front of the plant. The workers probably entered by that back gate where the shed was, and only the executives and bosses came in front. The double entry door had engraved brass panels and door knobs, as well as glass windows on it. Pretty fancy for a place that killed cows and pigs, he thought to himself. Then the thought crossed his mind…wondering what it would take to be the owner of a packing plant? Nah, that was not how he wanted to earn his Lincoln. He could come up with a better way than that. With some certainty, he told himself that meat packers did not get to work with people the way he liked to work with people.

As he continued to circle around the fourth side of the building, headed back to the gate, he saw a truck pull up and a man got out to unlock it. Well, then he knew he could not go back to wait by the shed. He looked around, and across the street was an abandoned gasoline station. Times were pretty poor on the east side and there were many small businesses that had gone out of business, he guessed. He decided to just go sit on the stoop of the closed station and wait.

Harley sat there all morning, through all the packers going in to work and then, hours later, coming out for lunch and smoking. He supposed they were not allowed to smoke inside the factory. Some of the tobacco might end up in the meat, or something like that, maybe. He wasn't sure, but it made sense to him. Also, he noticed there were not as many men working there as he imagined there might be, and not many trucks pulling up to unload animals. Charley had told him multiple times about how he would never take his cattle to the packing house in Perry on a Monday, because that was the busiest day. Sure didn't look too busy today, but that may have been the result of these horrible money times for everyone. Hardly anyone he knew could afford to eat meat unless they lived on a farm and raised their own animals to slaughter.

Harley was starting to get restless. He was anxious to get on a train and get going. He had been sitting around for almost twenty-four hours. Soon, the plant would be closing and it would start to get dark. He could have been past Omaha and halfway to Denver by now if he had left yesterday. This trip was not getting off to a start like he wanted. He'd better start figuring out how to get on a train and get out of this town!

Finally, a train inched up behind the plant. It only had six cars behind it, so there weren't many to choose from. Only the doors facing the plant were open. How was he going to get on the train without the other side of the cars being open? He had to figure out how he was going to get on that train, and he had to figure it out fast! It was not going to take them long to load it once they got started.

He crept along the side away from the plant and tried to find a way to get in one of the cars. There was not one door he could get open on his side of the train. He could have hopped on easily, if any of the cars had been open. Men were hollering about "Hurry up!" and "Time to be done!" and Harley still had no idea what to do.

School Improves and Mile Swim News

My grades improved. Basketball season helped keep me in shape, and I swam at the YWCA on Saturdays, but it wasn't anything like the competitive swimming I needed to be doing. It was the best I could do, so I didn't worry about it. Lesson learned from Mother and Dad. It was time to decide what to do for a spring sport. My choices were golf or tennis. Golf took more time, and tennis was obviously going to be more conditioning, so I chose tennis.

Burnie was really excited about playing his final season of baseball. He wanted to be the Dazzy Vance of Des Moines! The North High team only lost two seniors from last year, so they had a strong team with a good chance of winning the conference championship. His dad was having a scout from Purdue University come to watch him pitch sometime in the middle of the season. I was constantly pestering Burnie about going to the University of Iowa with me, but his dad and mom had gone to Purdue, so it was pretty much a done deal that he would be going there also.

My life was getting back to normal. Of course, it was never going to be the same without Dad, but Mother was a good sports fan and she was learning more and more all the time about basketball and baseball. I don't think she was ever going to be a big football fan. She thought it was too violent.

She was really getting interested in my sports, though. One day she came into the dining room, where I was sitting at the table doing my homework, with the Tribune in her hand.

"Mable, look at this! This article says they are going to have a Mile Swim in the Des Moines River! You don't remember it, because you weren't born, but they had it as an Olympic event in 1908, and again in 1912. They call it open water swimming," she informed me as she read from the paper. "You should enter!"

"May I see that, Mother? It sounds like fun!" I read the article. It was just a short quarter column on the third page of the sports section.

"Mother, the headline says MEN'S Mile Swim. Do you think they would let a girl enter?"

"I am quite sure they would let a girl like you enter. I'll bet you could even get Ted Ashby to talk to them if you needed to," Mother replied.

"You know, I think I would really like to do it. Maybe some of the other North swimmers would like to try it, too. There aren't any event distances that long in high school meets. How much time do you think it takes to swim a mile, Mother?" I asked.

"Look at the end of the article," she advised me. "I think it says right at the end."

"Yes, it does. The Olympic times in 1908 and 1912 were twenty minutes and forty-eight seconds, and twenty minutes and four seconds. That was for men, of course. And it was at the Olympics. I'll bet I could swim it in less than thirty; maybe close to twenty-five minutes," I boasted.

"Well, I hope we will have a chance to find out," Mother said. "I have a suggestion, Mable. Maybe you could telephone Mr. Ashby and find out how to enter."

"That's a good idea, Mother. I'll do that tomorrow right after school. I need to get this essay done for English, right now, though. Thank you for showing me that article. Can you cut it out of the paper and put it upstairs on my dresser?"

"I sure will, darling daughter. And I will call you when dinner is ready."

Mother was such a wonderful cook. I always thought it was a good thing that I was active in sports, or I would probably be really fat!

I was not going to get fat playing tennis, that was for sure. In swimming, I am always in the water, and even though I am swimming hard and giving my body a workout, I never really sweat. Tennis is not like swimming at all. I sweat like crazy! The courts soaked up the bright sun and then bounced it right back up in my face. Since it was a spring sport, I always remembered the weather being cool, not steamy. The temperature at our first match in April was seventy-eight degrees. It was ninety degrees at our last match in May. Those kinds of temperatures made for one extremely hot tennis season.

Burnie was having a very successful baseball season. Going into the conference playoffs, the Polar Bears were 17-6.

Riding West and Making Friends

As he was standing there, suddenly, the cars began to move forward. Harley knew he had no choice; he had to ride the top. His father had said that was the worst place to ride, but Harley knew it was the only way to get on that train. He raced up to the car closest to him. There were only four cars left coming, so Harley reached for the lowest ladder rung on the back. He missed, and almost fell forward. That was frightening; and could have been deadly. He stood there, realizing what nearly happened and the next car inched past him. Clearing his mind quickly, he looked back to see the ladder on the next car approaching. He had to get on that one! Harley's timing worked this time and he caught the second rung from the bottom of it with both hands. Again, he was jerked off his feet, but he hung on for dear life. As strong as he was, it took all his might to put one of his boots up on the side of the boxcar and use it as leverage to get his other foot up and move his hands to the next rung. Then he was able to scramble up to the top of the car. He laid down flat on his stomach and rested. He was sprawled out like what his father would have called "a drunk in the middle of the street," but Harley was on his way to Washington and he had actually jumped onto a moving train!

Just minutes later, after crossing the Des Moines River, the train pulled up to the Rock Island station and stopped. Then it backed up and three passenger cars were attached. He could see the roof of the station, but no people. He realized that the boxcar was so tall, that if he laid completely flat against the top of the car, no one on the ground would be able to see him. Even the people on the raised boarding platform would not know he was up there. He would have preferred, however, to be inside one of the boxcars. Even with the ice that was in there with the meat, he could stay somewhat warm with his bindle. The problem was, no one was going to open those meat cars at the passenger station. He realized he was not going to be able to get off the top of the train until the next stop, and he had no idea where that would be.

"All aboard! Train leaving for Atlantic, Omaha, and all points west… Bound for Denver! All aboard!" the conductor yelled. "Atlantic, Omaha, and all points west… Bound for Denver!"

How lucky could he get? Atlantic was only about one hundred miles west of Des Moines. The weather was not that bad. It would be a little bit cool, but it couldn't be cold enough to freeze him or anything. He felt around in his pack before the train started moving and found his work gloves. He would need those for sure, just to be certain that he could hang on once the train got up to full speed. When they got to Atlantic, he would definitely find a way to get inside one of the cars.

The train lurched again. Harley was not ready for it but he had centered himself on the top of the car. He scooted forward and actually had his fingers over the front edge now. It was a good handhold, but he was afraid if he was lurched forward again, he would go flying off the front of the car, so he tried to wiggle backwards. Now that the train had started to go forward, this was easier, but he still tried to hug the top of the car really flat. He had his stocking cap and his gloves on, and the sun was starting to go down. It would be totally dark when this train arrived in Atlantic and it would be easier to slip into one of the freight cars. This was the beginning of his rail riding adventure and he was on top of a boxcar, headed west to Washington! He wished his father could see him now. He also hoped his mother would forgive him for sneaking off. She would probably forgive him when he came home safely, with enough money for the first semester of college.

As it picked up speed, Harley could see by looking sideways, the train was going through Valley Junction. They would be totally out of Des Moines in about five more minutes. He had been awake a long time, having gotten up so early in the morning, and he was feeling tired. The clack, clack, clack of the rails could have been comforting and even put him to sleep if he had been inside a car. Out here, up on the roof, he didn't dare fall asleep. He could slide right off and be thrown to the side or slide backwards and be run over. His life certainly depended on him not going to sleep!

He tried to think of ways that he might be able to stay awake. He thought about counting animals he saw, but it would soon be too dark to see any. It might even put him to sleep faster, like counting sheep in bed. No, no counting animals. That could be a disaster. He settled upon singing. That's it, he could sing at the top of his lungs and no one could hear over the train noise! Most of what Harley knew in the way of music was old Lutheran hymns. He probably should have joined the Boys Glee Club at Roosevelt; he would know the words to more songs. *My Faith Looks Up to Thee* was his favorite, so he started with that. He knew all six verses, and sang the chorus every time, so it took a while. Then he sang Lena's favorite hymn, Fairest Lord Jesus, which also had six verses. When he finished that, he realized he'd skipped a verse. It certainly didn't seem right to sing them out of order, and he was so afraid of falling asleep, so Harley sang the whole song over, with the verses in the right order this time.

The sun was below the horizon, and it was rapidly getting cooler. This spring air was damp, and that made it seem even colder than it was. He figured they had left Des Moines about twenty minutes earlier, so they might be within forty minutes of Atlantic. Harley said a little prayer thanking the Lord for helping him get on the train safely, feeling like it had to be more than luck. He was going to have to get much smarter really fast. He thought that was strange, not running into any bums on the east side of Des Moines, and finally decided that it was because it had been Sunday. Most of the towns like Des Moines had several soup kitchens, and they probably put out a big spread on Sundays. Harley supposed most all the bums who were around would be going to those and not trying to get on a train on Sunday, or even Monday, like he did. They would most likely wait around and try to hop a freight on Tuesday. It didn't matter. Charley had told him that there were thousands of men and teenagers on the rails, so Harley knew he would have plenty of company sooner rather than later.

Harley sang another song or two and watched lights go on in all the scattered farmhouses he could see from the train. They looked so warm and cozy, but Harley knew that probably every one of those farm families was struggling just like his. Maybe they didn't have their house burn down, and maybe their father didn't have a stroke, but he figured they were struggling just the same. He prayed for them, for their children, and for their animals.

The train blew its whistle only twice so far. There was a road every country mile that crossed the tracks, but most of them were dirt roads. This was western Iowa, which was pretty sparsely populated. The only places the train blasted a warning were where it crossed an asphalt or paved road. When Harley lifted up his head to peek at the automobiles that were stopped, he was glad that he brought his stocking cap and not his seed corn cap. That cap would have blown right off!

Harley had been turning his head from one side to the other, watching farms in the distance and measuring the one-mile increments of country roads crossing the tracks, but he hadn't been counting the miles. How dumb was that? He could have had some idea of how far the train had traveled if he had kept track. Then he decided to raise his head just enough to rest his chin on the top of the boxcar, thinking maybe he could see ahead. That didn't work very well. All he could see were the tops of the cars in front of him. It might have worked if he had been lying on top of a car that was closer to the front of the train, but those were the passenger cars. It really didn't matter; they had to be getting to Atlantic soon, and then he could get inside and be safer. Hopefully.

Before Harley realized what was happening, his eyes closed for a moment. Startling himself awake, he burst into song again. He was not going to sleep until he got safely inside a boxcar! He tried to peek ahead again, and this time, there was a tiny glow on the horizon. All around him, it was really dark now, but that had to be a town. They had to be coming up to Atlantic. Then, like a wish coming true, the train started to gradually slow down. He realized he had a tremendously tight grip on the edge of the roof and that every muscle in his body was tightly wound up. Harley forced himself to release a huge sigh, and then another sigh. He tried to relax, but still hold on. The train was slowing down very gradually. This had been the longest hour, or maybe two hours, of his whole life.

Then he looked to his right and saw a water tower that had 'Atlantic' painted on the side of it. "Thank you, Lord," came out of his mouth. Then again, "Thank you, Lord." Not only had this been the longest hour of his life, but also the most thankful he had ever been. Here Harley was, only on the rails for a little over an hour, and he was already having peak lifetime experiences. This was going to be an incredible journey!

The train had started slowing down a long way outside of town, Harley figured out. It literally crawled into the station. He still could not see any people on the platform, but he could hear them. Some were saying welcome to those disembarking, and some folks were saying goodbye to passengers who were boarding.

He edged over to the far side of the roof, away from the platform side. He looked down over the edge and saw no one. Fearing he could not survive on the roof at night, all the way to Omaha or Denver, Harley had to get off the train and then find a way to get inside. He swung his legs over the side and climbed down the ladder. Then it occurred to him that there was no reason for anyone to open those freight cars, so he had nowhere to get back on.

Looking over three more sets of tracks beside him, he noticed that two sets over from where he was, there was another train. One of the boxcar doors on that train was slightly open and he thought he saw something inside it move. Harley strained his eyes, and saw it move again. A boy who appeared to be about Harley's age stuck his head out.

"Psst, hey you! Can you get the door open on that car you just jumped off of?" the boy hissed at him. "Hey, can you get that door open?"

"I don't know how," Harley hissed back.

"What are you, stupid?" the boy asked.

"Sorry! I rode all the way from Des Moines on the top of that car, for cryin' out loud!" Harley defended his intelligence.

"Shut up and get over here," the boy commanded him.

Harley cautiously ventured in that direction.

"Get in and be quiet! We'll go over and see if we can get it open. Stay here and come back over only when we call you."

The first boy and then another one hopped out of the car and the second one gave Harley a push towards the open door. "Get in there!"

Harley climbed in, just glad to be inside somewhere, and was not in the least upset by being bossed around by a couple of dirty strangers. He was exhausted. He watched as the boys expertly opened the boxcar door and then motioned at him to hurry up. Quickly jumping down out of the boxcar, he dashed back over to the car he had been on top of and they pulled him up into the car. It was full of dry ice and meat carcasses.

"Ugh, what the hell is that stink?" demanded the second boy, who was dressed all in denim and looked a bit older than Harley. "This car smells like something died in it!"

Harley let out a little chuckle. "A bunch of cows died. This car is full of beef carcasses. Probably heading west to be made into steaks and hamburger."

"Ain't nothin' funny, kid. This stink is awful. How far away is Omaha?"

Harley noticed the kid had a funny accent. He didn't even know how far away Omaha was. This fella sure was not from Iowa, or even anywhere near Iowa.

"Where are you from?" Harley blurted out.

"I'm from North Carolina, where it don't ever stink like this!" the boy replied, obviously annoyed. "I asked you, how far are we gonna have to ride in this gawd-awful smelly boxcar?"

"Omaha is less than an hour away from here," Harley tried to assure him. "Calm down, it won't be that long." Then he thought to add, "It doesn't really bother me that much. I'm from a farm near Des Moines."

"What's yer name, kid?" the first boy asked. This boy was shorter than the second one, and a bit huskier. He also looked closer to Harley's age.

"My name is Harley, what's yours?"

"I'm Clarence. And this here is Leo. I'm from Wisconsin. We got cows up there, but we milk 'em more than we kill 'em."

Leo spoke up next. "We'd better shut up with the fancy introductions and small talk. There probably aren't any bulls in this God-forsaken place, but somebody might hear us!"

Harley was wondering why they weren't shutting the door, when suddenly two more bums appeared in the door of the boxcar. "Room in here for us, Leo?" asked one of them. Both were older looking fellas.

"If you can stand the stink," Leo answered. "Git on in here if you're a-comin'. We need to get the door shut, but it smells so awful in here!"

Harley repeated himself, "It really isn't very far at all to Omaha. We will be there in less than an hour; maybe forty-five minutes."

The two new men eyed him carefully. "What are you, some kind of train schedule expert?" one asked suspiciously.

Catching the unpleasantness of their tone, Harley tried to smooth things over quickly. "I just studied this route before I got on the train. It starts in my hometown, so I know a little bit about it. After Omaha, I don't know anything about the trains."

"Hmmm, I 'spose that explains it. How long you been ridin, son?"

This was getting serious. Harley did not want them to know he just started. They might figure he had a stake of cash, or that they could trick him or take advantage of him. His father warned him to not tell anyone the whole truth about himself; Charley actually told him to lie, except he would have to remember the lies. Tell the same ones to everyone, he had told him. Harley should not try to change his story too often, or he would forget what he told different people.

The main problem was, he didn't think to make up a story ahead of time. Now he had to make one up on the spur of the moment!

"Well, a couple of months. That's how long I've been riding."

One of the two guys who got on last said, "You look like you just walked out your front door. I don't think you been ridin' for months, boy. No need to lie to us."

Harley thought more quickly that he realized he could, "I did just walk out my front door. I stopped in Des Moines to see my mother, give her a couple of bucks, and take a bath. You got a problem with that?" He added that last part just hoping they would interpret it to mean that they should not try to put something over on him. He did not want to challenge any of them; they may have all been traveling together and he was by himself. He had to stand up to them, but he knew he should probably try to get in with their group, too. His father had told him it worked out best for him to have a few good friends to count on.

The guy nodded his head, like that explanation was accepted and Harley tried hard not to look too relieved. This was going to be more complicated than his father had made it sound. Not being a grown man like his father was going to make him more vulnerable. Harley was beginning to understand why his mother had been so worried. This was going to be a dangerous trip to Uncle Gene's and Harley was going to have to make use of all the advice his father had given him. Trouble was, Charley had obviously not been able to tell him everything, so Harley was going to have to be cautious at every turn.

He decided not to talk any more for a while. Harley wanted their attention to go back to each other, or to the smell of the carcasses, or to how far Omaha was. They did start to talk among themselves and that gave Harley a few minutes to relax and warm up. He noticed that even though it was a refrigerated car, it was much warmer in there than riding on top.

He listened as the men talked among themselves. Most all of them had been down in either Texas or Florida for part of the winter. This long-term rail bum life seemed to have a seasonal route, kind of like the winter wheat circuit did. It all depended on the weather or where the crops were. Clarence was obviously just trying to run away from something. Leo was trying to figure out where to go to stay for a while, to really settle down and look for a job. Those two seemed the most hopeless, though, because the two older bums kept telling them that they were just dreaming if they thought there were going to be any jobs for them anywhere. Anywhere.

"Where you goin', bud?" Clarence finally asked him. "Where ya been?"

Harley was ready. He felt like he was getting better at making up stories about himself. "Doesn't matter where I have been. I'll tell you where I'm going though. I'm going to work on a sheep ranch in Washington and going to pick apples there, too. I know a guy. He's my uncle. Has a ranch in Chelan…that is where I'm headed," Harley told them, confidently mixing truth and fiction. What he was not going to tell them was that he was going to go to college in the fall. He was definitely going to follow his father's advice that would not be a smart thing to tell the bums he met about his college plans.

"Does he need more help? You know how hard it is to get pickin' jobs out there? Can you get us hired on?" one of the older guys asked.

"I suppose I can ask. Can't guarantee you anything. He has a pretty big place, though. When he wrote me last year he said there are a bunch of other big ranches around his and they are always looking for help. I heard more hobos go to California than go to Washington. How many of you want to go with me?" asked Harley.

All the men, Clarence, Leo, along with the older fellas, whose names were Adam and Ed, said they would go to Chelan with Harley. He started thinking they wouldn't really do it, but they had not been bad to him. Yet. Maybe his uncle could really help them. He was so new at this rail riding thing, it was hard to feel safe. These people were complete strangers. They helped him get inside the boxcar though. If they had not been there to help him, Harley would still be on top of the boxcar.

Senior Trip and Graduation

June, with graduation as its main event, was coming quickly. Final exams were pretty challenging, but nothing I couldn't handle. Burnie and I had studied together for all four years of high school, so we used our most successful strategies to study together for all the exams. I always had the most trouble with the mathematics, so with his engineering brain, he was the perfect tutor for me. He likewise relied on me for my expertise in English and literature. We both passed all our final exams and then we were free to enjoy ourselves on Senior Picnic Day at Riverview Park.

Riverview Park was the most fun place in Iowa to go! The businessmen who owned it were trying to make it like Coney Island in New York. There were all sorts of rides and shows. My favorite since I was little was the carousel. The first time Dad took me on that ride I was in seventh grade. I wasn't exactly a little kid, but that ride made me feel like one. With all the different wild animals, I felt like I was in an exotic jungle. They were all painted with crazy bright colors and decorated with colorful blankets, saddles, flowers, and fringe. My favorite was the tiger. His teeth were a brilliant white. That might sound scary, but he was really beautiful and exciting to ride!

Then there was the Jack Rabbit. As giant roller coasters went, it was spectacular. You could hear the people on it screaming in almost every corner of the park. We also loved going to Zindra's Palmistry Temple, but we would just wait outside to hear about the fantastic futures that our friends were told they were going to have. Both Burnie's folks and my mother forbade us to go in there. They said only

God knows what is in front of us in our life. If we wanted a better future, we were expected to work for it. Zindra was a very exotic looking woman who wore very colorful and strangely-styled clothes. She also wore a lot of gold jewelry, but Burnie said he didn't think it was real gold.

The Monkey Island was one place I could watch for hours. It was pretty good-sized and was surrounded by a wide moat. I guess that meant that monkeys couldn't swim, because I never heard about them escaping. The monkeys played with each other all day long. I couldn't understand how they seemed to never need a rest or a nap. They just played and played and played.

The last place we went before we ate the picnic lunch with our classmates was the Fun House. It had two giant clowns painted at the entrance. The banner said "A Laugh Every Second." It was silly to look at the weird mirrors, the goofy tricks they had set up, and the ridiculous games we could play. Burnie pretended he got hurt when he was walking through the mirror maze; he'd fall down when he walked into one of the mirrors and howl like a banshee.

The bathing beach opened on Decoration Day at the end of May, so it had only been open for a few days when we went. After lunch with our classmates at the Pavilion, and another stop at Monkey Island, we went to the majestic bath house to change into our swimsuits. It almost felt like we were at Coney Island. Riverview had a sandy beach they had built and also had a large filtered swimming pool. I preferred to swim in the river and use the beach; I swam in filtered pools all the time.

"So," Burnie inquired as we walked toward the shore of the river, "what did you find out from Ted Ashby about the mile swim? They are going to have it in the river, right?"

"Yes, he was so nice and very helpful," I said. "He said anyone could enter and mailed me an entry form. I have it filled out, but I haven't sent it back yet. The race isn't until the third of July."

"Did he think it was strange that you wanted to compete? Did he mention if any other women were going to enter?"

I was a bit offended, but did not want to let it show, so I controlled my tone, "Burnie, he met with me after the state meet and he wrote an article about me. He does not think I am strange. And no, he didn't mention any other women. What other women would enter?"

Burnie shrugged, "I don't know, I guess I thought there might be someone else besides you."

"I don't care if there is or there isn't. I just want to see how long it takes me to swim that mile, and I am going to try to win."

"Really, you think you might be able to win? That would be really nifty!"

"Well, Burnie, that's more like it, and listen, I am going to have to figure out a way to practice and time myself. I have never done a mile before, at least not in a river. That's over sixty laps in a twenty-five-yard pool like at the Y. But laps are really different than just a straight swim in the river. There is no turning at the end of every lap. I may need you to help me."

"You've been swimming plenty in the river before, Mable," Burnie said.

"Sure, I have, but only swimming from one side to the other side and back a couple of times. That sure wasn't a mile. In this mile swim, there's no stopping," I explained.

Burnie was getting interested. "So how long do you think it's going to take?"

I told him, "Mother said that back in the 1912 Olympics, it took the fella who won twenty minutes. I think I would like to try to do it in twenty-five or thirty minutes."

He was excited now. "I'd be happy to help you practice. We'd have to find a stretch of the river where it would be good. Do you know where they are going to have the race?"

"No, but I guess I can ask Mr. Ashby. He might know."

"Okay. Do that and then we can start after graduation. This is going to be fun!" Burnie exclaimed with glee.

We had a plan. Hopefully, it would help summer go slowly. I was not looking forward to being separated from Burnie in the fall.

Our North High graduation ceremony that next Sunday was inspirational, but at times, I felt sad, too. I missed Dad terribly, of course. The chorus sang our school alma mater beautifully. Students and parents were all hugging and crying afterwards. Mother invited Uncle Albert, Aunt Helen, and Grandma Von Dornum down to Des Moines for the festivities, which included a party at our house later Sunday afternoon. I was pleased to have them there when I walked across the stage to receive my diploma, and again when they announced all the college scholarships and I went on the stage for that. Mother was still beaming from ear to ear when she saw the list of senior accomplishments listed in the program and my two state backstroke records were there.

People who knew my dad also remembered my graduation. I received many cards, some with cash in them, from fellas Dad knew at the Water Works. There was also a twenty-five-dollar check from the construction company in Houston. That's a lot of money. It was comforting and thoughtful, and it would definitely help enormously with my college expenses. I was determined to succeed at Iowa and to make Mother and Dad proud.

When we got home from the ceremonies, Mother had everything ready ahead of time. She had prepared delicious finger sandwiches, potato salad, fruit salad, lemonade, and a fabulous German Chocolate cake. That was my favorite. She had a surprise for me, too. There was a large, heavy box sitting on the chair that was at my place at the dining room table. As we sat down to eat, she told me I had to open it before we ate. I opened it right there on the chair. It was a brand new portable typewriter! The portable versions, with their own carrying case, were the newest thing in writing equipment. They were much lighter-weight than the old desk kind like we had at school. I don't know where she got the money to buy it, but I guessed her secret stash in the sugar canister was empty.

I was feeling slightly guilty about her spending all that money on a gift for me because I knew it was for emergencies. I thanked her over and over and threw my arms around her for a giant hug. She hugged me back, but said, "Mable, surely you don't think I bought that all by myself? Where would I get that much money?"

I turned toward Uncle Albert and Aunt Helen, saying, "You helped Mother get this for me? Thank you, thank you, thank you!"

"No, it wasn't us, Mable," said Aunt Helen, shaking her head.

"Mother," I asked, "Who helped you afford this?"

"It was Mr. Ashby, dear. Look at the card inside the cover. He wrote you a little note."

There was an envelope taped to the inside of the lid. The letter inside was handwritten and it read, "Dear Miss Hall, Congratulations on your graduation. I also offer my congratulations for your successful senior year as editor of the Oracle and for your swimming achievements. This typewriter is a vote for your future success in the journalism department at the University of Iowa. I also know you will someday be an excellent sportswriter. Make sure to come and see me at the Tribune when you graduate." *He signed it,* "Your friend and fan, Ted Ashby."

Golly. This was unbelievable; I knew that his would be one of the first thank you notes I was going to write the next day.

I turned to see if Grandma was impressed with this fancy new typewriter, but she was not there. I asked, "Where's Grandma?"

Mother answered. "She went upstairs, but she'll be right back."

Sure enough, down the stairs came Grandma. She had a large wrapped package in her arms, with two smaller packages on top of it. I ran to help her; it was a large load for a tiny woman like her. I was pretty sure what was in the large one; it was my velvet quilt!

Grandma turned away from me as I came to help and headed into the parlor with the gifts. She ordered, "Zuerst essen wir!"

So that is what we did; we ate first. The conversation over those sandwiches and salads was all about the graduation ceremony, along with some college advice, and which of my friends were also going to school or those who were going straight to jobs in Des Moines. We even ended up discussing how much of the corn and beans the farmers in Iowa may already have planted and how the crops were growing, which was of great interest to Uncle Albert, since many of his friends were still farming.

There is a saying. "You can take the boy out of the country, but you can't take the country out of the boy." It seemed that even with Dad gone, and just Mother and me there to share with, Uncle Albert still needed to tell all the local farm news from Hardin County. Mother really was interested, because he brought news of many of her former Steamboat Rock friends and neighbors. We had moved to Des Moines only seven years ago, and she still had warm memories and connections to her hometown.

Mother listened intently and then added, "Be sure to tell all those ladies that I miss them, Albert." I could tell she meant it.

Everyone seemed to be eating very slowly and deliberately. I decided it was supposed to be one of those moments that Mother had told me I should try to "savor." Savoring it is trying to appreciate it while it was happening and enjoying the feeling that you get from it, for as long as possible.

What an amazing piece of advice my mother had given me; I decided to try savoring it, and it was miraculous. I looked around the table at all the members of my family. They were smiling and eating the delicious food my mother had lovingly prepared. I listened appreciatively as they recounted and praised my accomplishments, and shared silly stories of my younger years. Laughing their way through the simple meal, my family was celebrating me. I loved them as much as they loved me, and I savored it.

Eventually, someone mentioned the cake and all of us hurried to finish the food on our plates. There would be no cake until everyone was finished. Mother brought the cake out of the kitchen with great flourish and pageantry. Aunt Helen held the door open for her and Grandma's crystal cake plate sparkled beneath all the German chocolate grandness.

I had ice cold milk with my cake, but all the adults had iced tea. Dad would have had milk, too. No one seemed to be in a hurry to finish the cake like they were with their food, and I remember considering the possibility that they were all in a conspiracy to postpone the moment when I opened my beautiful, long-awaited quilt. They were enjoying their cake and tea, but I suspected they were savoring my unspoken anticipation, also.

Finally, Grandma Von Dornum cued Mother. It was just a glance, but I caught it. She edged her eyes toward the parlor, indicating that it was time for us to finally move the party into the other room. I know she saw me watching her, because after she signaled Mother, she directed her attention very precisely at me. She smiled at me, as only a loving and thoughtful grandmother could smile at her only granddaughter. It warmed me. It felt beautiful, like a soothing wave of love washing over me.

"Let's all move into the parlor, and we can discover what is in those lovely packages Bertha brought down the stairs," suggested Mother.

I just wanted them to hurry, so I started offering to pull out their chairs so they could more easily stand up from the table.

"I'm fine, thank you, Mable. I can get up on my own," Aunt Helen assured me. She half-laughed when she said it. They were tormenting me! I'm sure they meant it all in good fun, but I had waited half the school year to see that quilt. Time was up!

Grandma went into the parlor and took a place on the settee; it only seats two people. She motioned me to sit down next to her. I nearly fell over the coffee table trying to get there quickly. Aunt Helen, Mother, and Uncle Albert all sat across from us on the davenport.

Grandma handed me the biggest package first. She said, "Ich habe das für dich gemacht, Liebling Enkelin. Es ist für die Verwendung an der Universität. Sie sagen die Räume dort werden nachts Kalt."

I wanted to rip off the paper, like a four-year-old at Christmas, but I restrained myself. I carefully untied the exquisite bow, removed the tape from the paper on the bottom of the box, and turned it back right-side-up. I removed the green and pink striped paper with care, folded it in quarters, and handed it to Grandma. She would never want to throw lovely paper like that away. We were a family who reused many things, including wrapping paper. She put it in her lap and patted it gently, like she was so happy to be able to use it again. She thanked me.

"Öffne es jetzt," she urged me.

I opened the flaps on the box and pulled back the crisp white tissue paper. I think I must have gasped, or let out some other little noise, because Mother said, "What are you waiting for?"

I pulled out my quilt. My luxurious, glorious quilt. It was made of silk velvet. The quilt was a whirlwind of absolutely gorgeous colors; before my eyes were all the colors I had seen upstairs on the bed so many months ago. Some of the randomly shaped pieces were burgundy, gold, creamy white, emerald green, sable brown, gray, sapphire blue, teal; even the black pieces shimmered.

It was a crazy quilt, with no special geometric pattern. It was the most gorgeous thing I had ever owned. Even the thread she had done the featherstitching around the edges of each piece with was multicolored. Dyed like a rainbow, in no particular order, just like the quilt.

I pulled it to my face. It was so very soft; it felt like baby skin. The sheen on it reflected the afternoon sun and colored light landed on the wall at the end of the parlor. I hugged Grandma, tenderly, one of those gentle hugs like Dad used to give her.

"Thank you, thank you, thank you," I said, at least three or four times.

She replied, "Bitte," which I knew meant 'You're welcome', and then Grandma gently took the quilt away from me and replaced it with the smallest present. I gestured toward the medium-sized one, but she insisted, "Nein, Nein. Das kleine Geschenk, Kindlein."

So, I untied another lovely bow and also folded the paper, giving it to her to pat, just like last time. What I unwrapped was a little purse, pieced in that same gorgeous silk velvet, just like my quilt. It was about six by eight inches, with a zipper on one of the long sides. No strap; it was a clutch purse. I unzipped it. The lining was gold satin fabric, the same as the backing on my quilt. I put it in my lap and smoothed it flat again.

"Es ist für jene fantastischen Tanze, die sie an der Universität von Iowa haben.

Irgendein kluger Junge wird dich zu einen Tanz bitten," she explained. Then Grandma smiled widely at me and added, "Er wird ein Glückspilz sein."

"It's beautiful, Grandma. I love you so much." It didn't seem like enough to say.

"Öffne das jetzt!" she commanded, declaring, "Keine anderes Mädchen an

dieser großen Universität von Iowa wird so etwas haben." She triumphantly placed the final present on my lap.

I was trying to savor this moment, but that was difficult. I had no idea what could be in this package, that could possibly be more special and unique than the two gifts she had given me already.

"Grandma, this is too many gifts. You worked hard on the quilt and that purse is just…just…wonderful. I love you so very much," I blabbered.

Grandma was getting impatient for me to open it. She scolded me with, "Bitte höre auf zur reden und öffne das Geschenk von deiner Großmutter."

Uncle Albert and Aunt Helen burst out laughing at the same time. Mother had her hand over her mouth, stifling what I was sure was a rather large chuckle. Mother told me, "She said you'd better open it right now!"

"Okay, here I go."

I took off the bow and the paper but took no time to fold it this time. What I held in my lap appeared to be a piece of clothing, made of the same amazing velvet, also quilted. It was large, whatever it was!

"Hold it up, Mable," my mother urged me. "Stand up and move over to the end of the table, so we can all see it better, please."

It was so silky, it nearly slipped out of my hands. It's very difficult to try to explain how it felt to hold it. Like holding a cloud? That's close. I started to let it fall loosely out of my hands while hanging onto what seemed to be a collar. There was also a belt attached. It was a bathrobe; it was a crazy quilt, silken, rainbow-colored velvet, full-length bathrobe. It matched the purse and the quilt. The pieces were the same size and the same multi-colored embroidery floss had been used to feather stitch the pieces together. This robe, however, had a lining made of smooth black cotton. The contrast between the inside and the outside made it an extremely dramatic garment.

I was stunned at its beauty. I stammered, "Is this really for me, Grandma? For me?"

Grandma simply smiled at me and stood up. She was such a tiny woman, but she reached over and gave me a hug, while Mother stood up and wrapped my new robe over my shoulders. It was a moment I would treasure the rest of my life. Mother and Grandma were beaming. I was crying; that kind of love was incredible. So incredible.

Harley Hears Hard Stories

The ride to Omaha was educational for Harley. These fellas talked about all sorts of things they had seen while riding the rails. They exchanged some experiences about begging for food and running into dead ends on work leads they had, or some infrequent opportunities to work. Leo was most likely about five years older than Harley, and Clarence was the same age. The more they shared their stories with him, the luckier Harley knew he was.

Leo's life as a hobo started nine months ago, about the same time Harley started his wonderful senior year at Roosevelt. Feeling a twinge of guilt, although he knew none of the young man's miserable tale was his fault, Harley listened. Leo's father was a coal miner in North Carolina. There were seven children in the family. Leo's father came home one day and said the coal mine had been closed. He watched his mother and father hug each other and cry. His mother said there would not be enough money for food for the children. Leo left that night. He had five younger sisters and one younger brother. Leo said he decided he was not going to take food from their mouths. He left a note for his parents, telling them he loved them and that he would write them as soon as he found a job. He had not written them yet but was determined not to go home until he had some money for them.

Clarence left Wisconsin for adventure. His family's dairy farm had been auctioned off by the local bank. His parents moved in with his widowed grandmother, with no room for him. That was okay with him because his father was a mean guy, and sometimes got violent with him. He was supposed to go to Chicago to live with his aunt, but he decided to take off on his own. Clarence just hopped on a train and went right past Chicago, hoping to go to California. He had worked for a little while as a dishwasher in a restaurant in St. Louis but quit so he could head west.

The two older men had obviously been on the rails much longer. They were much thinner and their clothes were in pretty poor condition. Harley was pretty sure they were not as old as they looked; the fatigue and hopelessness was in every line on their faces. Both of them had some horrible experiences trying to earn a few dollars. Adam said he had worked all day to unload a truckload of coal for a man. It was cold and he worked hard to make sure he got it all thrown down like the man wanted it done. Then the man paid him with two tomatoes. In South Dakota, Ed had gotten a one-day job in a wheat field. At the end of the day, the farmer gave him five cents. Adam told the men, "I gave that nickel back to the farmer and told him to keep it, 'cause he needed it more than I did."

They all had stories like that. No wonder it all sounded so hopeless. The more they talked, the more Harley began to think that no one in the country had any money to pay anyone to work. He knew how it was around where he lived. People like Mr. Flynn were okay, and they worked hard to get there, but Mr. Flynn had savings, and owned a business selling something everyone needed: milk. Harley could see what appeared to be a deep division in classes; between rich and poor, but he had never seen people as destitute as these four fellas. At least, he thought, farmers can grow their own food. At least up until the day they lose their farm to the bank.

Ed told them what he thought was a foolproof way of getting a hot meal in a restaurant. He said he would walk back and forth in front of a restaurant, waiting for a man to sit down at the counter. Then he would go in, sit down next to the man, and speak to the waitress, giving her a sad story and then asking if there was a job he could do in exchange for something to eat. If there was work, that was swell. He did the job and they would give him a meal. On the other hand, if there was no work and the waitress turned him down, chances were good that one of the other people sitting at the counter would speak up and say, "Give him a sandwich, I'll pay for it."

Both of the older men said they could always ask other hobos where to find home-cooked meals, at regular folks' houses and farms, where you could go and sometimes get fed. They also knew the places to stay away from; where the man of the house kept a gun by the door. Harley also learned that hobos had a language of signs that they would leave for each other on fences and on other buildings, signs that left messages about food, police, and jobs.

Suddenly, Clarence told everyone, "Shhhh! All of ya, shut up! The crew is checkin' the cars. Take cover, don't talk!"

All of them moved to different corners of the car. Ed grabbed Harley, saying, "Git over here, ya dummy."

Harley didn't resist. He plastered himself in the corner next to Ed and barely breathed.

They heard someone rattling the door of their boxcar. "This is another cold car. It's shut tight," a guy hollered.

They all sat still and listened. The conductor hollered again, and then it got quiet. Leo spoke up, "We got a few minutes before we start movin'. Any of ya gotta pee, ya better do it now, or anything else, too. Jest hop out the far side here," he directed them as he cracked open the sliding door on the far side of the boxcar. All of them hurried out, and then hurried back in about a minute later, Harley included. It was quite a sight.

Then Leo informed them, "Looks like the next stop is Denver, because they have uncoupled all the passenger cars. They'll get picked up by the next train and be stoppin' in Lincoln and Crete and Hastings and McCook, I think, is the last one before Denver. Us? We is goin' all the way, non-stop!" Then he added, "As dark as it still is, I think I'm gonna curl up and try to get some shut-eye."

"How do you know all that?" Adam asked.

"This was one of the first routes I was on. Couldn't figger out why it never stopped all the way to Denver. Found out when I got there. Learned my lesson. Had to relieve myself in the darn car and then smell it all the way. Hooooey... won't do that again!"

The train gave its first lurch forward about four or five minutes later. The men stayed in their corners until the train was well underway. Curling up with their bindles, the hobos all hunkered down for some rest before Denver. Leo told them it was about a seven or eight-hour trip. From Denver, they would have to figure out how to get to Chelan, Washington. Harley noticed no one was complaining about the smell of the carcasses anymore. They must have either gotten used to it or they were too tired to notice. It still smelled like a lot of raw meat, though.

Harley slept a little, but he was excited about going to Denver. He had never been in Colorado before and neither had his father or mother. He figured he was now going to be the first person in his family to ever go that far west, except for Uncle Gene. He would like to get off the train for a little bit and look around but decided that would not be a good idea; he might lose track of his new-found friends, and that would cause problems for him and them. He would be all alone and these guys might get mad at him, thinking they got ditched. Maybe he could take a look around Denver on his way back home in the fall.

The rhythmic swaying of the train, once again, was comforting. He managed to sleep a little bit at a time but would then have to rearrange his bindle and pack of supplies and clothes. All the other guys appeared to be sleeping as though they were dead. He hoped they weren't.

Harley thought about his parents again, and about how he would write them. It wouldn't be easy trying to decide what to tell them and what to leave out. There would be a fine line between trying to impress his father with his bravado and trying not to frighten his mother with his foolhardiness. He also thought about what he would write to his Uncle Gene, if he even had time to do that. Harley had to find a proper way to ask if he had any extra jobs for a few more men who desperately needed work, but that might have to wait until they got there. He was hoping his uncle was as generous as Harley's mother, Lena. She was Uncle Gene's sister, after all. Maybe it ran in the family.

Lena's family was large and close-knit. His mother's four brothers and two sisters all lived in Iowa, except for Uncle Gene. He had moved to Washington to "protect his heart." Harley had overheard Lena talking to Uncle Lynn about it one day. He wasn't supposed to have heard the story, so he never told anyone he knew. Apparently, Lena's brothers Gene and Earl had fallen in love with the same girl. Earl proposed marriage to her and she accepted. Heartbroken, Gene decided he couldn't stay and see them together all the time, so he moved west. He eventually found another woman to love and marry, and was happy again, but he still did not want to see Earl and his bride together. He came back to visit family briefly about every five years or so. Well, now Harley would get to meet Aunt Lou and get to know Uncle Gene better.

As the hours passed, Harley alternately slept and thought. He noticed it was getting quite a bit cooler. Sometimes, he could actually feel the train going uphill. They must be coming to the mountains! He wasn't going to be able to see them until he was in Denver, when he would be in the middle of them. He started wondering if it was going to be much colder in Denver. Summer was starting, and he did not bring anything at all close to being a warm jacket. Surely it couldn't be cold enough there in early June to need a winter coat, but he was actually shivering a little bit. It wasn't just the coolness of the meat boxcar either; it was getting even colder than that in there.

Only because Ed woke up and saw him shaking with the cold was Harley able to catch any more sleep. He offered Harley an old gray blanket. That blanket looked

Country Boy, City Girl

like it had been worn for the past fifty years as a donkey blanket, but it also looked warm, so he accepted the offer. It was terribly itchy and scratchy but it was warmer than nothing and allowed Harley to get some rest.

When he awoke, the train had slowed but it was not pulling into a station. He looked over and saw that Leo was awake, looking up at the vent in the top of the boxcar.

"What's going on, Leo," Harley asked him.

"We is goin' up a mountain, Harley, goin' up a mountain. Gonna be goin' through a tunnel soon. A dang deadly tunnel, too," Leo replied, shaking his head sadly.

"You mean we're going to die?"

"No, I mean I knew a guy who did die in this tunnel. We are smart to be inside this stinkin' boxcar." He paused, then added, "Never thought you'd hear me say that, did ya?"

"How'd he die?" asked Harley, still wanting to be assured he was safe. He wasn't a fraidy-cat, but he certainly did not want to die.

"Well, last time I came this way, there was a fella like you who wanted to see the mountains. It was early morning when we left Omaha and he decided that when we got closer to Denver he would climb out and ride on the top of the train. As we slowed down to start up into the mountains here, he opened the door and he climbed out onto the roof of the car. I've seen lots of men ride up there when the trains in the harvest places get really full, but never seen a man get on top of one in the mountains. I told him he was bein' a fool and I was right." Leo almost sounded like he was boasting for being right.

Of course, he might be entitled to brag because if the other man had listened to him, he maybe would still be alive.

"Did he fall off?" Harley asked.

"Nope. Suffocated, the dummy. All the smoke from the engine filled up the long tunnel. Weren't nothin' for him to breathe but that black ol' coal smoke. There wasn't no vent in the top of that boxcar, so there was no fresh air anywhere for him to get. We could hear him yellin' about havin' trouble breathing, but we couldn't do nothin' about it. He was pounding on top of the car like a wild man, but we couldn't do nothin'. When we looked up there after we got outta the tunnel, he was gone. We was lucky there was no vent in that car. Now this car, it's got a big ol' vent in it."

223

All the men were awake now and heard about the smoke, so Adam and Harley started scrambling to boost Clarence up to the vent, so he could stuff their clothes into the openings in it. The train started to take a wide curve, causing the men to struggle with finishing their blocking of the vent, but they got it done. Harley felt a rush of relief.

"The tunnel is at the end of this curve," Leo told them. They all sat down and then decided to lie down. Harley figured they wanted to be as low as they possibly could in case any smoke came into the car during their trip through the tunnel. He laid pretty low himself, putting the old gray blanket over his head. He peeked out and saw they all had something over their head, or at least had their handkerchiefs over their faces.

A thought crossed his mind that maybe these men were all having the toughest, roughest of times in their lives, but none of them had it so bad they wanted to die. They were hungry, flat broke, wearing tattered clothes, with no place to sleep at night. Having abandoned any family they had, they were alone with no sure destination in mind like Harley had. A couple were sick, Harley was sure, from the coughing, wheezing, and moaning that he had heard come out of them, whether they were awake or sleeping. They were living a brutal life and he was off on an adventure.

Even Clarence wasn't in the same category as he was. He had heard the men talk about boys they had encountered on trains, who were trying to get out west to be cowboys or find their fortune in Hollywood. The hobos laughed about them, but none of them had laughed at Harley. He was tempted to tell them about college but didn't know if they would think he was crazy or maybe think Harley felt like he was better than they were. He did not want them to think either of those things, so he confirmed his initial decision not to let them know about his ambitions.

That got him thinking about his Lincoln. He was so certain that a new Lincoln every year was actually within his reach. He just had to keep the picture in his mind and keep his plan in motion. Start small, work hard. That was what Mr. Flynn had done and that is what Harley was going to do. He just had to get started on his plan. Money for college was the first step in that direction, so he knew he was in the right place. There was not enough money for him in Des Moines, Iowa, so he was going to Chelan, Washington and get it!

They got through the tunnel and uncovered themselves. A faint black haze remained in the car, but only Adam was coughing much. He was nearly choking and Harley imagined that was what it sounded like when the kid on top of the boxcar died. It was horrible. Then Adam spit a huge black wad of mucus against the boxcar wall, which ended his coughing and gagging. It was a nasty sight, but Harley was relieved not to have to listen to that cough any more. He made a mental note that as he returned home, if he came through the mountains again he would be sure there was not a vent in the boxcar he chose.

They knew there was maybe an hour left, so Ed said he wanted to share his story. Seemed like the two younger fellas had gotten a chance to tell theirs so he wanted to tell his. Ed said he was single and that he and his older brother had a stock market business in Kansas City, where Ed sold stocks and bonds. They were doing really well until a couple of years ago, and they lost everything on Black Friday…their main-street business, their big fancy houses…and they couldn't find other jobs anywhere. Someone in their family had a little cabin up in the Arkansas hills; it didn't even have running water or plumbing. They let his brother's family and Ed live there rent-free, but they still couldn't find any work. Ed said his brother never made another dime. Died of sadness and despair, he told them. They had gone from middle-upper class gentility to just being plain ol' scrabble-ass poor. All at once, just like that. As the surviving brother, he was the next logical bread-winner, so he hit the rails. He had no idea what had happened to his sister-in-law and two little nieces. He said he prayed every day that either someone took them in or that they found a charity mission to live at. Thinking that they were doing okay was the only way he could keep going, looking for work. It was the only thing that let him sleep at night. Harley's guts were in a knot when the guy finished his story. It was probably how the Great Depression got its name. Being destitute was depressing.

Gary, Indiana had been Adam's home. "I was a construction worker; really good at framing houses. Folks just stopped building houses." His voice was shaking, which surprised Harley; Adam was a tall, well-built man, in spite of that disturbing cough. He was not the crying type, for sure.

"I had to leave my Mina, she's my wife, and our six-year-old twins girls; Ruth and LuRae. I miss 'em so much! I need to get some money so I can go home. They are staying with Mina's mom. Her father passed away two years ago and left some money, but it ain't going to last all that long. I need to get some money and get back home!"

Adam wiped his eyes with his sleeves and blew his nose on a faded red handkerchief. As he stuffed it back in his jean pocket he was still whimpering a little, "I just want to go home." These bums seemed plenty tough on the outside, but all of them had been crushed on the inside.

The train started slowing down. All of the men, except Harley, knew they had to jump out of the boxcar before it actually arrived in the Denver station. Ed explained that the tracks would be busy and crawling with armed railroad bulls. He had heard many stories about men beaten and sometimes killed by the bulls, so he decided to jump off when the rest of them did. They laughed at his earlier lie about being on the rails for six months; they didn't care that he was new to this or that he had lied to them. He was young, and they were turning out to be pretty regular guys as far a railroad bums went, so Harley laughed at himself right along with them.

They jumped off in the outskirts of Denver. It wasn't too bad, Harley thought. It was not much worse that jumping off the moving tractor on the farm. There were some fields, a few pastures, and a couple of stores. It almost looked like Commerce, which was on the outer edge of Des Moines. Dirt roads, but otherwise some pretty serious attempts to look like civilization. Stores, a bank, and a block of little row houses lined the street near where they landed. It butted right up to a small ranch but it looked like the start of a town. There was a grocery store as well as a harness shop/gas station combination, too. Seems like the guy who owned the harness shop was ready to help folks with horses, as well as those with automobiles. Harley always admired a man with good business sense.

He thought it was about noon. Seemed like the people here had seen plenty of rail bums. In fact, Harley saw some fellas who looked to be in the same situation he and his friends were. They waved at each other and one of the other guys pointed and hollered, "We ate on the east side of town. You'd be better off on the west side now."

"What's he talking about," Harley inquired.

"Him and his guys hit the houses on the east side of town already. Begging for handouts and food. He thinks we should look on the other side of town," Adam responded.

"Well, I'm getting hungry. Actually, I'm really hungry," commented Harley.

So, the men walked through a back alley of what looked like the main street, heading to the west side, wherever that was. It was a windy, sunny day. It smelled like spring, but not spring on the farm. There were more pine trees than Harley had ever seen in one place before. Colorado looked a whole lot different than Iowa. He wasn't really paying attention to where he was walking; he was struck by the size of those mountains! So, these were The Rockies? Impressive! Nothing like this in Iowa, for sure. He was walking at the rear of the group and their dragging feet left a cloud of dust for him to walk through. He just followed. Then he started itching. His chest itched and then his legs itched. His feet itched. His head itched. What was going on? He kept stopping to scratch and was falling behind.

Leo called back to him, "What's goin' on, farm boy? We walkin' too fast for ya? I thought you was hungry!"

"I don't know what's wrong, Leo. I'm itching something awful!" Harley yelled, stopping again to scratch his head and his legs.

"He's prob'ly got them lice. I figure they was on that blanket I loaned him last night. I'm itchin', too," Ed offered.

"Lice? You loaned me a lousy blanket? Thanks a lot!"

"I found it just before we got on the train. Looked okay to me. I wanted somethin' warm if we was headin' to the mountains. Kept ya warm didn't it?" The bum didn't even apologize to Harley.

"Oh yes, thanks a lot! I was warm, but now we're crawling with lice. How are we going to get rid of them? I can't stay like this. I've never had lice. I know how we got rid of them on the pigs, but does mayonnaise and vinegar work on humans?" Harley was raving by now. The itching was getting worse and he didn't know what to do. His mother would have known what to do, but he was never going to let his mother know he got lice on him. She would kill him for sure, letting himself get that "dirty".

"Mayonnaise and vinegar works on lice, period. Pig or man, don't matter," said Clarence, slowing down to walk with Harley. He didn't walk very close to him, however.

"Where are we going to get mayonnaise and vinegar?" asked Harley. He wanted to do something quickly. "My dad told me that kerosene works good, too."

Clarence tried to calm him down. "We'll ask at one of the houses. We can offer to do some chores. For a dime we can get a quart of mayonnaise, and it'll only be a nickel for the vinegar. Folks want to hang onto their kerosene. They need it for light and fuel."

"Where's a house? Let's find one and ask. I can't stand this itching!" Harley was getting frantic. He had heard that lice carried disease and he didn't want to get sick now.

The men walked, scanning the area for a house that seemed like it might need some work. They saw a large house, back a ways from the lane, looking like it needed the crumbling wooden fence around it repaired. Clarence knocked on the door, as he was the most presentable of the crew. After gesturing and a lot of friendly nodding, he returned with good news; they would receive mayonnaise and vinegar in exchange for repairing the fence. On the back porch, there was already a stack of pickets they could use and they didn't even have to paint them. The woman also made them sandwiches! The men set to fixing the fence with the tools she laid out next to the pickets and they were done in about two hours. After giving them some vinegar and mayonnaise, the lady directed them to a nearby creek and the motley crew thanked her generously.

As he and Ed sat with mayonnaise and vinegar soaking on their hair and skin, Harley thought that the woman would have made a wonderful neighbor back in Iowa. He missed his mom for a few minutes, but then returned his thoughts to his reality. He sat on a towel and only had a handkerchief across his lap. The other men had built a little fire on the bank of the creek, but the two "lousy" men sat to the side so as not to infest the others until the gooey cure had about two hours to kill all the lice. It smothers them, and then they would have to spend some extra time looking for any eggs the lice had left and pick those off. It was a little cool to sit around naked, but they had to get the lice off their clothes, too. Those were washed in the creek and hung up to dry on tree branches. Harley just knew he had to get rid of these pests before he got to his Uncle Gene's ranch. His mother must never find out he had lice.

The raggedy band of rail bums decided to spend the night on the banks of the creek, so they added to the fire and laid out their bindles. Slumber did not come easily to the Iowa farm boy, as he still felt the ghosts of the lice all over him. He knew they were all dead, but a tingle here and there throughout the night made it an uneasy, interrupted sleep.

IF YOU ARE SICK, they'll care for you	DOCTOR HERE, WON'T CHARGE	FREE TELEPHONE	ALCOHOL IN THIS TOWN	YOU CAN SLEEP in HAYLOFT	
KEEP QUIET	HOLD YOUR TONGUE	BARKING DOG HERE	VICIOUS DOG HERE	BEWARE of FOUR DOGS	EASY MARK, SUCKER
THE SKY is the LIMIT	TROLLEY STOP	GOOD PLACE to CATCH a TRAIN	THIS IS NOT A SAFE PLACE	MAN with a GUN LIVES HERE	BE PREPARED to DEFEND YOURSELF
DISHONEST PERSON LIVES HERE	COWARDS, will give, to get rid of you	YOU'LL BE CURSED OUT	A BEATING AWAITS YOU HERE	POLICE HERE FROWN on HOBOS	AUTHORITIES HERE ARE ALERT
THERE ARE THIEVES ABOUT	CRIME COMMITTED, not safe for strangers	JUDGE LIVES HERE	COURTHOUSE; PRECINCT STATION	OFFICER of LAW LIVES HERE	JAIL

Birdland Pool Lifeguards

The Mile Swim

Mr. Ashby was keen about helping me plan for my mile swim. He jokingly told me that he was assisting me so I would agree to do another sports interview with him after I beat all the men and won. Taking that the way he said it, I went along with it as a joke, but Burnie kept insisting that Ted was not kidding. Burnie was convinced I could win, too. I just wanted to see how long it would take me in a competitive situation, because I learned a long time ago that the best way for me to improve my skills in anything was to challenge myself to personal goals along the way. Twenty-seven minutes or less was my target time. I think I was also secretly hoping that they would make it a women's sport in the Olympics, that I would be the first woman to win it, and that my time would be twenty-four minutes or less. Hey, a girl can dream, can't she?

Mr. Ashby helped us determine the stretch of the Des Moines River where they were going to hold the race. It would start just south of the Birdland Pool area and would end near the Grand Avenue bridge downtown. Naturally, it was the straightest part, but we decided to practice in another stretch of the river that was almost as straight. Burnie seemed to think it would be bad luck to practice in the same leg of the river as the real race would be held. I didn't think it would be fair. I suppose anyone could guess the planners of the event would use the straightest part, but as long as I didn't see anyone else practicing there, I felt like it would be a fair race.

Mother was excited about our summer river race project. She suggested we could borrow one of those distance measuring wheels the men at the Water Works used to lay out pipe lengths. We did just that and rolled through it through the weeds along the bank to measure out a mile. Burnie drove a stake in the ground at each end of the distance. Then all we had to do was figure out how to time my swim trials. Burnie thought he could just start the stopwatch when I started swimming, run along the bank faster than I was swimming, and meet me when I went past the ending stake. That sounded ridiculous to me, but I couldn't think of a better idea. It certainly wouldn't take him twenty-seven minutes to run a mile, so I had to concede that it would probably work.

One morning while I was giving swimming lessons, Burnie went down the bank with a scythe, or as I called it, a weed knife, and cut himself a crude running path along the bank. He said it was to make sure he didn't stumble and fall while he was timing me. I kept teasing him that he just wanted to make sure that he could run faster than I could swim!

My swimming lessons kept me busy in the mornings and lifeguarding at the pool occupied my afternoons. Fortunately, it stayed light so long in the evening that there was a lot of time to swim in the river before we went home for dinner. Burnie would meet me after I finished at the pool, we would go to our starting stake, and I would swim halfway out from the shore. It was too shallow near the shore for me to dive in. For the race, Mr. Ashby said they would have us diving off anchored pontoons out in the middle. We didn't have a boat, so I would swim out to the middle, Burnie would holler "Go!" and then start running down the bank with his stopwatch in his hand.

Twenty-eight minutes and forty-five seconds was my first time. Ugh! I knew I could do better than that! Even though I wanted to swim it again right then, Burnie convinced me that I should only swim it once a day. It was June 19th, and the Tribune's Mile Swim was on July 3rd. It was going to be part of the Fourth of July festivities in Des Moines. I was kind of excited that the race might get a little more attention because of that. It's not that I felt I needed publicity; it was because I wanted to make Mother and all the other supportive people in my life proud of me. It mattered to me what Burnie, Mr. Ashby, my aunt and uncle, my grandmother, and my coaches thought about me. I owed them a lot for all the help they had given me.

Burnie helped me practice almost every day until July 2nd, except when he had to go out of town three times for baseball games. I went to several of his home games on days when I didn't lifeguard. Those were good resting days for me. I still had lessons and lifeguarding, but no long swims. I didn't practice on July 1st either.

Watching Burnie's baseball games was like sitting in an oven. I think I picked the hottest days of the summer to attend them. Mother insisted I wear a wide-brimmed hat and take a fan with me. At first, I thought that made no sense at all, since I sat for hours in the hot sun when I was a lifeguard. She reminded me that most of the time I sat under an umbrella beside the pool, so I guess she had a point.

At two of the games I attended there was a coach from Purdue visiting with Burnie afterwards. They were busy talking baseball stuff and making plans for Burnie being on the team at Purdue. They were giving him a partial scholarship like the one I hoped for at the University of Iowa. I was proud of him, just like he was proud of me. I knew we would be friends forever, even though he was a goofy fella and decided not to go to the same college I was.

Each day my mile swim time went down. My last swim on June 30th took me twenty-six minutes and ten seconds. The main thing I was trying to do was learn to pace myself so that I would start out quickly, hopefully get ahead, keep swimming steadily, and then have some push left over for a sprint at the end of the race. I was so glad I was practicing. Burnie and I never saw other swimmers anywhere else in the river, but then we were only there in that one space for just a short time every day. Someone else could have been practicing anywhere. Burnie also said that he took some time off his weedy mile run time; it went from fourteen minutes down to twelve minutes. I had to take his word for it; after all, he was the one with the stopwatch. I razzed him about it all the time and we laughed like hyenas out there on the riverbank.

As July 3rd approached, Mother kept trying to get me to eat more. We had daily discussions about it.

"Mable, you should try to eat a bigger breakfast. You are going to have a busy day. You need energy," is what I had to listen to every morning.

It didn't matter that I gave her the same answer every time, "Mother, I am going to be swimming. If I eat that much food, I will get stomach cramps and sink like a rock."

She would reply, "Well, then make sure you get a good lunch." She would offer to pack me a lunch. She would spend way too much time in a hot kitchen those summer days to make sure there was a hearty meal waiting for me when I came home in the evening. I was pretty sure she missed cooking those kinds of meals for Dad. He had been a hard-working man, so he managed to stay pretty fit in spite of those daily feasts. At least he appeared fit on the outside. No one knew about his heart, until it was too late. I liked to think that he was rooting for me to win this mile swim race. He had always been my best cheerleader.

July 3rd finally arrived. Mr. Ashby said no one at the Tribune had mentioned that there was a girl registered for the race. He thought there were about twenty-five swimmers registered. The race would start at 6:00 P.M. so if there were fellas working during the day who wanted to participate, they could come after work. I arranged it so I had swimming lessons that day, but no lifeguard duty. Burnie insisted on that.

There was no baseball game that day either, so we just sat around in the shade on his back porch when I got back from giving lessons. He had offered to mow the grass in his yard and in ours, but it was so hot lately and nobody wanted their lawn cut any shorter. It was certain to turn brown later in July; there was no need to hurry it along.

"So, Burnie," I ventured, "how do you think they will line us up to start the race? I hope they have something sturdy for us to dive from."

He replied, "I asked Mr. Ashby. He said they were anchoring five pontoons across the river and each one would have five divers on it. They had a crew of men from the jail cleaning up as much junk and branches from the edges as they could. The water has been looking really good, don't you think?"

"I want to swim kind of in the middle of the group. I mean, dive off the center pontoon. It will be easier to see where the other swimmers are from the center," I told him.

"You don't think you'll feel surrounded or something like that?" Burnie asked.

"Oh no, I have always liked being in the center lane in the pool swims. It really makes me feel the whole competition more intensely," I confessed. "Besides that, they won't be surrounding me. They are going to all be behind me!"

"Hmmm, never knew that about you." He was attempting sarcasm, but I ignored that. "Do you think you can win?"

"I need to get the time down to under twenty-six minutes, I know that. I am counting on the competition to help me with that. You have to remember how competitive I am, buddy. I want to win. I want to beat my best time by a lot. An actual race is so exciting. I intend to get my fastest time and I intend to win!"

"What do you win, anyway? Do you know? Is it a trophy, or a ribbon, or what?" Burnie wondered.

"I don't really care, although it would be nice if there was some cash involved." I laughed, and then added, "How about all three? Cash, a ribbon, and a trophy? I mean, a mile is a long way! There had better be some good prizes!"

"And then," Burnie suggested, "Mr. Ashby can take a picture of you with your ribbon in your teeth, and you holding the trophy with all the cash sticking up out of it. Like they do at the horse races!"

We both laughed hysterically at the thought of a photograph like that. At the same time I was silently thinking, 'Yep, that would make a good picture!'

We ate around 2:00 P.M. Somehow, I convinced Mother that I should eat lightly, since it was a late lunch, so she made some ham salad tea sandwiches and cut up some celery and carrots. I ate two of the small triangular sandwiches and Burnie ate six. We thanked Mother and then decided to walk down to the spot on the river where the race would start, just to see if they were setting up the race yet.

There were big banners on both sides of the river. City workers had mowed a wide strip of the brush and grass on both sides, so that spectators could bring blankets and watch. There were actually some places where folks could have pulled cars up to the bank to sit in and watch. I had not given much thought lately to the fact that they were promoting this as part of the Fourth of July festivities in Des Moines. I began to wonder how many people would actually turn out to see it.

"Burnie," I wondered aloud, "how many people do you think will be here?"

He played it down pretty much. "I don't suppose there will be throngs of people lined up ten-deep on both sides, kiddo. It's a hot day. Some people are off of work. Some may bring their kids, although this isn't a really exciting thing."

"Not exciting? Are you nuts? How often can you watch someone swim a mile?"

Burnie was more sensible about this than I was, I guess. He observed, "No one is going to jog the whole mile, like I've been doing for you. I would think most people will be closer to the finish line."

"Should we go look down there? How are they going to end the race? What does the finish line look like?" I started thinking that these were questions I should have thought about earlier. I had just been so busy working my two jobs and practicing, too.

"I asked Mr. Ashby about this stuff a long time ago. I was wondering when you were going to ask." Burnie was chuckling a little.

"Really? What did he know? What did he say?"

"They are going to have a two-inch rope stretched all the way across the river, attached to buoys. You finish the race when you touch the rope. He's going to be there with his camera to try to photograph the winner touching the rope. That's what he told me, anyway."

Okay, those were all the details I really needed. The rest of the information was just going to distract me. I had to dive off the pontoon, swim faster than all the men, and touch the rope first. Now I had a specific goal. Oh, and I intended to do it in less time that I had ever done it. That seemed like the easy part. I knew I could beat my own best time. What I didn't know was if I could I beat all the other best times. Suddenly, some of Dad's best advice came back to me, "Whenever you're in a race," he would say, "always bet on yourself."

We headed back to the house. I was going to wear the swimsuit I wore in the state competition when I set my two state records. Mother called it my "lucky suit", even though I knew the religion in her heart didn't let her believe in luck. She had made arrangements with Burnie's mother to watch the finish together. It was nearly ninety degrees on the porch thermometer when Burnie and I left at 5:00P.M., and Mother said they were taking umbrellas and fans. They assured us they would find some shade and they would be just fine.

We arrived at the registration at 5:30 P.M. as directed. I walked up to the table with Burnie and the man sitting there said, "May I have your name, sir?" Burnie was dressed in a summer shirt and trousers. I was standing there in a swimsuit with a towel over my shoulders! Finally, the man looked up, when Burnie cleared his throat loudly, but didn't answer.

"Miss? Are you registering for the Mile Swim?" He sounded and looked totally incredulous. It was a little comical.

I replied, in a confident voice, "I am already registered, sir. Mr. Ted Ashby turned it in for me a couple of weeks ago. I'm certain you have it. My name is Mable Hall. Is my name there on your list?"

He looked at me, then looked at the list, and then looked at me again, replying, "Well, yes, it is on the list, Miss Hall. I guess I never really looked that closely before." He continued, "So you think you can swim a mile, huh? You must fancy yourself to be quite the little swimmer?"

"I have two state swimming records for North High, sir. I will be swimming for the University of Iowa next fall. Yes, I am quite a swimmer!" By now, there were fellas lining up behind me to sign in for the race. Burnie stood between me and

them, but I was pretty sure most of them had looked around and figured out there was a female in the registration line.

"Well, let's get you signed in and move this line along," the man suggested, this time with a big smile on his face. I smiled back and signed my name. To me, that smile looked like one of amusement, rather than a friendly smile. "We'll see who will be amused after the race," I thought to myself.

"Come on over here with me, Mable." It was Mr. Ashby's voice. "May I get a picture of you before the race?"

He had that nifty Leica camera with him again. We went over by the riverbank, so he could get the pontoons in the background of the picture.

"I understand you have been practicing. How has that been going?" he asked.

"Well, Mr. Ashby, I have cut almost two minutes off my time in the last two weeks. I have been focusing on getting the right pace, so I can start and finish the race strong," I replied. "I am planning on swimming my fastest time yet in the race today."

"I sure hope you do. I would love to see you win this," he said to me.

Then he turned and asked Burnie, "Do you think she can, young man?"

Burnie answered so enthusiastically, it caught me a little bit by surprise. "Oh, yes sir! I'm sure she'll win. You might as well just bet a pile of money on it!"

They started discussing the possibility that there would be some friendly wagering along the riverbank, among men whose friends or co-workers were competing. Both Mr. Ashby and Burnie doubted any of them would be betting on me winning. As I listened to their conversation, I kept wondering if any of them would be betting if "that girl" could even finish. It was that kind of internal competition within my head that motivated me even more. I was going to beat all their favored swimmers, and they would all feel foolish! The last thing I did before I left them was hand Burnie my hearing aid and towel, to give to my mother, so I could get them after the race.

We all lined up to get into boats, to be taken out to the pontoons. The pontoons were all in a row, roped together, and anchored securely. It was the hottest part of the day. Diving into the river water was going to be so refreshing.

Mr. Ashby had parked his car nearby and offered to drive Burnie down to the finish line after the race started. Burnie was going to start his stopwatch when I dove in, then they would get in the car and go. Burnie would clock my finish and Mr. Ashby would be able to get himself set up for taking pictures of the finish of the race. I was so determined to be the first swimmer to grab that rope!

The way the other swimmers reacted to me was interesting. Some tapped their foreheads, like they were tipping their hats to me, like a gentleman would do to a lady if he were wearing a hat. A few of them looked like they were saying something to me, but without my hearing aid, I couldn't make out what they were saying, so I just smiled and nodded. Just a couple of them stared, or glared. Most just gave me a puzzled smile.

We had all received numbers to pin to our swimsuits when we registered, but no one apparently cared in which order we lined up on the pontoons. The only expectation was that there were five on each pontoon. There was a starter on the middle pontoon, who cautioned us to not jostle each other in the water; to try to steer clear of each other. I did not laugh, even though I wanted to. I was pretty sure none of them would be close enough to me for any jostling to take place.

They must have been trying to make this look official, because the starter had on a referee shirt, with black and white stripes. First, they rang a bell to get everyone's attention. Then another man on the pontoon next to me hollered through a megaphone that we would be starting in one minute and that we should ready ourselves. I was ready. Boy, was I ready!

A minute later, the starter shouted, "Swimmers, take your marks. Get ready. Get set. GO!" He waved a starting flag and fired his gun.

Fortunately, there was no false start. That was encouraging. To me, that meant that none of them were really in very much of a hurry. I was grateful that even with my hearing aid off and a swim cap on, I could hear that megaphone and the starter clearly.

I had a smooth dive, and just started my strokes as soon as I came to the surface. It was a great dive, even though I had not practiced that much at all lately. I had to self-correct when I realized I was swimming much harder at the beginning than I had during my practice swims. Being in the lead was important to my plan, but I also needed to save some energy for the sprint at the end.

When I turned my head opposite ways each time I took a breath, about every three strokes, I could tell I definitely had one of the smoothest strokes. Some of these men were pretty large. Not heavy fellas, but above average height and fairly muscular. I was one of the first ten swimmers in the front of the pack. We were surprisingly even, with not more than about ten yards difference between the first one and the tenth one.

I just kept stroking, and for a few minutes, I really didn't pay attention to where I was. I just felt like I was swimming at the right pace to stay with the leaders. When I looked again, I was in fifth place! That was okay for now, because we had a great deal of the race left.

Being sure that Burnie and Mr. Ashby were probably already at the finish line, and perhaps even settling in with Mother and Mrs. Orwig, I started to realize that this race was mine to win or lose. "Whoa, girl," I thought to myself, "the word lose is not in your vocabulary." The mental gymnastics going on in my brain was crazy. I never thought this much when I was practicing. It was like I was extra alert; aware of everything going on. I was also totally focused on my stroke, my breathing, and my kick, all at the same time. This was different than any other race I had been in. I was swimming against adult men and I was on my way to having the lead.

I suddenly noticed that the other swimmers appeared to be slowing down. I checked my stroke to make sure that I had not started swimming faster and not realized it. That could rob me of my energy at the end. It became obvious to me that I was swimming at the steady pace I had practiced, and that the men around me were truly swimming slower.

Ha! They were adults, but they were not athletes. They might have been fit in their high school years, but most of them were probably not in peak shape now, like I was. These men were getting tired already, and I was just cruising along. I had been building up even more endurance for this longer swim in the past couple of weeks. I had been worried about making my time lower, but it was now obvious to me that some of them might have to start worrying if they were even going to be able to make it to the finish line! My confidence surged, but I was careful to stay measured in my strokes and steady in my pace.

As I swam along, I reached a point where I could tell that there were only two swimmers in front of me. Without my hearing aids and with the swim cap covering my ears, I couldn't hear anything, but as I turned my head when I breathed, I could see there were more people on both banks of the river. I felt like it had been at least ten minutes into the race, so I surmised that the banners and the people who appeared to be cheering were at the halfway point in the race. I thought I saw a large hand-lettered sign the said, 'You are ½ way there!' I just kept swimming.

I was in the middle of two men. Neither one was very close to me, so I was still confident that no 'jostling' would be happening. The water was the perfect temperature. There were only a few gradual curves where I felt like I was not swimming in a straight line and had to make adjustment in direction. This was so different that swimming in a pool. It was also different from the competition to which I was accustomed. Pool competition seemed so personal and close-up, because we were, well, close-up. This river swimming was like being a pioneer out in the wide-open spaces. Your nearest neighbor seemed miles away, instead of right there next to you in an adjacent lane. Also, there were no lanes. I could have swum anywhere. It was just strange, thinking of these things that I had not even imagined when I had been practicing for this.

I checked, again where those two men were. Now, I could see only one of them! We were almost dead even and I knew we were well over halfway to the finish line. It was time to depend on the internal pace I had worked on for the past two weeks. It was hard to tell exactly how much distance was actually left, but I could tell by my energy level that I had the push left inside me that would be necessary for a hard sprint against this fella if I needed it. I tried to tell by his strokes if he was getting more tired, but I just couldn't. I would have to count on my own strength to finish the best I could and not worry about what he had left in him. I was still burning with the competitive fire that pushed me to those state records. I knew that those records were nice to have, but I also knew that they were not going to be my greatest swimming achievements. I had more left in me!

The crowd on both banks started to get thicker. I could see them jumping up and down and waving their arms. We must be very close to the end. They could probably see it, which meant there had to be less than 100 yards left in the race. This was my sprint! I just let it kick in.

I cut the water with my fastest strokes, and my kick was controlled, but furious. I felt I was literally pulling myself through the river water. Of course, that's what swimming is; pulling yourself through water. I was not paying attention to that other swimmer anymore. I started looking for the buoys and rope. I just kept swimming, all the while, every third stroke of my arms I would try to look ahead instead to the side. Finally, I saw the buoys! They were probably fifty yards away from me, so I was really close to the end of this and I was going to win it. I swam faster than I ever had before. Maybe it just seemed like it, but I truly believe that it was the fastest. It wasn't like swimming in an indoor pool. In a pool you can see the end of the pool coming. In this river water, with the rope floating between the buoys, I had to just keep going until my hand hit the rope.

Then my hand actually did hit the rope! I grabbed it with both hands and hung on. I looked for a buoy; one was only about ten feet away from me. I pulled myself over to the buoy just as the second swimmer reached the rope. He was about ten feet on the other side of the buoy. He came up from the water and looked around. People were clapping and he started waving one arm at people on the west side of the river, while hanging onto the rope with the other hand. I realized that he thought he was the winner. When he turned to wave at the people on the east riverbank, he saw me hanging onto the buoy.

"When did you get here?" he shouted over the cheering.

"Right before you did," I shouted back.

"You won?" He sounded genuinely astonished.

"I got here before you did." Then I added, "Sorry."

Don't ask me why I told him I was sorry. I guess it was because he had thought he won, and I just informed him that he didn't.

He swam over right next to me. "How is that possible? You're a girl!" he said quite loudly; it was probably just his adrenaline.

"Don't feel bad. I'm a high school swim champion. I'm probably in better shape than you are." It felt like bragging and Mother would be very disappointed to hear me talking like that, especially to a complete stranger.

BIRDLAND SWIMMING POOL

Avoiding California

He shivered himself awake. Opening one eye, he saw a sliver of pink on the horizon, at the base of the pine trees across the creek. A shadow of a man, hunched over in the chilly air, was stirring up the still-smoking coals of the faded fire. There was no itching. Harley rested his head back down lightly on his rolled-up clothing that he was using as his pillow. Relief filled him, at a vermin disaster diverted. He said a quick prayer of gratitude for the woman and the picket fence, for mayonnaise and vinegar, and for the friends he had made who could help him get to Chelan. They were good men who had hard times right now. He would help them back by getting them some work if he could. His Uncle Gene would know how to help. Now, Harley just had to get his band of bums out to the ranch in Washington State, hopefully with no more lice encounters.

"Mornin'," Harley said, not knowing who the shadow man was.

The gray figure answered quickly, "Mornin' to you. Ya'll done with those itchy varmits?" Harley recognized Adam's voice.

"Yessir! We burned the blanket last night and that mayo and vinegar goop worked like a charm. Slick as a greased pig! There ain't no bugs on me," Harley reassured him.

"Why don't ya make sure all the fellas is awake, boy? We gotta try to hop an early train. Probably shoulda been gone an hour ago. Gets a lot harder in the daylight."

Harley shook out his bindle, quickly rolled it up, and went from bindle to bindle remaining around the fire, shaking shoulders and greeting each man in a sing-song voice, "Mornin' to ya, buddy. Time to get up and shake it off!"

There were a few groans and a few gollys. Most bums were used to sleeping on the ground, but the older the bum, the harder the dirt, especially in the cold mountain air up here by Denver. The other three rose up and staggered down to the creek to wash up and wake up.

Someone called up loudly from the banks of the creek, "Better get the coffee boilin'! We got coffee still, right?"

"Yep, but we need to get more before we leave town if we can. Hard tellin' where we will land next. Could be in the middle of the desert," Adam answered.

Harley did not drink coffee, so that conversation did not really concern him. He couldn't remember the last time he had a glass of milk and began to think that tea had even become an impossible beverage to obtain.

Harley thought back to sitting on the back porch with his mother. Each of them would have a giant glass of iced tea and be wiping their brows with handkerchiefs. They usually indulged like that on a blistering hot Iowa summer day, after a spell of hoeing and weeding in the enormous garden. Harley could practically feel the heat. Then he realized that the soles of his shoes were a little too close to the growing fire. He pulled back to a safer distance, knowing it would be bigger trouble than even lice if he wrecked his only pair of shoes.

That fence lady had given Clarence two cans of beans on the sly. Harley watched him slice them open with his knife and set them on a hot rock on the edge of the fire. The woman had told him not to come back for more in the morning, but for him to split the beans between the men. It was all she could afford to share.

"You men need to all get yer spoons over here and get yer share of these beans," commanded Clarence. "We can each take a spoonful in turn, until they is all eaten. Don't nobody need to be a pig about it, right?"

Harley dug in his bindle for a spoon as quick as he could. The men came scrambling up the hill from their washing up and formed a quick tight line, just like they were in the army or something. Nobody wanted to get left hungry, because no one knew when their next meal would be. The rails were harsh. Harley realized his father had been very truthful with him.

The beans disappeared as quickly as they had appeared. Clarence gave Harley one of the cans to scrape out the last bit of drippings from. Harley took a single swipe into the can, and then passed it to Ed, who was the thinnest man of the crew. He reminded Harley of the way his father had looked when he came back from the wheat harvest. Ed looked strong, but he was a little too lean to look truly healthy.

With the beans gone and their washing up done, the men gathered their bindles and begin to mill around.

"Where's our next stop?" Harley asked. Geez, that sounded dumb. He was the one who was taking them to Chelan and he didn't even know where he was going! "Remember, fellas, I'm just an Iowa farm boy. Really did not think this out very well when I got on the train in Des Moines."

"I've been west a few different times, and a few different ways," said Adam. "We got to get to Salt Lake City first, then we can decide where to go from there… west or north."

"Then our next stop is Salt Lake City?" asked Harley.

"Nope, we will be going through Grand Junction first…that's still in Colorado. At least we are done with the mountains, and let's hope we are done with the lice," Adam sneered at Harley.

"Those lice are dead and gone. I did not sit in my birthday suit in the freezin' cold, slathered in mayonnaise and vinegar, just to get lice again. I am done with that!" Harley replied, in a voice that made it plain he was not going to be ostracized for getting lice. He was done with them and he didn't want to hear any more about it. He wanted to forget it totally, if that was at all possible. Then he thought to himself that a fella like Adam ought to be nicer or he might not be getting any work at Uncle Gene's ranch, but he did not say it out loud.

They had to make their way back to the tracks on the other side of town. They had wandered pretty far to find the cure for the lice, but none of the others were complaining. It seemed like they were forming some kind of a team that was bent on getting to Chelan together so they could have work. That would have made Harley nervous, feeling like he had to find jobs for all these men, but in Uncle Gene's letter he said there were plenty of ranchers around him looking for good help also. These men did not all have to work for his uncle.

Along the way across town, they managed to beg food at some houses, and two houses right next to each other even had a sign out in front with an arrow pointing to the rear of the houses, saying 'Free food for bums. God bless you.' So, the men stuffed some of those goods into their bindles. There were a few more cans of beans, and some bread and some jerky. Stopping for food slowed down their trip to the train yard but allowed them to pack some extra food in their bindles for later. One of the houses even had a plate of cookies. The men ate those for their lunch. Harley figured those must have been good Christian families, like the boys his father worked with in the wheat fields. There sure were some nice people in the world, even when times got so bad.

It's gettin' to be late, fellas," announced Clarence. "We should lay low near the outer tracks until it gets darker. We can catch one of the late, slow trains that come through here. They don't really stop, but they slow down real good and the workers throw mailbags on and off the train as it passes the station platform."

So, they hunkered down outside the view of any railroad bulls and waited. It seemed like a good time to take a nap, since Harley had not slept much the night before. He closed his eyes and was asleep quite quickly. Curled up in his bindle, his fellow travelers left him alone. If he had been traveling with fellas he didn't know already, he would probably have been beaten and robbed or even killed. As it was, he was able to rest near his traveling companions and woke only when it was time to get ready to jump on the train they heard coming in the distance.

Leo tried to get it all organized. "We need to spread out and take turns climbing on. We don't want to rush the fella in front of us or one of us could fall and get killed."

Harley's ears perked up at the words "get killed." He certainly did not plan on that. His father had warned him and coached him about jumping on the trains. However, having done it only twice before, Harley still felt unsure of himself.

"I don't want to go first. I haven't jumped on many moving trains. I want someone already on there to help pull me up if I need it, okay?" He hoped they wouldn't think he was a sissy, but he did not want to die or lose his legs.

"You can be the last one on if ya want to, but ya gotta go way down the line. Start a trottin' down the rail a piece, 'cause we all want plenty of room to get a run at it," Clarence advised. "The rest of you follow Harley and space yourselves out. I'll pick out a good car as it comes by, and then you'll see me if ya keep watchin'. I'll be a leanin' out, so you know where to climb on, okay?"

Harley started down the right-of-way, as close to the trees as he could find clear space to run. Adam and Ed followed him, but not close. He had to keep looking back so he could see how far apart they were spacing themselves. It looked to him like they each had a different amount of territory they allowed themselves to jump on. It was probably based on how good they thought they were at leaping onto a moving train. Harley decided he wanted about a hundred yards. He couldn't believe any of the men would give themselves less than that, but they did.

It was harrowing. At first, he didn't think he was even going to get into position in time, and then when he did arrive at the spot, it seemed like the train was right there next to him. He wished he had run faster, but he simply had not known what to expect. He saw Leo, not Clarence leaning out of the train, and could not tell whether all the other men had made it or not, but there was no time to worry about that. The train came, Leo yelled at him, Harley heard men cheering his name, and he grabbed onto the foot rail at the bottom of the open railroad car door with both hands. He was yanked off his feet, but two men grabbed him by the shirt collar. They nearly choked him, but managed to drag him into the car, head first.

"Lucky little farm boy," Adam hooted.

"Good thing you ain't fat," joked Clarence.

"Where was you, Clarence, when we grabbed him?" demanded Leo. He sounded upset but he was smiling. Harley realized he had almost been killed and these fellas were joking about it. He was really gonna have to say some big prayers tonight! He gathered his bindle, thankful he had not dropped it, and curled up in a corner of the totally empty car to sleep.

Harley had no idea how much time had passed, but he awakened to, "Grand Junction will be coming up soon, son," Leo was saying as he shook Harley's shoulder. "Then it's on to The Great Salt Lake!"

"Do we have to chase the train again or can we just sneak on it? That was a close call for me. I don't want to jump on again, ever," Harley said.

Clarence spoke up this time, "Grand Junction has lots of trains that stop to load and unload. We can probably find one of those to get on."

Harley was relieved to hear that. In a short period of time, he gathered his belongings, such as they were. The men hopped off the train before it came to a complete stop. That was not quite as dangerous as hopping on the moving train, but more bums did it than Harley realized.

"Well," Harley spoke up again, "Let's find a train to get on and get to Washington. Every day we spend on the trains is a day less of work in Chelan. I want to get there as soon as I can. I came to work!"

"I like your spirit, boy. You got the right idea. I never seen a bum so anxious to get somewhere, Usually, they don't care what happens from one day to the next, or even from one week to the next," said Ed. "I seen men sit around in a hobo camp for weeks at a time…heck, I've been the bum that was sittin' there for a month myself. Down in Arkansas. It was just too darn hot to go anywhere."

"I'm with Harley," said Clarence. "Salt Lake City, here we come! Then on to Boise, Yakima, and Seattle."

That statement, as positive as it was and being all full of enthusiasm, caused an animated discussion among the men. Leo also wanted to go with Harley up north through Boise, Yakima, and Seattle, like Clarence said. The two older guys, Adam and Ed, wanted to head west to Reno and Sacramento and then take the trains up along the coast to get to Seattle. They had quite the argument and there were some harsh words exchanged. In the end, someone thought to ask Harley where he was going, since he was the one who knew where the "fer sure" work was.

"I'm going up north," Harley confirmed for them. "My father warned me about California. He said there are some bad people there. Cheaters and thieves. He heard about guys who went through Reno and they never even got to California… just disappeared at Reno. No one ever heard from them again. I promised my father and my mother that I would stay away from there."

"Don't they got earthquakes on the coast, too? Like that crazy big one in San Francisco back in '06 or '07? I don't want to fall in some big crack in the ground!" added Clarence. "No sirree, Bob! Not me!"

Trying to sound reasonable, Harley observed, "Well, we can't do anything about the cracks in the ground, but we sure can stay away from the crooks and thieves. I'm going north to Boise from Salt Lake City and anyone who wants a job in Chelan for sure will need to come with me. We stuck together this far. No sense in splitting up and wrecking our plan," Harley insisted. "I'm going north, period. That's where Chelan is."

It was like he repeated it twice so that neither of the older men would try to argue with him. Harley didn't want to argue with anyone. He did not have the energy and he really did not know either of them that well. He did not know what they were capable of if they felt threatened or if they wanted to fight him. Luckily, the bold declaration of his plans was accepted, and Harley practically felt like he was their leader now, even knowing that he was pretty much the youngest and definitely the least experienced of them all. He realized they were beaten down men and needed a leader. Harley decided right then that he would try to lead responsibly.

That raggedy band of bums on a mission to get to Washington waited all that next day in the shade behind a huge red dairy barn on Grand Junction's southern city limits. It was darn close to the track, and there was a small last stop station near there. It was almost dusk when the train pulled up and they managed to get on unnoticed. The plan worked perfectly again. Actually, it was more perfect, Harley realized, because he did not nearly fall to his death or dismemberment like when they left Denver on that moving train. He decided he was done jumping on moving trains. It was just not worth the risk. Since Harley was young and more justifiably fearful of death, the older men did not razz him. He was afraid they would, but they had accepted him as their leader and his flaws were overlooked most of the time.

Harley and his rag-tag bunch of men made all the other stops successfully. Boise, Kennewick, and Yakima went off without a hitch. It had been almost ten days since Harley had left home. He knew his mother was probably worried sick and he vowed to himself that he would call her as soon as he got to Uncle Gene's. The griping by Adam and Ed, who wanted to go through California, continued off and on, but never really amounted to a mutiny or anything serious.

The weather had been favorable and they had a fairly easy time finding trains that weren't being watched; ones they could just hop on. They also had a good run of panhandling for food. The three young men did a few odd jobs in Kennewick and the old guys found a mission in Yakima where they got good meals for two days in a row. Harley was sure he had lost weight because he had to pull his belt a notch tighter, but he never felt hungry or deprived. Mostly what he was missing was his mother's baking. He sure would have liked to have a lemon poke cake or a big bowl of tapioca with milk and peaches. He dared not mention his mother and her baked treats to the other fellas. They never talked about home, so Harley still was not comfortable revealing much about his family.

From Yakima, the rail riders had to pass through Seattle and then find a way to Chelan. Harley was trying to figure out how to let Uncle Gene know that he was so close and to maybe have his uncle pick them all up in Seattle. Perhaps he could call Gene when they got to Seattle…but he was not sure where to find a phone, and he did not know Uncle Gene's phone number. Maybe he could phone home and then get Uncle Gene's number from Lena. Harley decided to try that but did not tell the fellas yet. He wanted to find a way to call home without them knowing about it. Harley didn't like having to deceive people, but these were bums and even with all their travels in the past few weeks, he still felt some distrust. Bums were like that, Charley had told him. Trust came hard, if ever. Even as close as they were to their final destination, Harley knew he could not relax. He had a feeling, a premonition of sorts, that this was all going too well. Nothing horrible had happened since he got rid of the lice. His father had warned him about all kinds of things that could go wrong and to be careful of, but so far everything seemed under control. He was always waiting for the next dangerous hop or threatening encounter, but there was only calm and nearly effortless rail riding going on. It began to be in his thoughts nearly all the time. He waited for it…for the disaster.

The Mile Win

Other swimmers were finishing and the crowd just kept cheering as the stragglers touched the rope. There was a dock jutting out into the river where the buoys and rope were tied. The man with the megaphone, who had been at the beginning of the race, was at the end of the dock yelling at the swimmers to come over. I saw Burnie, Mother, Mrs. Orwig, and Mr. Ashby standing next to the megaphone man.

When I reached the dock and climbed out of the water, I was surrounded by all the other swimmers. We were dripping wet and people were trying to hand us towels. As the other swimmers moved towards the grass on the river bank, Mr. Ashby grabbed my hand and walked me towards the river end of the dock. At the end of the dock stood a man in a suit. He looked like he was hot enough to melt. In one hand he had a handkerchief to wipe his face with and that little piece of cloth was dripping wet. In his other hand he had a trophy. My trophy!

Mother was still clapping her hands together and beaming. Mrs. Orwig was clapping, too. The man in the suit handed Mr. Ashby the trophy and took the megaphone.

"May I have the attention of the spectators, please?" he shouted. "Welcome to the Des Moines Tribune's Men's Mile Swim." He looked quickly at me and corrected himself with, "I mean, welcome to the Des Moines Tribune's Mile Swim. We do have a little lady here. And she is our WINNER!"

Mr. Ashby held my hand in the air, like I had just won a boxing match. "Mable Hall," he whispered to the man in the suit. "Her name is Mable Hall. She just graduated from North High."

The man repeated it exactly into the megaphone. "Her name is Mable Hall and she just graduated from North High," and he added, "right here in Des Moines." He kept going, "Presenting the first-place trophy to Miss Hall is Ted Ashby, writer for the Des Moines Tribune."

More clapping. Mother was going to have sore hands. Inside the cup of the trophy were a blue ribbon and a ten-dollar bill. Burnie and I had been joking, but that was exactly how it turned out! I gave a little bow and thanked the man in the suit and Mr. Ashby. We walked off the dock and into the grass, moving towards the road. Mr. Ashby offered us a ride back to our house and we accepted. Along the way, mother handed me my hearing aid and I tucked it in the front of my swimsuit, securing the earpiece in my ear. It would have been nice to have it on during the trophy presentation, but I was dripping wet and that could have ruined my hearing aid. I was pretty tired; Mother and Mrs. Orwig looked worn out also.

When we pulled up to our driveway, Mr. Ashby got out of the car, too. I thought he was just dropping us off.

"Miss Hall, did you forget that I want to get your photograph? This is going to be a great story. I'm a little late for an appointment now, but I will telephone you tomorrow to ask you some questions if that's okay?" asked Mr. Ashby. "I'd like to take your picture now, while you are in your swimsuit." Then he turned to Mother and asked, "Is it okay if I take a picture of your daughter in her swimsuit for the paper?"

"Certainly!" Mother laughed. "There are so many pictures of her in her suit from swimming meets I can't even count them. There are several in the North High yearbook, too."

"Well, I suppose there are. That was kind of a silly question," said Mr. Ashby.

He asked me to stand under the big tree in Burnie's front yard. It was still mostly green and the front porch looked tidy in the background. He had me pose with my trophy in one hand, with the money sticking out of it, and my ribbon in the other hand. I finally remembered to take off my swim cap before he took the picture.

He started taking pictures and Burnie started laughing. It looked like he was trying to stifle them, but the chortles kept coming. Mr. Ashby was smiling, but not laughing. He had to hold still to take the photograph! I suddenly remembered something. This was exactly like the pose that Burnie and I had discussed when I was wondering what the first prize would be! Burnie had already found out from Mr. Ashby what first prize was before we had that talk. That rascal; he knew and talked all about it like he had no idea. Well, at least he had been confident that I would win, and I did.

I said, "Burnie, I should punch you! You knew what the prizes were all along when we were talking the other day."

"So what? I knew you would win. I just wanted to have some fun with you," he said in defense of himself. He laughed out loud this time. Mr. Ashby didn't get the joke, but Burnie told him about our conversation and he joined us in our amusement.

"I have to run now, kids, so I will call you tomorrow, Mable," said Mr. Ashby as he turned to go to his car. "I'll call early, about nine o'clock."

We waved goodbye from Burnie's front porch. I went home to bathe and change; I had to get that river water off of me. I told Burnie I'd meet him on his back porch in about an hour. It was too hot to shoot baskets but we could visit and make plans for tomorrow night. We were planning on watching the fireworks display put on near the Iowa Capitol building. We could see it every year from the backside of Burnie's house. The fireworks always looked so bright when they shone on the golden dome. As I thought about that, I imagined Dad watching them from up in Heaven.

The next day turned out to be a wonderfully traditional Fourth of July. There was a big carnival and auto races at the Iowa Fairgrounds. Riverview Park was packed and there was a super parade downtown. Burnie and I went to Riverview for a little while; we rode the carousel and the roller coaster. I had enough water yesterday so we skipped the beach. And we did stop by to check on the monkeys at Monkey Island! Mother and the Orwigs had a delicious picnic dinner for us that we ate in the Orwig's back yard. Then we just sat around in the shade, waiting for it to get dark. Burnie's house had a pretty good-sized balcony on the second floor of their house, off the back bedroom. We sat on the balcony and could see the fireworks at the Capitol perfectly. It was one of the benefits of living in Highland Park on the near-north side of Des Moines.

The next couple of weeks went fairly quickly. My picture was in the paper the Sunday following the mile swim. It read pretty much like the first article Mr. Ashby wrote. You know, how unusual it was for a girl to be doing a race like that, about my state records again, about me going to the University of Iowa in the fall, and about me wanting to be a sportswriter. I sent one to Grandma Von Dornum in Steamboat Rock and put one in my scrapbook, along with the first article. I decided that was the last thing I was going to put in my scrapbook. It had been my high school scrapbook. I was going to take a little bit of my swimming lesson money and buy a new scrapbook and use it for college. I was getting ready to fill a whole new book!

Unfortunately, and sadly, it ended up not being the last entry in my high school scrapbook. There was another tragedy about to happen in my life; one that might change my life again.

Cornered in Yakima and On to Seattle

The railyard in Yakima was small, but then Yakima was a small town. There was a crummy, run-down station and not much of anything around the place except scrubby trees. The main part of town was a good half mile away. It was almost like the founding fathers decided they were going to grow their town and built the railroad on what they thought might eventually be the edge of town. Seemed kind of backwards to Harley. He thought they would want the transportation close to the heart of the city. However, that remote location would probably make it easier to get on the train without being seen. There were not a lot of other men riding this direction. Maybe most of them went to California after all, in spite of the dangers. No wonder the ranchers up here needed help. There was not going to be much competition for any available work, that was for sure.

The men slept in an unoccupied old coach house that had been used more recently as a barn, behind a large home on the west side of town. It was the closest inhabited place to the rail station and appeared to be occupied by an older couple. The house had seen better days. Harley didn't see any signs of kids' toys and there were old-fashioned curtains in the windows. The paint on the house was looking neglected and the garden was too small to feed more than two people. Clarence and Leo were sure an elderly couple would be generous if asked for food. Maybe they were from a logging family or trappers, or even gold miners. Wherever they acquired their riches, it seemed like the house and property were on the decline. Perhaps their children had left home and they were too old to take care of the property. The men could maybe do some odd jobs for them and get another home-cooked meal before they got to Chelan.

Brushing large cobwebs out of the doorway, Ed led them into the building that was just south of the main house. There was a loft in the top, but the wooden ladder leading up to it had disintegrated and there was no alternate way to get up there. The only reason to go up to the loft would be to perhaps find some straw to cushion their sleep a bit, or to be up off the bare ground. It seemed pretty dry all around the building and the patch grass was about three feet tall. They were leery of starting a campfire because they were pretty sure the folks in the house didn't know they had visitors in the coach house. They were hoping to avoid having the sheriff show up and shoo them off, so the hobos decided to lay low for the night and approach the house in the morning, to maybe beg for a little breakfast or do some simple work.

The men all rolled out their bindles and slept on the dirt floor of the coach house. Harley had seen plenty of buildings like this on the wealthy side of town in Des Moines. Most of those were made of stone, but this one had was wood frame construction. These large structures used to stable the horses that pulled the carriages of the rich people. Later, with the introduction of motor vehicles, the horses were replaced with gasoline-powered automobiles. However, as he spread his bindle on the ground, Harley found the aroma of the horses still in the earth beneath him. That did not warrant even a slight comment from the Iowa farm boy, but the rest of the fellas had plenty to say about it. Somehow, eventually, they all fell asleep.

The barking dog wakened them. It was not simply barking; it was snarling, snapping, howling…all at the same time. It sounded to Harley like a one dog massacre. He ventured over to the door to peek through the one of the dirt encrusted windows on the door. Yep, it was a large dog. And it was right outside the door. They weren't going to get breakfast any time soon.

"What is that, a pack of wolves?" shouted Adam from where he was peeing, in the far dusty corner of the coach house. Hearing his raised voice from inside, the furious dog started clawing at the door, and barking even louder.

"Nope," Harley hollered back, "just one dog, but it looks like it could be part wolf." Hearing his voice right on the other side of the door, now the dog was determined to tear it down. Fortunately for the trapped men, it was a sturdy door, but the clawing gained in intensity.

Then came a sharp, high-pitched whistle; the kind you make with your two fingers between your teeth. The barking stopped. Everything was silent, except for the footsteps Harley heard crunching through the high dry grass.

A man's voice queried of the dog, "What ya got in there, Fang? Got a coon trapped, maybe a fox? Hope it's not a bear. I ain't openin' the door if it's a bear. Lemme get a look. Back up so I can get a peek in there."

Quickly, there was an old man's face staring at Harley through the window.

Harley thought perhaps he should duck down fast so as not to be seen, but he wasn't quick enough. Then he realized that if the man did not see him, he might open the door and let the dog in to get the critter. Harley didn't want the dog set loose on them, especially since he was the one right by the door!

He had to speak up. "Hey, mister. Please don't open the door. We bums just slept the night here. Didn't mean any harm, honest. We'll be leaving right away on the train. Promise."

The man looked square at him. "Ya cornered yerself some bindle stiffs, Fang. I'll be darned! Ain't never had no hobos here."

"We'll leave, honest, sir," Harley said again. He put his hands together up in front of the window, like he was praying. He did not want that dog let in. He could hear the dog start clawing at the bottom edge of the door this time and sniffing really hard.

"Don't reckon I need to turn the dog loose on ya, huh?" asked the old guy.

"No sir! Please don't. We don't mean any harm. We just wanted to sleep inside somewhere last night. We were going to leave right away this morning. There's five of us and we are packin' up our bindles right now. Just don't let the dog loose, please!"

"Whatcha doin' in Yakima? How come you ain't in California with the rest of the bums?" the old man demanded.

"I got an uncle who lives in Chelan. He's got a ranch. We are going there to work for him. I swear," Harley said through the crack. He was still eyeball to eyeball with the old man, with just a pane of dirty glass separating them. He noticed then that the man had a shotgun in his left hand.

"No need to be swearing, young man. I'll put the dog in the house again, then I want to see all of you before you leave. Don't be sneakin' off. I'll be right back," the old man cautioned.

He turned and left, taking the wolf dog with him. Harley let out an audible sigh of relief.

"Good thing you talk so good," said Leo. "You really saved us on that one."

"Are we waitin' for him to come back?" asked Ed.

"I gotta get my stuff together. I figure we ought to wait at least as long as that takes me," Harley said, noticing the rest of the men, besides Leo, were standing at the back door of the coach house with their bindles ready to go. "That old guy has a gun and I don't want to get shot in the back if he comes out and it looks like we are running away. If you fellas wanna look like criminals and run away, I can't stop you."

"Oh, hell," Adam exclaimed, "we'll wait, but he better not take too long. I want to get on a train. This place ain't no good no more."

The old man was already crunching through the grass by the time they all gathered together by the two big front doors of the coach house. He had a burlap sack in one hand and a pot of coffee in the other hand. Harley saw him first.

"He's bringin' us coffee!" Harley exclaimed.

The man heard Harley and added, "I got homemade biscuits in the bag for ya, too."

He stepped into the doorway and handed Harley the bag.

"Ya got coffee cups, don't ya?" asked the old man. The bums scrambled through their bindles for the cups they each had. In a flash, they all had a hot cup of coffee. They sat back down on their bindles and Harley handed out the huge biscuits. There were two for each man, with one left over. "I wasn't sure how many were hidin' in here, but I thought you said there was five of ya. I stuck an extra one in there for me. Gimme it." He grabbed the last biscuit and the bag from Harley, adding, "My wife wants the bag back."

"This is mighty generous of you," said Clarence, who was speaking up for the first time this morning. "Mighty generous, I'd say."

The other four men murmured, "Thank you," almost in unison. Ed said it a couple of times.

"Me and my wife is happy to help you out. My brother's farm went belly up a year ago. We managed to hang onto this place, but he had to hit the rails like you fellas. We ain't heard from him since he left. Just hoping he ain't dead, ya know?"

The generous man was a compassionate man. Harley figured he was doing for them with the biscuits and coffee like he hoped someone would do for his brother.

"I'll bet he's okay, sir," Harley replied. "I'll bet he's saving up his money and will be home real soon."

Clarence spoke next, "We need to be taking off, Harley. Those trains stop in this town a couple of times in the morning and then there won't be any more until late tonight. Let's get to Chelan."

The old man took the coffee pot from Leo. Harley thanked him again, and then all the other fellas chimed in with their additional gratitude. It was the first time anyone had given them food without them having to ask or beg for it; they didn't even have to work for it.

Their timing was perfect. It seemed like the train, unguarded in this remote little city, was sitting there waiting just for them. It could not have been more perfect. They climbed up and into the train. It pulled out almost immediately. Next stop Seattle, and then Chelan.

They would be in Seattle before dark. Summer was making the days longer, and it was getting warmer every day. They still needed their bindles for sleeping in the cool evening temperatures and spent their time in the rail car shaking them out and sorting their belongings. Pretty much like a spring cleaning, but without the house. No one found anything special in their stuff. Harley found a stamped envelope and some sheets of paper, but he had no writing utensil to use for his letter home. When he asked if anyone of the fellas had a pencil, Ed and Adam rolled over laughing in the back of the boxcar.

"That's real funny, kid. What the hell would we do with a pencil? We can't write. Hell, we can't even read!"

Harley wanted to tell them that he did not think that was a laughing matter, not being able to read or write, but they were his friends now, so he let it slide. His mother had told him that he would run into many people who did not know the value of education. That's why his quest for college remained a secret from the other rail riders.

Seattle came quickly because there was only one stop between there and Yakima. Seattle was a large railyard, and it took them about forty-five minutes to find a remote track and one without bulls. It took another hour to figure out the right train. There were not a ton of bums up here, but the bulls were always somewhere. When they found the right train, Harley would walk close enough to the station door to see the schedule, He would figure out when that train was leaving and then the men timed their last bathroom trip and got settled in a box car. There was no cover of trees or woods near these bigger cities, so they had to just get on the boxcar and hide. It was usually safe to get on one that had wooden crates or large trunks on it. They were less likely to pack last minute cargo on one of those, and it was easy for the men to conceal themselves.

Harley has so anxious to get to Chelan and then the next thirty miles to the ranch. In Iowa, the towns were not so spread out. It was hard to imagine a ranch with the address of a town that was thirty miles away. It was crazy, but things were about to get a lot crazier than that.

Steamboat Rock Disaster

There was no way to anticipate it or prepare for it. There was no way to prevent it, or to undo it. When the telephone rang on Sunday morning, August 1st, I answered, but Uncle Albert asked to talk to Mother without even really saying hello to me. I knew there was something wrong. Very wrong.

"Henrietta," he said, "there's been a fire. Mother's house caught on fire last night."

"Oh no," Mother shrieked. "A fire? Is there much damage?"

"Henrietta, the house burned completely down. It's gone. A complete loss," Albert reported.

"Mother got out, didn't she?" Mother asked, her voice trembling.

"Yes, she got out. But..."

"But what, Albert? Is she hurt?" Mother was panicking.

"She got out, but she went back in. She wanted to save the chairs that she and Klaas got as a wedding present."

"Oh, dear God, Albert, is she hurt? Is she okay? Is she alive?"

Mother waited for what seemed a very long time for the answer to come.

"She was alive, Henrietta. They took her to the hospital in Eldora, but she died shortly after they got her there. She breathed in a lot of smoke and had some bad burns on her legs and arms. She was already old and weak. She was unconscious. She didn't suffer from the burns, I'm sure of that."

Then there was a long silence from Mother. Finally, she whispered, "God rest her sweet old soul, Albert. God rest her sweet old soul." Mother sat down on the hallway bench and started to cry. She handed me the receiver.

"Uncle Albert, I don't think Mother can talk anymore right now. What is happening?"

"I am going to come to Des Moines this afternoon and pick up you and your mother, Mable. You'll be staying with us. The funeral parlor in Eldora is going to handle the arrangements. We have called the pastor at Bertha's church. He'll announce it during the service this morning, but this town is so small, everyone already knows. I expect the ladies will start bringing over the cakes and casseroles this afternoon, or tomorrow for sure. Aunt Helen is going to stay home and take care of all that business. There will be a lot of visitors at our house. Everyone loved your grandmother."

This was more information that I could remember all at once, but I said, "I'll let Mother know. She may want to call you back, if that's okay?"

"Tell her I am leaving in just a little bit. Aunt Helen will be here, if she wants to call her. Help your mother. You will have to pack a few things and plan to stay for a few days, until after the services. I'm going to hang up now. Be a good girl, like you always are, until I get there." He hung up.

I went over and sat on the bench. I put my arm around Mother's shoulder. She suddenly turned and grabbed me in a big hug. I started crying, too, and we just sat there, hugging and crying.

First my father, and now my grandmother. I was trying not to think selfishly, but it was hard. My poor mother. She had lost her mother and her husband in the same year. She was not taking this well. I had always thought of her as a strong woman, but in my arms right now, she felt drained and frail.

Uncle Albert arrived in record time. It was about 2 o'clock. His old Ford must have flown. We were ready. Mother was anxious to get there, and I think it was because she was having a very hard time believing it had really happened. She was almost in shock. We learned about that in first aid during health class at North. I had tried to make sure she was getting lots of iced tea to drink and even had her lie down in her bed for a bit before Uncle Albert arrived. She said she felt dizzy. She was okay by the time he got there, so Uncle Albert put our suitcases in the car and we prepared to drive off.

Suddenly, Mother hollered, "Wait!"

"Wait for what?" I asked.

"Mable, run back inside the house, write a note to Burnie's mother and put it in their mailbox. I don't want to bother them with this now, it will just hold us up from leaving, but I want them to know where we have gone so they don't worry."

That was just like Mother. I guess she was going to be okay after all. She was still her thoughtful, considerate self. Telling Burnie had not even occurred to me. I was too busy taking care of Mother and getting ready to leave. I ran into the house, wrote the note, and put it in their post box as instructed. I hopped back in the car and we sped away. Uncle Albert was not wasting any time.

The drive to Steamboat Rock was full of all the details of my grandmother's death. It was a horrible fire, and no one could tell how it started. It was Saturday night, so she may have been filling some of the oil lamps she used and spilled some fuel, which then got accidentally ignited. She didn't really trust electricity, so she very seldom used it, even though her house had been wired for several years. Grandma was pretty old-fashioned.

Her neighbors said that she ran out of the house, screaming in German. They came outside and saw the fire. A couple of them ran back into the house with her to help save some of her things and throw them into the front yard. After about two trips in, it became too hot and dangerous to go back, but again, Grandma yelled something in German and disappeared around the back of the house. The neighbor across the street from her speaks German, and thought she hollered something about her "wedding chairs." They tried to follow and stop her, but by the time they got around to the back, Grandma was already inside her flaming house again.

It was about that time that a few of the volunteer firemen showed up. They had buckets with them and were ready to start a line of men from the well in the side yard, but the house was almost totally in flames. The neighbors were screaming for Grandma to come out. What came flying out the back door was a wooden chair. Then a second chair came sailing out. The front of the seat of that chair was on fire, so one of the neighbors threw some dirt on it. Then Grandma came out and fell face down on the back steps. Fortunately, she was unconscious from that time on.

Her arms and legs were badly burned. Her shawl and her skirt had caught fire. Uncle Albert knew those chairs had been at the kitchen table. She may have caught her clothes on fire from the tablecloth when she grabbed the chairs. Running back and forth to the back door most likely fanned the flames on her clothes, but she paid that no mind. Her intent had been obvious; she had to save her treasured chairs. Well, they were saved, but my precious Grandma Von Dornum was gone.

Slowly, as Mother and I absorbed this horrible story from Uncle Albert, it all became more real to me. I knew it was true. No more pretending that maybe it was a bad dream or something. So, I asked about Grandma's hair. I have no idea what possessed me to do that, but it just popped into my head. My grandmother had beautiful, thick, long hair. That was pretty unusual for a woman her age. Most old women had thin graying hair, but not Grandma. She mostly wore it up, braided and twisted around the top of her head like a pile of halos. On Saturday nights, she usually took it down and washed it, so it would be nice again for church on Sunday. She never wore it down in public, just around the house on Saturday nights.

My relief was immense when Uncle Albert told me that she had her hair up in braids still and it was not down! He said he figured that if she was filling the oil lamps, she would not have taken it down yet. It would have been in the way as she went about doing that task; it was almost down to her waist.

By the time he finished telling us all the details, we were in Hubbard, with only about ten miles left to go to Eldora. I wanted to get there, but I didn't want to get there. I also didn't know what to expect, but I knew the first stop would be at the funeral parlor, because Mother insisted on that.

I said I would wait in the car, and Mother said, "Of course you will wait in the car. They are not going to let a child in there to see her before she is prepared for viewing."

That meant the embalmer had not done his job yet, but Mother didn't care. She had to see. That was it. No debating it. I was very happy to sit in the car. The only dead person I had ever seen was my father. Back then, I prayed that the rest of my family would live for a very long time; I really did not want to go to another funeral for many more years, and here my dear grandmother was gone just a few months after my dad. I started crying again.

Mother turned around from the front seat and looked sternly at me, saying, "Pull yourself together, Mable. Your grandmother was a Christian woman and is in a better place. She is having no pain. She is with your father. It is perfect in Heaven. Do not cry. Rejoice." Then she added, "And if you must cry, please don't cry in my presence. It just tempts me to cry. I have done my crying, and I'd like to keep it that way. From now on, I shall be rejoicing."

She certainly was German. Tough and resilient. Her mourning period had been longer for Dad, she spent about three days crying. I still cried sometimes when I missed him, like when I wanted to tell him something about baseball, or at graduation. I even thought about him after winning the mile swim. I didn't tell Mother that. I wondered if she thought about him now and then. I would never know, because even if I came right out and asked her, I knew for certain that she wouldn't want to talk about it.

We pulled up to the front of the funeral parlor. They had not been in business too many years. People used to have wakes in their homes. Funerals had always been held in churches. Lately, more people were using funeral parlors for wakes, but still having the funerals at the churches. Mother and Uncle Albert got out. Uncle Albert went up to the front door with Mother, and then they went inside. I could see Uncle Albert standing inside for the whole time. Mother must have gone somewhere to see Grandma, but Uncle Albert stayed by the front door.

After about fifteen minutes, Mother came back and they walked slowly back to the car. They were visiting quietly, and even paused on the sidewalk to finish their conversation before they got to the car. Mother was dabbing her eyes a little with her sleeve, but Uncle Albert did not reach out to comfort her. In fact, she even stepped away a bit.

When they got to the car, they were done talking and Mother was done dabbing. We drove silently to Steamboat Rock. The quickest way to get there was on a little road that went past, or really around, Pine Lake. There were a few picnic tables under some trees, but most of the woods around the lake were too thick for a picnic. You could barely see through them, they were so close together. That lake was good fishing. I remembered fishing there for what seemed to me to be hundreds of times with Dad before we moved to Des Moines. There were some men working on a huge stone wall by the dam going into the Iowa River.

As we drove into Steamboat Rock, we went past the little dirt road that went down to the banks of the Iowa River. There was a viewing point there where you could stand and see the actual rock that looked like a steamboat. Mostly it looked like the top of a steamboat, the tall part where the captain would stand and steer the boat. I always thought that rock was pretty nifty. When I moved to Des Moines and tried to tell my new sixth grade friends about it, they were not as impressed as I thought they should be. Then I realized they were comparing it to places like the Iowa State Fair and Riverview Park. That's when I learned what a sheltered life I had led for the first eleven years of my life. It was a good eleven years though. I grew up in Steamboat Rock, Iowa, learning to appreciate the simple things in life and knowing that I was loved.

Grandma's house had been in the northeast corner of town. We drove there first. Mother wanted to see what was left. It was the house where Klaas and Bertha lived when they sold the farm, after all the kids were grown. Uncle Albert stopped the car and we just sat there for a few minutes. None of us spoke. I wanted to ask some questions, but I knew it was not the right time. Finally, Mother got out. She stood in the front yard, and then walked to the back yard. I stayed in the car again, and so did my uncle. We both sensed that Mother wanted to be alone on this walk. As I was sitting there, I noticed that Grandma's beautiful floribunda rose bush was totally gone. It had been consumed by that house fire. The hundreds of blooms that were there this time of year, right next to the front porch, were gone forever. All that was left in that lot were the tall singed trees, most of the brick chimney, and the smoldering pile of ashes that used to be the house.

I could see the top of Mother's head over the smoky pile. She was looking at the hill of ashes, broken glass, and bricks. Then she would look down for a minute, almost like she was praying. It was sobering and educational for me. This had to be part of mourning the loss of her mother. My heart felt so heavy, but I knew I was not going to cry again right now, as I saw Mother heading back around to the front of the house.

She was walking rather briskly back to the car. She walked right up to the car door, swung it open and announced, "You know, Albert, there is one good thing I remembered. Do you recall two Christmases ago when you and Aunt Helen showed up with that cedar chest of our mother's? She wanted me to have it and you brought it down to Des Moines? You know, it has all her quilts in it. Every single one. She didn't keep even one up here for herself. They weren't in this fire and I am so glad about that. I'd rather have my mother than those quilts, but now I don't. I'm just happy to have those beautiful quilts. Those will be yours someday, Mable. You will have her quilts, like you have her name."

My name is Mable Bertha Woodrow Hall. Grandma's name was Bertha. I was proud to have her name and I would be thrilled to have her quilts . . .someday. However, Mother was right. I'd rather have my grandma.

Now we would be going over to Aunt Helen and Uncle Albert's house. Friends would be waiting there. Mother would not cry. I probably would, the minute I saw Aunt Helen. I would have to head back to the bedroom though, because Mother had made it plain that she did not want to see any more of my tears. I was a strong, resilient German-in-training, and I needed to act like one. Dealing with tragedy was relatively new to me, so I wasn't very good at it. These older people just seemed to know how to do whatever had to be done and then keep going.

Little Miss Mable Hall. I was an only child and had led a rather sheltered life. I wasn't like mother, who lost a little brother in his teens, whose deaf mother didn't speak English, or whose father died when she was a teenager. She became strong at a young age. I had experienced very few struggles in my life. Probably the hardest thing I had ever had to do, before Dad died, was to make new friends when we moved to Des Moines. Even that wasn't really difficult, with Burnie living right next door.

Aunt Helen greeted us at the door. As I peered into the kitchen, which was right off the porch through which we entered, I saw the old wood stove she still used. There were two ladies sitting at the kitchen table, which was laden with rolls, salads, cakes, and pies. I smelled the savory aroma of beef stew, or perhaps it was pot roast. It was Sunday, after all, so whatever meal was going to be served tonight was going to be substantial.

"Oh, Henrietta, this is so awful. And happening so soon after we lost John Henry. I am so sorry," Aunt Helen offered, shaking her head and hugging Mother.

"It's good to be back with family, Helen. Thank you so much for everything you are doing," murmured Mother, hugging her sister-in-law back.

Uncle Albert was bringing in our suitcases, so I asked him, "Do you need any help? Is there anything left in the car?"

He replied, "No, dear. You just stay with the ladies. I'm doing fine out there. You and your mother really didn't bring that much."

I followed Mother into the parlor. The house was just one story and much smaller than ours. They had a son and a daughter, who were grown with families of their own. This small three-bedroom house just fit their family. Most of the houses in town were very modest. Eldora had some really large and lovely homes, but not Steamboat Rock. Aunt Helen and Uncle Albert's children and grandchildren lived in town, but way over on the west side, on the banks of the Iowa River. I really shouldn't say "way over," because Steamboat Rock is only about ten blocks wide. Until Mother and Dad moved to Des Moines, the Von Dornums were a very close-knit family.

There were two more women in the parlor. Aunt Helen introduced them to me and to Mother as ladies from the church, Theresa Thierauf and her daughter, Rosemarie. They were there to pray. That was one difference between small rural towns and large cities like Des Moines. In Des Moines, people go to church to pray. In Steamboat Rock, people would know you so personally that they felt comfortable coming to your house to pray.

Rosemarie, who looked to be about thirty years old, said, "We are about to start another prayer. If you'd like, please join us."

Her mother started praying, "Dear Heavenly Father, we thank you for this family and for their faith in you. We thank you for this day of worship, and we thank you for receiving our beloved Bertha into your loving arms today. We know she is surrounded by your angels and resting with your son, Jesus. Bless this family in their grief, for they surely loved Bertha and will miss her greatly."

Rosemarie picked up where the older Mrs. Thierauf left off, adding to the prayer with, "And, dear Lord of all, please bless the firemen who tried to help Bertha, and the neighbors to ran to help her, too. Give peace to the doctor and nurse who cared for Bertha at the hospital. Let their hearts feel your love and purpose for them. They are your hands here on this earth. And most especially, Lord, we thank you for Bertha having her human fragilities healed up there with you in Heaven. We want to shout hosannas for Bertha being able to hear all your angels singing and all those heavenly harps playing. We shall sorely miss her, dear Father, and pray you will wipe away our tears."

She continued on with more supplication, "Do not let us dwell on our sorrow, gracious God, but help us rejoice with you that Bertha has come home; that she is now with her son Wiard and with her husband Klaas. Make us feel the joy and delight that you feel with her inside your golden gates. There is no greater happiness than to know Bertha is with you, her Creator and Master, as we pray these prayers. Please accept our eternal gratefulness and appreciation. In the name of your son, and our Savior, Jesus Christ, we pray. Amen."

I opened one eye and looked sideways at Mother. She was not crying, but there was a tear falling off her cheek. It fell on her bosom. She did not wipe her face, but she wiped her bosom. She looked over at me. We were seated on a settee, next to each other. She reached over and took my hand in hers.

She looked right into my eyes and said softly, "These are such good people, Mable. We are at home here. These folks loved Bertha. I do believe they are going to miss her as much as we are. This whole town loved her, you know."

I had to respond but was not sure what to say. I tried, "I'm glad we are here, too. I liked that prayer, Mother. These are really nice folks." Mother smiled a little and patted my hand, so that must have been the right thing to say. I was just not used to all this sadness. I was going to have to pass through this experience and learn from it.

This was very different than when Dad died. All his friends were there and such, but there was more banter and joking, not so much religion. I did feel more comfort now, just hearing about Grandma Von Dornum being in Heaven with Dad. Real comfort. The church women left with their husbands, who had been out in the backyard during the praying

We ate a huge dinner, which was good because Mother and I had not eaten lunch. The table was so heavy with food that I thought it would collapse. I think they were going to have to save those pies and cakes for the lunch after the funeral, because I was so full, I could not possibly have eaten a single bite of dessert. Several old friends of the family stayed for dinner, but there was plenty of food left over for meals in the next few days.

Mother and I were getting pretty tired and Aunt Helen could tell. "You two girls need to hop into bed. I put a warm bowl of water on the dresser, with a couple of towels and washcloths so you can wash up quick. We will need to go by the church early tomorrow and talk to Pastor Biddle about the funeral program and music. I sure did love what Mrs. Thierauf prayed about Bertha being able to hear in Heaven."

I never thought about that. I wondered if I would be able to hear perfectly when I got to Heaven.

"Well, goodnight and God bless," she said as she waved us to the back bedroom that had been her daughter's room. "Sleep as well as you can."

Mother and I got ready for bed pretty silently. I had a bunch of questions that I wanted to ask, but I knew this was not the right time. Mother looked very thoughtful and that was always a good sign she needed to be left alone. We were sleeping in the same double bed, so that meant being alone would be difficult unless I was extremely quiet. I saw a Bible on the nightstand, so I washed up, put on my night gown, and slipped into bed with the Bible. Mother got into bed and rolled over, turned away from me.

"Goodnight, darling daughter," she whispered. It sounded so soft and sweet. It was like she was imagining that her own mother was saying goodnight to her. Tears started to gather in my eyes, but I wiped them on the sleeve of my gown.

"Goodnight, dear Mother. I'm going to read the Bible and say my prayers, then I will turn out the lamp, okay?"

"That's fine, Mable. You are such a good girl. I am so proud of you." There was that feeling again. It was like she was saying the things she would want her Mother to say to her tonight. Sometimes she had told me that I had too big of an imagination. I don't think I was imagining this. I truly felt it in my heart. I know my mother's heart was breaking, and I could do nothing to help her; except maybe just be her darling daughter.

"I love you, Mother."

I love you, too, Mable."

I did not read or pray very long. I was exhausted.

Monday at the funeral parlor and at the church was no fun. I didn't really expect it to be, but the detais of a funeral and burial were too much. It was good that Dad had paid a funeral insurance policy for Grandma Von Dornum. All the expenses would be covered, so there would be no extra financial strain on Mother or Uncle Albert. The insurance money on the house would come later, at which time my mother and her brother would have to decide what to do with the burned down house and the lot upon which it sat.

The wake was going to be Tuesday night, and the funeral was Wednesday morning. We would be back in Des Moines late Wednesday night or Thursday. I would have so much to tell Burnie, I wouldn't even know where to start.

The rest of Monday and most of Tuesday was spent visiting with old friends of Mother's, eating cake and pie and salad. I also ate lots of sliced ham and deviled eggs. It seemed like I was gaining five pounds a day. I started to worry about fitting into my fall clothes for college. Mother seemed to be surviving on cookies and iced tea. Every time I looked, someone was bringing her a glass of tea and a plate of cookies.

The wake was held at the Eldora funeral parlor on Tuesday evening. The funeral was in the German Baptist church in Steamboat Rock on Wednesday morning. Some of the hymns were sung in German and some in English. The same thing applied to the prayers and the songs, some were in German and some in English. I had never been to a service like that. It was only the second funeral in my life, though. All I had to compare it to was Dad's funeral.

The pastor spoke in English; I appreciated that. I wanted to hear and understand what he had to say about Grandma. He spoke simply, but beautifully, about how so many people loved my grandmother. Nearly every store in Steamboat Rock and Eldora was closed for the morning. She had worked all those years at the dry goods store, so she knew everything about everyone in town, but she was kind and she never gossiped. As well as being friendly and fair, she was hard-working. Grandmother went out of her way to help people, including all sorts of neighbors when they needed assistance. She was usually the first one there when a family in Steamboat Rock had a crisis. Even though she could not hear, she made up for that with a sense of what was exactly the right thing to do in most every situation. I never knew all that about her. I just knew that I loved her. It was like a warm comforting hug from hundreds of people, to hear that the entire town loved and respected her.

The townsfolks of Steamboat Rock were so kind to us the whole time we were there. Mother wanted to stay a few more days, as she said she had to talk over insurance and other matters with Uncle Albert, the bankers, and some other people. I wanted to get home to Burnie; we only had a few more weeks to be neighbors before I left for Iowa City and he headed off to Purdue.

A few more days turned into two weeks. I began to wonder if we were ever going back to Des Moines. Oh, I enjoyed going swimming and fishing at Pine Lake and visiting with my cousins, but I was ready to go home days before Mother finally made her announcement, "Mable, I'm going to move back to Steamboat Rock."

"What?"

"I'm going to make Steamboat Rock my home again. Your father is gone, you are leaving for college, and there is really no reason for me to stay in Des Moines. It's far enough away from here that it gets hard for me to see the rest of my family. They are what I have left now, along with you, and I want to live here again."

I was stunned. Somehow, I thought to ask, "Exactly how is this going to work, Mother? When are you going to move? Where are you going to live?"

Mother had it all planned. "I will live with Uncle Albert and Aunt Helen until the new house is built. We will sell our house in Des Moines and with the insurance money from the fire, there will be enough money to build a new house where the old house was. Your Uncle Albert and his friends are putting together a big crew to help build the house, and I hope to move in by mid-December; we'll have a new home for Christmas."

"What about me and the University? How is that going to work?" I could not conceal the doubt and concern in my voice. Mother put her arm gently around me.

"It will work out fine, darling daughter," she assured me. *"We will be in the house in Des Moines until you leave for school. It will most likely be Thanksgiving before the new house is done."*

I'm sure I still looked puzzled, because she continued, "When you pack up your things for Iowa City in August, you can just pack up everything else in your room. We will move them to Steamboat Rock and everything will be in your new room when you come home for Christmas."

I just looked at her. She seemed to finally realize that this decision was a complete surprise to me. I had not heard her speak about this at all since Grandma Von Dornum's funeral.

"I suppose you are wondering when I decided all of this and why I didn't talk to you about it?" she finally asked. She answered herself. "I decided this at Grandma's funeral. All the folks in this town loved her and they kept asking about your father, and about you going off to college. They didn't want me to be all alone in that big house way down in Des Moines. I realized then that Steamboat Rock is home. I told Uncle Albert that I thought I should talk with you about it, but you know, he's a man, and he thinks those decisions are best left to the adults. He spoke with the insurance man and the bankers and all of a sudden there was a plan."

I understood. Mother had always loved her family and had not been able to see them more often than a few times a year. She truly would be alone in Des Moines. "I understand, Mother," I managed with a little smile. "I really love this little town, too. I know it's home to you."

Mother looked relieved and her shoulders relaxed with a deep sigh. "I know it will be a lot different for you. Thank you so much for understanding, Mable."

So, we left for Des Moines the next day. Mother and I had a long list of things to do to get me ready for the University of Iowa. Also, I could finally get back to Burnie, after our sudden departure. There was so much to tell him.

Into Chelan and On to the Ranch

The train between Chelan and Seattle was about the slowest train he had ever been on. The air was cool, so the fellas were glad that the doors on the rail car were closed all the way. The nights in Washington State, even in mid-June, were not like Iowa or Texas. It was more like being in the mountains of Colorado in May. Not freezing, but the kind of cool damp weather that gives you a chill.

The other men were not talking much to Harley. He wanted to ask them why but hesitated. He wasn't sure what was going on. Perhaps they were waiting for him to talk about working for his uncle. Maybe they were not sure if he would keep his word. He decided to get everything out in the open. That's what his father would have done.

"Sure been quiet, guys. What ya thinking about?" Harley opened the conversation with a simple question.

"Nothin'."

"Really, I've been thinking about why all you guys are so quiet. Nobody's talking to me. Did I do something? Are you mad at me?" Harley quizzed them further.

"I ain't mad," said Leo.

"I ain't mad," said Clarence.

"I ain't mad, either," said Ed.

"Me neither," added Adam.

"Well, then why the silent treatment?" pushed Harley.

Leo looked at him. Kept looking at him. Harley knew that Leo wanted to speak up.

Clarence noticed Leo's stare and said, "Go on, Leo, tell him what we is thinkin'."

"Well, alright. Here goes. It ain't bad, Harley, it's just tough. What if yer uncle can only hire a couple of us. Who are you going to choose? Or who is he gonna choose? We all came all this way together, and we wanna work together. But we ain't sure that's gonna get to happen, ya know what I mean?"

Okay, Harley thought. They are doubting my role here. I told them they would all get work and now they're wondering what this setup at my uncle's ranch is going to look like. They're right. We came all this way, and they all want to work!

Harley looked at them. Looked at them hard. They had believed until the barn. That dog was really the first bit of trouble they had together, and it had spooked them. These men were not confident at all. It had just been too long since they had an honest job that lasted more than a day. Each one had been beaten down so many times. Harley could not be mad at them for not talking to him. They didn't trust other people. They had not even talked much about this with each other. It was sad. Just plain sad. Well, he figured, they would be glad again when they got to Uncle Gene's. He was a generous man with a lot of friends. These four other fellas he was with had gone through some terrible times that Harley couldn't even imagine. They were unsure, anxious, and afraid to hope. He wanted to assure them of exactly what Uncle Gene would do or say, but Harley was not sure himself. He knew Gene would try to help, but there was no way Harley could give them a guarantee of a particular job at a particular ranch.

Ideally, they could all bunk and work together. Worst case, they would be working on separate ranches and only see each other once in a while, maybe once a month or less. Maybe they would never see each other again, but they would be working. They weren't family after all…what were they worried about? These guys were not as tough as they acted. They were worried about getting split up! Who would have believed that? Then Harley thought about what his father had told him about the wheat crew he worked with and how they had all gotten so close, sleeping together for all those months. And suffering the death of that guy by the twister. Men had feelings. He was going to have to stay confident that Uncle Gene could hire them all. They would find out soon enough.

He temporarily satisfied their concern with the assurance, "It's summer on a giant ranch. There will be more work than we can do." All four of them seemed to relax a bit after hearing that.

Clarence smiled a little and said, "Yeah, a big ol' ranch will have a whole lot of work to do."

Chelan came up fast. They hopped off while the train was slowing down, which was a good thing, because it never did stop. Shortly after they hopped off, it started to speed up again. Apparently this was just a mail drop and the train was gone. Got lucky on that one, Harley thought.

There sure wasn't much to see in Chelan. The railroad tracks were right behind the stores on the main street. Wagons and cars were on the street together. They still used a lot of horses here. Everyone was wearing cowboy boots. Harley had to find out where there was a telephone he could use. He had to get a message to Uncle Gene that he was almost to the ranch, and he needed to find out exactly where the ranch was.

He decided to go to the sheriff's office, or whatever law officer they had there in Chelan. He brushed his hair back and put on a clean shirt he had saved in his bindle. He looked pretty respectable, but what made him stick out from the locals was that he wasn't wearing cowboy boots. His regular leather shoes made him look like a city slicker, for sure. He got a few stares and a few smiles. Harley had a friendly face so he felt confident he would be able to find someone to help him. He left the other men out on the edge of the downtown buildings, near the livery stable and blacksmith. This was definitely not Des Moines. Not a lot of livery stables left there.

He did not see a sheriff's office so he decided to ask. He stuck his head into a barber shop. There were a couple of men in there, one in the barber chair and one waiting.

"I need to get a message to my uncle, Gene Van Voorhis, who lives about thirty miles east of here on a ranch. Any idea about how I could do it?" He decided honesty was the best policy, so he added, "I've ridden the trains all the way from Des Moines, Iowa to get here and I need to let him know I made it. I got some friends with me and we're gonna work on his ranch this summer. You ever heard of him?"

They started at him for a minute. Then they looked at each other. The barber said, "When's the last time you had a haircut, boy? Looks like it's been a month full of Sundays!" All three men laughed.

"Been a while, that's for sure. Probably since before I graduated from high school about six weeks ago. Been spending my money on food, not looking pretty."

"Don't worry, you ain't pretty, trust me, not pretty at all," said the barber. The men laughed again.

"My uncle?" Harley asked again.

"Oh yeah, I know him. Matter of fact, he was just in town a couple of days ago, but I'm sure he's back at his place by now. You should ask at the livery stable, boy. I think he bought some horses from Jack, the blacksmith. Maybe you could deliver them for Jack. That would give you a ride to the ranch. Jack's been puttin' new shoes on all of them before he takes 'em out there."

"Thanks, mister…maybe I'll come back and get a haircut in a while…like a month or something…I need to earn some money first. I'm gonna go see Jack now." He could hear the men laughing again as he dashed out the shop, nearly knocking over a chair just outside the door

Harley hurried back to the livery stable and right out in front was a burly man in in big black apron. It had to be Jack. Harley ran right up to him and introduced himself with, "Hi, I'm Harley Seibert, from Des Moines, Iowa. My uncle's Gene Van Voorhis. The barber just told me you sold him a horse or two last week. Are they still here? Can I take 'em to him?"

"Whoa, young fella!" The blacksmith had a blacksmith voice. It absolutely boomed and bounced off the walls of the surrounding buildings. It sounded like he was hollering down a big canyon.

"How do I know yer a tellin' the truth? You could just be a slick young horse thief from Sacramento for all I know!"

"Well, I am telling the truth. I've been trying to figure out how to get a hold of Uncle Gene to let him know I'm this close. I know he has a telephone, but I don't know his number and I don't know where there is a telephone in this town. Do you? I really want to call him 'cause he invited me. I just graduated from high school and I gotta earn some college money." Harley let that slip out by mistake. His hand flew over his mouth before he said anything else stupid.

"Slow down here, fella. That's too much to even remember. I can help ya find a telephone. Go straight across the square over there to the Blue Mountain Hotel. They got one. Tell them Jack wants you to call yer uncle. Then tell Gene to give me a call back at home tonight and if you is tellin' the truth, I'd be much obliged if you could take the horses out to him. Save me a trip. I'd even pay you a little something for saving me a couple of days and having to pay someone to watch the livery here."

Harley hollered "okay" over his shoulder as he ran across the square to the hotel. He had to slow down and catch his breath before he got inside though, because he could tell from the lace curtains in the front windows that is was a pretty fancy place for a town like this and he could not run in there like a crazy fool. He smoothed down his hair and tucked in his shirt a little tighter. He wiped the sweat off his face with his sleeve and put on a pleasant smile. He opened the door gently and stepped into a large lobby with a sweeping staircase off to the left. The front desk was on the right and there was a fortyish man behind it, writing in a ledger book like his mother used to keep for the lawyer in Valley Junction.

"Hello, sir. Jack from the livery sent me over just now to use your telephone. I am Gene Van Voorhis's nephew, and I have come to visit him. I need to let him know I am almost there." Harley said in his most mannerly tone.

"Well, come on in. I can arrange that. Did you take the train into town? I thought the passenger train came yesterday."

"Oh," Harley covered for himself, "I have been here a while now. I do need to telephone him, though."

"Certainly, I'm sorry. Come back to the office here." The man gestured Harley behind the desk and he followed the man into a small office.

"I don't know his number," Harley repeated himself.

"That's alright...Irene is our operator, and she will plug into your uncle's phone line for you. You just tell her his name and she will ring him for you. You have used a telephone before, correct?

"Oh yessir. I have. We have an operator, too. Marlys, back in Iowa. But I usually tell her the number."

"That's not necessary here, young man, Irene knows everyone's number. There aren't that many of us with phones."

Harley picked up the phone receiver and clicked it twice to signal the operator, just like at home. The clerk nodded his approval. A young woman answered and said "Number, please?" just like Marlys did at home.

"I don't know his number, but I need to speak to Gene Van Voorhis, please," Harley informed her.

"Certainly, one moment please sir." cooed the operator. She sounded pretty to Harley, but he did not know what made him think about that…about what she looked like. He guessed he had been hanging out with just fellas for too long.

Harley heard what he realized was his uncle's ring. It was 'three longs'. That's three long rings. His ring at home was 'one long, two shorts'. He waited and waited. It rang about ten times. Then eleven, then twelve.

"Do you want me to keep ringing for Gene?" asked Irene.

"Sure, if you have time," Harley replied.

"Sometimes it takes a long time for him to answer. He doesn't just sit around the house. He had a ringer installed outside on the back of his barn, so he could hear the phone, but then it takes him a few minutes to get into the house," she explained. "Sometimes, I have had to let it ring thirty times. Is that alright?"

"I don't want to bother him, but I really need to talk with him. So I guess you should just keep ringing."

Just then, he heard Uncle Gene's voice on the other end of the line. "Hello there," he said. "Who is this?"

"It's Harley, Uncle Gene, I made it! I made it!"

"Well, hooray for you, son, where are you?"

"I'm at the Blue Mountain Hotel in Chelan and using their telephone."

"How was your trip? Are you alright? Are you hungry? Shall I come and get you tomorrow?" Uncle Gene fired off questions like bullets.

"Well, that's why I am calling. I spoke with Jack at the livery stable. He wonders if I could deliver your new horses to you. He has new shoes on all of them. Do you want me to bring them tomorrow?"

"By yourself? You think you can do that by yourself? That's a big job, Harley. I know you are a farm boy, but those are four good-sized horses I bought."

"I met some fellas on the train, Uncle Gene. They can help me. They are good guys. We have been together on the rails since Omaha. I don't think I could have made it out here without them. They are hoping they can work for you too, or maybe for another ranch around here. Huh?"

"Let's get the horses here first, Harley. There is plenty of work around here this time of year. We can find work for them. How many?"

"Four other guys besides me, Uncle Gene. Two young guys like me and two are a bit older. They are all smart men, I think."

Gene was anxious to get his horses, Harley figured, because he had work for them to do. His uncle was done with the chit-chat. "Okay, Harley. Tell Jack I will telephone him tonight at home, and you and your crew can head out here with the horses tomorrow. There are five of you and only four horses, so someone is going to have to double up."

"It will work out fine. One young guy is little and he can double up with me. None of us are fat, after hoboing all the way out here."

"Well, I'm glad you are safe and I will see you in a couple of days. Tell Jack I will telephone him tonight about seven o'clock, okay?"

"Yessir, I'll tell him. Thank you! See you soon."

"Be careful. Watch for bears and snakes. Make sure you tie them horses up good at night; you will need to camp one night. Go to the dry goods store and tell the owner, Mike, that Gene Van Voorhis wants your supplies on the tab I have there. He can confirm it with Jack if he wants to. Get yourselves a decent meal or two so you are all ready to go to work when you get here, understand?"

"Yessir. I'll take care of everything! Thank you."

"Goodbye now, Harley."

"Goodbye, Uncle Gene. Thank you very much. See you soon!"

A quick click from his uncle hanging up was what Harley heard. His mother had always said Uncle Gene was a smart man and a good rancher, but he did not like to waste time on small talk. Harley had just discovered that was true. He decided it was probably a good idea to save all the hobo tales he had for when he saw his uncle in person, anyway. He thanked the hotel man and headed back to the livery stable.

The fellas were happy to hear they got to get some food from the store, but Harley had to warn them not to take advantage of his uncle's generosity. That would not be a good foot to jump off on. They arranged with Jack to sleep inside the livery stable in the tack room. That's where extra saddles, salves, and such were kept. It sure smelled fresh in there, a little bit like horse medicine, but clean. Not like horse manure.

Fortunately, all the fellas had ridden horses before. Ed said it had been about fifteen years; maybe even a little longer for Adam, but they did not seem worried. All five men went to the store before it closed for the night, so they could get a good start in the morning. They selected jerky, pickles, and bread, along with apples, and beans, of course. He also thought he'd better get a length of rope in case they had to tie the horses together at night. Harley had no idea how or even if they would be able to make a meal out of what they charged on Gene's account, but they watched what they spent while they also managed to get a favorite thing for each man. They all felt like rewarding themselves for such a successful rail ride to the west coast. All of them agreed it was a good thing they did not try to go through California. Who knows what disaster might have befallen them there?

They ate a cold dinner, not wanting to start a cooking fire in or even near the livery stable. It was the best they could do, and everyone was chatting about what warm home-cooked food they were going to look forward to eating when they had their jobs set up. No one seemed to care anymore if it was with Uncle Gene or not. When Harley told them that he was sure there was plenty of work on the ranches, the former hobos practically cheered.

They bedded down in the tack room for the night and were soon all sleeping. It was an uneventful night, which gave no indication of the trauma to be suffered soon enough.

Big Moves for Mable and Henrietta

We heard her calling, "Welcome home, Henrietta. Welcome home, Mable." Burnie's mother was walking across the front yard as Uncle Albert pulled the car up to the curb in front of our house. Our lawn had been freshly mowed, probably by Burnie. We had been gone nearly three weeks! Tomorrow was August twentieth and I had to be in Iowa City on the twenty-sixth. Burnie's dad was going to drop me off in Iowa City and then drive Burnie on to Purdue. I had to talk to Burnie!

"Is Burnie home, Mrs. Orwig?" I asked, apparently in an overly anxious manner, because she looked startled.

"He sure is, honey. He's cleaning the lawn mower blades out back by the shed. Why don't you just go on back there and see him? I will help your mother unpack the car." With that, she turned to help Mother out of the car and then gave her a long hug.

I walked slowly toward the back of their house. I didn't race back there, even though that's what I felt like doing. It's hard to explain, but even though I had so much I wanted to tell Burnie and so many things I wanted to talk about with him, I had not actually spent any time at all thinking about exactly what I was going to say.

I had seen him nearly every day of my life since we moved to Des Moines; we had never been apart for this long. There was never anything more than being friends between us. I just missed my best friend.

So, as I rounded the corner, there was Burnie. He had already cleaned the mower blades and was sharpening them with a big metal file. Both my father and his father insisted that the blades be sharpened right after every mowing. I could almost hear my father saying, "Burnie, it will make the job easier for the next person who uses that mower, and since it will probably be you, make 'em sharp!"

Burnie stood up and wiped his hands on the kerchief he pulled from his back pocket. "Come here, kid. Get a hug. You've been through a lot, I'm sure." Then he added, as he hugged me, "I'm so sorry about your grandmother. She was a very special person."

Of course, I started to cry, and Burnie tried to hand me his sweaty grass-stained kerchief. "Thanks, Burnie, but you can keep that dirty green thing. I have my clean handkerchief right here in my pocket."

"Can I get you some iced tea, Mable?"

We had a lot to talk about, so I knew I would need something to drink. I headed for the picnic table under the elm tree, saying, "Tea would be much appreciated, Burnie. Thank you."

What I really would have appreciated is some idea of where to start. How was I going to tell Burnie we were leaving Des Moines? I also wanted to tell him I was starting to get worried about going to college all alone, but I hadn't even figured out how to tell Mother. How would I make friends? There were going to be mobs of kids and I had a horribly difficult time hearing in crowds. I often felt left out and it wasn't easy or fun to always be asking people to repeat themselves. I wasn't worried about hearing in classes; all I had to do was sit in the front, but what about at parties, and in the dorm, and in the dining hall? Without my best friend, Burnie, who regularly helped me out in situations like that, how would I fit in?

Burnie came leaping off the back porch with two glasses of tea in his hands. They sloshed around but had a surprisingly reasonable amount of tea left in them as he set them down on the table.

"So, fill me in, kiddo. Tell me about the past three weeks. How is your mother doing? How are you doing? Is there anything I can help you with? We are both going to be getting out of this town pretty soon!"

I let out a heavy sigh, but I gave him a little smile with it so he wouldn't worry. "I really don't know where to start, Burnie. I really don't. But, I'm going to try."

So, I told him pretty much everything. Beginning, of course, when we got the phone call from Uncle Albert about Grandma Von Dornum's house fire. I gave the details of the trip up to Eldora, how the fire took Grandma's life, how she didn't suffer, and about her funeral service. I could tell Burnie understood when I told him how important she was to everyone in Steamboat Rock and Eldora, and how I had never really known about that part of her life.

I explained how Mother wanted to stay in Steamboat Rock all those extra days to take care of all the house and property details, and then I ran out of things to tell him. Still, I had not mentioned mother's decision to move there permanently. So, I dove into the truth about that because I could see in his expression that he knew there was more I wasn't telling him.

He was definitely surprised. "Are you saying your mother is going to sell your house and actually live in Steamboat Rock from now on? Are you going with her?"

"I'm going to Iowa City, remember? Going to college in six days...your Dad is still driving us, right?"

"Yes, but how did she decide to do that? That is one giant decision to make." Burnie looked right at me, like it was my fault.

So I told him how Uncle Albert, along with the insurance man, the banker, and the realtor, had persuaded Mother that it was the best thing to do and how she had not even let me know she was thinking about it before she made up her mind.

"She's not a modern woman like I am, Burnie. Women have had the vote for three presidential elections now, and she still hasn't voted! She just listened to Uncle Albert and those men. Mother's sure she will be happier living closer to the rest of her family and her old friends. I'm not going to be there most of the time, anyway. There is no changing her mind now; she's looking forward to it."

Burnie was really quiet for what felt like a long time. Then he said, "I guess your mother knows what she wants. Her brother wouldn't have her do anything that would be bad for her. How do you think it will work out?"

"Well, it will probably be very nice for Mother, but not for me. I always thought you and I could see each other during school breaks, you know, being right next door here. That's going to be different now. Much harder, don't you think?"

Burnie looked shocked and admitted, "Gee, I didn't think about that yet. That's not good. I don't want to lose touch with you, Mable. Friends like we are, well, they just don't split up because someone moves. We'll find a way. We will. I will make sure of that! And hey, I haven't even had a chance to catch you up on baseball! I'll betcha haven't had time to keep up on your Cubs, have you?"

Burnie was such a good fella; he was trying to make me feel a little better and knew I had to stop thinking about Mother moving. I had to start doing something about packing everything. Burnie and I both had a lot of suitcase packing and boxing up to do. I barely saw him for the next three days. Mother gave me a lot of time by myself in my room to think and pack, but a few times she needed my help with some big jobs. She was, after all, packing up the whole rest of the house!

All of my belongings that I was taking to Iowa City fit into one large trunk and one small trunk. I took my fall and winter clothes, the quilt and bathrobe Grandma Von Dornum gave me for graduation, and a couple of my swimming trophies. I also packed my good old Red Cross First Aid book. It had great information, as well as detailed illustrations that I thought might be helpful in my anatomy class. Even though I was majoring in journalism, my plan was to take a lot of physical education classes, too.

Two days before we were scheduled to leave, Burnie came over after supper. We shot some baskets and caught up on each other's packing progress, and finally, we had some time to catch up on baseball! My Cubs were leading their league and his Yankees were leading their league! They might meet in the World Series! We both had lots of players on our teams to brag about. Burnie mentioned that he wished my father was there to talk with us and he told me that Dad would really be laughing out loud at our crazy competition. I thanked him for that. It was nice to know Burnie still thought about my father, too.

Then Burnie said that Ted Ashby had called him and asked about me. He wanted to make sure he had my address at school and said that he would be following my college swimming career. Burnie told me that I needed to call Mr. Ashby and give him my school address and my Steamboat Rock address. I told Burnie I had no idea at all what the address in Steamboat Rock was, but he said I could get it from my mother. He was pretty sure the new house built there would have the same house number as the one that burned. That made sense to me.

When I called him, Mr. Ashby wanted to talk a long time. He gave his condolences for our loss of Grandma, which I felt was very thoughtful of him. He had some helpful advice for me concerning journalism classes and said if I could make arrangements for a place to live in Des Moines, I could work at the Tribune with him during my summers. I liked that plan! Maybe I could stay with Burnie's folks, visit Mother now and then in Steamboat Rock, and get real journalism experience, not just on the college newspaper.

The night before we were leaving on our college adventures, Burnie's parents took us all out to a picture show and dinner. We saw Huckleberry Finn, starring Jackie Coogan, at the Des Moines Theater. Then we ate dinner at The Chickadee over on 6th Avenue. It was a wonderful evening and of course Burnie and I received all of the very important advice our parents had to give us before we flew the coop. We pretended we were actually listening, even though we weren't. After all, it was a rehash of the same things they had been telling us all through high school. I really wished my dad had been there with us, because he always had the best advice for me. Missing him so much, I decided that night to make him very proud of me at the University of Iowa.

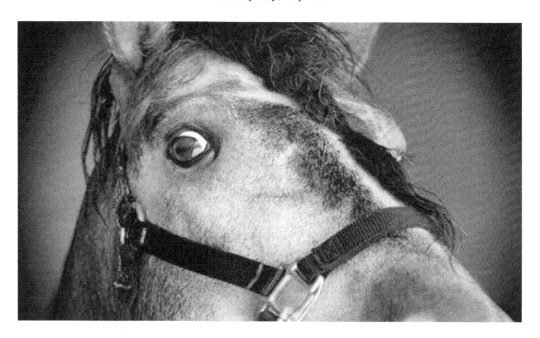

A Spooked Horse

With their stomachs full of biscuits from the store and a few cups of coffee from Jack's pot, the men were ready to saddle up and go. Jack drew them a crude map and also wrote out a page of clear instructions on how to get to Gene's ranch. He thanked them again for delivering the horses and gave each of them a dollar. Each man quickly tucked the money in their bindle. They agreed to follow Harley, since he had the map, of course. Adam and Ed rode behind Harley, each on their own horse. Leo was bringing up the rear and Clarence was on the back of Harley's saddle, hands grasping the rear of the seat. He said he didn't feel quite right putting his arms around Harley's waist, but Harley knew his arms would get tired or he would have a hard time hanging on going up or down steeper inclines they might come to. He told Clarence it would be okay…nothing personal, they were just riding a horse together.

In his mind, Harley wondered what kind of upbringing Clarence had that made him so skittish about touching other people. Probably from his dad beating him. Harley felt bad but did not want Clarence falling off the horse. He told him to hang on tight and grab him fast if he needed to. Harley was a good rider, but he could not hang on to Clarence. Harley had to hang onto the reins and Clarence was going to have to hang onto Harley.

So off they went, heading east out of town. It was about nine o'clock in the morning and there were clear roads out to the ranch. There might be a few cars going past them, but they just needed to stay along the edge of the roads and even move a little farther away if a wagon or automobile was coming past. Jack had drawn a shortcut that took them away from the road and along a creek for a while, if they wanted to water the horses or when they camped that evening. As they rode out of Chelan, it was a bright sunny day with fluffy white clouds already in the sky. Nice riding weather, for sure.

The men did not have much to say to each other. Most likely, they were all having their individual thoughts about their near future. They were no longer going to be hobos. Ranch work could be a twelve-month job. Animals, buildings, and equipment had to be taken care of year-round. These did not have to be just seasonal jobs. Of course, for Harley it would only be for the summer and a little bit into the fall. He was determined to start college at the University of Iowa in January at the latest, but the other men still did not know that. Harley hoped when they did eventually find out that they would understand. He also hoped and imagined that they would keep working in Washington State. It was quite a scenic place, he noticed, as they rode into some small hills. Growing up on the farm, Harley learned to love all the seasons; the dry, the wet, the snow, the baking heat. In this moment, Harley was truly enjoying his thoughts and the view on this trip.

"Hey, Clarence, check with the fellas how they are doing back there, would you please?" asked Harley. "Just give a little turnabout and holler at them."

Clarence did that. He looked over his shoulder and gave Leo a holler. He was on the last horse, but Clarence used a pretty darned big voice to holler back about fifty yards. Harley was afraid he was going to scare the horses with the really loud shout. "Tone it down, you'll spook the horses. They aren't that used to us. I don't want anyone falling off a buckin' horse. These are huge critters," Harley warned.

Clarence toned it down and Harley received a good report on everyone. The saddles were doing well and staying on tight. Ed and Adam, in the middle, were doing a fabulous job. Harley's horse was the largest one and he was under perfect control.

They just kept moving along. It was a good clip, but not pushing the horses. These horses had to look good when they got to the ranch. Harley wanted Uncle Gene to see he had taken good care of his valuable property and that the other fellas were responsible types who could be trusted. Hobos don't have a very good reputation lgg and Harley wanted his rail-riding friends to make a good first impression. He kind of felt responsible for helping them get off the rails. It was a good feeling. His mother and father would be proud of him.

They got to the creek that Jack put on the map, indicating a good stop for lunch and a break for the horses. The water there was clean; Jack had assured them that it was something both the men and the horses could drink. And drink they did. The men drank upstream and the horses drank downstream. The horses chewed on the grass along the banks and the men settled under a tree with their jerky and apples. Leo joked that they should have brought some apples for the horses; Ed and Adam agreed, but no one made a move to share their juicy fruits with the animals. After they got to the core, however, the men all got up as if they had the same idea at the same time and took an apple core over to their horse. Harley and Clarence's horse, of course, was the lucky one and got two apple cores. He was carrying twice the load, after all.

They spent about an hour by the creek and then remounted the horses and lined up again, in the same positions as the first part of the ride. Harley had forgotten about Jack's warning to watch out for bears and snakes. Mostly what they saw along the way were eagles, hawks, and rabbits; nothing much to frighten a horse. They were in wide open space and Harley didn't figure a bear would wander out there. And snakes like it warm, so they would probably stay near the warmer rocks, not along the side of the road in the cool foot-high grass where the men and their horses were riding. The afternoon passed with them telling a few tales about riding horses when they were younger and talking about the clouds and the smell of the leather saddles underneath them. Harley assured the others that these horses were going to a good owner. They were going to have great stables, lots of straw to sleep in, and lots of oats to eat.

It was about four hours more until they got to the next milestone on Jack's map, where the one road split off into two roads. They started to follow the road that went a little bit north, to the left. After a while, they began to discuss where to stop and camp for the night. The old guys wanted a place with a lot of trees. Leo and Clarence wanted some wide-open spaces, so they could see the stars. The four finally asked Harley to choose; after all, he was still their unofficial leader.

"Well, I prefer the open space. Better for a fire and gives the horses more grass to eat. Not too many trees near here now," Harley reasoned. "There's another creek up ahead on the map and I don't figure it's too far. Let's hustle these horses a bit and get there before dark."

After ten minutes of a faster trot, the men came upon the creek and found a small cluster of bank trees where they could tie up the horses. They scrounged for some wood branches and bigger wood to put a fire to. With a fire growing in warmth as the sun was going down, they sat down to heat their beans and rest their achy bones from a day of riding. There were backside complaints from all five of the men, because none of them had ridden a horse for a whole day in many years. Ed and Leo had the least experience on the saddle and were totally unprepared for how sore they were.

"How many more days are we doin' this, Harley?" asked Leo.

"One more day, buddy. We are half way there, I promise,"

"It may take me a day or so to recover from this," Leo warned.

"It's alright. Uncle Gene and I will have some time to visit. I am pretty sure he isn't going to shove us out the door into the barn in the first twenty-four hours. He knows I have been traveling a while. I'll talk to him, don't worry. We'll have time to rest up and get ready to earn our keep," Harley reassured all of them. "Remember, though, we came to work and earn us all some real money. There are men all over this country who would give their eye teeth for a real paying job like this. I hope you all remember how to work."

The men warmed up and ate most of the rest of the food from the store; then they laid out their bindles for one last night as bums.

Looking up at the brilliant stars in the night sky was a refreshing change from sleeping in a boxcar. The fresh air, with the scent of the grass and the rushing of the creek, was intoxicating. Even when the night breeze brought a whiff of the horses into Harley's nostril, he felt relaxed and even somewhat peaceful for the first time since he left home. He was one day away from being with family again. He was one day away from starting to work on his dream of college. He made a mental note to himself; he had to make sure Uncle Gene did not reveal his higher learning ambitions to his rail riding friends. Harley had become very fond of all these bums, even the two crusty old men. Adam and Ed traveled with the three younger men, but really stayed by themselves most of the time. The five of them were together, but something about the older men made them tougher to get to know.

His four hobo friends slumbered on their bindles, but Harley was having a hard time sleeping. It was not the snoring of Adam, and it was not the increasing buzz of the early summer insects in the grass. It was thoughts of his mother and father. He wondered about his father's health. He knew his friend Michael was working hard and probably having a good time playing at being a farmer…or else he was finding out how hard life on the farm really was. He could not wait to talk to his mother and get all the news. Finally running out of thoughts and plans, Harley closed his eyes and was asleep like the others.

The breakfast fire sent little tendrils of smoke upward. The men used their last bit of coffee and then tended the horses, making sure they had water. Clarence was thinking that maybe he could ride the fourth horse today and that Leo could hitch on behind Harley. Leo was not hearing any of that.

"That will be too much weight on that horse, Clarence. You are the little guy. I'm sorry, but you are gonna be hitchin' behind Harley again. It ain't right to ride that heavy on another man's horse. Just ain't right. I'm keepin' my horse to myself." Clarence had to concede that it was the right thing to do.

The men headed east into the rising sun. At the end of the day they would be home. Not their real home, of course, but to a place with a roof, running water, and plenty to eat. A place where they could get their humanity restored by proving their worth through an honest day's work. This was going to be a home with strangers, but kindly strangers who would treat them with respect. They would hopefully be working for Harley's uncle and Harley was a good fella.

The horses seemed happy to be moving again. Perhaps they could sense the excitement and anticipation from Harley and the others. The three younger men were a bit more pleased to be settled soon. The two older men wore the skepticism of many disappointments, and were obviously reserving their contentment for later when their situation could be proven. Regardless, the horses had their spirits up and so did most of the men. Clarence had resigned himself to being the smallest one and the tag-a-long rider behind Harley. He had gotten used to holding onto Harley's waist and Harley had adjusted also. Sometimes, just to change position, Clarence held onto the back of Harley's belt, but not so tight as to pull on it. He mostly reserved hugging Harley tight when they were headed up or down a steeper hill. They had a nice road to ride on, but it rolled with the terrain of west central Washington. It was warming up as they rode and the sky got brighter. There was not a single cloud or wisp of a cloud anywhere.

"You old guys ain't got much to say, huh?" Leo hollered to Ed and Adam, from the back of the pack.

"No, we ain't," returned Ed.

Old was relative here. Harley, Clarence, and Leo were all under twenty-five. Ed and Adam were probably in their forties but looked so much older. Their longer lives had been harder lives, obviously, and they wore it on their faces. The wrinkles of frustration and failure ran deep into their cheeks and foreheads. It was the times, mostly, but probably some of it was just bad circumstances. They did not come from the rich side of any town.

Leo could tell from that reply, and from them not turning their heads even a tiny bit to acknowledge his speaking to them, that they meant it. Clarence and Harley were riding where Leo felt was too far in front of the rest of them and he did not feel like yelling up there at them.

"Could you move along a bit faster and keep up with Harley?" Leo urged Ed and Adam.

There was no reply.

"We are falling behind. Let's scoot along quick for a minute and get up ahead with them, huh?" Leo tried again.

Still no reply, but he did detect a slight increase in speed. He settled for what he could get at that point. He had committed at the beginning of this journey, to Harley, that he would bring up the rear to be sure Adam and Ed were okay. Both of them had admitted to not having much riding experience. The blacksmith had called them "greenhorns" which provided the three younger men with quite a laugh. It brought only deeper scowling wrinkles to the old guys' faces. From the looks of it, it appeared to Leo that they might catch up with Harley and Clarence in about ten minutes. It was gonna be a slow haul, even after they picked up the pace a bit.

Leo hummed as he rode. Harley and Clarence were silent, as were the older men. Those men in the middle could see where the lead horse was, but they were not within shouting distance. It was not noon yet but getting close. The sun was high overhead and starting to bring the sweat out on the men and their horses. Leo wanted to know if Harley knew how much farther they had to go but guessed he would have to wait until they paused for their noon lunch break. Still, he really wanted to know.

Finally, Leo decided not to wait. He kneed his horse to get him to pick up the pace, and told the old men as he rode past, "I'm gonna go see how much longer we got 'til we stop. I'll either come back or wait for you up there. You gonna be alright back here?"

"We ain't babies," grumped Adam. "G'wan ahead. We'll be along right behind you."

So, Leo took off at a good trot and expected to catch up quickly with Harley and Clarence. He was nearly caught up with them. Clarence must have heard him coming and turned around to wave at him.

"Whatcha doin', Leo? Leavin' them old slow pokes behind?" Clarence hollered back at him.

"I got a question," Leo replied. He kept gaining on them. "I'll ask ya when I get up there, just hang…" Leo didn't have time to finish the sentence.

Suddenly, Harley's horse reared back with a frightening, squealing noise, twisting sideways and Clarence went flying into the air. He had let go to call back to Leo and had no way to guard himself against falling off the crazed horse.

"It's a damn snake," screamed Harley, who was holding ferociously onto the reins of the bug-eyed horse. The poor horse was frightened out of its wits by a Western rattler, lying low under the edge of a rock along that road.

"We riled up a rattler by ridin' too close to him. Are you okay, Clarence?" called out Harley.

Harley and Leo looked around. Clarence was lying in the scrubby grass along the side of the road, right where he landed after his sudden ejection from the back of the horse. He was not moving.

"Get up, fella, are you okay?" called out Leo this time. Still no answer and still no movement.

Harley got there first, but his horse was still jumpy and Harley didn't want to get off him, fearing the horse would pull the reins out of his grip and run away, so he tightened the reins and tried to talk reassuringly to the horse. This was difficult as the alarm for Clarence rose in him.

Then Leo arrived and was able to get off his horse. The offended snake was long gone, so he ran quickly to his friend's side. Leaning over Clarence, Leo shook his shoulder. Clarence's head moved in an odd way. Leo saw blood, and then felt Clarence's chest. He was not breathing, He looked for any sign of life, but found none.

"Harley, Clarence is dead! I think he done broke his neck in that fall! He's done kilt! Damn that snake!"

"What, what? Are you sure? Is he breathing?" Harley demanded.

"He ain't movin', he ain't breathin'. He's dead. Gone, dead, gone…gone…" Leo sounded stunned and panicked.

Harley finally got the spooked horse under control and rode closer. The horse still wanted to walk a little bit sideways, but Harley got close enough so he could see Clarence clearly.

"Come here and hold my horse, Leo. Come here and hold this damn horse," Harley said.

Leo came obediently and silently but said, "He's really dead, Harley," as he took the reins. He walked away with both his horse and Harley's, back towards where Adam and Ed were riding up to. He left Harley there with Clarence's body and proceeded to wave to the old men to hurry up. They did hurry up a little and got there in just a minute or two.

"A damn snake spooked Harley's horse. Stupid animal reared way back and Clarence went flyin' off! Broke his damn neck and is kilt. Clarence is dead, right here."

"What the hell!" said Ed

"Dead, right here?" asked Adam.

"Yep. Dead. What is we supposed to do now?" fussed Leo. "What are we gonna do now? Harley," he hollered, "what are we going to do now?"

Harley walked away from Clarence and approached the three other men.

"We are going to put him on the back of my horse again and take him to my uncle's farm. We sure aren't going to leave Clarence here. We don't have anything to dig a grave with, we only have about four hours riding time left, and we have to tell the sheriff in Chelan what happened. Maybe they can let his family know somehow."

"Geez, Harley, that's a lot of good thinkin' all at once," said Leo admirably.

"That is all just common sense, Leo," said Harley. "My mother says I have a lot of it. Got it from my father, I guess. This actually reminds me of a story my father told me about when he was working in the wheat harvest. A man died during a tornado, real sudden like this, and everyone was shocked. We didn't even have any time to pray over Clarence like my father did over that guy, though. I think we should say a prayer before we move him. He went so suddenly."

"We ain't doin' no prayin'," said Ed and Adam, at exactly the same time.

Leo and Harley looked at them.

"That was just plain strange," said Leo. "Sayin' the same dang thing at the same time. I don't pray neither, but it sounds like Harley prays, so let's have him say one and then get out of here with Clarence."

The three others silently followed behind Harley as he walked back over to Clarence's crumpled body.

"I'm just going to pray the Lord's Prayer," said Harley, which he proceeded to do.

"Our Father in Heaven, hallowed be thy name. Thy kingdom come, thy will be done on earth, as it is in Heaven. Give us this day our daily bread and forgive us our trespasses as we forgive those who trespass against us. Lead us not into temptation but deliver us from evil, for thine is the kingdom and the power and the glory forever and ever, Amen" ...and then he continued, "Bless Clarence as he comes up there to Heaven so suddenly, Lord. We are so sorry he left us like this. He was a good man."

For a few moments, no one moved. The rest of the men appeared to be waiting for Harley to be done. When he realized this, he said "Amen."

"How we gonna do this?" asked Leo. "I ain't never touched a dead body before."

"He's barely dead, Leo. Don't be a damn baby," commanded Adam. "This is Clarence, your friend. Pick up his feet and help us get him on the back of the damn horse."

Leo went right to Clarence's feet as directed, and helped Adam and Ed reverently hoist his body onto the horse, behind Harley's saddle.

"I'm going to have to tie him to the saddle so he doesn't slide off. You have some of that rope we bought, Ed?" asked Harley.

"I'll get it, hold on," Ed replied as he went back to their horses.

It seemed peculiar how calm all the horses were now. They had gathered together, making no attempt to run off or even wander away. Harley realized it could be his imagination, but he thought the horses looked a bit sad now. Not as happy as when they had started their sunny journey yesterday. Seemed natural, Harley supposed, since the fellas all seemed more solemn, too. Clarence was dead. Harley's mind flashed forward to having to explain this to Uncle Gene. He knew Uncle Gene would believe him, but it was going to be one heck of a thing to explain. He knew they would not get in trouble, but this was not how he wanted to start his visit to his uncle's ranch. Burying a dead hobo. But, Clarence was more than a hobo. Harley felt even more sad right after he thought that. Clarence had a family who loved him; he was young and full of adventure. His getting killed was just wrong, but it happened. Harley felt a twinge of guilt for not being able to control his horse, but he remembered how fiercely he had to hold on to that scared-witless horse and he had the reins to cling to. Clarence had no chance of staying on the horse, and Harley knew it wasn't his fault, but still, it was awful.

Harley tied him securely onto the back of the saddle, face down, and covered him with Clarence's own bindle. It was going to be a long four hours or so to the ranch.

"We should ride a little farther and then get a rest and something to eat. Horses can get some water, to," Harley suggested.

"Sounds good to me," answered Leo. "Sure enough, we do not want to eat around here. I can't believe what just happened, Harley. I can't believe it. So, now we're gonna move on, just go…like nothin' happened?"

Harley, thinking things had settled down, replied tersely, "We have to get to the ranch today, Leo. We have to bury Clarence. What do you want us to do? Build a church right here, invite a bunch of his family, and have a funeral?" Harley was perturbed with Leo. Leo had not wanted to touch the body but doing so had made this more real to him. Harley simply did not have the time or the patience to deal with Leo's reaction.

"I guess we have to go on, but this is just so bad. Clarence is dead. What else can we do?" asked Leo.

"We can try to notify his family after we get to the ranch. We know he was from outside Racine in Wisconsin. Uncle Gene can have the sheriff in Chelan contact their sheriff. I am not sure, but we have to stay practical, because there is nothing we can do to change this accident. That's what it was, Leo, an accident. He wasn't murdered or such. No gunfight or knifing, just a bad fall. A bad fall. At least he died quickly," Harley reasoned.

"Can we get movin?" Adam asked. "Can we just get goin' to this ranch and sleep in a bed tonight?"

"I agree. How 'bout you Leo, you ready to go now?" said Harley.

"You're right, we gotta move on. We really can't do anything to help Clarence now, except find him a good place to be buried," sighed Leo. "Let's just go."

They rode another forty-five minutes and finally came to a small creek. It was the size that probably dried up in the summer, but there was still enough water for the men and their horses. The last of the jerky was divided among them and the last can of beans was eaten. All of them were hoping, or rather counting on, eating dinner at a real table tonight. It did not matter if it was in Uncle Gene's dining room or in the bunkhouse, they just wanted a chair to sit in and a table to eat off of. It didn't seem real yet, but when Harley imagined his rear end actually sitting in a real chair, he knew he would have made it to where he needed to be for a while. He was hoping he could earn enough for a train ride back to Iowa. A real train ride in a passenger car, not a boxcar.

He did not share this thought with Leo or the old guys and he wasn't sure why. It may have been that the old guys were used to riding the rails, although they sounded anxious to settle down here for a bit. They never indicated they would be in any hurry to leave, but maybe they were just experts at leaving their options open. Leo, on the other hand, may have wanted a place to settle down. Sometimes on this rail journey they had all been on, Leo would start taking about meeting a girl, getting married, and raising kids, after he sent money to his parents, of course. No one took him seriously because he could not even get a job to support himself. What woman would want that? This Depression was going to keep a lot of men from having families, as well as take men who already had families away from them, like when Charley had to leave Harley and Lena. Harley hoped he would never have to do anything like that to his family when he had one. His family would have it better; that is what his mother always told him. She said to get his education, get a good job, and then look around for just the right gal to share it with.

He was starting to daydream a little bit about that girl, when he heard Adam talking to the horses.

"You're almost home, fellas. I guess your new owner is gonna be glad to see you and we hope he's also glad to see us. Shall we get on the road? Are you ready to ride?"

"I'm ready, fellas," said Harley.

"Me, too," added Leo.

They made sure all their gear was packed and Harley tugged gently on the ropes that secured Clarence. They rode off to the east again. By now the sun was on their backs, but Harley knew they would get to the ranch before dusk. There was not much conversation. Now and then, one man might notice a critter or an unusual tree, or a rock formation. No one mentioned Clarence, but he was most likely on all their minds. He had been the most eager to get to the ranch, except for Harley. Since Clarence was a farm boy himself; he wanted to see the ranch, herd a cow or two, shear a sheep, and other familiar farm duties he had grown up doing in Wisconsin. Now they knew that all Clarence could do was rest in peace.

Currier Hall and Registration

"Currier Hall...also known as the Women's Building since its construction in 1914...not even twenty years old ...still sparkling and eager to meet the needs of the young women of the University of Iowa." The orientation guide droned on and on; I just wanted to get in my room and unpack. I had this vision of how my marvelous velvet quilt would look on the bed.

Finally, when I did get there, the door was closed, so I knocked on the door before turning the doorknob.

"Come in, please," someone said.

The room was small, but well lit. A tall slender girl was sitting on one of the beds, which had a pale pink chenille bedspread on it. She smiled at me.

I smiled back. "My name is Mable and I'm from Des Moines. I like your bedspread." Then I immediately thought that was a silly thing to say. If I had used my good manners, I would have said, "It's nice to meet you." I decided I'd better start remembering my manners; I was going to be meeting a lot of new people in the next few weeks.

"My name is Dorothy. You can call me Dot. I chose this bed, if that's okay with you? I really don't care since both sides of the room are exactly alike. What do you think, Mable?"

"This other bed is fine, Dot. Thank you for asking. Are you all unpacked and everything?"

"I sure am, and I would be happy to help you if you want me to. I can make your bed for you," Dot offered as she stood up. "Wait, what's that wire coming out of your blouse?"

Well, I thought, I guess we'll get this over with right away. "I'm hard-of-hearing. It's my hearing aid. I wear it in my brassiere; it clips on, and the wire goes up to my earpiece. See?" I pulled my hair back from over my ear and showed her what it looked like.

"Why, I never would have known. Your hearing aid must work well. Can you hear anything without it?" she queried.

"I can hear a little, but I always wear it except for bathing and bedtime. Oh, and swimming, too. Lower voices are easier to hear. Higher pitched voices, like women's voices, are harder to hear. Men are much easier. I lip read a little bit, also," I explained. She seemed pretty interested, so I continued, "I must admit I am a little nervous about making new friends here. It's really difficult for me to hear when I'm in a crowd of people who are all talking at once. I don't hear very well at parties and places like basketball games."

"Oh, don't worry so much Mable. You are obviously a really nice person and you will make friends. Do you have a boyfriend?"

That seemed a little personal, but I had just told her about my hearing loss, so I thought this might be a good time to start getting to know each other. I decided to turn the tables on Dot.

"Not a boyfriend kind of boyfriend, but my best friend is a boy, if that counts. How about you? Do you have a boyfriend?" I asked.

"I sure do, but he's going to Iowa State in Ames. Don wants to be a veterinarian. He's a farm boy, but he doesn't want to farm. I miss him already," Dot whined a little bit at the end. "I don't think we will get to see each other until Thanksgiving. That seems like forever!"

"I miss Burnie, too. His father just dropped me off here and is driving him to Purdue. I'm pretty sure I won't see Burnie until Christmas. We have been best friends since sixth grade."

Dot was still smiling. I was thinking that we would be getting along swell as roommates. She quickly had the sheets on my bed and started looking around at what was left in the little trunk.

"Did you bring a bedspread?" she asked. "I don't see one in here with the sheets."

"Oh yes, I have one. It's a bit heavier, so I put it in the bottom of my large trunk over here. My grandmother made it for me for graduation." Somehow, I felt comfortable telling Dot more. "She just died in a house fire last month."

"My goodness, Mable. God rest her soul! I am so sorry to hear that. It's so sad. What a horrible thing to have happen. Was this in Des Moines?"

"No, it happened in Steamboat Rock. We just got back to Des Moines a week ago. I barely had time to pack for school."

We sat down on her bed and talked about all sorts of things. She told me she was going to study business, and I shared that I was going to study journalism. She was really curious about what it was like to go to a city high school in a big town like Des Moines. Her father was a banker in Mason City and she had two brothers. I told her that I was an only child and that my father died last year. She sat down on her bed, her hands full of my wooden hangers from the top of the big trunk.

"I am so sorry to hear that," she spoke very gently. "You must have had a very difficult senior year. And your mother; she is going to miss you terribly, isn't she?"

I thought for a moment how to answer her. I decided she didn't know what a practical family I came from and how my mother was such a strong woman...who wanted me to go to college more than anything.

"Yes, it was a shock when my father died suddenly, and of course, no one expected Grandmother's house fire. School is very important in my family, and that was always a priority. Senior year was very busy for me. I was sports editor for our school newspaper and I was on the swim team and basketball team. My father was always encouraging me in all my activities, and Mother supported me, too. She always said nothing was going to stop me from going to college, so here I am," I explained it all in as much of a nutshell as I could.

"But, isn't she going to be terribly lonely now?" queried Dot again.

"I doubt it. She's moving back to her hometown to be closer to her brother and the rest of our family. We only lived in Des Moines for six years, because of my father's work. I'll write her every week; she's going to be busy settling back in and getting together with all her old friends in Steamboat Rock. She'll be fine and I'm hoping to make some good college friends here, like you," I said as I smiled at her, and picked up few hangers to put my clothes on.

"Sorry, I guess I'm not helping much. I want to get all your clothes hung, get to the bottom of this trunk, and see that quilt your grandmother made for you," she said as she took a couple of dresses out of the trunk.

Dot and I finished hanging up my clothes in no time at all. I really didn't have that many. I always dressed pretty simply, mixing my skirts with different blouses and sweaters. She absolutely went crazy over the quilt and bathrobe when I took them out of the bottom. I let her try the bathrobe on. She was tall like I am, so it fit her well. I hung it up and then we decided to walk down to the office so we could figure out how to get something to eat in the dining hall. We didn't have to register for our classes until the next day, so after dinner we just walked along the river.

It was a pretty warm evening. I had not been that close to a river since the mile swim in Des Moines. I told Dot about it and she was pretty impressed. She had never played sports. She had just been interested in her school work. Her goal was to be a banker, like her father. It sounded boring to me, and it was a job that was mostly done by men, but she was excited about it. We had a lovely walk and visit. We saw some good-looking boys, but just in passing. There would be plenty of time later to meet boys at all the freshman mixers that the orientation guide told us about.

Before I went to bed that first night, I wrote to Mother. I told her all about Dot and my room. I also asked her to get me Burnie's address at Purdue from his mother. I had to keep in touch with him, and phone calls were going to be too expensive. Burnie had told me that he would write back to me, and I was praying he would keep that promise! I started a letter to him and figured I could write a little bit more on it every night, until I received his address and then I could mail it.

Registering for classes meant getting up early the next day and standing in long lines all morning in a gigantic gymnasium. It seemed like there were thousands of students in there, and they were all talking at the same time. It was a hearing aid nightmare. I had to tell every adult who tried to help me, when I finally got to the front of a line for my turn, that I was hard-of-hearing and then they all felt like they had to shout at me. That made everyone stare, or at least it felt like they were all staring. However, the registrars were helpful, and somehow, I got signed up for all my classes. Swim practice, when it started, would be early in the mornings, so it wouldn't interfere with any class schedules. I even managed to keep three afternoons per week open for working on the Daily Iowan, the university newspaper. I was excited! I was going to make my mother and father proud; Mable Hall, girl journalist and world-class swimmer!

Dot had also scheduled all her classes and, as we met up for lunch, we shared our registration horror stories. She agreed that it was terribly loud in there, and that she was a little intimidated, just like I was. That made me feel much better about the experience. We finally laughed about it and decided that by our senior year, we would be old pros at it, and probably be laughing at the poor little freshmen students!

That afternoon, I tried out for the synchronized swim team. It was called the Seals Club. Being on that team was a step towards the varsity women's swim team, which is where I needed to be to keep my scholarship money. The tradition was that you had to be on the Seals for at least one year before you were allowed to travel with the women's swim team and swim competitively. I had never done synchronized swimming before, so I had no idea how difficult it was.

There was a skills test that I had to pass in order to achieve active membership. I don't think I was the only freshman girl there who felt like she was about to drown! It was completely different than swimming a mile in the Des Moines River! Of course, I passed the test. It was in the swimming pool, after all, and I could do anything in the pool. At least I thought I could. All those underwater moves were new to me, and really didn't think that I did that well at first. Fortunately, I was able to laugh at myself, and the girls and our sponsor were really sweet to me. They knew I intended to swim at the collegiate level and I told them that I would learn to swim like a Seal as quickly as possible.

Most of the girls were curious about my hearing aid, and I showed them how I have to take it out right before I get in the water, and then put it back on as soon as I get out. I explained to Miss Camp, the sponsor, that most of her coaching for me would have to take place before I got into the water, and the girls said they would all be happy to point or demonstrate any instructions given after we were already in the pool, to help me out. Almost immediately, I had a swell bunch of new friends.

The Seals Club went to team competitions also, so I could keep my competitive edge sharp and be ready to win my individual races next year. Between swim team practice and Seals Club practice, I was going to be swimming a lot this semester.

A Green Valley Welcome

They came up a final steep hill and paused at the top. Before them was a paradise - a green valley, more lush than any they had seen in the past two days. It was just like Jack had described it. This valley was deep and wide. The hills on the backside were low and tillable. There were fields with cattle grazing on them and a hillside full of sheep. A generous stream ran right through the middle of it all. In the far distance, Harley could see the orchard. It was gigantic and just now turning the dark summer green, instead of the bright and light spring green when the trees just start to bud out. They were most likely done blooming and already starting to set fruit on their branches. Harley had never seen so many apple trees.

"I'm pretty sure this is it, fellas. Welcome to Chelan Butte Ranch. We have arrived!" announced Harley. All of them sat still on their horses and surveyed the valley for several minutes. Words were not needed, really. It was an incredible sight.

Finally, Ed spoke, "I ain't never seen nothin' like this. It looks like Heaven. We can bury Clarence in Heaven. He woulda liked that, huh?"

"Yes," said Harley, "and we had better get down there to the main house and find out what to do with Clarence before it gets dark."

"I just hope we ain't missed dinner, Harley!" chimed in Leo.

"I'm sure there's no shortage of food here, Leo. We'll be eating well, I'll guarantee you that."

Harley waved them forward and continued to lead the way down from that last hillside. Everything was so green and pastoral. It was like a museum painting, Harley thought. He had never actually been in a museum or seen one of the paintings there, but he had seen pictures of paintings, and he was sure he was right.

The horses must have sensed they were near the end of their journey also, or perhaps they detected the scent of the other domesticated animals, because all of a sudden, they were also in a big hurry. It was like they knew where the barn was and they knew that they belonged there. There was no holding them back!

As Harley got closer, he could see a few people moving around and one figure waved to the men on horseback. He waved back, even though he was not sure who it was. In another minute or two, he could hear a dog barking. They had to ride alongside a fence for about a half of a mile until they found a gate. There was a crude sign there that commanded people to close the gate behind them. They entered the gate and dutifully complied with the command once they were all inside the fence.

 Harley wondered if the fence was meant to contain the space, or to keep something or someone out. It certainly wouldn't stop a person or a wild animal, so he decided it was to delineate the property boundaries. Then he wondered if it went all the way around the property. That seemed hardly possible, with the size of the ranch. Surely not all of it was contained, but he supposed he would have to wait and see or ask Uncle Gene. He had never known anyone who owned a piece of land with these enormous dimensions.

As they made their final approach, it was easy to tell which cowboy was Uncle Gene. He was the tall man, in middle of the lineup of curious greeters, wearing a white hat and spectacles, and looking like a twin brother to Harley's other uncles, Mark and Earl. Uncle Gene stepped forward as the four horsemen neared the ranch house.

"You will have to excuse all these nosy gawkers, Harley. They just want to see what a teenage boy who is brave enough to ride the rails halfway across the country looks like. Now you have seen him, men, so you sheep fellas can get back out to the north pasture. You have a good hour of sunlight before we are done for the night. Let's round up the rest of those sheep. Don't forget to make the dogs do most of the work. They are a lot smarter than you are!" He laughed and took off his hat. He put it on Harley.

"Here's a great hat for you, Harley. A little gift from your old Uncle Gene,"

Then a look of deep concern swept across his face and he asked, with alarm, "Whoa, son, is that a body on the back of your horse?"

"Uncle Gene, that's Clarence. He was riding behind me earlier today, and the horse got spooked by a rattler. He reared up and Clarence went flyin' off the back. Broke his neck. He was dead where he landed. We couldn't do anything to help him, but we couldn't leave him there."

"You have a plan for him here?" asked Gene.

"Well, sir, we thought the sheriff could try to locate his family in Racine, Wisconsin. And we were hoping we could bury him on the ranch somewhere, or it could be off the ranch. We want it to be a nice spot, not just on the side of the empty road where he died. Okay?"

"Okay," said Gene.

"Okay?" asked Harley. "Really?"

"Sounds like a practical plan to me, son. I was raised by the same father who raised your mother, remember? You should not be surprised that we think alike. That's one reason why I am so glad to have you on the ranch. You will be able to figure out how to do lots of things here, without me having to tell you every single thing to do. Let's put him in the hay barn tonight. We can lay him on the straw bales and find the right place first thing tomorrow. We don't want to have to be digging a grave at high noon. I'll bet it's gonna be a warm day tomorrow!"

"Gee, Thanks, Uncle Gene. And, sir, I have some fellas I would like you to meet. Step up here, fellas," Harley said as he motioned to his friends. Leo, Adam, and Ed dutifully lined up.

Uncle Gene proceeded to circle up the remaining farmhands. Their clothing, beards, and demeanor were markedly different than those of the hobos. They stood straighter, so Harley pulled his shoulders back. They had tucked-in shirts and nice belts. He sort of shoved his hands around the waist of his trousers and hiked them up a little bit. He had a scruffy beard started, mostly because of his age. It was not a man's beard, and his mother would be horrified if she knew he had one. Uncle Gene might tell her, so Harley decided to shave it off at the first opportunity he had. He would ask Uncle Gene to loan him a razor before they bedded down for the night.

Harley's crew all shook hands and started some small talk with a few of the farmhands. He guessed they had been coached by their boss to be welcoming. The four new fellas were lowly bindle stiffs, but one of them was his nephew, so Gene wanted them treated respectfully. They tied the horses up on the fence rail by the horse barn and then followed the foreman, John, to the bunkhouse. Harley was surprised there were enough bunks for all of them, and a few extra beds left over. Maybe they would all be able to work for Uncle Gene and stay together!

It was a remarkably well-furnished bunkhouse. It had running water and a clean outhouse. There were burlap curtains on the windows, and the lighting was fairly bright. A couple of mirrors hung above two washtubs, and Harley could see a rigged-up clothesline out the back window. It was better than he had expected for way out here in the west.

About seventy-five yards east of the bunkhouse was the ranch house, an amazingly large log cabin with a porch that wrapped around the front and one of the sides. It looked like a rugged lodge that he had seen a picture of in one of the National Geographic magazines that his mother had. There was a warm, home-like glow coming through the windows, as it was quickly becoming dark.

It seemed to Harley that the country's bad economic times had not touched his uncle's prosperity. He appreciated the opportunity to work for his college money and not just ask for a cash handout. Uncle Gene would most assuredly not respect him if he had done that. He was determined to work hard the next few months to earn his uncle's respect.

The men all put the bindles down on their chosen bunks.

"Can we wash up right now?" asked Leo.

"Sure," replied John. "We already ate, but I think the boss is going to have some sandwiches sent out here for you," he added, as he gestured towards the large wooden table and chairs in the far front corner of the bunkhouse. "We eat our meals over there. Don't eat on your bunk; it'll draw critters and bugs. We keep this place dang tidy and clean and expect you men to do the same."

Harley felt like an affirmative response was needed, so he came out with, "That sounds swell. No one likes critters or bugs. We will keep it clean, right guys?"

Leo, Ed, and Adam all added a "Yes, sir, John." John nodded at them, with a friendly glance. Not a smile, but a positive mien. Harley thought to himself, "so far, so good."

With just two wash tubs, the men had to take turns washing up and did so quickly. Harley washed up last and decided to ask Uncle Gene for a spare razor when he saw him; hopefully before bedtime, whenever that was. It was nearly dark now, and Harley thought he had better check on the whereabouts of Clarence's body. He mentioned it to John and was told that it was in the hay barn like Uncle Gene had said, and they could bury him first thing tomorrow morning.

"Is it okay if I go up to the main house and talk to Uncle Gene?" inquired Harley.

"Well, go on up there, and knock on the door, since you are family. He might not know it is you, so if they don't answer the door, you will find a little wooden box with pencil and paper nailed on one of the porch posts. He lets us leave messages for him in there; then he gets back to us as soon as he can," explained John.

"That sounds like a good system. Thanks," replied Harley.

"I'll be back in a few minutes, fellas. Maybe I can pick up some sandwiches if they are ready," Harley said over his shoulder, as he closed the bunkhouse door behind him.

He strode towards the main house, which appeared even larger the closer he got to it. He could see the shadows of a person in the front room, so he was hoping Uncle Gene would answer his knock. He had gone about three-quarters of the way from the bunkhouse when his uncle stepped out on the porch.

"Comin' to get your dinner, nephew?" hollered Gene.

"Yessir, and a spare razor if you have one. I can't have you telling my mother I grew these whiskers."

"We can take care of that, for sure. I sure as heck would not want to be you, young man, if your mother saw you looking like this!" His uncle let out a hearty laugh, and Harley thought it sounded a lot like Uncle Lynn's laugh.

Gene quickly disappeared into the house and reappeared with a plate full of beef sandwiches and handed it over to Harley. He said there was a cupboard with drinking cups in it in the bunkhouse, and went back in, returning with a pitcher of milk! Harley had expected to be drinking coffee or water, but Gene said, "You are still a-growin', son, so you need milk. It won't hurt the fellas with you, either."

Then he pulled a razor out of his jacket pocket. "Don't try this until tomorrow morning, when there is some daylight. I don't want you chopping up your face."

"Thanks, Uncle Gene, and I have a couple of questions. Well, first I want to tell you how nice the bunkhouse is. Are you short on hands? There seem to be some empty bunks, even after us coming in?"

"Well, yes. I am missing a few men, Harley. Since you called me from town, three of my men got the California bug. They knew you were coming, so they just up and took off. Guess they did me a favor, since they really weren't my best workers," Gene shrugged. "How are the men you brought with you? Are they going to be slackers or workers? How well do you know them?"

Harley replied, "Well, they have been with me since Nebraska. They have helped me out with riding the trains and being safe. They are all regular guys whose families and lives fell apart the past couple of years. We all pull together, and they are really eager to prove themselves and settle somewhere to work. They are kind of hoping we could stay together. Could you use all of us, or do you know other ranchers around here who could use them?"

"Are they going to leave when you leave?" queried his uncle.

"No, I doubt it. They want to settle down. They aren't like the bums who enjoy riding the rails. Uncle Gene, they don't know that I am planning on going back to attend college. I will tell them soon and talk to them about staying here, but just let us get settled in around here first. Do you need all of us, or just me?"

"With the men who just took off for California and the bumper crop it looks like we are going to have, I have plenty of work for them. You can vouch for them all?" Gene raised a questioning brow in Harley's direction.

Harley chose his words carefully. "I have known them for about three weeks. They saved me from going under a train, they protected me from bad bums, and they prayed with me over Clarence's body out there on the trail. I believe they will work hard with us."

"You sure?"

"As far as I can tell. They have all had some hard times the past few years, but every chance we had to work somewhere the past three weeks, they took it. They just want a fair chance."

Gene concluded, "Then I will give them a chance. I am a fair man. You get your crew outside right after breakfast. At the edge of the grove on the far east side of the bunkhouse, you will find a couple of marked graves of other hands who died here. Bury Clarence next to them. I'll see to getting a grave marker, and you can call the sheriff on my telephone tomorrow night and let him know. Maybe they can let his family know. Clarence is wrapped in a horse blanket in the hay barn. Go ahead and bury it with him. Shovels are in the tool shed next to the barn. We have pretty rocky dirt here, so it will probably take you until noon to get the job done. Make sure it's deep, because we have a lot of critters out here, okay?"

Harley agreed, "We will get it done just like you say, Uncle Gene. Hey, do you think I might be able to call my mother tomorrow? I have truly had no way to let her know how everything is going since I left."

"Sure," Gene replied. "You go eat dinner and then bring the empty platter back up here. We can call your mother then."

"Will do, sir." Harley affirmed and briskly marched back to the bunkhouse to share the sandwiches and milk.

When he got to the door, it was a bit ajar and it sounded like the farmhands had returned from putting the sheep up for the night and were being regaled with hobo stories. These men were obviously born and raised around the area, or at least had come west some other way than riding the rails.

Leo and the other two had more tales to tell than Harley, so he just put the sandwiches on the table and said, "I have to take this plate back to the house when we are done. Let's dig in, fellas."

He did not want to let them know he was going to call his mother. He wasn't ready to explain the college plan; he wanted to focus on working with them on the ranch. When they got to know him better they would understand, and hopefully be happy for him. The new men made short work of the sandwiches, and the other hands got ready to play some poker. The game would not last long, as tomorrow would be another work day full of tending the sheep, cattle, and the apple orchard.

Harley took a lantern that was by the door and headed back to the main house.

His mother cried when she heard Harley's voice, but calmed down and was able to give him news from home. According to Lena, Charley was gaining strength every day and Michael was turning into a fine farmer. She scolded Harley for not contacting her but was completely overjoyed at his safe arrival in Chelan. He did not tell her about Clarence but did describe the way he led his new friends to Chelan instead of California, thinking that would please her.

"Well, I am glad you didn't stop in California on the way to Gene's, but maybe you will have time to stop and see Aunt Polly in Sacramento on your way home," suggested his mother. "You know, she is the reason I met your father. I will have to tell you that train station story again sometime before you see her. That way you can thank her properly!"

"Sure thing, Mother," Harley agreed. "I'm getting tired and I think the fellas in the bunkhouse will be wondering if I got lost. I'd better bed down here soon. I love you, and tell Dad that I love him, too. Please say hello to Mike for me. Do you want to talk to Uncle Gene?"

"Just thank him again for taking you on and thank him every day. Let's not run up his phone bill. We love you." With that, Lena hung up. She had a habit of doing that. She never said "goodbye" when she was talking on the telephone. She just quit talking and then hung up. It was different, but also funny to Harley.

Daily Iowan and Missing Burnie

Baseball was big this fall. It was difficult to focus on school. Most of the girls I knew were not at all interested in baseball. They didn't know a foul ball from a pop fly. I didn't have a hard time meeting boys, because there were a lot of them in my classes. In journalism, it was mostly men. Very few women went the journalism route in college. There were women authors and poets, but most people thought of the newspaper business as pretty gritty, thus making it an unsuitable career path for a girl. I loved to write and I loved sports, so there just didn't seem to be any other choice for me.

Without Burnie to talk baseball with, I had to strike up conversations with some of the fellas in my classes. I only had one journalism class that first semester, and I was the only girl in it. As a freshman, the expectation was to take only general liberal arts requirements, but since I was going to be on the Daily Iowan staff right away, they let me take Journalism 101. I had to submit a portfolio of articles I had written for the North High Oracle in order to be accepted by the Daily Iowan, along with a letter of recommendation from my journalism teacher at North.

When I listened in on the baseball conversations of my classmates, I discovered that they were mostly Chicago Cubs fans, but there were a few St. Louis Cardinal fans mixed in. One poor fella was from Canada and didn't get much of an opportunity to contribute.

One time, when the fellas were talking baseball, I had a chance to tell them about one of the most interesting men in baseball. He was Burnie's favorite pitcher from the Brooklyn Robins, Dazzy Vance. Well, now they were called the Dodgers. First of all, he had a nifty nickname and he was from Iowa. Second, he had some amazing records. Dazzy had won the National League MVP Award in 1924 and also won the Triple Crown, with the most wins, most strikeouts, and lowest ERA! You had to respect a man who could do that, even if he beat up on my Cubs! He fanned FIFTEEN of them in one game in that year. That same amazing year, he also struck out three Cubs batters with only nine pitches in one half-inning. He had one out of every thirteen strikeouts in the National League. It was an astounding year.

Dazzy Vance always wore a shirt when he pitched that had a tattered sleeve. Some managers complained about it, because they said it distracted the batters when he threw the ball, but Dazzy told them there was nothing in the rule book against it, so he kept wearing it, as his 'lucky shirt.' He pitched a no-hitter in 1925, and in 1926, my Dad told me about how Dazzy was one of three runners who ended up at third base at the same time in a game against the Boston Braves. Fellas like him made baseball the best sport ever!

All the DI guys were a bit surprised that I knew so much about baseball, but it didn't get me any interesting reporting assignments. The other DI staff told me that I would not get any real assignments to cover around the campus until my sophomore year. That was disappointing, but none of the other freshmen got assignments either, so I believed it was just their policy. I had to pass Journalism 101 first, they said. That class was a snap! I had scored an A on all my work so far, so all I had to do was wait until next year. It seemed like a long wait.

So, I enjoyed my classes, except anatomy, but I was not enjoying the Daily Iowan as much as I hoped I would. Running errands and making coffee were my major responsibilities, and that was quickly becoming tiresome. The only other girls in the DI office were the girlfriends of the writers. I began to wonder if it was the same in a real newspaper office.

My letters to Burnie gave him the scoop on all of this. We actually both got pretty good at letters. It was strange after just being able to stroll across our front yards and knock on his door to tell him something. That first long letter I wrote had to have three stamps on it. I decided not to do that again now that I had Burnie's address and he had mine. We both agreed that our letters were too short, but a little news was better than no news. Some of my letters to Burnie were more like short notes, but I appreciated his and he appreciated mine. It was difficult to wait for those letters to be delivered to my dorm postbox, but it was always worth it when they came. I also received letters from Mother at least once a week.

I was a bit homesick, or at least that's what I thought it was. Even though I was busy with going to class, swimming with the Seals, doing my little jobs at the DI, and keeping up with my homework, I missed my mother and Burnie. Dot was fun to be around but she was busy, too, and the only time we were certain to see each other was after the 10:00 P.M. curfew when we had to be in our dormitory.

I wouldn't say I didn't like the University of Iowa, but I started feeling that college in general was getting to be too much for me to handle. It was exciting all right, but maybe it was more excitement than I needed after the difficult senior year I had.

Dad's sudden death, the house fire killing Grandma Von Dornum, and then mother selling the house in Des Moines and moving back to Steamboat Rock; it felt like I never had time to recover. I had only been back in Des Moines for a week before I had to leave for Iowa City. Mother and Burnie had been supportive, but now I didn't have them around. Dot was a good listener, but it wasn't the same as having my mother and my best friend to talk to. I was feeling pretty down in the dumps, and then it happened.

Burying Clarence and Thinning Apples

Harley, Leo, Ed, and Adam put Clarence's body in the wagon and walked the horse, pulling it up to the corner of the property that Uncle Gene had told them about. Like Uncle Gene had said, it took until almost noon to dig the grave six feet into the rocky soil. They took turns, in pairs, filling in the soil over him, just like they had taken turns digging. Harley led them in another prayer after they laid him in and mounded the soil over him, and they solemnly led the horse back to the barn. Uncle Gene had taken care of notifying the sheriff, who would contact the Wisconsin authorities. Harley really hoped they could find Clarence's family.

There were many tasks to be accomplished on the ranch. It was like a small town of its own. There was the stable for the horses. Several of the horses were used for herding the sheep and the small herd of cattle, as well as for Uncle Gene's trips across the ranch. They also pulled wagons during the apple harvest.

Then there were the hundreds of sheep. They foraged the hills and valleys of grass, being watched by hands on horses and herded by the dogs. The corn and oat fields would be harvested for the animals to eat in the winter if the grass was covered by snow. The manure from the animal barns was used as fertilizer on the crops. The animals and crops fit together like a giant agricultural puzzle. This enormous operation was much more complicated than Charley's small pig and corn farm in Iowa. Harley was anxious to see where Uncle Gene thought he would fit in.

The orchards were enormous, containing apple trees by the hundreds. Nine hundred and forty, according to Uncle Gene. There were Red Delicious, Grimes Golden, Courtland, and King David. The apple blossoming went well in the spring, and the thinning of the apples was started. The hands who took off for California were supposed to have finished it, but left it undone. Uncle Gene needed Harley, Leo, Adam, and Ed to finish it immediately. Harley had no idea that there was so much to do with apple trees. They had a couple on the farm at home, but they certainly did not get much more than a trimming every other year or so. Betty's husband Jim always took care of that from the back of his pickup. The two neighbors shared the apples every year. Uncle Gene's apples went to a huge distributing wholesaler in Seattle and were shipped east from there.

These apple trees were shorter and wider than the ones in Iowa. They had been carefully pruned to be easier to harvest. Uncle Gene had very specific instructions, to insure the best crop. Harley knew that he was about to be schooled by an expert.

"Men, what is known as 'June drop' is over. That is when apple trees just naturally drop some of their apples. Mother Nature is an ambitious woman and would like each tree to produce hundreds of apples, but she forgot to make the trees strong enough to hold all those apples. So even after some of the extras fall off in June, we have to remove the rest of the excess apples, or our trees will break." Uncle Gene had his hands on his hips, and paused, obviously waiting to see if we had any questions.

I ventured to ask, "How do we know how many to take and how many to leave?"

"I want you to leave eight inches between each apple. Don't leave any clusters, like two or three apples coming from the same small branch. The branch can hold three tiny apples, but only one mature apple," Gene explained. "A man should be able to thin a tree in about ten minutes. Those fellas who just quit only finished thinning about one hundred trees. There are about 850 trees left to thin and there are four of you. Six trees an hour, eight hours a day, so all the trees should be done in how many days, Harley?"

Harley was an absolute whiz at figuring numbers in his head and was doing the math as his uncle was talking. "About four and a half days, sir," he quickly answered.

"Whoa!" exclaimed Adam. "That was darn fast, young fella!"

"Good answer, Harley. I guess those Iowa schools did their job," said Uncle Gene, who was as impressed as the other men, and also obviously proud. He repeated himself with, "Good answer."

"So, when do we start?" asked Ed.

"Well," Gene said, "Clarence is at rest now, so I want you fellas to go get some lunch at the bunkhouse, then get one of the horses hooked up to the apple wagon. Ask John which horse; you will be able to easily spot the apple wagon, trust me. All the extra apples you take off the trees get tossed in there. We grind them, add them to the silage and split it between the horses and the sheep. You can get four hours in after you eat, then finish up tomorrow, Friday, Saturday, and Monday. No work here on Sunday."

"So, what do we do on Sunday?" asked Leo. "Town is pretty far away, but we ain't got no money anyhow."

Gene reassured him, "You can do nothing or you can do plenty. I run a short prayer service at ten o'clock, at a little chapel on the back of the main house, and by the time that is over, most all the hands are up and around. Some go for a ride, some pitch horseshoes. Some play cards; but there is no gamblin' allowed on the ranch. It's your day to do what you like. Town is really too far, unless you leave on Friday after dark and ride all night and all day Saturday. About once every six weeks, if we can make it work, we don't work on Saturday. That's the time to go to town."

"Sounds good to us," said Harley, looking around at the men and getting the affirmative nods he wanted from all of them. "Can we ask what the pay is for the men, Uncle Gene?"

"We'll be talking about that tomorrow, fellas. Let's see what kind of work your crew can actually do in a day first," his uncle replied.

"Let's get goin', then," urged Ed. "Those apples ain't gonna thin themselves!"

The four men strode back to the barn, looking around for John as they went. They spied him entering the bunkhouse with a large pot in hand. Another hand was behind him with an armful of what looked like bowls and bread. They hurried up their pace a little, wanting to make sure they got a seat and a bowl of soup. Earlier, breakfast had been left on the bunkhouse steps; biscuits and gravy. They made their own coffee on a hotplate in the bunkhouse. This sure was better than grubbing and begging for meals from strangers.

The other hands were pretty friendly. It might take a while to sort out who wanted to talk and who didn't, but most of these guys seemed to like each other and to be open to the newcomers. Harley was pretty sure Uncle Gene had been kind of picky when he hired men, because there didn't seem to be any really mean or angry fellas. He just wanted to work for Uncle Gene, earn his money, and get back to Iowa.

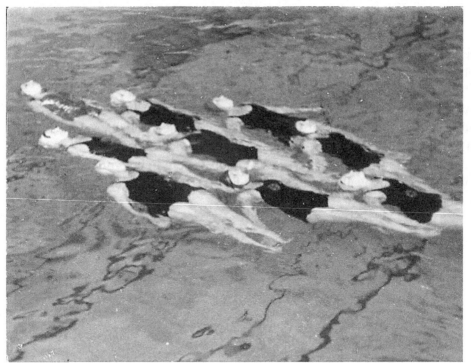

University of Iowa | digital.lib.uiowa.edu/wpe

Bad Grades and A Surprise

A low C? How was this possible? What was I doing wrong? My academic advisor had said that anatomy would be a hard class for a freshman, but with my interest in the subject, I was sure I would do well. I knew all the bones in the body, but really did poorly on the part of the first exam about muscles. I thought the Latin I took in high school would get me through, but obviously much more studying was needed. It was early in the semester, and the grades in my all other classes were A's and B's. Even one C was going to be totally unacceptable to Mother. I decided to tell her it was my hardest class and promise to study more earnestly. Mother believed in me, so I had to believe in myself!

That darned World Series was going to make it hard to concentrate for part of October, but there was plenty of time to recover after that. Miss Camp, coach of the Seals, said she would help me study for the next anatomy test. I really wanted to get the Red Cross First Aid Instructor certification the university offered. I thought that would allow me to work at a higher paying job when I went back to teach swimming in Des Moines the next summer. That little brown Red Cross book went with me everywhere; I read it and re-read it. I studied all the anatomy diagrams, copied the drawings in my notebook, and even slept with the darn thing under my pillow. I wrote to Burnie what I was trying to accomplish and explained that I hoped the extra knowledge would also help me raise my summer paychecks. When he wrote back about that was when I realized I was not really thinking quite straight. He asked me who I was going to live with in Des Moines during the summer.

I had not thought about that. I had not connected the fact that I wanted to work at the pool in Des Moines again, and with Mr. Ashby at the newspaper, but my family did not live there anymore. It hit me like a brick. Where would I live? If I lived in Steamboat Rock, the only place to swim was in Pine Lake. I never heard of them offering swimming lessons or first aid classes there. Where would I go when school was out for the summer?

Mother was not the one to bother with this dilemma, as she was still trying to get the new house finished and settle in. However, I had to talk to her about it before I could discuss it with Burnie. He, of course, immediately offered to let me stay at his house and I am quite sure that he had not even asked his parents. I know they would say I'd be more than welcome, but it seemed like I would be abandoning my mother.

She always wrote to me about how she wished she could give me a hug and a kiss, how much she missed me, and how she could not wait until I came home for Thanksgiving. She never tried to make me feel guilty and I was sure her affectionate expressions were not intended to do that, but I could not help feeling pangs of guilt. I missed her as well and told her so in my letters to her.

Her letters smelled like the cookies I always got when I went to Aunt Helen's house. Mother was living there while the new house was being built, so that made sense. The thought even occurred to me that she wrote the letters in the kitchen on purpose, so that I would get homesick for those cookies. When I told wrote Mother of my suspicion, she wrote back that my very active imagination was to blame, but I don't think it was my imagination at all.

Swimming with the Seals was much more work than I had planned. Afterwards, I was often too exhausted to give my backstroke laps the full measure of effort they warranted. By the time I got back to the dormitory for dinner, I was frequently too drained to go eat. That's when Dot would sneak back a little bit of food for me from the dining hall. They had rules about taking food out of the dining hall, so usually it was something like a roll with a chunk of meatloaf shoved into the middle of it, and sometimes just a few pieces of cheese and a piece of fruit. She never let me go without dinner, bless her heart. If there was a cookie to grab, I always got one of those, also.

I kept going, just thinking about making it to Thanksgiving. Our Seals Club meets would not begin until after the holidays in December. I just had to keep studying, swimming, and get through another three and one-half weeks until I could go home for a break. It was Halloween Eve when the fateful letter from my old newspaper buddy Ted Ashby arrived.

Meeting Aunt Lou and Salary News

John said to take Sadie, whose name was on her stall. She was cooperative, but pretty darn tall for a mare. Harley showed the other fellas how to put the harness on and hook her to the apple wagon. Someone, probably Aunt Lou, had painted the wagon green and decorated each side with a big red apple, so it was easy to spot behind the barn. There were four long burlap bags in the wagon bed, with shoulder straps on them. The other three men each grabbed a bag and hopped in the back of the wagon. Harley guessed they wanted him to drive, so he did.

Uncle Gene had said they would be able to tell which trees had already been thinned and which ones hadn't, which was true. It was astounding how many little apples were on those un-trimmed trees. Harley figured there were at least 200 extra apples on each one of them. They started slowly, not wanting to break the branches; Gene had warned them about that. As they went along, however, their technique improved. Several times they shared tips with successful ways they found to do the job more efficiently. Harley was proud of his crew and encouraged them.

It did turn into a long four hours after lunch, though. Most of the work was over their heads, but within their reach. They were using arm muscles which had been loafing for months and sometimes years. Now and then, one of the fellas might take a break for massaging his own arms. Ed and Adam both expressed out loud that they wished there was a tub for soaking in at the bunkhouse. Harley had not really noticed and neither had the others, but they were all praying there was one. They had worked for what seemed like more than four hours, when they heard the big bell clanging by the bunkhouse.

They were about a half-mile away, but it was loud and clear. The truck was nearly overflowing with apples. It was a good thing the young apples were tiny, or they would have had to empty the wagon at least a couple of times. As it was, he drove Sadie back slowly, so as not to drop any on the ground. That horse sure was patient. The men had all given her a pat and some chat when they emptied their shoulder bags into the wagon bed, and she was a sweet horse. Leo, Adam, and Ed had to walk the half mile back because the wagon was so full, but no one complained. Adam remarked that it actually felt good to stretch out his legs after standing all day.

Dinner was lamb stew and Aunt Lou's delicious biscuits. Harley figured her main jobs around the ranch were taking care of the main house, tending the giant garden, and cooking for the hands. He was glad there weren't so many hands that Uncle Gene had them cook for themselves because he sure did like Aunt Lou's cooking. It was almost as delicious as his mother's. He had heard about her in letters that Uncle Gene had written to Lena over the years, but still had not had a chance to meet her. Maybe next time he went up to the main house to call home, he could meet her properly.

Fortunately for the four new hands, there was a tub and a big hot water tank. All four took their turn to soak and took some razzing from the other hands for being soft, weak, and several other names. Harley knew his friends and that they would be proving themselves eventually.

Friday and Saturday were good days. They were ahead of the schedule Uncle Gene had laid out, probably because they worked faster than those quitters. Whenever mention of them came up in any conversation, no one on the ranch used their proper names; they just called them quitters, and sometimes spit on the ground in disgust after speaking it. Gene had himself a crew that valued hard work and it appeared as though they could finish by Monday noon, instead of using the whole day. Harley would have mentioned it to his uncle if he was one hundred percent sure, but didn't want to jinx it, so he kept it to himself. The thinned apple trees looked happier, or at least that is what Harley knew his mother would have said. He was thinking he could learn a whole lot about growing better apples and take it back to his mother for their trees.

Sunday turned out to be exactly like Uncle Gene had described. Some men went riding, some slept in, and some played cards or horseshoes. A few were seen writing letters, and one fella even wrote a letter for another hand who said he couldn't read or write. After the church service, Harley wrote to his mom and then went out to watch horseshoes. Leo tagged along. Harley had seen men at the Iowa State Fair in horseshoe competitions, and these fellas were not that good, but Harley knew they were better than he was, so he just observed. Leo actually asked to give it a try, and the other hands had many suggestions for him, but he had a long way to go before he would be ready for a real contest. He was able to laugh at himself and seemed to fit in well with the other hands. This was encouraging for Harley, who really hoped that all three of his rail-riding friends would want to stay on the ranch when he left and not return to the disappointing lives they had previously experienced.

Harley wandered up to the main house in the middle of the afternoon. He wanted to ask Uncle Gene about the pay. He had promised his friends he would do that when they were picking apples on Saturday. He knocked, and then started to write a note for the message box when Aunt Lou came to the door.

"Is that you, Harley honey?" she asked sweetly.

"Yes, Aunt Lou, er… I mean, ma'am, it's me…straight from Iowa to Washington." He added, "This is some kinda ranch, ma'am!"

"Aunt Lou, Harley, not ma'am. Call me Aunt Lou!" she laughed.

"Yes, Aunt Lou, I will. It is so nice to finally meet you." Then he blurted out, "You sure are a fine cook!"

She laughed again. "Thank you, Harley. Were you looking for your uncle?"

"Yes, ma'am, I mean Aunt Lou, I wanted to ask him a question about the pay…for the new men. He said he would talk to me, but he didn't get around to it yet. I know he's busy, and I don't want to bother him, and we know he'll be fair…" Harley knew he was rambling on, so he decided to wrap it up. "Is Uncle Gene available for a minute?"

Aunt Lou was amused and understanding. "I will get him. Why don't you come in and sit down here in the front room, Harley?" She motioned him into the entry way and pointed to the right. "Just find yourself a seat in there and he'll be right down."

Harley found the front room quite spacious, with chairs covered in leather and decorated with horns of different styles. There was an enormous ram's head above the massive stone fireplace. Harley supposed it was a mountain sheep, but he had only seen photos of them in his mother's National Geographic magazines. He was surprised to see a painting above the fireplace that was signed by Lou. It showed the entrance gate to the ranch and was, by Harley's untrained taste, a beautiful rendition of just the way it looked to him when he arrived. He stood admiring it, when Uncle Gene entered the room.

"Having a pleasant day of rest, young man?" Gene inquired.

"Yessir, Uncle Gene, very pleasant. I hope I'm not bothering you."

"Not at all. I'm sorry I forgot to talk to you men yesterday. Pay here is generous, as long as you keep working the way you have been. I went out to the apples, and it appears to me that you fellas are going to be finished early. What do you think?"

Harley was taken off guard. "Yessir, I was hoping to have that be a surprise for you on Monday. We should be done by lunchtime, sir."

"I really like that kind of work ethic, Harley, but I don't like surprises, even good ones like that. I need you to communicate with me about things, because I have a lot of jobs here to plan for and knowing who is going to be available ahead of time helps me plan better," Gene said.

"Sorry, uncle. Really sorry," Harley said, hanging his head a bit.

"No need to apologize, Harley. Just so you know now, alright?" Gene reassured him.

"Thank you, sir. I will update you whenever there is a need," Harley promised.

Gene invited him to sit down with, "Try out one of these custom-made hide chairs, Harley. I think you will find them quite comfortable."

Harley sat down, resting each forearm on one of the enormous cattle horns on each side of the chair, and Gene sat in the matching chair across from him.

"I pay twenty dollars a week, to start. After a month of dependable work, it goes to twenty-two dollars. After three months, it goes to twenty-five dollars, and that's where it stays. There is a Christmas bonus that I pay on the first of January. I don't like the way some of the first hands I had here spent their bonuses on foolish things in town, so I pay it after the holiday. If a man wants to buy gifts for someone special, he will need to save his salary up for it." Gene leaned forward intently and asked, "How does all that sound to you?"

"That's a very generous wage, Uncle Gene." Harley was stunned. That was over three dollars a day to start with. He had heard that men in California were fighting over jobs that paid $1.50 per day. "The fellas I brought with me are really fine workers and they will earn it, I promise."

"I have noticed that, Harley, and I have noticed you are a fine leader for them. I plan on keeping the four of you together as a crew whenever I can. Would you like that? Oh, and by the way, pay is in cash, the last day of the month," added Uncle Gene. "So, you will all have your first pay next Friday. It will be twenty dollars, because you will have only been here a week, right?"

"Sounds good, Uncle Gene. Thank you. I am going to head back to the bunkhouse now." With that, Harley stood up and put out his right hand. His uncle stood up and took it. He had quite a grip, but Harley did not let on as he felt it tighten. He strengthened his grip a bit to try to match the older man's.

"That's a fine handshake you have, Harley."

"Thank you, sir. That means a lot to me," Harley replied.

"Come and see me after lunch tomorrow, when you do get those trees finished. If you can't find me near the barn, just ask John and he will have your crew's next job ready," Gene added as they reached the front door.

"Yessir. Thank you again."

"Harley, I am so glad I am in a position to help you get your higher education. I can see, just from the short time you've been here, that you are going to be successful in whatever you do," added Gene. "Keep up the good work." Harley stepped out onto the porch, as his uncle smiled and closed the door.

Harley stood up even straighter. He knew he was fortunate, especially in these times, to have family who cared, and friends who helped. Sunday was a good day to be counting his blessings. He hurried back to the bunkhouse to tell his crew about their pay.

To Des Moines to See "The Babe"

Babe Ruth was coming to Des Moines in a week! He would be there on a baseball barnstorming tour with the Bustin' Babes and Larrupin' Lou's. The Yankees had skunked the Cubs in the World Series 4-0 and they were touring the country, celebrating and bringing big league baseball to the common folks. Ted had actually arranged for me to meet Mr. Ruth!

I read the words over and over, sitting stunned on the side of my bed. A low-lying late October sun shone into the dorm window and glistened on the shimmering velvet quilt. It looked like the fields of Iowa farmland, and then suddenly a green patch on the quilt seemed to change into a baseball diamond. Talk about an active imagination. In spite of the words being right on the paper in front of me, I could scarcely believe I was going to get to meet Babe Ruth, the Bambino, the Sultan of Swat.

Mr. Ashby had thought of everything. Burnie's father was going to drive to Purdue to get Burnie and then swing by Iowa City to pick me up. Burnie's mother had written to my mother and asked her to have Uncle Albert drive her down to Des Moines to meet us. Ted was aware that Babe Ruth personally knew the new Drake University football coach, Bill Williams, and the coach had invited Babe to scrimmage with the Drake football team while he was in Des Moines for the exhibition game. Their baseball game was scheduled for Saturday morning and the football scrimmage was on Sunday afternoon. Babe Ruth said he had never played football, so thinking it sounded like fun, Babe accepted. He would be playing football, wearing a Drake football uniform, scrimmaging with the Drake team, and Ted was going to interview him. Ted had already told the coach about me last year, when I was trying to get on the boys' swim team. He asked if he could bring me along, since I was such a huge baseball fan.

I was crazy with delight. My squeals brought girls from way down at the other end of the hallway. Our tiny room was packed, and with all of them talking at once, it was hard to tell what they were thinking. I had a chance to explain my squealing as they quieted down, and even though none of them squealed about my big news, I could tell they were impressed. There wasn't a person in the whole United States who didn't know who Babe Ruth was. A few gals patted me on the back and congratulated me. I didn't feel like I quite deserved congratulations, but it was so sweet of them. As they left in small murmuring groups, I had the feeling that lots of other people would soon know, and I was right.

When I went to class the next morning, several other students came and asked me about my upcoming opportunity. Word certainly travels fast on even a large campus like University of Iowa. By the time I got to the Daily Iowan office after lunch, the guys stood up at their typewriters and applauded me as I came through the door. That was a surprise! Before, it seemed like they only noticed me when their coffee was cold. Now I was getting lists of questions they wanted me to ask Babe Ruth, as well as requests for autographs. I told them I would try to ask him some of the questions, but that I was not at all sure if I could even get an autograph for myself. They urged me to try and I smiled gamely.

All that day, after the word of me meeting Babe Ruth got around campus, I felt happy for the first time in at least a month, but I knew the reason, so my college pressure only subsided temporarily. I had my next anatomy test in the afternoon, and even with all the studying and help from Miss Camp, I had the feeling I could have done much better on it. I would not find out the grade until after I got back from Des Moines the following week, so I decided to just put it out of my mind.

I got busy getting ready to go meet The Babe. I made an appointment to get my hair trimmed and I shopped for a nice pair of gloves. Ladies still dressed like ladies, especially when meeting such a luminary person as Babe Ruth. I made a quick call to Mother to make sure the arrangements had been made, and she assured me that we would be staying overnight that Friday at Burnie's house. That made me smile. Some time to spend with Burnie was just what I needed. And time with my mother, of course, but some of the things I'd been feeling were not ready to be revealed to her. Mother would not want to hear that I was thinking about quitting college for now and taking the time with her that I didn't get in the fall. I knew I simply needed more time to recover from everything; I just had to find the right time to tell her. For sure, I had to talk to Burnie first.

Days went more quickly than I thought they would that week. Seals Club practice and my swimming laps were done in a blur. Swimming was going well. I was an athlete, after all, and counted on my fitness level to get me through rough practices. During practice I focused on practice, and then it flew out of my mind the moment it was over. The same went for my classes. I gave them my complete attention at the time, and then my mind went back to Babe Ruth, Burnie, Mother, and Des Moines.

"I thought you would never get here, slow poke," was what I greeted Burnie with as he pulled up with his father right after lunch on Friday. His father assured me that Burnie kept on him the whole way to driver faster.

"He didn't want to be late, Mable. Sorry, it was my fault."

I reassured Mr. Orwig; I was just joking. I was very grateful for the ride and I let him know that Mother was going to give him some money to help pay for the gasoline. I told him right away that there should be no arguing with Mother about that either. She told me on the phone that she would help pay and she would not take "no" for an answer. Period.

All the way back to Des Moines, Burnie and I exchanged stories about our roommates, classes, the World Series, and new friends. It sounded like he had a lot more new friends than I did, but then he was not on the newspaper staff or involved in two sports as I was. He had more time for parties and such. His father had been listening to both of us, and chimed in, "Sounds like you are making a name for yourself ON campus, Mable, and Burnie is making a name for himself OFF campus."

"But, Dad! I'm doing great in my classes!" Burnie protested.

"Wait until baseball starts in the spring, Mr. Orwig, he will be the Big Man on Campus at Purdue," I assured him.

"Well," Burnie posed, "it might take more than one baseball season to achieve that. I really just want to help them win games. I can't set any records by myself like you can, Mable."

"I'm nowhere near setting any records yet, Burnie. I spent the first two weeks of Seals Club practice trying not to drown myself or anyone else. I told you that in my first long letter! Next year will be the one when I hope to have a chance to compete at the Intercollegiate Telegraphic Meet and set some records there, if I'm still at Iowa." Too late, I realized I had said too much.

"What? What do you mean, if you're still at Iowa? Huh?" Burnie turned and faced me directly from the front seat. "What do you mean?"

I had to cover my slip! I could not have Mr. Orwig saying something to my mother about this.

"I mean if I don't drown myself this year with that synchronized swimming jazz. That is nearly killing me. My leg muscles are starting to get muscles."

There was a moment of complete silence. I couldn't even really hear the engine of the car.

Burnie said under his breath, "Well, that makes more sense then." Unobtrusively, he gave me a glance that told me we would be talking more about this later in private. I wondered if perhaps he had read between the lines of some of my short notes to him and had already sensed my dissatisfaction with my college life.

Mr. Orwig changed the topic back to baseball, and we jabbered long and loud about that all the way back to Des Moines.

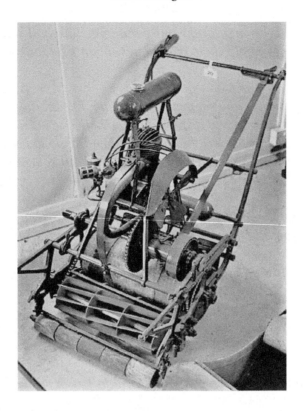

Spraying, Mowing, Shearing

When the four men finished the apple thinning, they learned there was even more work to do with the apples. As the weather warmed up, the bugs came out. The apples needed spraying. There were several diseases that could seriously affect the apple crop. His mother just sprayed soapy water on the trees at home whenever bugs became a problem, which wasn't very often. John told the crew that the bugs out here knew there were a lot of apples, and just hung around waiting for them to nibble on or spread disease to their leaves.

The men had to wear masks to keep the spray out of their lungs. The backpacks with tanks on them were heavy, but the spraying went faster than the thinning. They sprayed the trees in just two and one-half days. Harley could guess, and he found out he was right, about the next task concerning the apples. He could tell that walking around the trees was becoming more difficult, because the grass in the orchard was getting longer every day. They had been there two weeks, and it was prime growing season. The grass was growing like gangbusters! It needed to be cut, and although the sheep would make good lawnmowers, Harley was pretty sure that Uncle Gene had a plan for mowing the grass and he was right.

Uncle Gene had 950 trees on twenty-five acres of orchard. Harley had only mowed his own small front and back yard on the Iowa farm. They had a push reel mower that Charley had purchased at one of the bankruptcy farm auctions for a dollar, and he sure hoped Uncle Gene had a bigger mower than that!

It turned out that Gene had four mowers and they were imported from England. They were the Atco brand, and were apparently used to trim golf courses over there. He bought them off a train in Chelan, where they showed up by mistake. Apparently, the shipping labels and information were lost. Gene supposed they were originally destined for some fancy Hollywood estate in California, but no one could trace it. Harley had never been on a golf course, but he had seen pictures. He sure hoped Uncle Gene did not expect his orchard grass to look like a golf course! He knew the apples were a critical crop on the ranch, but he pictured himself cutting grass continuously for the rest of the season, and it was not a pretty picture.

Fortunately, John explained that the mowing took about a week, and only had to be done about every three weeks. As the summer got hotter and it was now nearing the end of June, the grass would slow down in growth, and there would be many chores to fill in their spare time between mowing days. So, the men learned how to use the Atco mowers, and headed out to the bushy green grass under the trees. John said the orchard definitely did not have to be groomed like a golf course and showed the men how to raise the cutting level to the highest mark. The mowing went pretty darn quickly at that setting, but twenty-five acres was still a lot of mowing.

Harley really enjoyed his Sundays, especially every other week when he called home. Lena was thrilled to hear his voice and Harley wanted to be updated on Charley's health. Lena and Harley determined that he would have to wait until second semester to enroll. He was also wondering what his folks were going to do when Michael left for the University of Iowa in September. Harvest season would be approaching and he worried that they would be short-handed. He learned that one of Betty's nephews from her mother's side of the family was coming to work for Jim, and he would be helping Charley also. That was one less thing for Harley to worry about. He was aiming for college to help his family. He did not want his quest to harm them in any way.

On one of the Sundays, all the fellas decided that they would hike up to the hill where Clarence's grave was. They had not heard anything back from the sheriff about any relatives in Wisconsin; they just felt like a visit from old friends was called for…so he wouldn't feel forgotten. Uncle Gene had put up an oak cross like he said he would, with Clarence's name and date of death on it. It matched the other three crosses up there, only it looked newer, of course. Weeds had started to grow along with the grass over it. Harley wished he had thought to bring some trimmers, but he vowed to himself to remember next time they came. He sure as heck wasn't going to push one of those big Atco mowers up here. As long as the crosses could be seen above the grass, that would have to do. The men all agreed that it was a fine spot to be buried.

Having completed the first round of mowing the entire orchard, Harley went to John to see if he knew what task Uncle Gene had for them next. He had hoped it wouldn't involve anything else in the orchard right away, and it didn't, but then he learned to be careful what he hoped for. They would be helping shear the sheep.

Harley did not like sheep. Not at all. He hadn't said anything to either Uncle Gene or to his crew, but Harley thought sheep were the smelliest and most brainless animals alive. At one point, Charley brought a few sheep home from the auction in Perry, Iowa. Those sheep were so dumb. They would bust out of the snug warm barn during a heavy spring snowstorm to give birth to their lambs, in the middle of the night. Harley found seven dead lambs in snowdrifts the next morning. Lena was stomping mad, and it really took a lot to get her that mad. She literally stomped around the house that morning. Harley would do whatever Uncle Gene wanted done, but mowing the orchard again was now something he was looking forward to.

There were several crews on the ranch who did nothing but herd, feed, worm, and well, do basically anything else with the sheep. There were about 300 sheep to keep track of. Just the thought of that many sheep in one place disgusted Harley. John said they needed extra hands for shearing because while they were shearing some of the sheep each day, the other sheep still needed to be watched, fed, and taken care of as usual. He volunteered to watch the sheep instead, but John said those men had a routine; the sheep and the dogs were used to them. John kindly, but firmly, declined Harley's offer. Then John confided to Harley that shearing was his least favorite chore on the ranch because he also hated the way they smelled. At least John understood, but he still expected the fellas to do the required work, and Harley assured him they would do whatever needed to be done with shearing.

What needed done was stinky and repetitive. The regular herders would bring fifty sheep in the main corral each morning. Once they were in there, a hand would have to single one out, put a rope around its neck, and bring it out of the corral to a ramp parked next to the corral gate. The sheep was led (dragged) up the ramp, to stand on a wooden platform. If it would not stand still, men were required to help the shearer move the sheep into the best positions. Then the trimmer, who held the shears, would shear the sheep. He trimmed as quickly as he could. The men helping would have to keep their arms and hands and heads out of the way so they didn't get cut, as the man who was shearing went quite fast. This was not easy work, it was not fun, and the sheep wool smelled awful to Harley. Sometimes it had feces stuck to it, but mostly it was that greasy lanolin smell that he hated. He put a bandana over his nose and just did the job. Uncle Gene passed by the second day, giving Harley a nod and a smile.

"I don't like the smell, either, son," he said. That really did not help Harley feel better at all, but he nodded and smiled back.

About every third sheep, the men had to stop and shove the trimmed wool into bags. It made Harley think about the Baa Baa Black Sheep nursery rhyme. They were certainly going to have more than "three bags full" after shearing three hundred sheep! The bags were tossed up into the lower hay loft and when the shearing was all finished. A truck would come from a woolen mill near Seattle to pick up all the wool and pay Uncle Gene. Harley had no idea how much Gene would be paid per pound, or per bag, but he knew it was a big money-maker for the ranch.

Charley had always told his son, "Whatever is worth doing, is worth doing well," so Harley sheared the sheep well. He hated it, but he did his best. He, along with Leo, Adam, and Ed, were learning how to ranch. Learning about new machines, learning about how to do jobs efficiently and on time. There was never really a schedule on the farm in Iowa, he and his father had always just done what needed to be done as the time came. He never thought of it, but here in Washington State, there was a definite rhythm to the work. He was getting in rhythm, he figured. That couldn't be a bad thing, because it felt good. He had never felt so productive, and at the same time, he felt like he was not just helping Uncle Gene, but also his rail-riding friends.

Somehow, the sheep finally got sheared. It was getting warmer every day, and if sheep can look happier, these sheep did. Harley was just happy it was over.

The apples became his focus again. Uncle Gene said it looked like they were headed for a record crop. Uncle Gene was not the kind of man who patted you on the back and praised you for doing a good job. Harley, in his head, felt that was what his uncle was trying to tell him as he sized up the large crop of apples.

The men mowed the apple orchard again, and then went through to do a final thinning, making sure none of the branches had more weight than they could bear. Too many apples on a branch always hurt production that year, and the next year, also, is what he learned from Uncle Gene.

When the mowing and apples were taken care of again, Uncle Gene put Harley's crew to work checking the fences. Harley knew that this was an 8,000-acre spread, but he had not given much thought to how much fence there would be on a piece of land that large. Their farm in Iowa consisted of three different pieces of land, all near each other just outside of Grimes, but there was only a total of 240 acres. Most of it, besides the barnyard and house areas, was tilled Iowa farmland. Uncle Gene had 800 acres of oats and corn, the twenty-five acres the apples were on, and pastures for the sheep. The rest of it was a series of valleys and buttes; it was wide-open western land. Not at all like his father's little farm. Harley now knew the difference between a farm and a ranch; a ranch had a whole lot more fence!

He did enjoy doing the fences with his crew. They took out two horses pulling a wagon full of posts, fencing, barbed wire, and tools. Uncle Gene was quite particular when he was showing them what to do. There should be no breaks, no sagging, no leaning wire or posts. Everything had to be tight and square.

Gene told them, "We don't only have sheep, we also have some cattle. These fences have to be able to hold anything."

Gene came out about once every three days, checking on the work that had been done, and suggesting the next area he wanted checked. Harley was impressed at how Gene knew so much about every aspect of the ranch.

Harley was also amazed at how much stronger he seemed to be getting. Working all day, every day, he felt like he was in the best shape he had ever been. At home with his folks, he had never worked this hard for this long. He'd take a half-day to go fishing, or his father would take him to Des Moines or Perry with him. Lena would send him to the bank or grocery store, or there might be an afternoon now and then to lie around and read. On this ranch, Harley's only free time was on Sundays, and he had learned to treasure that. Aunt Lou loaned him books from her library. At first some of the other hands made fun of him a little, but they found out it didn't really bother him, so the razzing stopped.

July turned to August. Harley turned nineteen on August 11th, and Aunt Lou surprised him with a birthday cake at lunch. She made a large spice cake and all the ranch hands got a piece. She baked cakes for them sometimes for a special dessert, but Harley could tell that she had put in a bit of extra effort on this one. That was the day Harley chose to tell his friends that he was not going to stay on the ranch.

After lunch, the crew was on horseback, riding through the orchard, having been sent out to look it over by Gene. They paused for a moment about halfway through their patrol.

"Say, fellas?" Harley began, "May I talk with all of you seriously for a minute?"

"We got apple trouble?" asked Ed.

"No, no trouble, just something I need to tell all of you. I have not been quite honest," Harley admitted.

"Not honest? Ain't never thought you was a liar," said Leo, with a truly pained look on his face. "You ain't no liar!"

Ed and Adam rode over nearer to Harley, as if they wanted to look more closely at him. They looked confused but said nothing.

"It's called lying by omission. There is something that I haven't told you," Harley explained.

"You ain't on the run from the law, is you?" asked Leo. It was apparent he was going to be doing the talking for the rest of the crew. Ed and Adam just sat on their horses, listening. They had looked up to Harley, even though he was younger. He had changed the path of their lives these past few months. They had a good job, money in their pockets, and the security of 'place' that so many men were missing in these tough times.

"No, no, no," Harley assured them. "Nothing like that. I want to start by saying that you fellas have been great friends to me. I have learned so much from you. You know, I am the youngest among us and an only child and being with you fellas has been almost like have a couple of big brothers, honestly."

"Ok, so just tell us," Leo urged him.

"Here's the deal. Everything I told you about my folks is true. My dad had to ride the rails, our house did burn down, he did have a stroke. And I set out to hobo to earn money…" he paused and looked at their intent gazes which were fixed on him. "But I need the money for college. I am going back to Iowa to start college in January. That has been my plan all along. I am so sorry I kept it secret."

"Why didn't you tell us that to start with?" asked Leo.

"I don't know. I was afraid. I didn't know you fellas would help me so much and get to be such good friends. I have grown up the past few months, a lot, and you have been so helpful," Harley kept talking, hoping he could explain all his thinking.

"I have been poor. Our farm is small and the past few years we have been on the edge of losing it. My mother went to college, and she wants me to have a better life than the farm. I don't want to be poor my whole life. I know how to work hard and I want to own my own business," he blurted out all at once.

The men stared at him. They took in this new information. Harley watched them as a slow smile grew on each man's face.

"That ain't no bad lie, kid," said Leo. "Is that the best lie you got? You are a pathetic liar, if it is!" The horses kind of shuffled around with their feet, like they had listened to enough and wanted to get on the move again and finish their walk through the orchard.

Ed looked thoughtful for a minute, "So you gonna leave the ranch in January?"

"No, I have to be back in Iowa in January. I'd really like to be back for Christmas. I will probably have to leave pretty soon after the apple harvest is over. My mother wants me to go to Sacramento and visit her Aunt Polly while I am out here. That will take a couple of weeks, and then I have to get back to Iowa," Harley explained.

"You gonna ride the rails back? You gonna ride the rails to California?" Adam asked.

"Oh, no. I am not riding the rails without you fellas! The only reason I got out here alive was because of you… and Clarence. Uncle Gene is buying me a train ticket from Sacramento to Des Moines, and I am paying for my own ticket to get from here to Aunt Polly's. My hobo days are over, and that's the other part of this, too…" Harley said.

"What other part?" asked Leo.

"Well, I am hoping, and so is Uncle Gene, that your hobo days are also done for. He wants all you men to stay here and not wander off when I leave. He says he would be in trouble if you fellas left him. Most of the hobos are still going to California, or headed down south for the winter. He won't have enough winter hands if you leave. He even told me he would gear you fellas up with winter clothes if you will stay." Harley sincerely wanted these friends to have the life on the ranch that was being offered to them.

"I ain't goin' nowhere. Where would I go? This place is like home now. If yer uncle is gonna keep us, I'm gonna stay!" said Leo. Ed nodded his agreement enthusiastically.

Adam spoke up. "I been sending good money back to my wife and girls and would be darn happy to jest go home now, but this money is too good and the wife says she wants me to keep sendin' money. She says to stay here for now and let her save up. We hope to get a house someday. Ed and me are stayin'," added Adam. "Right, Ed?"

"Fer sure," exclaimed Ed. "I ain't leavin'!"

Harley was so relieved at their reaction to his revelation. "Uncle Gene will be so glad. Is it alright if I tell him that all three of you will be staying?" asked Harley.

"Sure," said Leo. "Tell him we will be proud to stay. You got a fine family, Harley, ya know that?"

"Yes, I do. And I also have fine friends. Best friends a fella could ask for," added Harley. "Let's finish this orchard trip and put these horses up proper before dinner."

With that suggestion, the men got their eager horses on the way, and completed the orchard check. They started the route back to the barn in contemplative silence. Each man was thinking about his own future, for sure, and counting the blessing of good friends and continued prosperity. None except Harley were looking more than a year or two into the future. Harley, however, was dreaming of his name on the sign above the door. A building all his own. A business all his own. His Lincoln parked on the street out front. His mother in a fine dress. His thoughts stopped short of his father in a fancy suit; he knew that was not going to happen. Charley was too comfortable in his shirt and overalls. His dad owned one suit and it would probably last him the rest of his life. That was fine with Harley. His father was a farmer and he was proud of him.

Back in Des Moines

Mother was waiting on the front porch of Burnie's house when we drove up. I did not recognize the lady sitting between her and Burnie's mother on the porch swing, but I was immediately introduced to Mrs. Smith, a lovely retired teacher who had purchased our house. She had the kind of bright eyes and charming smile that must have made her a wonderful teacher. Mrs. Smith excused herself, despite an invitation from Mrs. Orwig to stay for dinner. She insisted she had sewing to do and a pie to bake for a church auction and supper on Sunday. That seemed strange for a Friday night activity, but she was adamant. She had lunch and cards on Saturday with some of her retired teacher friends, so both those tasks had to be done tonight. She waved one more time as she entered our front door. I mean her front door.

It felt a little strange seeing someone else going into our house. She was such a friendly lady, though. I was glad Burnie had such a nice new neighbor and I knew how lucky she was to have the Orwig family next door to her.

Dinner was delicious and our room was very comfortable. Mother and I had a long visit after dinner, before bed, but she did most of the talking. There was a lot to tell about all the goings-on in Steamboat Rock and about the new house. She was very excited for me to see it and assured me it would be all ready for Thanksgiving in a few weeks. I kept the little bits of any information that I told her pretty vague. Of course, I was terribly busy with my activities and class, I really enjoyed my roommate, and my work on the paper was not fulfilling, but it was only for a year, and then I could contribute the way I wanted to. That all seemed to satisfy her for the time being.

Mother rolled over and said "Goodnight, darling daughter." I leaned over and kissed her on the shoulder. I didn't realize until that moment how much I had really missed her.

It was actually pretty hard to go to sleep that night. I was tired from the long car trip and all the chatting, but what kept me so sleepless was having so many scenarios going through my head of what the rest of the weekend would actually bring. I had to decide what to wear. I had those new gloves I had purchased in Iowa City, but I had not given any thought to what outfit I would be wearing when I shook hands with the great Babe Ruth.

I was also trying to sort out all the questions given to me by my newspaper comrades at the university. I could not possibly ask them all. Maybe I could only ask one question. Which one? I had three hand-written pages of questions. Some were about him, some about baseball, some about politics, some about Ty Cobb, some about Lou Gehrig, and some really strange ones, like about his superstitions and such. How could I choose one or two questions out of that whole mess? I finally decided I would show the list to Mr. Ashby tomorrow when he came by. He would know what to do. I did not want to make a fool of myself.

Mother was sleeping quite peacefully. I strained to look over her at the clock by the bed. It was nearly 2:00A.M. I closed my eyes, said my grateful prayers to be back in Des Moines with the people who loved me the most, and added in a big thank you, in advance, for getting to meet Babe Ruth. I don't remember fading off to sleep, but it probably happened the instant I closed my eyes.

Harley Heads Home

August slid into September, then October. The days were still fairly warm, but the nights were getting cooler in the valley. The apples were red and heavy on the limbs of the carefully tended trees. Harley felt proud of the way they looked. Uncle Gene, of course, did not praise much, but the look of approval on his face when he went through the orchard was enough for the crew.

The picking of the apples called for many more men to be assigned to the orchard. Even though Harley had been in charge of the maintenance crew all summer, John assumed the leadership role for the harvesting. John knew everything about everything. He was a leader all the hands looked up to, including Harley. He was definitely the boss when Uncle Gene was not around. A skeleton crew was left to care for the sheep, and at least fifteen extra men were moved to the orchard. They used huge shoulder bags to drop the apples in. The men were showed how to pick fast, but not be too rough with the branches. Breakage would negatively impact next year's harvest.

The shoulder bags got heavy quickly and had to be laboriously carried to the apple wagons to be emptied regularly. Not all the varieties of apples ripened at the same time, so John had made a map of where to pick each day. Uncle Gene wanted to maximize the harvest, so the men had to examine the dropped apples that fell naturally from the tree and add them in the wagon if they were clean enough. The bags were taken to the long white barn south of the orchard and inspected; then they were put in stackable wooden crates.

The size of the apples was impressive and the size of the stacks of apple crates was staggering. They were stacked in an area roped off beside the barn. As the crates of apples were stacked higher and higher, Harley became curious about what would happen to all of them. Uncle Gene explained that trucks from a wholesaler would take the crates and then sort and grade the apples. They would be taken as far east as Indiana to be sold. He had one of the best apple farms in Washington State and was very proud of his "extra fine" apples. Each apple that was picked and placed in a bag, and then in a crate, and then in the truck, put Harley closer to the date of his departure for California. That thought always left him both anxious and excited. Mike had written him a letter, asking him to pick up some gold for him when he went to California. Harley knew that was not going to happen, but it was good for a laugh. Although he sure would like to pick up a little gold trinket of some kind for his mother.

It took over three weeks to finish the apples. The last ones ripened and were harvested just before Halloween. The changing leaves in the valley were gorgeous, and made Harley miss the smell of burning leaves that he remembered from his mother's backyard pile each fall. He was fairly sure she would have them burned before he got home. He was still aiming for before Christmas, but he had to get safely to Aunt Polly's and then home. Home, and get to work on the next step of his plan.

The fellas were quiet as he packed his sparse belongings on his bunk. Uncle Gene had loaned him a small canvas one. Harley promised to bring it back or ship it back. He really wasn't sure he would ever come this far west again, so he planned on shipping it. He didn't want to hurt Aunt Lou's feelings by refusing her open invitation to return soon. She had no idea of the long-term mission Harley had put in front of himself. He had a business to start and a car to buy, after he finished college. If he ever did come back, he would be driving his mother out to see her brother's beautiful ranch in his new Lincoln. Harley had come with only a hobo's bindle but was leaving with so much more. He had more life experience, more work experience, and more determination. He counted his friends and his blessings as he packed. He especially remembered Clarence, whose grave he had visited last night, just before dinner. He didn't look forward to saying goodbye, but he felt like he needed to give his crew a proper speech before he left. Uncle

Gene told him to be up at the house at 8:00 A.M., right after breakfast in the bunkhouse, so he knew now was the only time he would have.

He started by clearing his throat. That worked to give the fellas a 'heads up' that he had something to say. "I have to be up at the main house right after we eat, so I want to give you fellas the proper goodbye you deserve. You are a special bunch of men, I hope you know that. If you didn't know it before, now you do," he added as he peered up sheepishly at them. He really was not the speech-giving type, but here he was, giving one anyway, as they sat at the breakfast table.

"I told you before, you are the main reason I got all the way out here to this valley alive. You are a great bunch of fellas, and I thank you kindly and sincerely for your friendship. Now, before this gets all mushy, let me also tell you that you had better not start loafing around when I leave. My uncle is counting on you. You are important to this ranch," he reminded them, lowering his voice and trying to sound serious like Uncle Gene.

"That's right," piped in John from across the room. "No loafing!" Then he let out a chuckle. "You sounded just like your uncle there, Harley. Good one!"

"Well, John, these guys think of this place like home, and I know you'll keep treating them well. But right now, I'm done packing and I'm heading up to the house." He stood up, walked to their chairs, and shook each man's hand. "God bless all of you, and I hope we meet again someday," Harley said over his shoulder, as he walked over to the door and stepped out of the bunkhouse.

Gene and Harley took two of the horses and a buckboard wagon. Harley did not have much to take with him, so the horses' load was light; mostly the weight of the two men. His uncle had thrown an old tent in the back, along with some campfire supplies, because they would be sleeping under the stars one night, just like when Harley made the trip from Chelan to the ranch. For at least the first two hours, Uncle Gene was silent. Harley followed his cue, thinking the rancher had a lot on his mind about the coming winter preparations. When His uncle did speak to him, he wanted to know about Lena.

"I know I kept you busy, Harley, but you also know the ranch is a huge enterprise and I don't get much social time myself," he began. Continuing, Uncle Gene was obviously concerned about the effect of the dire economic conditions on his sister's family. "Are your folks going to be able to keep the farm, all of it? Or at least 160 acres? Ya can't earn a living on much less than that."

"We have a good herd of animals, and our expenses are pretty small. Mother gardens and works part-time for a lawyer in Valley Junction," Harley tried to assure him. "Things are much harder since Dad had his stroke, but our friends and neighbors help. My best friend Mike has been doing all my chores while I've been here."

Uncle Gene pressed Harley a bit more, "I just want to be certain that your mother and father will keep their farm. If Lena needs any help, you need to tell her that she has to let me know. I don't want them to have to auction the land, you understand?"

"Yessir," Harley replied, feeling somewhat uncomfortable under his uncle's piercing stare. "I understand and I will tell Mother that." Harley knew that both his parents would be too proud to ever take a penny from her brother, but he had promised Gene would tell her, so he would, if it ever got that bad. He hoped, in that same moment, that they would never be so close to losing their land that Harley would have to give his mother that message.

Having settled that concern, Uncle Gene started an inquiry into Harley's college plans. "Let's talk about your big plans for the money you earned here," Gene commanded. "How far into the University of Iowa do you think that cash will get you? What are you going to study? What's your plan for when you graduate?" He wanted some good answers, that was obvious!

"Well, Uncle Gene, I'm sure it will get me two semesters of tuition and some books. I am going to find a job over there for my room and board money. My friend Mike that I told you about, his dad knows a guy who owns a restaurant over there and he'll hire us both as waiters. We can eat there and live in the apartment above the restaurant."

Looking thoughtfully at Harley, his uncle replied, "Sounds like you have everything all planned, but you do know, don't you, that most times things don't always work out the way you plan them, right? What happens if that restaurant closes? What happens if the place burns down? What if…?"

Harley cut him off right there. "Uncle Gene! I know things can go wrong, but I'll be ready. I'll keep some savings, I know how to do lots of different jobs, and I am determined to make it through college! I'll *make* things work out!"

"Okay, okay, you sure do sound determined, and you have showed me in the past few months that you know how to work plenty hard, but what's your grand plan after you are done with all this schoolin'? What good is all this learning going to do you in the world?"

"Don't laugh, and don't tell my mother, but I want to own my own business. I think I want to sell floors, maybe furniture, too, but floors for sure." Harley glanced up at his uncle to gauge his reaction. He thought briefly that he might tell Uncle Gene about his dream of owning a Lincoln but held that back.

"That's interesting, but why not tell your mother? You think she expects you to come back home and clean a cattle barn with a college education?" Gene pulled the horses to a hard stop and turned to Harley.

"You must know her better than that. She wants more for you than farm labor, Harley. She wants you to take your education and your work ethic and make something big for yourself, don't you know that?"

"Sure, I know that, but I really love being on the farm. I love the smell of fresh hay in the barn loft, taking care of the animals, and being out in the open air all day long. I like a hard day's work. Honest, Uncle Gene, there has never been a single day when I wished I lived in town instead of out in the sticks on a dirt road. But, I know there is more in life for me than that, and I want to be able to help out my folks, especially now that Dad has had his stroke. They are going to need my help. I want to be in a position, financially, to give them what they need… and to let them enjoy life. My folks deserve that!"

"So, what are you going to be studying? You have a major picked out?" questioned Uncle Gene.

Harley had a quick answer for that. "Business and accounting, sir. I took a business class my senior year at Roosevelt, and I got an A. It was interesting and it was easy for me, and it all made a lot of sense. My teacher said I've got what it takes to run a business!"

His uncle looked over at him thoughtfully. Harley could tell Gene had been listening carefully to his plans. "I tend to agree with that teacher, Harley. You showed a lot of leadership at the ranch. You wrangled that odd assortment of hobos all the way from Iowa to Washington and helped each one acclimate to ranch life. Makes me feel proud of you, and proud of your folks for raising such a fine young man as you."

"You're giving me way too much credit. The trip out here was a team effort, really. When I hopped on that first train out of Des Moines, I had no idea what I was getting myself into, and I most definitely would not have made it on my own," Harley admitted, shaking his head.

"Give yourself more credit, son. I'm sure you had to scramble on your way out here, but you pulled together a group of hopeless men from all over and created a crew with a common goal. I'm glad and just plain lucky you brought them all to the ranch. You basically hired three new ranch hands for me, and you did a darn good job of it." The rancher gave Harley a hearty slap on the shoulder and said, "Let's pull up here and set up camp for tonight. There's a little creek just a bit south of here where we can water the horses. We can get up early and be in town before noon. The train thru Chelan comes pretty much on time, right around three o'clock."

Late afternoon came quickly as the two men set up a simple campfire site, but then the sun seemed to move slowly on its way to settle behind the horizon. Harley was glad to unhitch the horses and walk them over a small ridge to get water. He was somewhat leery of rattlesnakes, but his uncle assured him that as the day cooled off, the snakes would not be out sunning anymore. They would be trying to find a warm rock to wind up close to for the night and would be no threat to him or the horses. Still. Harley was watchful.

It was a perfect time to enjoy the quiet that was peacefully settling in as the horizon darkened in front of him. The horses were quite cooperative and sidled down the bank to the creek. Harley stood to the side and tried to understand the feeling of total happiness that had suddenly seized him. He smiled broadly and felt as satisfied and calm as he had in a long time. Sure, it was beautiful country and nature could bring that feeling, but this seemed different, and more. He thought a bit harder and realized it was an overwhelming feeling of accomplishment. He had overcome a mountain of difficulties and now he had his tuition! Back in Iowa, he'd had this crazy idea to go west and work for his uncle, earn college money, and cast a future that could help him reach his goals and help his parents. Those horses must have sensed the feeling, also, or else they were just happy to have a filling drink of water. They both tossed their heads toward Harley and almost seemed to grin at him. He could see their teeth, anyway, and he smiled back at them.

"Let's get back to the boss, fellas," he said, as he pulled on their halter ropes and walked them up through the tall grass leading away from the creek.

Uncle Gene had started a small fire and unpacked some of the leftover food Aunt

Lou had packed in the wagon for them. As they ate, both were silent, enjoying the peace and quiet. With the horses secured and settled in, the two men unrolled their sleeping bags close to the fire. Harley stacked on a few extra logs before climbing into his bag for the night and Gene thanked him.

"It's been a pleasure to spend the past couple of months with you, Harley. When I moved out here from Iowa so many years ago, I knew I would miss the family, but it has been a blessing to have the ranch and my independence. I was pretty darn young when I made my choice, but it turned out alright, I guess," Gene mused.

"Why did you move so far away, anyway?" Harley inquired, wondering if that was too bold of a question.

"Got my heart broke real bad in Iowa, son, and I just had to get far, far away from it. Simple as that," the rancher explained. "Lucky for me I met Aunt Lou out here. I would have had a miserable life without a woman like that. I have no regrets, that's for sure."

"I'd want to stay in Iowa when I graduate, but I guess I haven't really planned out where that might be. I suppose I don't have to plan that far ahead; I need to graduate from the university first." Harley was fishing for a little advice, and Gene knew it.

Gene was ready to share an idea he came up with while Harley was watering the horses. "Des Moines is a big enough city to have a successful business in. Grimes isn't that far away. You could get a few acres out by your folks and have your business in town." He paused, then explained more. "You'd have that country feeling, as well room to grow a family, if you find the right girl."

"Golly, Uncle Gene. You have it all planned out for me! How many kids do you reckon I should have?" Harley joked.

Harley and Gene both laughed. "You'll know what's right when that time comes, Harley. Just find the right girl first; that's the hard part. They rest comes naturally." The rancher turned his back to the fire and bunched up his pillow, which was really just an extra blanket. "Let's turn in now. We need to get going early to get you on that train."

"Goodnight then, sir, and thank you for the advice." Harley also bunched up his pillow, which was really just a blanket, and turned his back to the fire.

TO MY
FRIEND

FRIENDS MAY COME
AND FRIENDS MAY GO—
THE OLD FRIENDS
AND THE NEW,
BUT THROUGH THE
YEARS I HAVE
COME TO KNOW
THAT THE BEST OF
THEM ALL IS YOU

Reconnecting with Burnie

I don't remember dreaming anything, but I remember Mother gently and persistently shaking my shoulder.

"Mable, Sweetie, time to wake up. We have a baseball game to watch," Mother was whispering in my ear. "We need to get downstairs for a good breakfast. It's going to be a busy day."

I opened my eyes when I heard "busy day." It dawned on my sleepy head what that meant. I am going to see both Babe Ruth and Lou Gehrig today! I sat right up on the edge of the bed. It took me a minute to get my bearings. You know how when you wake up in a strange place and you are really not completely sure about where you are? It was like that. Then I remembered I was in Burnie's house. That felt good again.

"Okay, Mother. Do you know if the bathroom is available?" I asked.

"I'll check, dear. Do you know what you are going to wear?"

I started to answer her, but she had already headed down the hall to check on the availability of the bathroom. What she didn't suspect was that I had not given any thought at all to what I was going to wear today. I spent most of my time thinking about what I was going to wear tomorrow. It actually surprised me, when I thought about it, that Mother even cared what I wore. I thought she knew me better than that! Oddly enough, then I started thinking about it. What would I wear?

"Bathroom is available, Mable. I'm ready, so I'll just meet you in the dining room. Anything I can do to help you? Do you want to lay out what you are going to wear on the bed?"

"No, thank you, Mother. I haven't decided what I'm wearing yet," I told her as I whisked past her and down the hall. "I can take care of it. Don't worry, I'll be right down."

As I washed up and ran my brush through my hair, I looked at myself in the mirror. I smiled, practicing what I would say to Mr. Ruth when I met him. I tried several different greetings, but they all sounded fake. I decided to just see how Mr. Ashby greeted him, and then just say the same thing! Brilliant, Mable, simply brilliant. Well, even if it wasn't brilliant, it was the best I could do for now. We weren't going to catch up with him until tomorrow after the Drake scrimmage, so I had almost two days to come up with something appropriate and original.

When I returned to the bedroom, resplendent in my velvet robe, I thought maybe I could just wear my spectacular robe to meet him. The Babe would certainly never forget me! Geez, I had strange thoughts pop into my head sometimes lately. It had to be my nerves. Then I thought about how I hoped I could get my photograph taken with him. Surely Mr. Ashby would have his camera with him.

I had to get dressed. I opened my suitcase and looked at my dark green dress. It would look really nifty under my North High letter sweater. I was the only girl in my class who had one. After all, I was the only one who had lettered in practically every sport they had for girls. It would probably be getting a little cooler after the scrimmage tomorrow, and I would be nice and warm. Maybe Babe Ruth would ask me about my letters and chevrons and medals. Wow, I must have been going nuts. Only a hammerhead would be thinking like this. 'Get dressed, Mable, and get downstairs,' I told myself. 'Focus on the game today and quit worrying about tomorrow.' For today, I chose a blue skirt, white blouse, and a blue sweater. Good enough for a baseball game.

Everyone else was already down in the dining room, of course, and practically finished with their breakfast. Burnie's mom directed me to the kitchen and asked me to help myself to the French toast and bacon slices that were in the warmer on top of the stove. French toast! That was downright fancy for a Saturday breakfast. I thanked her several times for going to all the trouble, but she said she really enjoyed cooking for a crowd. And we were a crowd, with Mother and me, Uncle Albert, and the three Orwigs. It all felt good, though, like family.

The exhibition baseball game was going to be at Holcomb Park on 6th Avenue, home of the Des Moines Demons, at 11:00 A.M. This was also known as the Western League Park, where in May of 1930, they played the first-ever night baseball game under permanent lights. I didn't get to go, as the crowd was nearly double the capacity of the ballpark, but I sure would have loved to be there. Baseball Commissioner Kenesaw Mountain Landis even came to town to see it!

I loved watching baseball, and had not seen a real live game for what seemed like ages. Last summer had been so hectic, what with all the things going on in my life. Since Father passed away, baseball had almost slipped out of my life, too. Father would not have liked that. I was thinking how swell it would have been for him to be here today to see Babe and Lou, not to mention meet Babe tomorrow. Golly, I really missed him. My life was so busy and I was doing everything Father wanted me to be able to do, but he wasn't here to see it.

I had all these thoughts running through my head and realized that Burnie was trying to talk to me.

"Hello, hello, hello, Mable? Are you here?" he said it in a rather sing-song voice, so I reasoned it was not his first attempt to get my attention. Oops.

I apologized. "Sorry, Burnie. I have all sorts of different thoughts going through my head. I'm really sorry. What were you saying?"

"I was saying how they must be starving you at that university. You really goofed down that French toast! How much bacon did you eat?" he asked.

"I only had three pieces. How many did you have?"

"Not that many," He let out a little oink sound, like a pig, and I knew he was trying to be funny. I, however, was not amused.

"Well, I'm in two sports right now, smarty pants. I'm hungry. Is that alright with you?" I realized I sounded pretty defensive, but Mother just patted my lap.

"She's tired and cranky, still…not awake maybe. Do you want some nice cold orange juice, Mable? It certainly woke me up." Mother was trying to make up for my meanness.

"I really am sorry, Burnie. I have a thousand things going through my mind. Maybe we can find some time to talk before we leave for the game?"

Burnie's mother interjected, "Why don't you two go for a walk over past your old school? You can catch up with all of each other's news on the way?"

I wiped my hands and mouth on the cheery yellow cloth napkin and pushed back my chair. "May I please be excused? I'd like to go for a walk."

Burnie pushed his chair back also. "May I please be excused? I'd like to go for a walk."

"Please go, kids," ordered Mr. Orwig. "Have a great time. It's 9:30 now, so try to be back in about forty-five minutes. We need to all be in the car and heading down to the ballpark by 10:30, okay?"

Burnie's dad was so organized. He had a schedule for the whole day, I'll bet! Burnie grabbed his baseball cap on the way past the hat rack in the front hall, and we went quickly out the front door.

We had walked nearly a full block before Burnie said anything. I knew that he knew. He knew I was unhappy. I knew he was going to make me tell him everything. Well, he really wouldn't have to make me tell him. I needed to tell him all of it. The problem was, I wasn't sure where to even start.

"Just spill the beans, Mable. You can't fool me," Burnie said rather flatly. "Just spill all of them."

"I don't know where to start," I said quietly. They were very tiny, quiet words that came out of my mouth. It surprised me. I actually had a pretty loud voice. I didn't even sound like me.

"Just start. We can put it all in order later. Start anywhere. I want us to have a special day, and you are definitely not going to have any fun today with all that bother bottled up inside. It's not like you at all," coached Burnie, sounding more like a brother than he ever had before.

The next breath I took was so deep, it even surprised me. I stopped on the curb at the end of that first block. I let out that breath. We just stood there, not even crossing the street. It was a quiet and peaceful Saturday morning, but I knew that in many of the houses all around us, people were getting ready to go watch Babe Ruth play baseball in Des Moines, Iowa. I felt part of all that. It felt familiar and comfortable again. This was the perfect place to tell Burnie everything I was thinking.

I started right at the beginning. I told him about moving in with Dorothy and about how well we got along. The registration story had him nodding his head. I know he was sympathetic with my struggle to stay oriented in that huge, loud registration auditorium. Continuing with my Seals Club tryout and my disappointment at not being able to compete in the backstroke my freshman year, I let out my frustrations and felt my voice getting stronger and louder, more normal, but shaky. I tried to stay calm and not cry while telling him how I thought about Grandma Von Dornum every morning when putting on my robe and every night at bedtime when I slipped under my beloved quilt. I told him, with no small amount of embarrassment, about nearly getting a D on the first anatomy test. I explained how it was impossible to get even one tiny byline on the Daily Iowan, just because I was a freshman, and that I had a growing dread that as a sophomore next year, I was going to be given all the 'girly' articles and not get to be anywhere near the sports page.

In addition to that, I continued, that synchronized swimming stuff was taking a lot of time that should have been spent swimming my laps and sprints. I was truly afraid of not being ready to compete for national records next year if I didn't do more actual swimming. All the time, I kept remembering how proud of me my dad would have been and I did not want to disappoint him. I really had not made any other friends besides Dot. My journalism class was all fellas. My anatomy class was a lot of fellas going for pre-med. Dot was thinking of pledging a sorority, and I knew for sure that was not a route I was interested in. I felt lonely and I was terribly worried about my mother, although she kept telling me in her letters that she was just fine. How could she be fine? Her husband died and then her mother died.

Tears welled up constantly now as I spoke and I did not want to go back to Burnie's house with red eyes! I could not help myself. Burnie stood there in front of me, with his hand on my shoulder. I was hoping he would have some magic solution for me. The only solution I could think of was to move to Steamboat Rock with my mother. Maybe I could go to the Iowa State Teacher's College in Cedar Falls. I didn't want to be a teacher and I was pretty sure I had never heard of a national level swimmer from there, but it was the closest college to Mother's house now. It was a state school so the tuition would be the same, which was reasonable, but I would have to work to save up for it, because there was no way that school had swimming scholarships. They probably had a newspaper, but there was no way it could be the same caliber as the Daily Iowan.

All of this information and a rambling train of wild thoughts poured out. I looked up into Burnie's eyes a few times. Mostly I just looked up at the leaves on the trees across the street. They were turning colors and some were falling down around us. I felt like I was falling, and failing. I had never really failed at anything and my world was turned all sideways. I stopped talking.

"Mable, that's a lot of brutal stuff going on. I had no idea from your notes that you were that unhappy," Burnie offered. "I am so sorry."

"Well, I'm sorry, too," I sobbed. "I'm sorry I hate everything I'm doing right now. I always have done what I like to do, and I've been good at it, and I have had fun doing it. I'm not having any fun right now, and I don't like doing any of it, and I just want to QUIT! I need to quit and do something else. This is not the right time for me to go to college. It's too awful to keep up. I feel like I'm on the losing team every day, with everything I do. It's no fun to lose and I need to quit. Just quit now, and go live with Mother until I'm ready to try again."

Suddenly Burnie grabbed both my shoulders with his hands.

"No way. I hear you saying you are all tooted out and just exhausted, but you are tougher than this, Mable. You are talking like a lardhead. Your father would not be listening to any of this gibberish. Harry Hall would tell you to 'put your shoulder to the wheel' and to 'give it some gunch'! He would not listen to any of this nonsense for even a minute. Where on earth did you get a dumb idea like quitting?"

"I don't think it's dumb. It makes perfect sense to me. Nothing, absolutely nothing about my first year of college is going the way I thought it would. Everything is wrong. I just need to start over, that's all," I explained. "Just quit right now and start over. I think after your dad drops me off in Iowa City tomorrow I will just pack up and have Uncle Albert pick me up. Be done with it as soon as possible. I need to go home to my mother."

Bernie was really scowling now. He asked me if I had told Mother, or Mr. Ashby, or my Seals Club coach, or anyone. Had I told Dot already?

I told him I hadn't told anyone but him. Why would I be stupid and tell anyone before I told him?

"Well," Burnie began slowly. He was talking to me in a tone of voice that I interpreted like he was talking to a really stupid person. I did not appreciate it, and I told him so.

"Well," he began again in the same tone, totally ignoring my complaint. "I don't think you are stupid, but you are thinking like a hammerhead."

"Hrumph! You are not being much of a friend. I thought you were on my side." I scowled at him this time.

"There are no sides, Mable. You are just wrong. I am your best friend and I have been and will always be for you...when you are right. This quitting foolishness is just that...foolish. You won't be hearing me say it is a good idea at all. No one else will either. It's quitting. You don't quit. I don't quit. We don't quit. It's the worst idea I have ever heard. There isn't anything you have told me that can't be cured by either giving it a little more time, or a little more effort." Burnie had his hands on his hips now and was staring hard at me.

"What time is it?" I asked.

He pulled out the spiffy pocket watch he had received for graduation in May. It glistened in the mid-morning sun.

"We need to head back. We will talk more about this later. This discussion is not over, trust me," he said sternly. Now he sounded more like a parent than a brother.

I nodded, saying nothing. I could see he was pretty upset, but I couldn't help it. I was pretty darned upset, too.

Burnie switched over so he was walking on the street side of me, like a gentleman was supposed to do. I thought I heard that the custom of the man walking between a lady and the street was from back years ago. The carriages on the muddy streets might splash a person as they drove past, and the man was supposed to protect a woman from getting wet or dirty. I liked it, but it was bound to be a bad deal for the fella. I guess it could still happen with passing cars or bicycles.

Just as we approached his front yard Burnie said, "We are not going to discuss this in front of our families. We both need to do some thinking and we can talk about it again later, okay? Let's just go have a heck of a day at the ballpark. Deal?"

"Deal," I mumbled. I felt a little bit better getting it all off my chest, but I still felt extremely unsettled. I was looking forward to the baseball game for sure, so I knew I had to let go of my worries for now or I would spoil the whole day for myself and for everyone else. I did not want to do that. The adults in our lives had gone to a great deal of inconvenience and expense the past week arranging all the transportation and such to get Burnie and me to Des Moines to see the game and meet the great Babe. We were done thinking and talking about it for now. I stopped and peered into the entryway mirror as we passed it to make sure my eyes were not red.

Disaster on The Way to Sacramento

The two men arrived in Chelan with time for a short goodbye and lunch at the hotel before the train left. Harley made sure his uncle knew how appreciative he would always be for the time they shared together on the ranch.

Harley certainly had a different view from the passenger train than he had from the boxcars on his way out to Uncle Gene's ranch. This passenger car was much quieter than a boxcar, and he was higher up from the level of the tracks. It was almost like being a chicken on a roost, instead of on the ground. He could see the horizon more easily and noticed again the differences between the terrain out west and the cornfields of Iowa. Sacramento was in northern California. Harley had heard about all the farming and the masses of migrant workers and bums competing for work in the agricultural fields.

The fields he saw were stretching from the railroad tracks to the horizon, in all directions. Most appeared to be sugar beets, sunflowers, and various types of berries. There were vineyards and pear orchards. He saw one enormous operation that looked like it had hundreds of workers picking tomatoes. Most of the people in the fields looked like migrant workers, not hobos. He was grateful that he and the fellas had gone straight to Chelan and did not try to compete for a job in these fields.

Several times, when they stopped quickly in a few of the small towns of northern California, Harley was able to hustle out to the steps at the front of the car and observe the area around the station. He was interested in trying to see some of the local hobo jungles, if there were any. He only managed to see one, near Susanville. It looked like it was about a quarter of an acre and had many low shrubs growing around it. He could see a couple of fire pits, no fire in them. There were four or five bums sitting around, near the edges, and none of them were looking towards the train, but he imagined the hopeless looks on their faces. His hobo days were thankfully over and he was headed home with the $325.00 he needed to get through the first two semesters of college at the University of Iowa. He might have to work someplace in town for his room and board, but his college tuition and books were paid for. As he rested his head against the side of the doorway in the passenger car, he imagined his mother's smile. He closed his eyes and imagined his first Lincoln. He imagined his store and his own business. Harley had begun thinking it should be a furniture store or maybe a hardware store. He would seek advice from other people, and of course, he had to get to college first. Being young, Harley often found himself planning too far ahead of where he actually was in his plan, but he was keeping his dream alive. His dream was big, but his determination was even bigger.

The train started to move forward, departing Susanville and heading to Sacramento. First there was a small lurch, then a larger jerk. Harley grabbed for a vertical handrail and continued to look out at the hobo habitat as the train steadily rolled past the station, past the water and telegraph tower, and quickly picked up speed. Finally, he stepped toward the door into the car. He really did prefer being a regular passenger and not a stowaway.

Walking down the aisle to his seat, he did not see his jacket over the back of it. He thought he had been in exactly the middle row. Perhaps it had slid down on the seat, or he was looking at the wrong row. He hurried to the spot where was sure he had been sitting, and there was no jacket, and no suitcase! The man who had been sitting next to him was gone.

Harley looked at the remaining people sitting near his seat, desperately asking, "Where did this fellow go? Did any of you see him leave? My coat and bag are gone!"

They shook their heads. One woman said, "Sorry, I did see him get off the train, though. When he left, he had a coat and suitcase, but I assumed they were his. He walked to the rear of the car. I guess he got off."

"He stole my suitcase. He stole my coat!" Harley started to panic. "He stole my money!" He felt sick. His money was gone. His future was gone. How could he have been so foolish as to leave his bag unattended? What was he going to do?

The people on the car with him looked down. It seemed like no one wanted to make eye contact with him or help him. One man in the back spoke up, finally. "You should let the conductor know. He can let the manager of that station know. Although..." he added, "that thief has probably run off already. Your bag and money are gone, I'd bet."

Harley felt his face getting red. He felt like screaming or crying. "I worked all summer for that money. It was my college money! How could someone do that?"

"It's hard times, honey," an older woman in a green hat offered. "People do horrible things sometimes. Do you have far to go? Do you have someone to help you?"

"Yes, I'm going to see my great aunt in Sacramento, and I have a ticket home, but I need my money. I need my clothes," Harley explained. He patted his sweater pocket and was relieved to confirm that his train ticket home was indeed still there. His shoulders and arms felt so heavy, and his legs made him just plop down in the seat nearest him. "I don't know what to do," he said, as every bit of hope he had escaped from his body.

"There might not be anything you can do, except let the train people know," someone said. "I'll get the conductor for you, young man." A short middle-aged man got up and headed to the front of the car. "I believe I saw him go forward earlier. I'll be right back"

Harley wanted to thank him but was too stunned to speak any more at the moment. He would thank him when he returned, he thought. His brain was racing, but no clear thoughts were evident. He had never felt like this before. No one had ever done anything like this to him his whole life. Is this what the world was like? How had he been so careless? All he had was in the suitcase. He had not told anyone he had money. He had merely greeted that man next to him in a cordial manner. Was he a professional thief? Was he a desperate man? Was Harley lucky that he had not been robbed at gunpoint or knifepoint? How could someone do that to another person, just take everything and leave them nothing? Questions with no answers; that was all Harley had left. What would he tell Aunt Polly, or what would he tell his parents? He nearly felt like crying, but he was not going to let that happen. He rubbed his eyes, ran his fingers through his hair, and sat up straight. The other passengers were all looking out the windows. They had nothing to offer him in the way of comfort or explanation. What was there to say?

The short man came back with the conductor right behind him. Harley answered the conductor's questions as well as he could. The man's description, the name of the town, how he had left his suitcase unattended, how he came back to find his belongings gone; it was not helpful to retell his huge mistake. The conductor tried to explain what he would do with the information, but it was clear to Harley that he should not expect to see any of his belongings again.

Telling Aunt Polly would be easy, because she would wonder why he had nothing with him when he got off the train. He would need to confess immediately, right there on the platform. The difficult part would be when he had to let his parents know, or let Uncle Gene know. They would all think he was such a fool. Who would just leave everything they had sitting in a train car with a bunch of strangers? It would be embarrassing, if it wasn't so sad. He tried to stop thinking about it and decided perhaps he should try to sit down and relax. He felt slightly dizzy and emotionally drained, but it was such an unfamiliar feeling that he was not sure exactly what to do. He sat back in his seat with his hands folded and head down. It occurred to him that the other passengers might think he was praying; perhaps that is what he should do. So, he gave it a try, but it did not go well. He started thinking, instead, that he would like to get his hands on the culprit and strangle him. That would not go over well with the God that Harley knew, so he pushed the angry thoughts of violence out of his mind and decided to take a few deep breaths and try to nap.

He awoke as he heard the conductor pass by announcing, "Next stop, Sacramento! We will pull into the station in about fifteen minutes, folks."

His waking thoughts were fuzzy; then he remembered what had happened to him. He was now numb with the reality. In a few minutes, he would re-tell the story of his foolishness to his great aunt. It was his first trip on a train, as a real passenger. It dawned on him that he might actually have been safer riding as a bum, with his hobo friends to watch out for him. He surely was a failure at his first effort at watching out for himself. He shook his head.

The woman in the green hat spoke up again. "Young man, are you going to be alright?"

"Yes, ma'am. My great aunt will be at the station. She will know what to do. I just feel so foolish for letting this happen. I was so careless, and now I have lost everything I have." Then Harley realized how empty that statement sounded, and added, "Well, I still have my family. I will be alright, thank you." He managed a weak smile for her.

She smiled back a little bit, adding, "I'm sure you will be, but I am so sorry for this happening to you. Don't give up."

Mable and the Kids at the Game

We had to take two automobiles to the ball park. It was becoming a glorious warm fall day. The sun was bright and Mother ran back into the house to get her umbrella. She didn't want to get too much sun, she said. She really had never been an outdoors type of woman, even though she had lived on a farm as a young girl. Father had turned her into a city girl. It was definitely surprising that I became such a tomboy.

When we got to the ballpark, it looked like a beehive. Swarms of people were streaming into the gates. The level of excitement was quite high. There were many young boys there and I was sure they were eager to see their baseball hero. Babe was known for his hard-hitting and for all those home runs. People quoted him all the time; he could be very inspiring and entertaining.

One of my favorite quotes was when Babe said, "I swing big, with everything I've got. I hit big or I miss big. I like to live as big as I can." Babe was a big character, and characters always made writing about sports easy. It was the daily stories that challenged any writer. As I looked around for Mr. Ashby at the main gate, where we had arranged to meet him, I was thinking that he was a great sportswriter because he made every article interesting. He made any athlete or any game he was writing about come alive.

Holcomb Park was wonderful, for a minor league park. One upper tier of seating with about twenty-five rows, wrapped around from far right to far left field. It had standard seating for a municipal ballpark and then there were more low bleachers and some standing room areas stretched all around the outfield. It had a capacity of 5.000 fans! The ads on the outfield fences were colorfully painted and neatly redone before every season. The playing field, on the other hand, showed signs of regular and hard use.

"Over here, Mable." I heard Mr. Ashby call out from behind us. He was running toward us as we stood there by the ticket office. Mother having her flowered umbrella up probably helped him spot us. He had his camera in one hand and his press tag flapping around his neck. He was always ready for a story and a picture.

We all got to our seats and then he asked me to go to the field with him. It surprised me when Mr. Ashby told Mother that we might not be back until after the game, and to meet us at the cars in case that happened. I had been hoping he would get to talk to the two big Yankee stars, but I discovered he was intent on getting a story from one of the kids swarming around the edges of the field. I knew I shouldn't have been surprised. After all, he did a story about a girl swimmer and I was definitely not a star of any kind. He thought I was interesting and that he could write a compelling story about me that people would like to read.

"Look for an interesting kid, would you Mable?" he asked. "Let's find one who is different from the rest of them."

I looked around. There were hundreds of people, but not as many children as I thought there might be. I had read in yesterday's paper that they were expecting at least 8,000 fans today, but it seemed like many more people than that were already there and it was still at least thirty minutes before the game. The teams were already warming up.

I did see a tall, slender girl who looked like she was about thirteen or so, and she had a little brother on each hand. It appeared to me as though she was trying to find a good spot in the standing-room-only outfield area from which to watch the game. She would have to be right up to the fence or the little boys would never be able to see. There were already about three rows of taller folks in front of her, so she was craning her neck to see if there was a better place to try.

"Mr. Ashby, what about that girl over there? The one with the two little boys? She's trying to find a place to watch from. Maybe we could help her," I pointed and explained.

"I see her, Mable. Looks good to me. Let's go," Ted agreed.

I went over towards her and tried to get her attention by waving and she looked at me, but of course she did not know who I was or why I was waving at her. She made eye contact with me for just a few seconds, and then began looking around again. Again, I waved, but I also called out to her this time.

"Little girl, let me help you," I told her, in a rather demanding way, now that I think about it.

"I want my brothers to be able to see," she answered and pointed towards the rows of adults in front of her.

Ted caught up with me as I pressed towards her. "I can help you get in the front, young lady," he assured her and held his press pass up in front of himself as he weaved us through the crowd.

"We need to get to the bullpen, folks, Press. Press here, please let us pass through to the bullpen," Ted kept repeating authoritatively. People just stepped aside for him. A few said, "Hi, Ted." Or "Quite a crowd, huh, Ted?" They either knew him or recognized him from his picture that was next to his column every week. It was unusual being with a celebrity. I guess that's what you would call him. He was famous, at least in Des Moines. It was exciting.

Ted kept leading the girl and her brothers, and I followed along on their heels. I didn't want to get lost and be left alone in that crowd. I didn't have any idea where our seats were from where we were now, but I was confident that Burnie would take care of Mother for me and get everyone else in our families to their seats for the game. I had never seen this ball park so jam-packed.

Ted maneuvered us to and through the gate in the fence by the bullpen. The bullpen is where all the relief pitchers warm up and wait to get their chance to pitch sometime during the game. All the players in the bullpen were Demons. Babe Ruth and Lou Gehrig were nowhere to be seen. Ted saw the disappointment on my face.

"Mable, we are here to write about the game. We will catch up with the Bambino tomorrow at Drake. We can't be bothering him during the game. He and Larrupin' Lou have a home run hitting show to put on. Looks to me like there are at least 10,000 folks here who came itching to see some hard-hittin' baseball. Babe doesn't have time for us now, for sure."

The girl quietly asked, "Are we going to stay here and watch the game?"

Ted turned to the pitching coach, who looked like a growly old bear. "Hey, Joe! Okay if I let these three little baseball fans stay here for a good view? Too many big folks are hoggin' all the fence space."

Joe hooted back, "Okay with me, Ted. Any friends of yours are friends of mine. This ain't no official game no how. No harm...let 'em sit down and watch from the end of the bench down there."

All I could think came from my writing brain. 'This ain't no official game no how.' Wow, three negatives in one sentence; Miss Hawn would have flunked him in English for sure! Anyway, I made sure the kids were comfy on the end of the bench, then started looking around.

Ted was starting to take pictures. He took quite a few photographs of the players in the bullpen, and then stepped onto the outfield to take a few shots of the crowd. The ball park was certainly completely over-capacity, and we had the best seats! We were practically right on the field. I hoped Burnie could see well and that Mother was in the shade.

I was gawking at everything there was to see, when I felt Ted right behind my shoulder. He said, "Mable, go talk to that girl, and find out her story. Where are their parents? Are those her brothers? How old are all those kids? Do they usually come to games? We have a story to write here!"

I thought I heard "We have a story to write here." I knew that's what I heard! He said "we," right? Was he going to let me help with the story? Jiggers, that would be wonderful! There might be words that I wrote, printed in the Des Moines Register and Tribune. I was going after my first real story!

I weaved through an uneven row of potential pitchers, none of whom looked too overly eager to be sent in to pitch against Babe or Lou. All big-time talkers, suddenly turned into big-time gawkers. I smiled to myself. It was amusing, seeing these full-grown baseball fellas turned into little boys again. I moved alongside the dark-haired girl and asked if I could sit down with her. She wasn't really watching the game; she was just watching the two younger boys watch.

"My name is Mable," is what I opened with. Seemed harmless enough.

She answered me with, "I'm too tired to talk right now." She really did look tired, too. The minute she sat down and had an opportunity to let go of the boys' hands in a safe place, she hunched over and looked like a much older person. I noticed then that she had dark circles under her eyes. She was also pretty pale for the end of the summer. All three of them were. It looked like they never got outside.

"Could you please just tell me your name?"

"Edith."

"What are your brothers' names? They are your brothers, right?"

She glanced sideways at me. "I am really tired, but their names are Levi and Paul, okay?" She let out a huge sigh.

She really did not want to talk to me. I decided to give it a break: I'd move to the other end of the bullpen and watch the game for a few minutes, then try again.

Ted came over by me and started listing all the fellas on each roster for this game. Babe Ruth and Lou Gehrig were the only Yankees actually playing on this barnstorming tour. The rest of the players in each stop on the tour were recruited from the local ball club. The Des Moines Demons were pretty evenly split in ability, between the two stars' teams. Stan Keyes was the star of the Des Moines Demons. He had hit thirty-eight home runs in the 1928 season and had a batting average of .369. That was impressive, considering he was the second oldest member of the Demons. No other players were even close to those stats, and he was about ten years older than they were.

Ted then changed the course of the conversation.

"Mable, go ask those kids if they would like a red hot. They look hungry to me. Maybe they want a fizzy soda, too. Go ask 'em. Hurry back."

I hustled back over to Edith's side. "My friend Ted wants to buy you kids each a red hot. Would you like to have a fizzy soda, too?"

Her eyes brightened a little bit. She turned her head and looked right at me for the first time. "Sure, we would. You call him Ted? He's not your father?"

"No, he's a newspaper writer that I know. We are friends. He wrote an article about me last year. I am going to go tell him you want to eat. I'll be right back," I said, hoping she was now in the mood to talk to me. Ted was counting on me to get her story. I had to get busy!

I told Ted that the kids would love red hots and sodas, and he excused himself to go get the concessions. I headed back to learn more about these three children. I was an only child. Burnie was like a brother, but that was not the same. This trio of children was beginning to pique my interest.

"Edith," I began, "do you live near here? How did you get here? Are your parents here somewhere?" I realized almost immediately that I had asked her three questions and not even given her a chance to answer the first one. I was a better interviewer than this! She kept watching the game and acted as though she had not even heard me.

"I'm sorry, Edith. How did you get to the game today? Just wondering?"

She turned slowly to face me. "We walked. We live over on the other side of East 14th Street. Just south of the river. Over by the junkyards."

"That's over a mile away. Do you come to many of the games over here?" I asked.

"We came to just a few games this past summer. We mostly sit outside in the grass and listen. Tickets cost too much. My father saved up for our tickets this time." She smiled.

"Your father sounds really nice. Is he here, also?" I asked.

"No, he's working today. He works every day. He has two jobs and works really hard," Edith offered. "He works for the city, and he works at the junk yard on the weekends."

"Interesting," I thought out loud. I always wanted to go explore in a junk yard, but Mother and Father would never let me. In fact, they strongly discouraged it; they said it was dangerous. "What does he do for the city?"

"He is a garbage collector. He picks up your garbage, well, everyone's garbage." Then she added, rather matter-of-factly, "Our mother died five years ago."

"I am so sorry to hear that. Really sorry," I told her. "It must be very hard for your father and you."

"Oh, we get along okay. Dad and I get Paul ready before school in the morning. The neighbor lady is like a grandmother to us, and she watches him while Levi and I are in school. I watch them both all summer; they are good boys," she started explaining.

She went on, as we watched a rather uneventful first inning, to explain how she and her brothers became motherless. Her mother died of complications from childbirth after Paul was born. She was eight at the time and basically became a surrogate mother to her two younger brothers. They were now five and seven and she was thirteen. No wonder she looked so tired.

"Oh, look at this, Babe Ruth is going to pitch! He hasn't even bothered to get warmed up!" Edith exclaimed. She suddenly leaped up to her feet and dashed to the end of the bullpen.

I followed her and so did the little brothers. Just then, Ted entered the bullpen from the other end. His arms were loaded with red hots in steaming fresh buns and a large carton of soda.

"Red hots, anyone?" he sounded like the red hot salesman who roamed the baseball stands. It was funny. "Red hots? Get 'em while they're hot." He stood there, arms laden with that all-American baseball staple, and the boys rushed over to him. Levi brought Edith's to her and then went back to claim his own. Ted handed them out to the boys, and then brought me one, also.

"You didn't have to get me one, Ted, but thank you very much. I am a bit hungry." I said, as I began stuffing the bulging red hot and soft, warm bun into my mouth. It didn't have ketchup on it, but it was quite tasty. As long as it didn't have mustard on it, I could eat almost anything.

Ted took a few pictures of the boys and Edith watching the game, and a few more of all of us eating the red hots. I was trying to scan the crowd for Mother's umbrella. I thought I spotted it once, but then realized it was not her. I was probably not going to get to see her or Burnie until after the game; we would just have to meet them by the car.

Being on assignment with Ted was almost as much fun as just watching the game; there was so much going on. Bath Ruth pitched two innings and Lou Gehrig pitched two innings, but neither of the big Yankee stars had hit a home run yet. Every time one of them got up to bat, the crowd cheered and hollered, but to no avail. They each got some base hits and drove in a few runs, but no balls were going over the fence. It was easy to see the disappointment in the faces of the two little boys. Their big sister Edith was obviously a more seasoned sports fan like me, and she took the let-down in stride. She would glance sideways at me now and then. I didn't know whether she wanted to talk some more, or if she was just checking to see if I was still there. Either way, I had dropped our conversation in the middle of an interview and I had to get it back on track.

The red hots were devoured and washed down with the fizzy soda. Ted offered to take the boys to the men's room, so Edith and I were left side-by-side at the end of the bullpen bench. Most the potential pitchers looked more and more relieved as *the game wore on...they would not have to pitch to the two greatest hitters in the history of baseball; they were very happy to just observe.*

I had to get Edith talking again. There seemed to be more to her story. Perhaps it was the sad look in her eyes or the premature curve in her back when she sat, but I didn't know exactly what it was. I had to ask.

"Edith, how are things going with school? Paul will be going into kindergarten in the fall, won't he," I inquired. "Is Levi in second grade?"

"They are doing well, Mable." She smiled slightly, but it did not last very long. "Levi really loves school." Her smile once more appeared briefly and disappeared quickly again.

"Is there something wrong, Edith? I feel like you are really sad about something. Can you tell me? Everyone says I am a good listener."

"I wish I could tell you, I really do. I am not sure what it is, and I really can't describe it. I just feel sad, and like giving up, but I know I can't." Now Edith looked even more sad. "And I don't have anyone to talk to, and here come the boys, so never mind, but thank you." She stood and greeted her brothers with big hugs, and ushered them right back to the near fence, so they could see the whole field again. She peeked back over her shoulder and gave me a wink and a faint smile.

I looked at Ted. "Ted, I have been talking to Edith, and these kids have no mother. Their father works two jobs and she seems so sad. We really didn't get to talk about baseball that much, I'm sorry."

Ted shook his head a little, took off his hat, ran his fingers through his hair, and put his hat back on. "Mable, there is a big lesson in this for you."

"A big lesson? About writing? About sports? Tell me, Ted, please," I asked him. "I'm here to learn!"

"Listen, Mable, because this is important. At any given sporting event, not all the stories are about sports. Sports always involve people, and people are human. The most interesting and most compelling part of sports is nearly always the human part. Everyone at this game has a story, Babe has a story, you have a story, Edith has a story, even that goofy relief pitcher over there with his socks and shoes off has a story. It's our job, as reporters, to dig up those stories and bring them to the light of day in the newspaper. That's why I love this job!"

Wow, I had to talk some more with Edith. She definitely had a story.

In Sacramento With Aunt Polly

Aunt Lou had told him that Aunt Polly would be wearing pink. It was her favorite color and was a large part of her wardrobe. Harley had no trouble spotting her. It seemed like nearly everyone else on the boarding platform was dressed in black, brown, or gray. She looked like a single flower in a bare garden. She was beaming at him as she approached, but he could hardly muster a grim grin. He was fearful she would know something was terribly wrong right away and it would ruin their first meeting. She was so special to his mother, and now he had to bring this disaster to their brief visit.

"Harley, dear, it is so wonderful to finally meet you!" she gushed, giving him an arms-wide-open embrace. He hugged her back, and as they parted, she looked at him quizzically. "Are you not feeling well, Harley?"

"I'm so sorry, Aunt Polly. I let something horrible happen on the train, and I am feeling awful about it. It's a mess now, and it just happened about an hour or so ago, and I'm angry and mad at myself and I really don't want it to spoil my visit, but I don't know what to do at all," Harley rambled on as he held her hands in his. "I'm just so sorry."

"My goodness, I don't know what to say. What are you talking about, dear?" She stepped back just a little bit and looked up at him.

"I left my suitcase on my seat and stepped out of the car at the last stop. When I came back, it had been stolen. My jacket, my clothing, and all the money I earned at Uncle Gene's. It's all gone," he confessed. "It's all my fault."

"My word! How awful. Did you tell anyone?"

"The conductor took all the information, and relayed it back to Susanville, where it happened, but he thinks there is little that can be done. It was probably an experienced thief. I can't believe that fella sat next to me almost all the way from Chelan. We didn't speak much, but he had no reason to do this to me," Harley explained. He felt so naïve. "I guess I appeared to be an easy victim. And I suppose I was."

"I'll tell you what," said his great aunt, "Let's get back to my house, have something to eat, and try to figure this out." She tugged at his arm and guided him away from the train. He followed her through the station and to her car.

It was a nice gray Ford. Really clean and shiny. She offered to let him drive, but since she knew better where she was going, he declined. He thought maybe he could see more of the sights if he was not driving. Plus, he was still having difficulty thinking of much else than being robbed, so he would be a distracted driver. Harley had not driven much in the city, either. Most of his road experience was on dirt roads or in the small town of Grimes, having only driven in Des Moines three or four times. He was definitely not ready for the streets of the capital city of California!

Aunt Polly's house was a white cottage with a red-tiled roof. The yard was bursting with colorful flower beds that his mother would have loved. The driveway was crushed white rock. The inside was welcoming and there were a lot more windows than there were in the replacement farmhouse they had built after the fire. Someday, he would make sure his parents had a really beautiful home like this, he thought.

She ushered him into the sunny front room. It was nearly four o'clock in the afternoon, so she said that a piece of pie and a cup of tea was in order. Harley took a few minutes to look around the room as Aunt Polly went to the kitchen to prepare his treat. It was tidy and organized. His great aunt did have a large stack of books and magazines piled next to what was obviously her reading spot, so she was definitely related to his mother. Other than that conglomeration, everything else was quite symmetrical and well-appointed. The furniture and wall decorations were floral and color-coordinated. Harley was no expert of décor, but it clearly reminded him of the tasteful rooms he had seen in some of the magazines that Betty sometimes brought over to show his mother. Betty was somewhat into trying to be more modern in the decorating of her house. Lena's house was functional and everything had a purpose. There were not many frills in his upbringing. He enjoyed the looks of Aunt Polly's house, but decided his home in Iowa was more suitable for his taste.

The windows in this house really made the difference. It was almost like he was sitting outside. That was probably the intended effect and he did appreciate that part. He usually wasn't much for sitting around inside.

Aunt Polly returned with pie and tea, as well as a plate for herself. It was served on one of those little oval carved-glass trays with a matching cup, like he had seen the ladies at church teas use, or like they put out on the cake table at the graduation party he had attended at the church in Grimes. His mother owned nothing like these and he was surprised his great aunt had her own set. He thought they were just used at larger gatherings. Pretty fancy, but of course Aunt Polly was a widow who had inherited good money, so she could afford special things like this.

"I made the pie myself, Harley. Do you like it?"

"It's a delicious pie, ma'am. As good as my mother's, and that's darned good," he replied.

"Well, thank you for that, Harley. That's quite a compliment, because Lena does make delicious pie," Polly answered. "Are you feeling a little better?"

"I honestly don't know," Harley ventured. "I am very disappointed in myself, and I don't know what I am going to do, but I do dread telling my parents what has happened. I want them to know, but I don't want them to find out. That doesn't make any sense, does it? I'm so sorry to come here in these circumstances. I thought this would be a grand visit and then I would get on the train to Iowa and be college-bound. I have gone through a lot of difficulty to earn that money. It's quite a story, and now it's all for nothing."

"Listen," Aunt Polly spoke firmly but quietly. "This is bad, I will admit. It is hard to hear and you are clearly so unhappy. I understand. Gene told me how hard you worked and also some of the very difficult times you had just getting to Chelan. Especially with that friend of yours who fell off your horse and died. That must have been terrible. I understand, but I can only imagine a little bit of the disappointment and loss you are feeling."

"I would give anything to get my money back, Aunt Polly."

"I could replace it for you, Harley," she replied.

"Oh no, we can't do that. I mean, that is very generous, but I want the money that I earned to pay for college. I cannot just have someone give it to me. Thank you so much, but I never intended to impose on you like that. I can't."

"Of course, you can. I am family, Harley," Aunt Polly insisted.

Harley was just as insistent. "No, just plain no," he stated. "I will find a way to earn it again when I get home. There is always a way to earn money if you really need to."

Aunt Polly looked at him for what seemed a whole minute. He had to look down at his pie. Then she told him how she admired him, and she knew his parents had 'raised him right'. She told him there were long bread lines in downtown Sacramento, and really no jobs here. Almost 90,000 people lived in Sacramento and she was one of the lucky ones. The way the economy was, her money wasn't worth much, but she could get through all this and had no desperate need like so many people. She offered to drive him around and show him, but he declined.

"I have seen enough struggle," Harley explained. "Let's just get to know each other. Maybe you can tell me some stories about my mother and father, if you like. Or, tell me about how you came to live in California, all the way from South Dakota. I really just need to relax and figure out what to do when I get home. We have two more days to get acquainted, so let's just do that." He hoped she would not be offended and respect his desire to just try to take it a bit easy.

Aunt Polly was sweet and certainly seemed to understand. He had a comfortable bedroom to himself, with a wonderful east-facing sunny window. Waking up in that room reminded Harley of his parent's bedroom. His father had always told Lena how he liked seeing the sun come up every morning right away. Harley missed his parents badly, the most since he had left Iowa. He figured he had just been too busy before now, and it seemed odd that he was so anxious to finally be home again, while at the same time dreading having to face them and tell them about his stolen college money. He tried not to think of it too much, but it inevitably creeped into his thoughts several times a day.

Aunt Polly was a delightful hostess. They went fishing once, but she was the only one who caught anything. Harley made the excuse that he was out of practice and vowed to her that he would catch one next time. She also regaled him with stories of his mother as a young girl on the farm in South Dakota. He learned more details of their life as neighbors living in their sod houses and toiling to scrape out an existence on the bleak South Dakota farms of their parents. Aunt Polly obviously had the same level of adoration of the old draft horses as his mother did. Harley felt blessed to have such a large family with a strong work ethic. It gave him encouragement that he would find a way to regain his money for school.

Her version of how his parents met at the train station in Des Moines differed considerably from his mother's tale. Aunt Polly was not as sure of the "love at first sight" as Lena was. Polly saw a pretty rough-looking farm guy on that boarding platform, and Lena saw her true love. It turned out that both women were right, Harley told her, and she did have to agree with that.

The pair ventured out one more time in her Ford, so Polly could show him the state capitol. There was no way for them to avoid seeing Sacramento's astounding "Hooverville", however. It was large and sprawled for many acres across a hillside not far from downtown. It was full of tents, crudely-built shelter shacks, and hundreds of homeless folks. She avoided driving right along the side of it but got plenty close for Harley to get the feeling of dire poverty that rose up from it and hung thickly over the entire area.

Harley rode along silently for a while, then he spoke up. "I will not be like that, and I will not allow my parents to be like that," he firmly told his great aunt. "I told you about my plan to own my own business, to help my parents, and to have a car just like Mr. Flynn. I mean it, with every bone in my body. I will be successful, no matter what."

"Well, I know you don't mean, 'No matter what,' dear. You will work hard, be honest, and gain your fortune in a way that will make us all proud." Harley straightened up, smiled at her, and Aunt Polly continued, "I hate to bring this up, but we have not spoken of it for quite a while since you arrived. Have you given more thought about where your college money will come from?"

"Yes, I have, but I will keep the details to myself. I'm sorry to seem secretive. My ideas are still working around in my head. I have some people, like Uncle Lynn and Mr. Flynn, who I think I might speak to about this when I get home. I'm sure my mother will keep you posted, since you know all about this now. I truly appreciate all the accommodations, delicious food, and the pleasant time you have helped me have during my visit here. I'm going to be sad to leave tomorrow. Do you know what time my train leaves?" Harley inquired.

"Ten o'clock sharp, in the morning. I have a canvas valise you may take your things in, dear. Please keep it," offered Aunt Polly.

"Thank you so much and thank you for getting me an extra change of clothes. Are you sure you don't want the valise back? I have imposed on you quite a bit already."

She insisted, "Please take it to the university with you, Harley. That would please me very much, really,"

Harley gave her a smile. Her kindness was so comforting as he continued to contemplate telling his parents about his disappointing loss.

They drove back to Aunt Polly's house and Harley spent the rest of the afternoon doing some yard work for her. It felt good to have chores to do. He wanted to stay busy and he was pleased to be able to help her out. Her yard was small but had several different beds of flowers in the front that needed weeding and a bank of bushes in the backyard that needed trimming. She brought him out a glass of lemonade just as he finished, so he was sure she had been watching him from inside the house.

"I'm going to write your mother and ask her if I can borrow you for yardwork more often," joked Aunt Polly. "Your folks sure have taught you to work hard. Uncle Gene told me what a go-getter you were, but I had no idea! This work would have taken one of my local yard men a couple of days. You did it in one afternoon!"

"Happy to help you out, Aunt Polly. It feels good and will help me get ready to pitch in again when I get back to Iowa. I'd better finish off this lemonade and get cleaned up for dinner. Is there anything in the kitchen I can help you with?" asked Harley.

"Golly, no, Harley. Thank you, though. You have helped me plenty. Just go wash up. I have dinner almost ready."

After cleaning up, Harley ate dinner with his great aunt. Their conversation was pleasant and the unfortunate theft of his college money was not discussed, but it was all Harley was thinking about. He would have more time on the train, but he knew he had to come up with a plan for getting more money. Harley went to bed that night, thinking about it; he woke up the next morning, thinking about it.

Aunt Polly gave him a tight little hug at the train, and he climbed aboard with his gift valise. She had given Harley a twenty-dollar bill for his afternoon of yard work, which was like a week's pay at the ranch. He thanked her repeatedly for all her hospitality and especially for her generosity. He promised to give Lena a hug for her and waved out the window of the train one final time as the wheels started turning. He was going home.

Mable and Edith

Resting my hand gently on Edith's shoulder, I sought to resume the interview. "Could we talk a little bit more? Your family is so interesting," I offered, hoping to cajole her into sharing more of her feelings.

"Interesting? I don't know about that. Frustrating and exhausting, for sure," sighed Edith.

"You look tired, Edith, you really do. I don't know how you do everything for your dad and brothers."

"I don't know how I do it either, Mable. I'm pooped. If it wasn't for the boys, I think I would run away. It's like I am just going through the motions at home, and I just don't have time to even have friends or any fun at all. I am so tired," Edith confided. "I'm so tired, all the time."

"Have you talked to your dad about how you feel?" I asked.

"My father is so busy, and he's tired, too. If I just ran away, the boys could maybe go to the neighbor's or live somewhere with a nice family. It's just too hard," Edith said quietly, so her brothers could not hear.

"Oh, no! You can't do that. Running away is dangerous, and your brothers and dad would miss you so much. You can't quit," I blurted out. No sooner had "you can't quit" come out of my mouth, and I realized I had more in common with this little girl than I knew before. She felt trapped and overwhelmed just like I did!

"Edith, you need to talk to your neighbor lady, or maybe your teacher at school. Do you know any ministers? I know there are people in Des Moines who could help your family. They offered us help when my father died. People care and running away is not the answer at all. You are too young to give up. You just need to ask for help," I assured her.

I moved a little closer and put my arm around her. "I am going to ask Ted to give you his business card. He knows lots of people. I think he knows almost everyone in Des Moines. I will ask him to help you find people who can help your family, without you running away and quitting!"

Edith looked over at me, but it was a doubtful glance. "I don't know Ted, and I don't know you. I don't think anyone can help us."

"Oh, yes they can! Ted has helped me a lot, and he can help you, too. He's a great guy and he loves baseball just like you kids do. Trust me, no quitting! Promise?" I looked her right in the eye and she returned my gaze with a small smile.

Letting out a big sigh, Edith agreed. "Okay, no quitting, and I will listen to Ted. You have been so nice to listen to me, Mable, and I should say thank you. And thanks for letting us hang out with you during the game. I can't wait to tell Father about this!"

"You are welcome, Edith. And you need to tell him how you feel, also. Talking helps when you are worried and being willing to let other people help is important, too," I reminded her.

She was so young to have to deal with this. I was older, but not that much older, and I was trying to run away, too. I had some place safe to run to but had not talked to anyone but Burnie. I also had not asked anyone else for help, so where did I get off giving her that advice? I decided I had some more thinking to do, but there was no time for that now. The Demons just made their last out, and the crowd was standing up to go. There was a low level of grumbling that could be heard, what with no home runs by the Babe and Lou.

Eight thousand people, maybe a few hundred more, streamed out of the ball park, and you could hear the disappointment all the way.

"Not a single home run."

"Might as well of stayed home and watched the leaves fall off the trees."

"Can't believe I paid money to watch that."

"Weren't Babe Ruth and Lou Gehrig supposed to play today? Who were those two jokers?"

"They couldn't bat their way out of a paper sack."

Fans could be cruel. I would have enjoyed seeing a couple of home runs, too, but it was enough fun just to see those two giants of baseball in person. The thought of meeting Babe Ruth tomorrow popped back into my head. How strange that it had ever left. What this whole afternoon had become so far was not about baseball. I thought it was supposed to be about baseball, until I met Edith and her brothers.

Mother and Burnie were right there by the car. Ted and I had been delayed saying goodbye to Edith, Levi, and Paul. I wrote down her address and told her that I would write to her from school, or home, or wherever I landed next. Ted told her to watch the newspaper in a day or two for the pictures he took of her and her little brothers. He also gave her his business card, as well as getting their phone number. Burnie was leaning on the car, acting impatient, but he was just joking.

We apologized for being late and packed ourselves into the cars. Ted leaned into our car window, asking Mother and Burnie what they thought of the game.

Mother simply said, "My dear John Henry would have been very disappointed in this game. Before the game, I was wishing he could be here with us to see it, but now I'm rather happy for him that he missed it."

I started to say that he really didn't miss it, that he could have been watching it from Heaven, but then I changed my mind. Saying that would have upset Mother, I was sure.

Burnie had a different perspective. "I love baseball games. This was a great game. I got to see Babe Ruth and Lou Gehrig. There's a lifetime event right there! Stan Keyes hit two home runs. Jevers stole a couple of bases, and it was a warm sunny day at the ballpark with my favorite people. I am as happy as if I had good sense, as Mr. Hall used to say. I had a great time!

Mother asked me, "Where did you and Mr. Ashby spend the game, Mable? You two took off and we never saw you again until now."

"We went looking for a story, Mother. I found a young girl, Edith, and her two younger brothers. They walked to the ballpark from over on the other side of East 14th Street, just to see the game. Ted made arrangements for all of us to watch the game from the bullpen. He even bought us all red hots and fizzy soda! I interviewed her a little bit. It was just like being a writer for the Tribune and I loved it," I rambled on. "She was just standing there trying to help her little brothers see the game, so we helped her. It was really swell!"

Mother and the Orwigs all laughed at my excitement. It didn't bother me, however, because I was too jazzed up! I knew they were supportive of me, so it was fine.

I kept talking. "Tomorrow we are going on a wonderful picnic, right? Then the football game? What time are we leaving?" I asked Mother.

"I am pretty sure Mrs. Orwig said we would head over to Union Park about one o'clock. Then at four o'clock, we will go to Drake's football team scrimmage," Mother replied.

I picked up the plan. "And then we will be the first people to ever see The Bambino play football! I don't care if he didn't hit a home run in that game we just watched and I don't care if he doesn't score a touchdown in the scrimmage, I'm going to get to meet Babe Ruth!" I finished with a sort-of "so there" sigh and fell back against the seat of the car. I thought that I should probably try to relax for a few minutes. It was going to be tough to sleep tonight.

Everyone else got quiet, probably mulling over their thoughts on the baseball game we witnessed and maybe anticipating the meeting with greatness that was coming tomorrow. We rode the rest of the way home in silence.

'First professional baseball night game under permanent lights.
Holcomb Field, Des Moines, Iowa   May 3, 1930

Tales of the Trip Home

Harley boarded the Southern Pacific "Overland Route" in Sacramento, rode through Carson City, Salt Lake City, and Denver. It took a short jog south to Colorado Springs. There he boarded a Rock Island Line train that went through Lincoln, Omaha, and to Des Moines. He held his valise in his lap the whole trip. Aunt Polly had packed him a grub sack of sandwiches and fruit. Actually, it was a tin lunch box. Harley had left his grub sack on the ranch. He was careful and only spent about fifty cents of the money she had given him. He felt like he wanted to have a little cash to show his parents when he explained what had happened to his college money.

Arriving at the Des Moines station, Harley was surprised when he saw his friend Mike first, towering above the other people on the platform. He must have been home early from the university for Thanksgiving Break. Lena was right next to him, but barely visible in the quickening dimness. The train was arriving later than scheduled; about three hours later, so it was nearly dark at six. Next week was Thanksgiving and the days were getting shorter quickly. Harley took the last step off the train and realized Mike had steered his mother so she was right in front of him. Lena gave him a warm hug and stepped back to take a look at him.

"None too worse for the wear," she observed. Then she chuckled, "You and Mike here are going to have to have a wrassling match to see who is the strongest now, after all the work you two have done since graduation! It appears to me, son, that Uncle Gene took good care of you. I cannot wait for your father to see you. Is that little tote all you have?"

"Gee, Mom, you didn't want me bringing all my dirty clothes home, did you? Remember, I didn't take much with me. I was traveling with a bindle, Mom. I just had the basics, and I left most of that in Washington." Harley did not want to have to explain right there at the train, about how he had everything stolen. "How did you two get here? How are we getting home?" Harley asked, hoping to change the topic.

"We brought my dad's sedan. Jim is working on your dad's truck right now. I'll take Dad's car back to him in the morning," explained Mike.

"What's wrong with the truck, Mother?" asked Harley.

"Nothing big. Nothing Jim can't fix right away. Your father asked him to take a look at. Mike said it was making too much noise, that's all. Probably just a muffler."

"Or," Mike added, "it could just be needing a different oil or something for the cooler weather. Jim will have it taken care of by noon tomorrow. Don't worry about it."

They got into the sedan, with Mike driving and Lena in the front with him. Harley slipped into the back seat with his little valise and laid his head on the back of the seat. "I'm really tired, Mother. Do you mind if I just close my eyes for a few minutes?"

Lena answered quickly, "You close your eyes all the way home, Harley. You can greet your father when we get there, and then sleep tonight in your own room again. I put a cot in there for Mike. He is going to stay through the weekend, so you just rest, starting right now."

"Thank you, Mother...and Mike," Harley murmured as he closed his eyes and was quickly sleeping.

Mike drove carefully out of the station parking lot and guided the car towards Grand Avenue, heading west. He could take Grand to 8th Street in Valley Junction, head north to Buffalo Road, drive about a mile west on that, and then head north again on Clive Road. It was about four miles farther north from there to Meredith Drive, and then he would turn north one more time on Seibert Road. Two and a half miles north of Meredith was where Charley and Lena's farm waited.

Lena had some chicken and noodles in a pot on the stove, ready for an easy welcome-home dinner. It was one of Harley's favorites, so she knew he would eat it, no matter how tired he was. Harley was thrilled when he got home; as they drove up he could see his father sitting is his old red leather lounge chair through the living room window. The last time Harley was home, his father was still not getting around much except for the brief graduation outing. Harley leaped out of the back seat, ran up the stairs on the porch side of the house, through the kitchen and into the parlor.

"Hey there, son," Charley greeted him, "slow down a little bit. Did you wipe your feet, even?" Then he laughed heartily. "Come on over here, boy, and shake your old man's hand. Welcome home!"

Harley shook his hand, firmly, the way Uncle Gene admired. "You are looking good and strong, Harley. Did it go good on the ranch?" his father inquired.

"Yessir, I sure did learn a lot about apples and sheep. It's a whole different kind of crop and a different kind of critter," Harley informed him. "I'm happy to be back to corn and hogs, that's for sure!"

Lena and Mike caught up with Harley. As they watched the reunion of father and son, Lena said, "Why don't we hear all about this grand adventure over dinner, boys? Everything is hot and ready."

Harley was ready for his mother's cooking again, but not quite sure he was ready to give them the bad news about his college money. He hoped he could wait until tomorrow morning, after Mike took his father's car back. That's what he decided he was going to try to do. They had plenty of things to talk about; the rail riding, his hobo friends, his ranch adventures, his visit with Aunt Polly…lots of other topics, he hoped. He hoped correctly. Lena was horrified by his train-hopping stories and Mike wanted all the details about Leo, Adam, Mark, and Clarence. Charley wanted every second of the horse and rattlesnake incident retold a couple of times. And Lena, of course, listened intently as Harley relayed his time in Sacramento. It was so wonderful to be home, that for just a few moments, Harley actually did not think about his missing money.

Lena had made an apple pie and after Mike and Harley had two large pieces each, there was none left. Charley grumbled a little, but Lena assured him there would be another pie tomorrow night. Harley finally knew he had to get to bed, so he excused himself, kissed his mother goodnight, gave his father a hug, and shook hands with Mike.

Heading down the hall with Mike, Harley hollered over his shoulder at his parents who were still sitting at the kitchen t able, "It sure is great to be back home!" Lena heard the click of his bedroom door closing.

Almost whispering, she said to herself, "It sure is great to have you back home."

Harley's head hit the pillow, and even though he had assumed he would be kept awake all night worrying about how to break his bad news to his parents, he was soundly asleep within minutes.

Mable Contemplates at The Picnic

Sunday was a lovely day for a picnic. It was even a bit warmer than yesterday. Actually, the weather was unseasonably warm for early November. The trees at Union Park were a little late getting color. Most of them appeared to be oaks and they always turn plain old brown anyway. It was still beautiful, though, with the sun sparkling through the leaves. It was a heavenly day to be eating outside. No bugs. No big breezes. No loud children. It was very relaxing, except I still had not decided what questions I wanted to ask Babe Ruth.

Union Park was on the east side of Des Moines, and Drake Stadium was on the west side, at 27th and Forest Avenue. It was practically brand new, having been built and dedicated in 1925. My father had helped build it, so I was excited to see it. We had driven past it a few times on the way to Valley Junction to watch the trains, but I had never been to a sporting event there. I was way more interested in baseball than in college football. High school football was a favorite of mine also, but I think that was because I knew the young men who were playing in the game. I just thought the whole game of baseball was more interesting in general.

I had put off thinking about the Babe Ruth questions while talking to Burnie on our morning walk yesterday. I had no time to think about it during the ballgame. After yesterday's game, I briefly thought about asking The Sultan of Swat what had happened to his "swat," but decided that would be too harsh of a question. I considered asking him about what it was like to travel from city to city. That seemed exciting to me, but then I realized that baseball players did that all the time during the whole baseball season, so he was probably used to that kind of life. I wanted to ask him about his family, too, but then realized he might be offended by too personal of a question. I only had about one more hour to come up with my questions. I decided to go off by myself for a few minutes and think. I told Mother that I was going over by bandstand, to sit myself down and figure out what to ask.

The grass under this tree was extremely lush and green. It was a perfect place to escape and create my interview plan in my head. This had to go better that my last plan. I didn't even have a plan last time, when I spied Edith and her brothers at the game. I just had a hunch they would be interesting and they truly were, but I certainly could have done a better job on the interview. I just stumbled through the questions I had asked and left myself with so many unanswered that I would have to go back and see her, or write to her, to get the rest answered.

As I sat there, looking up through the leaves, my mind was going like crazy. I was actually more worried about how I was going to tell Mother that I wanted to drop out of college, than I was about what questions to ask Babe Ruth. Then, I started to wonder what he would think of my dilemma. He was competitive, like I was. I wondered if he had ever quit anything. I knew he quit pitching early in his career and now he just did it on the barnstorming tour for the fun of it. I had read all about how he came to live in the orphanage, which made me wonder if he missed not living with his parents, or why he became such a troublemaker at such a young age. Those questions were probably too personal.

With all those possibilities in my head, I could still not escape my own question; if I should quit college. That was what was on my mind all the time now. I realized this was the first real life decision that I had to make. Everything else had always just seemed like the next natural step to take. Whether it was going out for a sport or trying to get the sports editor job on the Oracle, or which college to attend; these choices seemed like they practically decided themselves for me. I was going to have to decide whether to drop out of college or not by myself.

Mother would not like it, Burnie already didn't like it, and I doubted that Mr. Ashby would think it was a great idea either. They would probably all be asking me the same question, "What are you going to do instead?" I had spent considerable time thinking about that, but still had no clear plan. At first, I thought that I could just get a job writing for a local newspaper. There were local papers in Iowa Falls and Eldora. At least that way I could get more experience. Then I thought that finding someone to hire me might be a problem, with the economy going down so fast. Jobs in general were nearly impossible to find. Actually, more folks were losing jobs than were getting jobs. What was I thinking? A man would be hired before I would. A college graduate would be hired before I would. Even if I did get hired at a local paper, it would not pay very much, since I only had a high school diploma. They would probably rather hire someone who grew up in the local area, not an outsider like me. Rats, I was going to have a hard time helping Mother without a job.

So, if I quit college, I would probably not be able to get a real job. Perhaps I could do laundry or iron or clean houses. I wondered how many people in Steamboat Rock or Eldora could afford to have someone else do their laundry or clean their house? Surely there were not many, if any, who had that kind of money. I knew nothing about farming, so I certainly would not be able to work on one of the local farms. This line of thinking was going badly.

Okay, why was college so horrible? What exactly did I dread returning to on Monday in Iowa City? Well, to start with, I missed Mother. Her calm voice, constant encouragement, and reassuring hugs had always meant so much to me, and now I was going for months without any of them. I also had grown to hate synchronized swimming. It was an obstacle to my swimming competition. It was not real competition. All that work was not easy, but it was helping keep me in good physical condition, but basically all I did was swim around in circles.

My anatomy class was a nightmare. I used to enjoy classes like biology, and I knew a lot of Latin, which should have helped me. Nothing helped me. It got more difficult every day. I was taking it because I thought it would be easy and help me with my Red Cross certification.

There was another problem with college. I was a journalist who was not allowed to write or publish in The Daily Iowan. I was only a freshman, so no bylines for me! They had an underclass poetry journal that was published every year, but I did not write poetry. I wrote sports news, or any other kind of news, but not poetry.

I really hated making coffee and running errands for the men at The Daily Iowan, also. They were a bunch of fellas like the ones who were on the North High Oracle staff. They only wrote about sports and they had never really played them. Most of their articles about sporting events were either just about the statistics or they were personality pieces on players, and not at all about sports. They simply did not know any good questions to ask. I thought they were pathetic. I know this makes me sound like I think I know it all, but really, those fellas were the ones who should stick to writing movie reviews and horoscopes.

I must have fallen asleep while doing all this thinking, because I was totally startled when Burnie bounded over to the tree and said my name, "Mable, Mable! Nap time is over and it's time to head on over to Drake Stadium!"

I opened my eyes quickly but was not quite alert yet. At first, I was not sure where I was. So many things had been swimming through my brain, I will admit I was a little disoriented. Then I remembered that I had sat down under the tree to do some serious soul-searching, and then I suddenly recalled the question I wanted to ask Babe Ruth. I was ready to meet him now.

BAND STAND, UNION PARK, DES MOINES, IOWA.

Telling His Folks About the Money

Harley was up early, thinking he would make coffee for everyone else. When he got to the kitchen, Mike was there already and had the coffee pot on the stove. He decided to talk to Mike about the money. It wasn't going to be easy, but he hoped Mike would understand.

Harley began, "Mike, I have something I have to tell you before my parents get out here. It's pretty bad, but just hear me out, please."

Mike looked at him with surprise. "Did you kill someone?"

Harley whipped around where he stood and asked, "Are you crazy? How do you figure I killed someone?"

"Well," asked Mike, "you said it was bad. I just figure killing someone is pretty darn bad."

"Believe me, I did not kill anyone. But someone killed my dream of college for right now," Harley explained.

"What? How's that?"

"Mike, I had $325.00 I earned at my uncle's ranch. He bought me a ticket to Sacramento to see my mother's Aunt Polly. I had the money in my suitcase, and it was stolen on the train trip to see her. It happened at one of the stops and by the time I discovered it was gone, it was too late. The thief had gotten off the train at that stop and there was no way to locate him. All of my money for the University of Iowa is gone. There is no way I will ever see that money again, and I have no idea how to tell my mother and father. No idea…what am I supposed to do?" Harley pleaded with his friend.

"Heck, that won't be easy," Mike agreed. "It's going to be rough on them, buddy. Are you going to tell them this morning? Do you want me to hang around or do you want me to go? I could just go start the chores; you could come and get me when you are done. Your mother's is going to be walking out here any minute."

"Thanks, Mike, I was thinking you would be heading home with your dad's car. It would be super if you could stay." Harley hesitated, then suggested, "I kind of want to do it alone, but I really want to talk to you some more about this. Could you start the chores and I'll holler down to you? I want to get this over with first thing this morning, okay?"

"Absolutely, Harley," Mike agreed. "And I want to hear more about your trip. More about the rails, the ranch, everything. I'll head down to the barn and you go wake up your folks, or just start the sausage. That always wakes up your father!"

"Thank you, Mike. Really, thanks a lot," Harley said as he took the sausage from the icebox.

Mike went down to the barn and Harley started the sausage. He heard his father making his way down the hall to the bathroom with his cane. Harley smiled as he thought about how his father had beat the doctors' predictions that he would never walk again. As he took the eggs from the ice box he marveled at the parents he had, at the personal trials they had survived: the fire and rebuilding the farmhouse, his father riding the rails to the wheat fields, and his father's stroke. His mother and his father had overcome all of those things. It was terribly hard times all over the country, and especially for farmers, but his folks still had their farm and each other, and they believed there had to be better times ahead.

Harley also knew that his parents planned on him being an important part of those better times. He was supposed to go to college and have an easier life than Lena and Charley. Even as he was thinking that, a bolt of optimism hit him. He would be going to college! He was going to have to tell his parents about the theft, but then he was going to find a way. He was!

"Harley, is that you out there in the kitchen?" Lena's voice came from the back of the house.

"Yes, Mother. I have the coffee and sausage started. Dad is in the bathroom," he answered.

"Don't start the eggs yet, son. Sometimes your father is in there for a while," Lena informed him.

Harley poured himself a cup of coffee and turned off the sausage. It could wait in the pan. As Harley sipped his coffee and waited, he gradually realized that he was now looking forward to telling his parents about the money. Yowzah, that was a strange feeling! He couldn't wait to tell them! He thought for a moment and figured out what was going on in his head. It had to be the beginning of the answer to his problem. He would tell his parents and then go into town with Mike. He wanted to see Mr. Flynn, who had told him to let him know if he ever needed anything. Harley needed advice! Mr. Flynn knew how to make money, and Harley needed to learn how right away! Surely Mr. Flynn would have some ideas. His parents might have some ideas, too, and of course he would listen to them first, but money came slowly in the farming business, and he needed money before second semester started in January.

When his mother came into the kitchen, she gave him a hug around the neck from behind. He reached for her arm and squeezed it affectionately.

"Good morning, son," she said.

"Good morning, Mother. Is Dad coming soon? Should I start the eggs now?"

"Sure, go ahead. He will be here when he hears the sizzle, trust me," Lena laughed at bit. "Your father is not a man who would miss a meal, you know that!"

Harley laughed, too. He was now excited to talk to his parents about his problem. He was looking forward to solving it. He actually felt energized. On one hand, this newly-found optimism seemed strange, but he also looked forward to the challenge and felt totally invigorated. He realized he was actually smiling.

Charley appeared in the doorway. "Good morning, Harley. How are you? Well, that big smile tells me a lot! Glad to be home, son?" asked his father.

"Yessiree! I am, Dad. Ready for breakfast?" Harley answered.

"Yep," Charley answered, as he made his way to his usual place at the kitchen table. He leaned his cane in the corner by the door. The square table had one side pushed against the wall, so there were only three chairs. It was covered with a piece of dark blue and white checkered oilcloth, just like when he left months ago. There was a black and white cow cream pitcher with a matching sugar bowl. The salt and pepper shakers were two roosters, and there was a simple pressed glass toothpick holder. The painted cast iron napkin holder had a meal blessing written on it.

Harley had the sausage and eggs on three plates almost instantly and put each at a place on the table. He made sure his parents each had a fresh cup of hot coffee in front of them, and then he pulled up his chair and reached for a napkin to put in his lap. He knew his mother would still expect him to use the manners he was taught.

"These eggs look wonderful, Harley," complimented his mother.

"So, fill us in on a little bit more of your trip, son," instructed Charley. "Then we need to get on with those chores!"

"Mike is on the chores right now," Harley explained. "He went on down to the barn quite a bit ago, so I could talk to you two alone."

"Why?" asked Lena, "You have a secret or something?"

"No, Mother, but I have something more I need to tell you."

Harley began by giving a few more details about his hobo friends. Lena's concern about his companions showed on her brow, but Harley kept smiling at her, hopefully relaying the positivity he was feeling. He again skipped over the parts when he got lice from the blanket on the way to Denver and the time when he almost didn't make it while running to board the train on the way out of Denver. Harley gave a few more details about caring for the apples and the sheep and about how the other men were going to stay on permanently for Uncle Gene. By then, his mother was nodding with approval. Charley appeared to be proud of a son with so many new ranching skills. Harley felt ready to get to the bad news.

"So, I was on the train to Sacramento to see Aunt Polly. We stopped at some little town just briefly and I stepped out on the platform at the end of the passenger car. I could see one of the hobo jungles, and I stood there for a little bit counting my blessings. When the train started up, I went back to my seat. The fella who had been sitting next to me was gone, and…so was my suitcase. He stole it and got off the train," Harley said, pausing and looking at his parents.

"Where was your money?" Lena asked, her voice changing pitch. She cleared her throat. "He didn't get your money, did he?" She looked at him pleadingly.

"Yes, Mother. He stole my money. All of it. $325.00."

Lena's head sank onto her crossed arms on the table.

Then Harley hastened to add, "But, it's going to be all right, Mother. I am going to college still! Don't worry."

"Don't worry? Have you gone plum crazy?" Lena was sputtering. "What do you mean? Did you get the money back?"

"No, the conductor wired back to the station where the thief got off, but he was long gone. I won't see that money again, but I am going to get more money, you'll see. I don't want you to worry!"

Lena started to say something else, but her husband waved his hand to quiet her. Charley asked, "What is your plan, son? Where is that much money going to come from? That was four months of earnest labor, and you only have about six weeks before the second semester starts in Iowa City. There's no paid farm work to do this time of year!" Both of his parents seemed pretty alarmed and upset. He tried to calm them.

"Listen, I know this sounds bad. I basically have to start over, but I am healthy and smart. I kind of have a plan. I am going to talk to Uncle Lynn and Mr. Flynn. They are both good businessmen, and they both offered me advice and help if I ever needed it. I sure do need help now, so I am going to try to go see both of them today. Mike will drive me when we finish the chores if that's okay with you. I mean, I really need to get started."

Lena asked quietly, "Started at what, Harley? How is this possible?"

"Mother, I don't know yet how it is possible, but I believe that it is."

She spoke again, "Is there some way your father and I can help you? You know we don't have any money to spare at all right now."

Harley looked at his mother's sad face. "Please, I guess you are going to have to believe, too. Don't be sad. Smile. I am going to go to college. Just believe in me."

Charley finally spoke again. "You know, Lena, this boy has accomplished a lot already. He helped rebuild this house, he finished high school. He went clear to the west coast and earned a lot of money. I believe he can do whatever he sets his mind to. We believe in you, son. Right, Lena?" He reached across the table and took Lena's hand. "Right, Lena?" he repeated.

"Yes, we do," confirmed Lena. "You let us know what you get worked out, Harley. We believe in you and will help any way we can." Sadness and shock still dominated her face, but she managed a tiny smile of encouragement.

Harley was overwhelmed with appreciation. He grabbed his parents' hands where they were clasped in the middle of the morning meal. "Thank you. Thank you," he said earnestly. "May I go help Mike finish now? I'll tell you all the rest about California and Aunt Polly tonight, I promise!"

"Get goin', son. Those animals need breakfast, too," urged his father. "We'll talk some more when you get home. You'll be home for dinner, right? I'm gonna need some help with the evening chores."

"I'll be back as quick as I can," Harley assured them. "Chores will be done before dinner."

Harley bounded down the back stairs and headed for the barn. He suspected Mike had finished with the chores a long time ago and was just waiting for the signal to come back to the house. As Harley raced around the corner of the garage, there stood Mike. He nearly knocked Mike over!

"Mike, are the chores done? How soon can we leave for town?" Harley asked.

"Let's get cleaned up and go," answered Mike.

They raced to the house and Harley won, so he had dibs on the first shower.

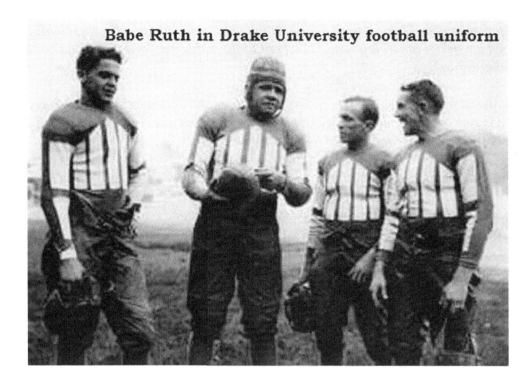

Babe Ruth in Drake University football uniform

Watching the Game at Drake

I helped clean up the picnic supplies. There weren't any food leftovers to worry about because Mother had shared them with kids who came to play on the swings and ride their coaster wagons down a few of the steep hills at the park. She was always so generous. We shook the leaves off the blankets we had laid down in the grass and then folded them. With the car loaded, we proceeded south to University Avenue and then west to Drake Stadium, to meet the greatest baseball hitter ever, Babe Ruth.

The closer we got to Drake, the more I talked. I was going over Babe's statistics out loud, and it was driving Burnie plain crazy. "I know he had fifty-four home runs this year. No, it wasn't the sixty he had last year, but it was a lot. I know he scored the most runs he's ever had, at 163. I love baseball, too, remember?" Burnie said impatiently, then queried his father, who was driving, "Are we there yet?"

Burnie's mother laughed out loud. Actually, she laughed so hard, she nearly snorted out of her nose! Mr. Orwig was laughing, too. Burnie's mother said, "Where did that come from? You haven't asked us that since you were about eight years old!"

His father added, "I don't think Mable is the only baseball fan who is excited. I know I am, too. I am trying really hard not to floor this gas feed pedal and run all the stop signs."

That was a scary thought! "Oh, please don't do that," I pleaded. "I want to get there in one piece. Remember, we don't get to meet and interview him until after the scrimmage, so we have some football to watch first."

I was thinking that the scrimmage could be pretty interesting, even if Babe Ruth had not been playing in it. I told them that Drake University had quite a football team the past few years. They were completely undefeated back in 1922 and even got invited to the White House. They were also the first college football team from Iowa to play in the Rose Bowl Stadium. It wasn't for the Rose Bowl game, but they had beaten UCLA 25-6 in front of 40,000 people! The Bulldogs were also the first Iowa team to go all the way to Hawaii to play. Now Drake football was about to make another big splash in football history, having a scrimmage with Babe Ruth during the Homecoming festivities this weekend. I was so excited, and Burnie's mother was totally surprised to hear that I knew all these facts. Thanks, Dad!

Uncle Albert's car, with Mother in it, was right behind us. Mr. Ashby had pulled out of the park before we did and his car was nowhere in sight. He most likely wanted to get there ahead of us, talk to Drake's coach, Bill Williams, and make sure all the post-game arrangements were in order. Ted was very professional about his interviews. He never wanted to inconvenience any of the sports figures he wrote about. He told me that it was because he wanted them to think well of him in case he ever asked for another interview, or some free tickets to a game.

Back when he told me that a few months ago, I didn't understand why he would want free tickets, because he had a press pass and could enter any event he wanted to attend for free. He explained that he gave those free tickets or passes to disadvantaged kids, ministers, or high school athletes. I told him I guess I should have met him sooner and then I would have been able to go to more free sporting events when I was in high school! Ted laughed and agreed. He was a wonderful role model for me.

We approached Drake heading west on University, turned right just before the stadium and parked the car on 27th Street. There was quite a bit of a downhill slant there, so Burnie's father double checked the emergency brake and then pulled a couple of bricks out from under the front seat. He put them in front of the wheels headed downhill, just for good measure. He had already turned the wheels toward the curb, so with three-way protection, I was absolutely certain the car would be where we left it when we came back. Burnie and I piled out of the back seat while he was arranging the bricks and Mr. Orwig asked us what we thought.

Since neither of us were licensed to drive yet, we were not quite sure why he wanted our opinion, but it made us feel more grown up. My second thought was that he intended this to be a learning opportunity, for our future reference when we did begin driving. It was most likely the latter.

Ted hollered and waved at us from the east side entrance to the stadium. That is usually where the visiting team's entrance was, but the only visitor today would be Babe Ruth. I remember thinking that I hoped they let him come in the main entrance and not the side door! The main entrance was on the south side, but Ted motioned for us to come over to that east door. Burnie and I raced over, hoping maybe The Babe was there with him, but he wasn't. Burnie's mom scolded us from the other side of the street for not looking both ways for cars before we ran across. Golly, one minute Burnie's father was treating us like grownups and the next minute his mother was acting like we were five years old. What a strange day.

We waited for the Orwigs, Mother, and Uncle Albert to join us, then Ted led us all down a brick-lined outer passageway that went along the north end of the stadium. We could see into the stadium through some brick archways but could not see the street. It was much cooler in there, probably from the bricks providing shade from all directions. It was not wired with electricity, but there was plenty of daylight left. Ted escorted us to some seats on the west side of the field. There were a couple of hundred Drake students on the east side. The stadium would have held thousands more, but regular folks were not being admitted. You had to be from Drake or you had to be invited, as we were. Ted told me he thought it was because Babe Ruth had never played football before, and he was a tiny bit unsure of how he would look. He had to keep up his all-star image, I suppose.

When we reached the west side of the stadium we went down the steps to the section they told us to sit in. Since it was on the west side, we would be facing east, so Mother did not have to worry about being in the sun, and we did not have to squint into the afternoon sun in order to watch the scrimmage. Ted told us, as we took our seats, that the Drake "blue" team, which was the varsity, and the Drake "white" team, which was the sophomore team, would take turns with having the ball on offense. One team would get it for a certain amount of time and be given the chance to score, and then it would be the other team's turn to be on offense. That sounded fair to me.

"What position do you think Mr. Ruth will play, Ted?" inquired Burnie's father.

"I heard that he wanted to try kicking and running. The coach said he was told that they didn't want to put Babe in the position of being tackled hard or getting hurt," replied Ted, "and that makes good sense to me. How 'bout you?"

Mr. Orwig agreed, "I would bet they have talked to those burly Drake boys long and hard about taking it easy on Babe, for sure."

"Yep," added Uncle Albert. "Sure bet they do not want those big ol' Iowa boys bringin' Babe Ruth down. He might not be able to get up."

Those were the first words I had heard out of Uncle Albert all day! He is not a very talkative man, and I guess I was so wrapped up trying to figure out how to tell Mother about my quitting school and figuring out what to ask Babe Ruth when I finally met him, that I really did not think about my mother's brother. He had gone to a lot of trouble to bring my mother down to Des Moines. He was not a crazy baseball fan like my father was; he drove all that way to make my mother happy. I thought for a moment about what a wonderful family I had, and then the crowd suddenly stood up and started to cheer and clap wildly.

The Drake football team was running onto the end of the field. There were players in blue and white striped uniforms and players in white uniforms, running side by side. When they reached the far side of the field, they split apart, with the crowd cheering the whole time. The striped team turned and ran down the far sideline to the visitor benches and the white team kept trotting straight across the field, to our side of the stadium, and ran down to the home team benches. When both teams were in their places on each side, the announcer began to speak from the press box that was set high in the bleachers behind us. The clapping and cheering became an expectant hush.

"Ladies and gentlemen, welcome to Drake Stadium, home of the Drake Relays and home of the Drake Bulldogs. This afternoon we have a special scrimmage for your viewing pleasure. The varsity and junior varsity football teams of this wonderful university will scrimmage, and will share the field with a very distinguished teammate for this once-in-a-lifetime event. Please give a warm and resounding welcome to The Sultan of Swat, the Great Bambino... Mr. Babe Ruth of the New York Yankees!"

The crowd went into a clapping and cheering frenzy. There was yelling and whistling. Men wildly swung their hats over their heads and women waved their hankies high in the air. One lone player, helmet still on, stepped forward out of the line of striped uniforms on our side of the field. He took off his helmet and waved back at the crowd, facing us, and then turned to wave to the fans on the other side. It was then that I realized that we were sitting in the home bleachers with the other non-Drake people who had been given special invitations, and that the Drake students were all sitting on the other side.

I looked around me for the first time. I saw the mayor, players from the Des Moines Demons, and Governor John Hammill! He was a Republican and my parents really liked him. I liked him even more because he had introduced a constitutional amendment that allowed women to be elected to the Iowa General Assembly. Mr. Ashby had arranged for us to be included in a notable group of football fans, or maybe they were just Babe Ruth fans. I really doubted if those men would all have been there for a simple Drake scrimmage without Babe Ruth. It did not really matter, it still made me feel extremely special. I elbowed Burnie, who was still cheering and waving his hat. He looked at me and I pointed to the governor. Burnie nodded his approval. As the cheering subsided and Babe put his helmet back on, the referee blew his whistle.

Drake had striking uniforms. The striped jerseys had bright Drake blue shoulders and five wide white stripes running down a blue background on the chest and in the back. They came to an arrow point right below the neckline. They wore blue pants. The white team had white sleeves and three thin blue stripes running down a white background. They wore white pants.

I saw Mother lean over to Mrs. Orwig's and heard her say, "I would hate to be the washwoman who has to keep those white trousers clean!" They both giggled like little girls.

The Babe's striped team, the varsity, got to have the ball first. The white team lined up to kick it off to them, but Babe Ruth was the one kicking the ball. He was kicking off for the white team and for the striped team, the announcer informed us. He apparently fancied that kicking was a part of the game he would be good at, so they were going to let him try. Well, his first kick went fairly straight, but not very far. The crowd cheered anyway. After all, it was Babe Ruth.

There was some hard-hitting tackling, but none of it happened anywhere near the New York Yankee. Those Drake boys had been instructed well on how to protect the baseball star, which was good because he was on the field almost the entire fifteen minutes that the varsity Bulldogs had the ball. They scored one touchdown, just as the time ran out.

The Babe had played a few different positions and carried the ball twice for a total of twelve yards. A humble beginning, but a beginning for sure. Burnie thought he should have been able to get a lot more yards since the players had been discouraged from any real tackling of him. They just sort of caught up with him and pushed him over. It did not look like college football, but I kept reminding everyone that Babe Ruth had never played football. I thought it was a respectable first half for him.

There was just a brief break at the end of fifteen minutes, not a real football half-time. Then Babe Ruth kicked off and the white team had the ball. This time his kick went much farther. He came out of the game after the kickoff. Mr. Orwig was sure it was because the Yankees did not want their most famous and much beloved slugger to get hurt. I told Ted that I thought Babe looked tired and they decided to give him a break. Even though he was an incredible athlete, he was nearly twice the age of the Drake boys.

He came back into the game when the white team was about twenty yards away from the goal line. The quarterback lobbed him a little pass on the far side of the field, and The Babe caught it easily and ran for the touchdown. The crowd went wild, and I could tell by looking at him that he was ecstatic with himself. Both teams played well, but the white team did upset the blue team, with a score of 13 to 7.

As the clock wound down, I started paying less attention to the game and was thinking more about my questions. I fumbled around in my bag to make sure I had my notepad. I felt around and also located my pencil. Everything I needed was there, but both Ted and Burnie noticed my fidgeting.

Ted leaned over and said to me, "Relax, star girl reporter. Take a deep breath."

Burnie elbowed me. Thinking it was a payback for me elbowing him earlier, I ignored it. Then he gave me a wink and a smile, with "You can do this, Mable."

That wink instantly reminded me of Father. That wink. Burnie knew what it meant to me, and he knew I knew. I smiled back, but was totally unable to reciprocate the wink, as usual.

"I am as ready as I will ever be, you two." I was reassuring them, as well as myself. "Don't worry. I won't embarrass anyone. I'm actually thinking that maybe if I write this interview up correctly, I could get it in the Daily Iowan. They should be begging me to put it in, and they would have to give me a byline! Really, fellas, I can do this, you'll see."

We had seen Babe Ruth play both ways, watched him punt, and he even caught a pass and ran for a touchdown for the white team. No one had hurt him, so the Yankees would be pleased. Baseball was definitely his game, not football. However, for the age he was and for playing with a bunch of college athletes, he showed well.

When the final whistle blew, everyone stood and cheered again. They announced that he would be shaking hands and meeting spectators at the front gate after getting his street clothes back on, so folks should line up out there. There would not be time for autographs, they added, but he would definitely stay there until everyone who wanted to had greeted him. I could hear some people grumbling *about the no-autograph part, but I also heard others appreciating how he would shake hands with everyone.*

Ted then told me that we would have about ten minutes with Mr. Ruth after he changed out of the uniform, but before he went to the gate. Ted said my family and Burnie's family could go along, and greet Babe, but then Ted and I would take him aside to interview him and get a photograph. Mother was beaming. I could just tell she was thinking about how it would have been wonderful if Father had been there to meet Babe Ruth, but I know her smile was also for her pride in me. I hurt a little bit when I briefly contemplated telling her about my decision to quit the University of Iowa. I had to push that quickly aside in my head. First, I had to get this interview right.

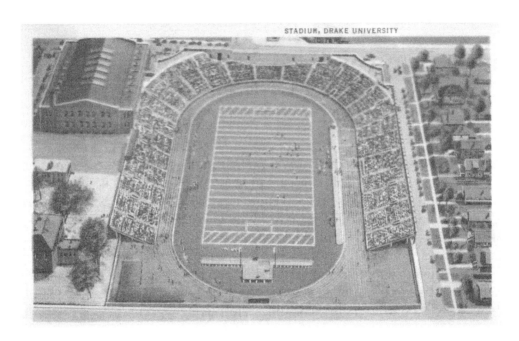

Uncle Lynn and Mr. Flynn

Harley wanted to talk to his Uncle Lynn first, so that is where Mike dropped him off. It was Sunday, so his uncle was sure to be home. Harley was hoping that Uncle Lynn would not have some odd chore he needed help with because he had dressed up, in anticipation of seeing Mr. Flynn later. He didn't want to get his good clothes dirty. He had to roll up the sleeves on his dress shirt, however, because they were quite a bit shorter than they were when he wore the shirt to graduation. Either his mother shrunk the shirt or his arms had grown longer over the summer. Mike told Harley that he looked taller than when he left. Maybe that's why his good trousers looked a little short in the legs, too.

Harley knocked on the side porch door, where he knew Aunt Alice would answer, since she was probably in the kitchen. She saw him through the window panes and ran to the door.

"Harley Van Seibert! When did you get home?" she squealed.

"Last night, Aunt Alice. Is Uncle Lynn around, please? I came to get some advice," Harley revealed.

"Sure he is, honey. And you know he loves to give advice! I'll go get him. Better yet, grab a cookie from the jar there and follow me," she told him over her shoulder as she headed for the library. "I think he's in here with his third cup of coffee."

There he was, sitting in an over-sized black leather chair with his feet up on an ottoman, reading the Sunday edition of the Des Moines Register. Uncle Lynn read the Register first thing every morning. He always said he wanted to know the latest news before he started his day. He figured someone might want to stop and chat with him, and he wanted to be able to discuss, intelligently, whatever was going on in the world, or in Iowa, or in Des Moines. Harley was proud that all of his mother's brothers and sisters were so well-educated. It was part of his motivation, too.

"Hello, young traveler!" Uncle Lynn whooped, as he rose to shake his nephew's hand. "When did you get back?"

Aunt Alice beat Harley to the punch, "Last night, Lynn. This young fella hurried over here this morning to get some advice from you. I'll let you two be. Let me know if you need anything. We just got back from church, but you've had breakfast, right, Harley?"

"Yes ma'am. Thank you," he replied.

As Aunt Alice left the room and closed the door behind her, Uncle Lynn returned to his chair and said, "Pull that other chair over here, young man. Tell me what's on your mind and please tell me about your Uncle Gene. Does that big brother of mine have a nice spread out there?"

"Yes, sir. He sure does. That ranch is enormous. He has more than 8,000 acres. It's a giant spread!" answered Harley. "There was no shortage of work out there, either. I learned all about apples, and even sheep. Uncle Gene is quite a rancher."

"That's good to hear, Harley. Hope I can get out there some day to visit him and Aunt Lou. Are they both feeling healthy and looking good?" asked Lynn.

"Yes, sir. They are."

"Great. Now, I am wondering what you're doing here so early. It's not a milk route day. What can I do for you?" Lynn peered at Harley over the newspaper, then folded it up and put it in his lap.

"I need some advice. I talked to Mother and Dad this morning and had to tell them that the $325.00 I earned for my tuition at Uncle Gene's was stolen from me on the train in California," Harley said.

"What the hell!" exclaimed Gene. "I'll be damned! What kind of low-life would take a kid's college money?"

"I don't know. He sat next to me all the way from Chelan, and the minute I turned my back, he stole my suitcase and got off the train. I'll admit it was just plain stupid to leave it like that, but where I come from, people aren't stinking thieves," Harley countered.

"Well, you are young and trusting, Harley. Trusting is usually a good thing, but not in this case, that's for sure. I am so sorry. So, is this what you want advice about?" asked Uncle Gene.

"Yes, please. I went to talk to Mr. Flynn before I left for Washington," Harley revealed. "Don't worry, I met him at Roosevelt's graduation. Then we met at his house. He told me all about his business and how hard he worked to get that car. I told him I have always wanted one since I saw his when we started the milk route. I told him how it was helping motivate me to go to college. Then he let me drive the car around the block! He was so nice. And when we were back in his driveway, he told me that if there was ever anything he could help me with, to please come and let him know."

"So now you want to ask him for college money?" Uncle Lynn was scowling.

"No, never!" insisted Harley. "I want his advice on how to earn more money as quickly as possible. My hobo days are over…no more begging for handouts for me!"

His uncle looked puzzled, "So what is it you want from me, then?"

"You are a good businessman, too. Look at how successful you are! You have your farm, the milk route, and your mail route. I wanted to come and ask you for advice before I went to Mr. Flynn," answered Harley.

"That's very flattering, Harley. Thank you. It means a lot to me."

The young man continued, "You don't have to come up with something right this minute. You can let me know after you have time to think about it, but I hope you have an idea or two pretty soon. I only have about six weeks before I need to be in Iowa City. I can come back tomorrow or call you."

"Call me. I will have some ideas. By the way, how did you get over here today?" asked Gene.

"My friend Mike drove me. He was going home to see his folks. I guess I didn't think this out very well. I was so anxious to see you and Mr. Flynn," admitted Harley.

Uncle Gene laughed a little. "I understand. Listen, why don't you take the milk truck to Mr. Flynn's, drive it home after that, and bring it back tomorrow morning for the milk route. You are going to be helping me on the route again, instead of Mike, aren't you?"

"Yes, I am, and that's a great idea, Uncle Gene. That's exactly what I'll do. I'll bring the truck back tomorrow. Thanks so much!"

"You had better get going before Alice tries to make you stay for Sunday dinner," Gene told him. "Get on out of here and go talk to Mr. Flynn. I'll talk to you tomorrow."

Harley hustled out of the parlor and through the kitchen, pausing only for a second to give Aunt Alice a peck on the cheek. "I'd stay for dinner, but I have an important errand. I'll see you tomorrow morning."

Surprisingly, there was no argument from Aunt Alice, just "Okay, Sweetie, see you tomorrow morning!" as he hurried out the door.

Harley hopped in the milk truck, which was emptied of all the milk crates and coolers, so it bounced a little more easily over the road out of Uncle Lynn's. The farm was in the far southeast corner of Polk County and it was about a forty-minute drive to Mr. Flynn's house in Des Moines. Harley arrived right after noon. He hoped he wouldn't be interrupting their Sunday dinner, but he also didn't want to waste time, so he pulled up and parked on the street in front of the house and turned off the truck. He sat for a minute, thinking about how he would start the conversation. Then Harley realized how dumb he was being. He could talk to Mr. Flynn just like he talked to Uncle Lynn. He'd just be honest and state his purpose.

Then Mr. Flynn appeared right next to the truck!

"Hello, there, Harley! Are you just back from your trip? Milk delivery is tomorrow, not today, right?" Mr. Flynn smiled and laughed. He could tell he had startled the young man.

Harley fumbled for the door handle and managed to unload himself from the front seat. He felt awkward and uncoordinated. He straightened himself up and reached out to shake hands with Mr. Flynn.

"Hello, sir. Yes, I just got back last night. I wanted to come and talk to you as soon as I could," Harley blurted out, as they shook hands.

Mr. Flynn wanted to hear all about Harley's trip, so he invited him inside and before he knew it, the young man was at the Flynn dining room table with some sandwiches in front of him. As they ate, he began to retell his experiences on the rails and on the ranch. Then he told about the theft of his money. Then he stopped.

He stopped because Mrs. Flynn gasped, and Mr. Flynn abruptly rose to his feet.

"I will pay your tuition, Harley!" said Mr. Flynn.

"No, sir. Please. Sit down. That is not why I came here. I need to pay my own tuition. I just need some help with an idea of how I can earn that money again between now and January, when second semester starts."

"Let me think a minute. Let me think," murmured the businessman, as he sat down and looked at his hands in his lap.

Both Harley and Mrs. Flynn remained very still. Several minutes passed, and finally Mr. Flynn looked up, directly into the still-hopeful eyes of the young man before him.

"There is one opportunity I can think of, but it is going to demand a lot of hours and some serious physical labor, Harley. Will you still be helping on the farm and helping with the milk route? This will take up your nights," warned Mr. Flynn.

"I still have to help my dad and my uncle, sir, but I will work anywhere and anytime. I'm plenty used to hard work, I just told you. I'm young, I don't need that much sleep. If this is a night job, then it will be perfect! What is it?" he asked. Harley was excited!

"Calm down. I am pretty darn sure I can get you in, but it starts right away. Could you start tomorrow?" inquired Mr. Flynn.

"I can start today, sir," insisted Harley. "Where is it?"

Mr. Flynn was still looking right at him. "It's down at the Ford Automobile plant on Grand and 18th Street."

"But I don't know anything about making cars, sir. Won't that be a problem?"

"No. Harley. You won't be making cars. They have decided to close the car plant, but Ford is making it into a place where they will have offices," explained Mr. Flynn.

"Do you know anything about office work, Harley?" asked Mrs. Flynn.

"Not really. My mother worked in a law office, and I am really good at reading and writing. And math," he added.

"Not office work, either," Mr. Flynn informed both his wife and Harley. "They have thousands of square feet of concrete floors in the factory that they are going to need covered with linoleum, so they can turn that area into office space. Do you know how to lay down a floor, Harley?" asked Mr. Flynn.

"Well, I laid down the floor in my folk's house after we rebuilt it, sir." Harley did not mention that it was license plates and not linoleum. He felt a little twinge of guilt for the partial truth he just told. In his upbringing, a partial truth was called a lie of omission. It was a lie, plain and simple, but he really wanted that job. Harley felt it was justified because he knew he was smart and that he could learn whatever he needed to do very quickly.

"It's long hours, overnight, and I am pretty sure they don't pay overtime for even this late work. But, it's a job where you can get lots of hours and earn back the money you need," Mr. Flynn explained.

"How do I apply? How do I get the job? How do I start tomorrow?" Harley fired one question after another.

"Just go there tomorrow at seven o'clock, in the evening. Ask for a man named John Betz. I will be telephoning him and tell him you are coming. He owes me a favor for giving his crews a break on the lunch truck sandwiches and milk that I send over there every day. You will probably work from eight o'clock in the evening until about four o'clock in the morning. How will you get there?"

Harley spoke right up. "I'll be there at seven, Mr. Flynn. I can take my dad's truck. And that will get me home in time for chores and the milk route, too. How can I ever thank you?"

"That's easy son. Just get yourself to college and pull up in this driveway some day in a Lincoln." Mr. and Mrs. Flynn both let out a little laugh.

Harley couldn't get a laugh out, but he did have a large smile to share with them. He thanked and thanked Mr. Flynn many times, until he was finally asked to stop.

"I just never imagined it could be so easy, sir. Jobs are so hard to find; you know that. How can I get a job so easily?" Harley wondered.

"Sometimes," Mr. Flynn explained, "It's not *what* you know, it's *who* you know. Good business is often the result of good connections. People are willing to help other people, especially those they know and trust. They also know that those same people will help them when they need it."

"You are helping me," Harley noted, "but I don't know that I will ever be able to return the favor."

"Really doesn't matter, son. However, my money would bet that someday you will," Mr. Flynn assured him. "Someday, you will."

"Right now, I am going to get home and tell my parents about this. I know my mother is upset and worried. This will mean everything to her. I can't wait to tell her," gushed Harley, as he rose and extended his hand to Mr. Flynn,

Mr. Flynn rose and shook his hand. Then he pulled Harley toward him and gave him a hug. "You will make us proud and you will make your parents proud, Harley. Hurry on home and give them the good news."

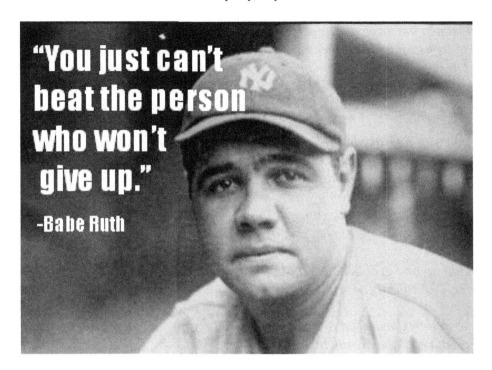

Interview with Babe Ruth

The trip to the press area in front of the locker room took us back along the south side of the stadium again. The lockers were in the back area of the Drake Fieldhouse, adjacent to the stadium. They played basketball in the fieldhouse and had an indoor track. It struck me that Drake University did not have a swimming pool. I could never have attended Drake. I needed to be in the pool every day.

In the press area, there were a few wooden chairs in one corner of the room, positioned around a sturdy square table. A stack of newspapers and magazines were in a semi-straightened stack on top of the worn table top. Ted motioned me over there with a wave of his pencil. We sat down and I retrieved my notebook from my purse again. It occurred to me that I might want to jot down the questions I had decided to ask, as I felt the anxiety rising in my neck and face. It felt warm and probably looked red, but I took a deep breath and took my pencil in hand. I turned to a clean page about halfway back in the notebook and wrote "Babe Ruth" at the top of the page. It was a milestone in my life as an athlete, as a journalist, and as a baseball fan. A huge milestone. Bigger than I knew at the time, for certain.

I wrote down the three questions, one at the top of each page, leaving plenty of room to transcribe his answers. I was ready. I closed the notebook, and then closed my eyes, feeling a little prayer was in order to calm my nerves. I would tell you my prayer, if I could remember it. Even though I cannot remember it, I am quite sure it was answered.

The door with a Drake bulldog face emblazoned on it in thick blue and white paint swung open wide. The Coach Williams stepped in and the Great Bambino was on his right. It was momentous. Ted caught the eye of the coach and waved him over to us. Mother, along with Uncle Albert, was seated on a long navy-blue davenport along the wall next to our table. Burnie and his parents were standing right next to them, with Burnie sort of leaning against the wall.

Ted stood up and grabbed my hand. "Let's go meet Babe Ruth, star girl reporter," he said.

The coach introduced Ted to Babe, and then Ted introduced my mother, the Orwigs, Burnie, and my uncle to Babe.

"This is the young lady I wrote to you about," Ted explained. Babe was smiling and nodding.

"The swimmer?" asked Babe Ruth. He already knew who I was? Ted had not told me that!

The Babe continued, "This is the sports editor <u>and</u> the little girl who beat all those men swimming?"

Oh my, I must have let my mouth fall open. Questions raced through my brain. How did he know all this? Ted wrote to him about me? Why hadn't Ted told me? How much did Ted tell him?

Both Ted and the Babe must have seen my gaping mouth or at least recognized my enormous amazement, because Ted quickly explained.

"I needed to let them know that we wanted a special interview, Mable; that there was a reason to set aside a few extra minutes for this," Ted explained. "The Babe here was all for it and looking forward to talking to you, from what he wrote to me."

That world-renowned baseball giant was just standing there grinning at me. I smiled back. Then I stuck out my hand. "I am very pleased to meet you, Mr. Ruth. Thank you for accepting this invitation to meet with me. I just have a few questions for you, for the Daily Iowan."

I fumbled to reach back to the table where I had just been sitting. I needed to get my notebook. Burnie reached over, grabbed it off the stack of newspapers, and shoved it into my hands. I mumbled my gratitude, I think.

Babe spoke right up, "Not so fast, Missy. I have a few questions for you first. We'll talk about me soon enough."

Coach Williams from Drake spoke up, "We have people waiting outside, remember?"

"Oh, there will still be plenty of them when we get out there, pal. I want to talk to Mable first. I promised," was Babe's retort. Then he winked at me and added, "Never break a promise to a lady, coach." He continued, "So you followed all the sports in your high school, and were a sports editor, huh?"

I nodded.

"And you beat a bunch of men swimming in the river?"

I nodded again, nervously.

"And you broke a bunch of swimming records and tried to get them to let you be on the boys' swimming team?"

I kept nodding.

Babe let out a big belly laugh. "Good thing I'm not the reporter," he chided. "You sure aren't giving me any answers I could jot down in my notebook!" Then everyone in the room laughed.

He calmed the laughter with a little clearing of his throat. "Well, that is very impressive for a teenage girl, Mable. You are quite a sports hero yourself, aren't you? And now you are in college, so to top it all off, you must also be an excellent student, huh?"

Ted stepped in, trying to take the focus away from me. I appreciated all of Babe Ruth's kind comments and the fact that he took the time to read what Ted had sent him, but Ted could tell that all the attention was flustering me.

"Why don't we step over here to the table and have ourselves a little interview, Mr. Ruth, so Mable can ask you her questions for the Daily Iowan?" Ted suggested.

"Oh sure," Babe replied, "but you had better start calling me 'Babe', or we cannot really be friends. That 'Mr. Ruth' thing is just too formal, as well as I feel I know you Des Moines and Drake folks. We have had ourselves quite a fine weekend of sports here in the middle of Iowa. I will not be forgetting this beautiful city, the sporting baseball fans and," he added, "this Drake team. Great young fellas! What an afternoon of fun I have had!"

I decided to start the interview.

"May I quote you on that, Babe?" I asked quickly, whipping open my notebook and starting to write.

"Sure you can, Sweetheart. What else would you like to know from ol' Babe?"

I flipped back to the pages where my questions were.

"Well, first I would like you to tell me about your most important sports memory, or perhaps accomplishment. What do you think if you had to pick just one?" I asked in the most professional interviewer tone I could muster.

I think it stymied him for a moment, as I hoped it would. My journalism professor at the university told us that a common question was okay to start an interview with, but we should try to make it so the subject would have to give a narrow answer…a specific answer. It would make them pause and think for a moment, instead of giving a "canned" answer to an often-asked question. From the look on his face, I think I succeeded in making Babe pause for a moment before he answered.

"Hard to choose just one," he started with.

"Sorry, but you must choose just one for this question," I replied, feigning an apology.

"I got ya," he said, "Give me a little minute, here."

I waited, we all waited. Babe Ruth had rolled his eyes upward and appeared to be looking for an answer written on the ceiling.

"It has to be today. It has to be. I know I have set records in baseball, but today I played football for the first time in my life. Wore a real uniform. Ran fellas down and tackled 'em. Got tackled, or should I say pushed down? And I scored a real touchdown. Caught the pass by myself and ran it into the end zone. That honestly felt as good as when I set the homerun season record. It was a big ol' first for me. Probably won't ever do it again, either. I hope to set some more baseball records,

if that old buzzard Ty Cobb will let me, but I most likely ain't gonna be playing much more college football or any other kind of ball with a pigskin. Just ain't my game, but today it was. Yep, thinkin' about what I did this afternoon, it is by far the best sports memory I have."

What a great answer! I was writing as fast as I could.

"I got that last part, Mable," Ted assured me. "If you have the first half, I got the rest. Next question?"

"Are you ready, Mr. Ruth?" I asked.

"Is that the next question?" he joked. "And don't forget my name is Babe, Missy."

I countered with, "No sir, I'm sorry, I won't forget and don't you forget my name is Mable, Babe." I pointedly spoke his name.

Everyone laughed heartily again. He was an entertaining man. A heck of a funny fella, and the greatest baseball player ever. No wonder people all over America, and the world, loved him.

The Drake coach was still looking at his watch, even though we had been promised ten minutes and I had only used maybe two minutes to ask and get the first one answered. Perhaps he was including all our introductions in the ten-minute count. I had to finish.

"My next question is, have you ever quit anything? I mean quit something you started because it was too hard, or took up too much time, or maybe even wished you had not started?" I looked right into his startled eyes, beneath his bushy brows and sun-wrinkled forehead, He did look surprised. So did Ted, when I looked at him, and so did Burnie.

"That's a different kind of question, Mable," he began. "I am gonna have to think about this one, too. You got a special skill at askin' hard questions?"

I did not answer that question, thinking it to be rhetorical. However, I nodded in an affirmative manner.

"All right, then. I'll answer. Nope, I never quit nothin'. Ever. Never quit nothin' in my whole life. I don't quit." He looked back at me square in the eyes. "Babe don't quit. Write that down, Mable. I never quit nothin' in my whole life. Ya got it written down?" he asked firmly.

"Yessir. I have it written down." I replied firmly. He had gotten so suddenly serious.

The Drake coach tried to lighten the moment, I believe, by chiming in with, "That's why he made such a good Bulldog today. Bulldogs just don't quit, right Babe?"

"Nope, they don't," he said, but then he pressed harder, "because it don't matter whether you are a bulldog or a goose. Ya should never quit nothin'. If ya start somethin', ya need to finish it...no matter what. Why the heck would you start something, and then quit. That ain't no way to win, that's for sure."

He was so adamant, Ted felt compelled to step in also, injecting, "I think she was just curious, Babe. You know some people get beat down and quit one thing, but it makes them more determined and successful from then on. Is that what you meant, Mable?"

Babe spoke up, this time in my defense. "Oh, I'm sure she didn't mean no harm. I just got this thing about quittin'. Never believed in it. Never will. There ain't no good excuse for quittin'. I ain't offended, Mable. Don't you worry." He smiled at me and gave me a nod and a wink. I smiled back quickly and then immediately glanced over at Burnie. My buddy Burnie had seen the Sultan of Swat give me a big wink and so he was also grinning broadly.

I dove head first into the ongoing fray I had created with, "I think what I meant was have you ever felt beaten down by things going on around you and it was difficult to go on? You have honestly never felt like you might want to quit?"

Babe nodded affirmative, several times. "I get what you mean, Mable. You want to know if I have ever been tempted to give up? Huh?"

"That's exactly what I mean," I replied, relieved that I had salvaged this question, with help from Babe Ruth himself.

"Yes, I have been tempted. I was tempted when I first got into major league baseball. I pitched damn good for the Red Sox that first year with them, but the bums said they had too many players on their roster and moved me down to the minor leagues, to the Providence Grays. It was a dark time for me. I thought hard about giving up...about quitting, but Brother Matthias at the boys' home had always called me a winner. He believed in me. I owed a lot, and I still owe a lot, to folks who have believed in me all along the way, clear to today. I helped that Providence team win the pennant, and the Red Sox was real glad to get me back I'm sure glad I didn't let that little setback make me quit."

"Do you mean 'owed' like a debt? Like you had to pay them back for believing in you?" I asked.

"Well, kinda, but not exactly. I worked hard to get where I am and to get people to believe in a bum like me. I feel like the only way to get beat, for me, is to quit. So, I never quit. No one can ever beat me." He almost bragged. "No one can ever beat me. You cannot beat a person who won't give up, Mable. Cannot beat 'em."

"Wow, that is a whole different way of looking at quitting." I said, awestruck by his strong feelings about this. I had stirred up a beehive in him. He spoke with such passion. It was like he knew that I was thinking about giving up, and was telling me not to. Had someone told him? Ted did not know, Mother did not know. The only one there who knew was Burnie, and he had been with me all afternoon. With no opportunity to speak to the Babe alone. It was like Babe Ruth could read my mind.

Babe Ruth was watching me, even though the coach was looking at his watch.

"I hope you are not still getting hassled because you are a girl, are you Mable?" he asked me suddenly.

"No, no, not at all...well, maybe a little at the Daily Iowan, but I can handle it, and I think they will be begging to print this story."

"Is the swimming too hard at your university? Did you make the team?" He kept pressing me.

Out of the corner of my eye, I saw Mother and my aunt and uncle perk up their ears. This was becoming a case of Babe Ruth interviewing me!

"No, sir, freshmen can't swim on the varsity or in meets. I'm not allowed to compete this year at all, except in synchronized swimming."

"You ain't thinking about quittin' are ya?" he just asked me straight out!

"Well, some of my classes are really hard...I'm not getting the grades I want right now, but I know I can, someday." Boy, I was really trying to come up with excuses fast. This interview was not going like I thought it would!

He proceeded to hit the nail on the head with, "Well, you ain't quittin', Mable. You ain't giving up. When you quit, they win. Those swimmin' folks who won't let you swim, those writer fellas who think you can't write, and those classes you got...you seem purty smart to me. This ain't no time to quit. Like I said, you can't beat a man who won't quit. That goes for you, too. If a girl won't give up, she can't be beat. Ya hear me? They can't beat a girl who don't quit." His eyes drilled me with a look he usually reserved for pitchers like Lefty Grove of Philadelphia.

I stammered, "But, when I am at the university, I miss my mother. Besides that, my father and grandma just died this year. It's hard."

"Don't matter how hard it is, little lady. You don't quit. Quitters quit, not you. You already beat all those men, and you set records. That ain't easy. You are tougher than you think. You ain't quittin'."

"I don't know," is all I could say at that point.

"I know! I know for sure you will be beat if you quit. Your pa would not want you to quit, I am sure of that. Right, Ma?" as he glanced at Mother.

She slowly shook her head in a 'no' gesture. She was almost stiff with fright. Not of Babe Ruth, but at the idea of me quitting. I had really made a mess of this, and the coach kept looking at his watch and trying to guide Babe Ruth over to the outside door, where hundreds of fans were waiting.

"Any other questions, Mable?" asked Ted. Now it was my turn to simply shake my head 'no'.

"Then thank Mr. Ruth for his time and his wise advice, girl reporter, because he has to go now," said Ted.

I stuck out my hand to the larger-than-life Babe Ruth. He grabbed my puny hand in his large paw and held it firmly. His eyes grabbed my eyes, and he said, "You can't beat a girl who won't quit."

His eyes continued to hold mine, then he loosed his hand from mine, gave it a fatherly pat, and winked at me again. "You go get 'em, Tiger!" he said, and then he was gone. The blue door closed and I stood facing it, with my back to everyone else in the room.

I had interviewed Babe Ruth. He had just changed the course of my life. I felt it deep inside me. Turning around, I saw Mother hug Uncle Albert. Burnie's parents hugged him. Ted and Burnie shook hands, then they both came to me and put their arms around my shoulders, one on each side of me.

"Great interview, star girl reporter," Ted said. "That sure will give you plenty to write about. I expect I will see that on the front page of that Daily Iowan rag."

Burnie laughed. "Don't suppose you will have to have that "I want to quit" talk with your mother now, huh?"

"Okay, all of you. I am not quitting. I am done with thinking about quitting. We are done talking about quitting. No one will be beating me at anything, any time soon. You heard the Babe," I reminded them all, "You can't beat a girl who won't quit."

Sharing the Good News

That truck of Uncle Lynn's seemed to glide down the roads back to the dairy farm. He didn't need to take the milk truck home with him now. He decided he could drive his father's truck to his new job that evening. Harley was at his uncle's farm in no time at all, giving him the great news, and Uncle Lynn was as happy as Harley was for himself. Aunt Alice started to cry, which gave Harley a hint at what his mother's reaction might be. He and Lynn climbed in the truck and headed north towards Grimes. As Lynn drove, he gave Harley a brief verbal tutorial on laying linoleum. Lynn has laid his kitchen, porch, and bathrooms with linoleum, so he could explain most of the details to his nephew. It didn't sound too hard, except for all the time on his knees. Uncle Lynn said he would go to his basement and get out the knee pads he had purchased for himself when he did his floors and would let Harley use them.

The conversation made the trip home go quickly. They arrived in less than forty-five minutes, and Harley jumped out of the truck.

"I will see you tomorrow morning, sir," shouted Harley over his shoulder, as he yanked open the screen door on the back porch and leaped up the two stairs towards the inside door. "Bright and early!"

Lena heard all the shouting and came out of the parlor into the kitchen. "What's all the hollering about, Harley? Sounds like something crazy is going on!"

Harley could not contain himself. "It's not crazy, it's unbelievable, Mother! Mr. Flynn has found a job for me, and I start it tomorrow!"

"Wait, not another word," said his mother. "Come out to the parlor and tell your father, also. We could really use some news like this, Harley! What in Heaven's name has happened?"

Harley grabbed her hand and hustled into the parlor, dragging her behind him. He stopped in front of his father's overstuffed leather chair and wrapped his arm around his mother's waist, hugging her tightly.

"I have incredible news. I can still hardly believe it myself. Mr. Flynn knows someone who has a job for me, starting tonight."

Harley dared not stop to barely even take a breath. He wanted to explain the whole story before his parents started asking questions.

"I can do this. It will be a lot of work, but it's going to get me to Iowa City in January. That's all I care about. I can still do the chores here, morning and night. I can still do the milk route with Uncle Lynn." He took a quick breath.

"I can sleep in the afternoon. I start at the Ford plant at seven o'clock tonight. I will be laying linoleum floors for their new offices. They are not going to be an automobile factory any more. I can learn how to lay that stuff quickly; I know I can." Harley took another breath.

"I'll be done there at four in the morning, Mr. Flynn says. I can come home, do chores, and help Uncle Lynn work the milk route after that. I'll need to drive the truck back and forth, but I'll put gasoline in it. I will save all the rest of my money. What do you think?" Harley finally took a deep breath, and looked at his father, waiting for his reaction.

"Charley?" Lena asked.

Charley was looking out the front window, towards the narrow gravel road that passed by in front of the little white farm house.

He spoke in a measured tone. "I think you are going to wear a lot of gravel off that road out there, but if you end up in Iowa City, then I say ya oughta go for it, son. But you know, your mother will have the final say on this; she always does." Charley gave Lena one of those familiar two-eyed winks.

"I say it's a God-sent job, Harley. I can barely believe it. How can Mr. Flynn make something like this happen so soon?" asked Lena.

"Mother, he's a successful business man. He knows a lot of people. This fella at the factory owes him a favor, and he's using it to get me this job. I would love to have you meet him. He and his wife are just swell people!" said Harley.

"I'm sure they are, son. We're not in their social circle, but I sure do want you to thank them for us all," instructed his mother.

"Oh, I have thanked them over and over. He finally had to tell me to stop saying 'thank you' to him. I'm just going to show my appreciation by doing a great job there, that's all I can do right now," said Harley.

Charley spoke up again, "This is wonderful, Harley. Not a lot of good things been happenin' to this family the past couple years. We're still together, and now this comes to you. You worked hard for that money that got stole, and I'm glad you have a chance to earn it back. Really glad."

Harley let go of his mother and stepped beside where his father sat. He leaned over and hugged Charley's shoulder.

"Thanks, Dad. I will make you proud; I will," promised Harley.

"We're already proud of ya, Harley. So proud. Yer a good son, and we're blessed by that every day," said Charley.

His father wiped his eyes, but Harley couldn't tell if it was just a rub, or if there was a tear there. He knew Charley was a strong, tough man, but the times had been pretty hard on him. He did not think one whit less of his father if it was a tear. He turned to hug his mother again, and she was wiping her face with her apron.

"It's okay, Mother. It will all be okay, really," Harley assured her.

"I know, Harley. That's why I have these tears. I am so relieved. We are so blessed. Blessed by God, blessed by you, and blessed by the Flynns. Mightily blessed and so grateful." Lena folded her hands in front of her tear-stained face and prayed, "Thank you, Lord."

In the same breath, both Harley and Charley said, "Amen."

Epilogue

Harley Van Seibert 1916-2009

Harley earned his tuition money for the University of Iowa at the Ford factory. He enrolled and attended for three years. While in Iowa City, he waited tables while going to school. Harley met his future wife, Mable Hall, in that restaurant, and played amateur basketball on a team with his life-long friend, Mike McMichael. He then moved to Chicago and started laying floors for the General Floor Company. He married, moved to Des Moines, Iowa and started his own flooring company, Seibert Distributing. Harley had great personal and business success, raising three daughters with his wife and buying a new Lincoln every year. He took good care of his parents, buying land and building his own home just a mile from the house where his parents lived. He laid a linoleum kitchen floor for Lena with a black and white checkered pattern, and a single red rooster tile, that his mother chose, in the middle of the room.

Mable Bertha Woodrow Hall Seibert   1914-1983

Mable went on to graduate from the University of Iowa with a degree in Journalism. She swam in many national collegiate swim meets and after graduation she set several national AAU women's records in the backstroke. She also showed her skills in swimming exhibitions held all over the Midwest. After graduation, Mable moved to Chicago and worked writing copy for several publications there. She taught private swimming lessons at a major hotel in Chicago, and in 1936 Mable participated in the US Olympic Swim Team Trials, where she came in 4th place in the backstroke, earning a place in the Berlin Olympics as an alternate. A young man she met at the University of Iowa, Harley "Van" Seibert, also moved to Chicago, where they married in 1939. A few years later, the young couple moved back to Iowa, bought forty acres near Grimes, and built a home. Harley established his own flooring business and Mable stayed home to raise their three daughters. She was a life-long sports fan. In 1970 Mable reconnected with Burnie and they exchanged a few letters, until her death in 1983.

Translations

p.99-100

"Oh, meine süße kleine Enkelin!
Ich habe dich so sehr vermisst. Du bist so groß geworden!"
"Oh, my sweet little granddaughter! I have missed you
so much. You have grown so tall!"

"Berühre nicht die Soirte dieser Box. Es ist für dich, aber noch nicht. Du wirst
es bekommen, wenn du graduierst."
"Don't you touch the string on that box. It's for you,
but not yet. You will get it when you graduate."

p.104

"Bei Donner!," she yelled out. "Sollte das deine Abschlussüberraschung sein,
kleine Schnüffelnde Maus." She called out to Aunt Helen, "Komm schnell her,
Helen!"
"By Tunder!" she yelled out. "This is supposed to be
your graduation surprise, little snoopy mouse." She
called out to Aunt Helen, "Come here quickly, Helen!"

She said, "Du wirst überrascht sein, meine süße Mable. Es wir schön sein, genau
wie du."
She said, "You will be surprised, my sweet Mable. It
will be beautiful, just like you."

Aunt Helen said, "Bertha, Henrietta hat Mable hier heraufgeschickt, um dir zu
sagen, dass das Abendessen in fünfzehn Minuten ist."
Aunt Helen said, "Bertha, Henrietta sent Mable up here
to tell you that dinner is in fifteen minutes. Come
and knock on our door when you are ready and we will
all go downstairs together."

p.214

"Zuerst essen wir."   "First we eat."

p.215

"Ich habe das für dich gemacht, Liebling Enkelin. Es ist für die Verwendung an der Universität. Sie sagen die Räume dort werden nachts Kalt."
"I made this for you, darling granddaughter. It is for using at the university. They say the rooms there get cold at night."

p.216

"Öffne es jetz.," "Open it now."

"Nein, Nein. Das kleine Geschenk, Kindlein." **"No, no. The little gift, child."**

p.217

"Es ist für jene fantastischen Tanze, die sie an der Universität von Iowa haben. Irgendein kluger Junge wird dich zu einen Tanz bitten," she explained. Then Grandma smiled widely at me and added, "Er wird ein Glückspilz sein."
"It's for those fancy dances they have at the university, Mable. Some smart boy will ask you to a dance," she explained. Then Grandma smiled really big and added, "He'll be a lucky boy."

"Öffne das jetzt!" she commanded, declaring, "Keine anderes Mädchen an

dieser großen Universität von Iowa wird so etwas haben!
"Now open this" she commanded, declaring, "No other girl at this big University of Iowa will have anything like this!"

"Bitte höre auf zur reden und öffne das Geschenk von deiner Großmutter."
"Please stop all this talking and open the gift from your grandmother!"

I hope you have enjoyed the stories of Harley and Mable. Please go to my Amazon author/book page and leave a review. It will be very much appreciated.

Any comments you have about the story will be very helpful as I write the next part of their story, to be released in 2019.

To keep informed about the upcoming book, please leave your contact information at TeresaHolmgren.com and I will send you a link to my blog.

If you enjoyed this book, please try my first book, <u>Never A Dull Moment</u>. Available on Amazon and Kindle.